W9-DEW-438

ALSO BY AMY SOHN

Run Catch Kiss
Sex and the City: Kiss and Tell

MY OLD MAN

A NOVEL

AMY SOHN

SIMON & SCHUSTER

NEW YORK   LONDON   TORONTO   SYDNEY

SIMON & SCHUSTER
Rockefeller Center
1230 Avenue of the Americas
New York, NY 10020

Copyright © 2004 by Amy Sohn
All rights reserved, including the right of reproduction in whole or in part in any
form.

Simon & Schuster and colophon are registered trademarks of
Simon & Schuster, Inc.

For information regarding special discounts for bulk purchases, please contact
Simon & Schuster Special Sales at 1-800-456-6798 or
business@simonandschuster.com

Designed by Karolina Harris

Manufactured in the United States of America

10 9 8 7 6 5 4 3 2 1

Library of Congress Cataloging-in-Publication Data is available.

ISBN 0-7432-3828-1

This book is a work of fiction. Names, characters, places, and incidents are products
of the author's imagination or are used fictiously. Any resemblance to actual events
or locales or persons, living or dead, is entirely coincidental. Although several well-
known people appear on these pages, the references to them, their conduct and
their interactions with other characters are wholly the author's creation.

One thing I feared, and it befell,
　　and what I dreaded came to me.
No peace had I, nor calm, nor rest;
　　but torment came.

— THE BOOK OF JOB

MY OLD MAN

BAD THINGS

WH Y is this happening to me, Rabbi?" the dying man moaned from his bed.

"I'm not a rabbi yet," I said. "I have four more years to go."

"Well, that's soon enough," he said, "so tell me: What did I do to deserve this? Why does God want me to die before my time?"

His name was Neil Roth. He was a married father, thirty-nine years old, and he was dying of leukemia. I was in my second semester at the Rabbinic College of Reform Judaism, visiting him at Memorial Sloan-Kettering as part of my pastoral care internship, and Neil was the first patient on my list who'd been conscious.

When I saw that he was awake I'd opened with, "How are things going?" and Neil told me his story. He was a computer programmer on the Upper West Side, a lifelong loner, and he had just resigned himself to the possibility that he might spend the rest of his days single when one day he walked into a flower shop in midtown and exchanged a glance with the curvaceous Costa Rican manager, Angela. She was a knockout in her early forties, and as Neil ordered a bouquet of mixed roses to have sent to a sickly aunt in Miami, Angela smiled at him with such unguarded warmth, he knew right then they would marry.

They had a whirlwind romance and got married six weeks later. She moved into his place on Riverside Drive, and a year later they had a baby girl they named Ruby. Each night Neil would come home from work to the sight of his wife nursing his baby, a sight he had never thought he'd see, and then one night as he was getting ready for bed he saw these black-and-blue marks he couldn't explain.

The doctors diagnosed him with leukemia, and though they put him through chemo, he didn't respond. Now they were saying he'd be lucky if he made it three months. Angela had been at the hospital with him every night this week but had gone home to get a little sleep.

"You didn't do anything wrong," I said, trying to sound rabbinical and authoritative even though I was scared out of my mind. "God doesn't have a plan for us. We make our own paths and the reason we can experience great joy is because we can also experience great heartbreak."

Neil was wearing a Yankees cap to cover his bald head, and his cheeks were sunken and gray. He breathed irregularly, almost randomly, which I found unsettling although I tried to act comfortable. He had no eyebrows but his eyes were bright and confrontational. "Why would a just God let a decent person die?" he asked plaintively, in a hoarse, faraway voice.

I cleared my throat, stalling for time. I knew that Jews liked to ask questions, but I hadn't been prepared for anything so hard-hitting. "Many people have struggled with the very same questions as you," I said. "They wonder, *If God is omnipotent and just, why would He bring sudden tragedy into the lives of decent human beings?* Since they can't find a reason, they tell themselves that they must have sinned in some way, and that they're being punished, or tested."

"Exactly," he said. "I have a brother I don't speak to—we had a falling-out over money twelve years ago—and I was thinking maybe this is God's way of telling me to make up with him. I don't want to, but if this is a test I might. So am I being punished?"

"A time of great illness is certainly a good time to take stock of one's relationships, but no, I don't believe you are being punished." Rabbi Freedman, one of the chaplains at Memorial, had told us that when patients tried to blame themselves, they wanted to be assured that they hadn't erred in some way. "Given the paradox that God is just but evil exists, some choose to believe that the reason tragic events can befall good people is because God is beneficent but not, in fact, omnipotent. God is engaged in a work of creation that is only partially finished, one that struggles against the forces of chaos."

He rolled his eyes. "But every page of the Torah is all about how powerful God is. And you're telling me He's not omnipotent?"

Neil was the dying one but he was killing me. This was even more sweat-inducing than the Rorschach test I had to take to get into rabbinical school. "A conversation about my own beliefs in God is probably a lengthier one than we have time for today," I said, "but the short answer is that people pray to God for solace. As Rabbi Harold Kushner wrote in his classic text on suffering, *When Bad Things Happen to Good People*—"

"Don't even talk to me about that book," he said wearily. "I have eleven copies."

"Then you probably know that Kushner has some wise insights. He likens the human-God relationship to that between a teenager and his parents. The teen is aware his parents are not all-powerful, but still he seeks out their protection and care."

"But this God hasn't protected me. I'm thirty-nine and I'm going to die." His voice was weak but very clear. "My daughter's going to grow up without a father. It's like God has slapped me in the face."

I racked my brain, trying to think of something to say, anything, that would help. "Abraham Joshua Heschel suggested that both life and death are aspects of a greater mystery, the mystery of being, the mystery of creation. Death is not a defeat but an arrival, a reunion with God." We had studied Heschel's essay on death with Rabbi Freedman and I'd found it brilliant and insightful, but as I said it, it sounded hollow and half-baked, like a lame answer to a perfectly fair question.

"So I'm supposed to be *grateful* about what's happening to me?" He seemed to get a little color in his blue cheeks and then he said slowly, "Are you insane?"

This was the hardest question of all. If I were Neil I wouldn't have been reassured by any of the things I was saying either. I wanted to write him off as a cantankerous jerk but he was obviously intelligent. He was staring at me coldly, like he was beginning to wish his last name hadn't been so overtly Jewish so he wouldn't have wound up on my rotation list.

The week before, Rabbi Freedman had had us write down sayings on cards, from different philosophers, that he thought might help us in the hospital rooms. He said not to think of them as cheat sheets but resources, to be tailored to the individual patient. I lowered my eyes and slipped one out of my book bag. "'Sometimes there is no reason.'" Neil's mouth was thin and expressionless. I flipped to the next one. "'God does not bring misfortune upon us. He is in the love between us and our loved ones when we are suffering.'" I smiled. "He is with Angela and Ruby. With you."

He slumped even further in his bed with a frown. Flip. "'A time of suffering can be a time to renew one's relationship with God.'" He shook his head like I was a bad Bible salesman and stared out the window. I'd never had trouble believing in the power of the Almighty myself, but both my parents were living and nothing traumatic had ever happened to me or even anyone I knew. At twenty-six the most faith-shaking event I had experienced was getting a C– on a BC Calc exam senior year of high school. I'd never had to deal with anything real.

"Why won't you give me any answers?" Neil said.

"My role is really just to be with you, and to listen."

"I don't want your company! I just want to know . . . *why is this happening?*"

"A more useful question might not be, 'Why is this happening?' but as Kushner suggests, 'God, see what is happening to me. Can You help me?'" Neil was blinking at me slowly, unimpressed. The steady line of his faith was starting to dip below stable, and I felt my own blood pressure rise in response.

"There would be no life without death," I offered. "The two go together. It is because tragedy can happen that the good things can happen too."

"That may be true," he said, folding his hands over his stomach, "but it's not very comforting."

I shrugged stiffly, feeling like the room was very stuffy, and said the one thing all rabbis say when faced with questions of doubt, the one they think gets them off the hook: "There is a great history of doubting Jews. So you're in good company." It was the keeping-up-with-the-Joneses of theodicy: if everyone else doubted God, it wasn't so bad that you did too. "Job's servants, sheep, and ten children were killed and then he caught a terrible disease. In his dialogue with God he comes to see that Man is powerless in the face of God's might. It's sobering but in another sense, comforting."

"It's depressing is what it is," said Neil. He listlessly picked up a *Macworld* magazine on his tray. Religion was losing to technology.

"If you would like," I said, leaning over, "I can say a Misheberach for you, the prayer for the sick."

"I don't want you to pray for me," he spat, licking his lips. "I already know I'm going to die!"

I felt lost, like a total fraud. This wasn't theodicy; it was the idiocy. Rabbi Freedman said that in tough moments it could be good to be honest, and real, not to feel like we had to be pillars of wisdom. Maybe the best thing I could do for Neil was level with him.

"You know what?" I said. "You're right."

"What do you mean I'm right?"

"I'm seriously striking out here, aren't I? You're throwing me good pitches but I haven't been doing a very good job."

"No you haven't," he said after a beat.

I shoved the cards back in my bag. "I guess if you want to know the truth, my own God-vision isn't all that strong. That's actually true of a lot of rabbinical students. We can talk about the dangerous rise in interfaith marriage or the binding of Isaac or Jewish views on homosexuality and abortion, but nobody really talks about God."

"You don't think there's something wrong with that?" he said.

"It's not an easy subject! What kind of person do you think applies to rabbinical school anyway? People that think they *are* God. Half my classmates are completely meshuggeneh!" His eyes were wide and frightened, like what I was saying was more upsetting to him than death itself.

"Look," I said, "it's not like I don't try. I get up there and do my exegesis, put as much passion into it as I can, but so far, God's been the most elusive part of rabbinical school. I study really hard and do well on tests but most of the time I can't feel God at all. So I don't know why bad things happen to good people. In fact, the tragedy around us is pretty good proof that there probably *isn't* a higher power. I don't know what I was thinking trying to put a positive face on death. What you're going through is so depressing I can hardly even imagine it. You'll never get to see your daughter grow up. It totally sucks!"

"What's wrong with you?" he said.

"What do you mean?" I said. "I'm *agreeing* with you! You wanted answers. I'm giving you answers."

His face contorted into a grimace and he moaned, "Ohhhhhh." His lips were turning blue and dry. I couldn't tell whether he was in physical pain or just aghast at my honesty. I had expected my awakening to energize him too, but instead he looked sicker than he had the whole time I'd been with him.

"Are you all right?" I said, touching his arm.

"You . . . " He pointed his slender finger at me unsteadily and leaned back like I was the devil.

"What is it?" I asked hoarsely.

"You are . . ." He heaved in and out and his face got even paler than it already was.

"Yes? Yes?" I felt that he had something to communicate, something vital and true that would change my life forever. "I'm what?"

He gulped in some air agonizingly slowly, determined to get enough in his lungs to speak. "You are the worst . . . rabbi . . . I ever . . . met." With that he turned a dark gray, his head fell back on the pillow, and he stopped moving.

"Neil?" I said, shaking him. "Neil?" He rose up again for a moment and gasped violently for breath, as I leapt back with a scream. Then he was still.

I raced into the hallway and up to the nursing station. "Come quick!" I said to the pixie-ish blonde behind the desk. "Something's happened!"

She ran with me into the room, checked his pulse and breathing, and lowered her head. "Aren't you going to defibrillate?" I asked.

She gave me a funny look and said, "No. He's DNR."

"He's DNR? But—but can't you make an exception?"

"It's not your decision," she said, and left.

I stared at Neil's body, praying it had all been a mistake, that it wasn't the end. They had to bring him back, if only so his last words wouldn't be "You are the worst rabbi I ever met."

She came back in with a short Indian doctor with big ears. He went to the body, checked some vitals. Then he drew the curtain and disappeared behind it for a few minutes with the nurse.

"Are you family?" he asked when he came out. His look wasn't accusatory so much as befuddled.

"No, the rabbi."

He jerked his head back in surprise and said, "I didn't know there were—"

"There are female rabbis, yes."

"So what happened?"

"I—I don't know. His wife went home to get some rest. We were talking—and he just—went," I said weakly.

"Sometimes they do," he said, nodding. "They wait till the family goes because they can't die in front of them. Is this your first?"

I nodded. "The first one's always the hardest," he said. His pager beeped and he checked it and walked briskly out the door.

I followed, feeling stunned. As I moved slowly down the hallway toward the elevators, I realized that though God hadn't been able to send Neil Roth a message, he'd chosen instead to send me one, through him: Rachel Block was not leadership material. I'd been sure my honesty would serve as a comfort, but what kind of dying man wanted to sit with a faithless rabbi? I'd been so inept I'd made him croak months before his due date, his wife not even there to hold his hand. She was going to come back only to find that he'd gone. I was a reverse rabbi. Instead of creating miracles, I caused premature death.

As I went down to the lobby and out into the spring sun I wondered two things: what a rabbinical school dropout could possibly do next, and how I was going to tell my parents.

THE HISTORY OF
THE PENCIL

Oh barkeep!" a hulking young Italian was shouting, doing the twenty wave with his hand. "I'd like a Metropolitan."

"Would you happen to know what's in that?" I asked, moving down the bar.

"A Metropolitan," he said more loudly, like my problem was hearing and not comprehension. "That's not a complex orduh."

It wasn't an order a heterosexual male should have been proud of either, but instead of saying that I just said, "I'm new here."

"They don't train youse?"

"They did, but most people order beer."

"Triple sec, Kurant, and cranberry," he said with a sigh. He had a few buddies with him, all sporting a faux hip-hop look. I tried to mix like I knew what I was doing, and when I shook the mixer up and down he said, "You look good doing that."

I wanted to think of a wisecrack but I can never think of anything smart to say on the spot. I always think of my best comebacks a year after the initial insult, when they do me no good whatsoever. I poured the drink through the strainer, stuck in the straw, the lime. He lowered his mouth to the glass, smacked his lips, and said, "Do you taste this good?"

I didn't say anything. I just wiped off the counter. "Why you bothering ha, Gallo?" said one of his friends, who was heavy and had a face like a pig.

"She's cute. And she looks Italian."

"Whaddayou want an Italian girl for? When's the only time it's OK to spit in an Italian girl's face?"

"When?"

"When her mustache is on fire." They howled and howled, in a way that made it clear they had told this joke before. For a second I wanted to go back to rabbinical school.

My bar was called Roxy and I'd been working there two months. It was on Smith Street in Brooklyn, two blocks from my apartment. I'd gone in a few times after I dropped out of school to shoot the breeze with the bartender, Caitlin, a former model from Kentucky. One humid night in July she mentioned that one of the other girls had quit because of the cigarette ban, and I realized bartending might be a good thing to do while I figured out what to do next. I went in to meet with the owner, Mike, a skinny guy with an unshaven face, and when he asked if I had experience, I said I'd bartended at my alma mater, Wesleyan. It was only a semester, through Cardinal Catering at school, but I omitted that detail and he hired me a couple days later. Caitlin had to reteach me how to mix drinks, and when I finally admitted my rabbinic past she laughed and said most nights she felt like she was hearing confession herself.

Though my first few shifts solitary were a nightmare, I'd finally gotten the hang of all the basics and was learning how not to dive down under the bar when customers came in, but I still hadn't gotten the hang of fending off assholes. At least half a dozen guys propositioned me each shift, with varying degrees of shame and subtlety—middle-aged married men who insisted they just wanted to buy me dinner, fresh-out-of-college boys looking for a Mrs. Robinson, thirtysomething yuppies looking to turn me from a barmaid to a wife. "What time do you get off?" or "All the men in here are jerks. You need to be with someone who can protect you." It didn't matter what I wore or whether I remembered their drinks, if I wore my hair down or gave them lip. It wasn't me they liked so much as the erotic appeal of the bar. It was like being a stripper except the pay was worse.

My looks fall somewhere on the spectrum from cute to pretty, but the guys that have said I'm beautiful said it weightily, like they wanted to be rewarded for their creativity of thought. I'm five-six, which is tall for a Jewish girl, I have a decent rack, 36D, and my butt

is a slightly smaller version of J.Lo's—not as round but ample
enough to catch the eye of an ass man. I have green eyes and curly
dark brown hair down to my shoulders, and though it has on occasion been called pre-Raphaelite, if I don't put any product in I look
like the bastard love child of Rosanne Rosannadanna and Marc
Bolan.

"Rachel?" a voice called from down the bar. I was gritting my
teeth, trying to figure out how another customer had learned my
name, when I saw that it was Joey Yatrakis, this theaterfuck I knew
from Wes. He looked good—generic, too skinny, and Caesar cut—
but good. I went over and hugged him.

"I'm so confused," Joey said as he pulled away. "I thought you
were a rabbi."

"It didn't work out."

"Why not?"

"I didn't feel comfortable as a messenger of God."

"That's deep," he said. He'd been a stoner at Wesleyan and evidently the New York theater world hadn't reformed him. "But isn't
bartending a little badass for a former rabbi?"

"I'm questioning a lot of things in my life right now," I said with a
shrug. "So do you live in the neighborhood?"

"No, my girlfriend does. I was on my way to the train and I saw
your sign for margaritas."

"You want one?" I said. "It's one of the few drinks I do well." I
mixed him one with orange juice, the way Caitlin had taught me—
and though he tried to pay me I waved off his money. Since he
seemed relatively chipper I decided to broach the most dangerous
topic you can ask a New York City actor: "Are you in anything now?"

"Yeah!" he said. "I got cast in this play by Hank Powell. It's called
The History of the Pencil."

"Hank Powell wrote a *play?*" I said. "Isn't film to theater the
wrong direction?"

"He says he believes in downward trajectories."

"That's so Powell," I said. "What's it about?"

"A suicidal writer who's losing his mind and money."

"Is it autobiographical?"

"What do you think? *Everything* Powell writes is autobiographical."

"What's he like? As crazy as all his characters?"

"Crazier. He reads you like a book. It's like he can see into your soul. But he's got his own drama going on all the time too. He's half gypsy, half schizo."

"That doesn't surprise me," I said. "Powell knows people. How old is he?"

"Fifty-one."

"Really? I assumed he was younger." All the characters in Powell's movies were in their early thirties, and though he had been writing and directing for fourteen years it never struck me that *he* had to age, even if his protagonists didn't.

"What does he look like?"

"Mustache. Black hair."

"Is he hot?"

"I'm a guy!" Joey was young but old-school and hadn't yet realized that in this century a man could comment on another man's attractiveness without being branded a *fegeleh*.

"Come on," I said. "You gotta give me something."

He thought for a second and said, "For a middle-aged guy he's in pretty good shape."

I decided he resembled a more rotund Gabriel Byrne, funny-looking but with an innate sexiness that shone through in spite of his girth. "Is he married?"

"Divorced." It figured. The men who write women well can never get it together with them in life. "We close Sunday. Afterwards there's a cast party in a loft near the theater. You can come if you want. My girlfriend was supposed to be my date, but we're going through a trial separation."

"That's too bad."

"No it isn't. I can never have a girlfriend when I'm working. Too many stimuli for me to handle. So are you single?"

"Absolutely," I said.

"Don't tell Powell," he said, shaking his head. "He's a devil with the women."

"Really?" I said, wondering what to wear.

Hank Powell was the nation's most prolific indie auteur, the neo-Cassavetes, the Queens Godard. His first film was the seminal *Leon and Ruth* (1989) and since then he'd made eight others, all brilliant in different ways. He cast big-name stars before they were stars and shot on mini-budgets on the streets of Little Italy, Hell's Kitchen, and Jackson Heights, Queens, where he grew up. He wrote and directed all of them himself, and though none made a ton at the box office he had a devoted following of art-house hipsters like me who felt he was the last shining god of character-driven cinema.

I had seen *Leon and Ruth* in eighth grade on a date at Cobble Hill Cinemas with a guy named Colin Anderson who didn't appreciate me. He was in my class at Packer Collegiate, the private school I went to till ninth, and he was a shining squash star, nationally ranked. We had tried to get into an Australian thriller but it was sold out so we saw the Powell instead. It starred a then-unknown Julia Roberts and Don Cheadle and was about a waitress in love with a guy who had just gotten drafted for Vietnam. Right when Leon and Ruth were having the tearful good-bye that put Hank Powell on the map of indie cin forever, Colin whispered, "Would you consider blowing me?"

"I'm trying to watch the movie here," I said.

"How about a hand job?" he said.

From that night on I saw Powell films the night they came out—at the Quad, or Cinema Village, with no popcorn and no date. Each was written like a highly stylized stream-of-consciousness id with long monologues where the characters addressed the camera in highly poetic terms about their relationship to God and the soul. *Lydia's Chest Wound* (Annette Bening, Steve Buscemi) was about a down-and-out female taxi driver with a bee-bee lodged in her left areola; *Knock for Greenberg* told the tale of a hermetic landlord (Ron Silver), cold to the world until he had an aortic aneurysm and got nursed back to health by a Puerto Rican nurse (Rosanna Arquette with dyed-black hair); and *Difficult Women* (Lena Olin, Michael Imperioli) was about a Latvian cocktail waitress in love with a low-level Russian Jewish mafioso. All of his women characters were fierce and tough and I loved how he got them so well.

In the mid-nineties he branched out into book writing—there was the collection *Powell: Six Screenplays* and a book of poetry, *Scratchiti,* that had Beat aspirations but was as static and pretentious as his movies weren't, and a horrendous coming-of-age novel, *The Stoop Sitter,* which I'd bought for a buck at the Strand. I prayed the play would be better than the books.

The Guido down the bar beckoned me for a refill and I told Joey I'd be back in a minute. As I mixed it I got a head rush and not just from the shaking. For the first time in months things were looking up. I was going to meet Hank Powell.

T H E next night I went to meet my parents at Banania, a French restaurant, to celebrate my dad's fifty-fifth birthday. I had lived eight blocks from them since I graduated college, and saw them on a weekly basis. I couldn't help it: proximity makes elusiveness harder to justify. I am of that small breed of brownstone Brooklyn seventies kids who were born into a neighborhood that twenty years later happens to be experiencing a hipster influx. We holdovers are in a difficult bind. While our small-town peers spend their lives trying to get as far away from home as possible, we have a double motivation to stay: placating our parents and taking advantage of the cheap rent. Cobble Hill is a lot like Grover's Corners. It's tedious and repetitive, but it has a hold.

Though I didn't like to admit it in mixed company, I was one of the few twentysomethings I knew who actually liked spending time with their parents. I was always the center of attention and they always got the check. They could be annoying sometimes, prying even, but they listened when I talked and now that I could drink with them we'd sometimes laugh for hours. It was like those magnets you see on lesbian refrigerators: "The more people I meet the more I like my cat." That was how I felt about my mom and dad.

But it didn't hurt that right after I graduated Wes the neighborhood took off. The hipster influx began in 1996, when a guy named Alan Harding opened a restaurant on Smith Street called Patois, and the honkeys started coming out to play. Within a year a dozen more restaurants, yoga centers, craft shops, and clothing boutiques had sprung up, and within five years realtors were advertising apartments as "just steps from Restaurant Row." Parents bought their babies onesies that proclaimed "bklyn" and "718" like they were all down with the posse when in truth there was no posse left to be down with; all the Puerto Ricans had long ago sold their religious article shops and hightailed it back to the island.

I arrived at Banania ten minutes late, but my parents weren't there yet. A snot-nosed toddler in a booster seat at the next table was wailing at the top of his lungs as his mom wiped his nose with a napkin. One of the downsides of living in Cobble Hill is that the whole hood's a maternity ward. A waiter came over to my table—tan, shaved head, French accent. One of the upsides of living in Cobble Hill is that there are so many hot waiters. He asked if I wanted "someseen to drink" and I ordered the most expensive glass of white wine, since my parents were paying.

As I was sipping it something caught my eye on the wall by the bar. It was this weird decoration: a racist caricature of a dark-skinned black man, or Turk, it was hard to tell. He wore a red fez and was drinking from a teacup, smiling gleefully with bright lips and gleaming white teeth. It was so offensive it made Aunt Jemima look like high art. Banania was a French-owned restaurant and I figured the coon-on-the-wall was their idea of cute. Frogs aren't just backward; they're backward with pride.

The waiter brought my wine and my parents ambled through the door. "What took so long?" I said.

"Sorry, sorry," said my mom. They sat down noisily, their faces flushed and eager to see me. They always look like that when I'm around. Sometimes I feel like I'm their drug of choice.

My dad had a salt-and-pepper beard, square 1970s-style glasses, and the worst fashion sensibility known to mankind. He worked in computers at Bear Stearns. My mom was the kind of semiliberal that bought hemp drawstring pants without being fully aware that she was wearing marijuana. She taught second grade at PS 41 in the Village. They listened to Arlo Guthrie and thought Garrison Keillor was the Messiah, and though they looked younger than they were, they both had guts and moved more slowly than they used to.

"What took so long?" I said.

"Dad was looking for his glasses," my mom said.

His face flushed and he spun his head in anger. "If you didn't feel the need to do spring cleaning in *every season,*" he said, "I'd have some idea where my things were." He always got mad at her for throwing stuff out even though his side of the bedroom always looked like a tornado hit it, which to me was proof that she left it alone.

I put my present on the table. "Happy birthday, Dad."

He gave me a big smile, a hundred and eighty degrees opposite of the scowl he had just shown her, turned the box over, and ripped it open with venom. "Wow!" he said. "What a *great present!*" He says that every time, no matter what I buy him. I felt good about this year's gift, though—a pair of black biking gloves and a little electronic timer that attached to the handlebar. Over the summer he'd gotten into biking around Brooklyn on little-known paths, and he was always calling obscenely early on weekends, hounding me to join him.

"You put that on your bike and you can see how fast you're going," I said.

"I *know!*" he said. "It's exactly what I need." He put his hand into one glove even though it was still attached to the other one. "Don't I look cool?" My mom rolled her eyes but he didn't notice.

"So how's Roxy?" he said.

"We had a little adventure last week," I said. "This transvestite ex-con from the projects came in and got in my face."

"Did he hurt you?" said my dad.

"She tried to. She said she didn't like the look of me and took a swing but Jasper pulled her off me and eighty-sixed her." Jasper was a heavy six-and-a-half-foot-tall gaffer from Minnesota who came in almost every night and worked as my unofficial bouncer.

"I wish you weren't working so close to the projects," my mom said.

"Most of the PJ guys are actually pretty cool," I said. "Stuff like that hardly ever happens."

My dad looked off to the side, all furrowed brow and grave. He had not been handling my new career well. In a matter of months his only child, his pride and joy, had gone from woman of the cloth to woman of the washcloth.

When I was growing up, our synagogue in Brooklyn Heights, Brooklyn Rodeph Shalom, had been the center of my family's life. My dad was on the religious school committee, my mom helped with fund-raisers, and I was pretty much the star student from the moment I entered in first grade till the final youth group Shul-In in twelfth. In tenth grade I was elected president of Brooklyn Rodeph Shalom Temple Youth (which, unbeknownst to the rabbi, we nicknamed BReaSTY since every female member wore a D cup or bigger). In college I ran WesJAC, the Wesleyan Jewish Action Committee, and I went to services every Friday night, even when the only other attendants besides me were the homeless woman who came for the free wine and an overweight guy named Zeke Shnayerson who had eczema all over his hands.

After I graduated I took a job at a nonprofit in midtown called the Jewish Culture Foundation, where I helped Jewish film festivals secure funding, ran conferences for Jewish museums, and organized retreats for Jewish artists. But after four years of getting intimately acquainted with the bureaucratic politics of nonprofit institutions, I decided to do what I knew I always would: become a rabbi.

I got into the Rabbinic College of Reform Judaism the first time I applied. (Everyone called it RCRJ, or Rick-Ridge, because the only thing leadership-oriented Jews love more than God is acronyms.) My dad was so ecstatic when I got my acceptance letter that he got a custom-made T-shirt that said "BLESS ME—I'M A RABBI'S DAD" on the front and "SHE AIN'T BAD-LOOKING, EITHER" on the back, in big, felt block letters. Wherever we went he'd tell people I was going to be a rabbi—cab drivers, waiters, the Lubavitchers over at Court Street Stationers, anyone. My mom gabbed about it with all her friends and colleagues, delighting in the fact that I'd still be living in the hood since RCRJ was in the Village, and before I even started classes she asked whether I thought this might mean they'd get front-row seating at High Holy Day services.

So it wasn't a surprise that when I dropped out after just a semester and a half they hit the roof. My father kept saying, "Shouldn't you give it more time?" and, "If you stayed I'm certain you'd see things that would make you feel as full of faith and optimistic as the hospital made you depressed!" My mom would begin sentences with "When you go back to school . . . " instead of "If," and I'd always scream and correct her. They'd quieted down about it for the past couple weeks but evidently they hadn't put it to bed completely.

"I don't see why you have to stay at the bar," my dad said, frowning. "I was browsing through the *Forward* classifieds and I saw an opening for religious educator at Central Synagogue."

"I don't want to teach Hebrew school!"

"Leave her alone," my mom said. "This is just a temporary thing. To tide her over until she figures out what to do next."

"Did I ask you?" said my dad. "Did I say your name?" They'd been bickering like this a lot lately. I had no idea my job insecurity could be so bad for my parents' marriage.

"I don't think you should be giving her grief about her career," she spat. "Especially when—"

"Especially when what?" he shot back.

"Especially when she's only just reentered the job market."

I knew something else was going on. "What are you guys talking about?" I said.

"Nothing," my dad said. If he didn't want to talk about something there was nothing you could do to make him. "I just don't understand why you won't go back to school. They'd take you back in a heartbeat! Tell them you went temporarily insane from the radiation at Memorial!"

"Maybe you should talk to some of your old friends from school," my mom said. David might have some insight. Have you talked to him since you left?"

David Peres was a redheaded cantorial student with whom I'd had a brief affair, and like a moron I had made the mistake of introducing him to my parents after just one month. Naturally they fell head over heels. The problem was, I never did, and when I dumped him shortly thereafter because I knew I'd never love him, they went ballistic.

"No, I haven't talked to him," I said, "and I don't plan to either."

"Maybe he could talk some sense into you!" my dad said. "You didn't realize what a good thing you had there!"

My mom shot him a look like he should calm down. "Have you given any thought to what you might want to do with your life?" she asked, trying to sound nonconfrontational. They always did good cop, bad cop.

"Not really," I said, "but until I figure it out I have to have a shit job and I'd rather sling brews than anything else."

"You're twenty-six years old!" my dad shouted. "You do shit work when you're twenty-one!"

"Not true!" I exclaimed. "Haven't you heard of the quarterlife crisis?"

"I saw that book on the Staff Picks shelf at Bookcourt the other day," my mom chirped, as though the brutal diagnosis for my generation was secondary to the fact that we had a shared reference point. "The flap copy was very intriguing."

"What are you talking about?" my dad asked. He hated to be in the dark about anything.

"The quarterlife crisis is like the midlife crisis," I said, "only cooler. Like countless Gen Xers I went into the career I'd always dreamed of, only to realize that first choice might not have been the right one." They were staring at me skeptically, the way Neil Roth had. If I could convince them my job flux was not something to be ashamed of but part of a bona fide national trend, maybe they'd get off my back. "So now I'm standing at a crowded intersection trying to hail a cab. But they all keep passing me by. It's a shift change and they all have their off-duty lights on. I don't want to walk all the way home, but suddenly I'm having to face that prospect, daunted by the notion of what a long and tiresome road I have ahea—"

"All right!" he said. "I get it!"

"Don't dismiss," I said. "The quarterlife crisis has been severely underresearched and underappreciated. Yet it's just as common as the midlife, if not more so."

"You can have a quarterlife crisis without becoming Carla on *Cheers*," he said.

"Carla was the waitress," said my mom. "Sam was the bartender."

He glared at her but before "Family Court" could continue the waiter came over and asked my parents if they wanted any drinks. My dad got Scotch and soda. My mom said what she always says: "Just water to start with." She has this principled resistance to saying yes on the first ask.

"So you wanna come away with us this weekend?" my dad said. They had a place up in the Berkshires, and they always tried to get me to go up with them.

"I don't think we're going," my mom told him. "I have too much schoolwork."

"You can do it there!" he whined. He hated it when she wouldn't go because then he couldn't. He didn't know how to drive and they rented a car every weekend. "You've got to come, Rach! You can drive me."

"I work Saturdays," I said. "And besides, I'm going to the theater on Sunday."

"Whatcha seeing?" my mom asked.

"The History of the Pencil."

"Oh, Rachel," she said, like I'd told her someone was dead.

"What?"

"Dad and I walked out at intermission. I wouldn't recommend it *at all.*" Strike one for the Rachster. It did not bode well for a future with Powell to find that my parents had gone exeunt on his work.

"Come on," I said, eyeing them warily. "Was it really that bad?"

"A train wreck," said my dad. "Long, self-important, and hard to follow."

"Why'd you go in the first place?"

"We subscribe."

I wanted to tell myself they were being overcritical but they'd been going to the theater for thirty years, all the way back since the early seventies when they'd second-act whatever Broadway shows they could. They knew this arena better than I did. "Well, I'm going to see it anyway," I said, unfolding my napkin. "I'm kind of a fan of Hank Powell's."

"He's written other stuff?" asked my dad. "That play was so catastrophic I assumed it was a freshman effort."

"No," said my mom. "Remember, Richard, in the *Playbill* it said he was a screenwriter."

"That hack got people to finance a film?"

"Nine films!" I shot. "And he's not a hack. Didn't you guys see *Leon and Ruth?* Julia Roberts was in it after *Mystic Pizza* and before *Steel Magnolias*. Remember when she won her Oscar a couple years ago how she said, 'I owe my career to Hank Powell'?"

My mom jolted to attention and snapped her fingers. "That's right," she said. "He was her gay theater teacher!"

"No, that was Tom Hanks."

"Tom Hanks is gay?" my dad said. I put my head in my hands. Talking to them about popular culture was like teaching retarded kids to swim.

"What are his other movies?" my mom asked.

They stared at me cluelessly as I rattled off the titles. *"Lydia's Chest Wound; Knock for Greenberg; Difficult Women; Kid First, Then Husband; Love Is a Sad-Eyed Bassett Hound*, which won an Independent Spirit Award—"

My dad nodded eagerly and said, "I loved that film!" but when he started reminiscing it turned out he was thinking of *Love and Death on Long Island*.

I hated what I had to do next but I needed to restore some cachet. "Did either of you see *Flash Flood?*"

"Yeah!" my dad exclaimed, as my mom frowned, unsure.

"What was it about?" my mom said.

"Helen Hunt and Jeff Goldblum are vacationing in the Bahamas one summer with their kids when—"

"Oh yeah!"

"He wrote that too. It grossed a hundred million dollars and that was all the way back in 1994."

"Dad saw it at Cobble Hill Cinemas in the dead of winter," my mom said. "The heating system was broken and we had to sit there shivering in our coats the whole movie. I got bronchitis the next day. It was one of the worst experiences of my life."

Just as I was about to strangle myself with my napkin I heard someone at the door shout, "Racheleh!"

It was my upstairs neighbor, Liz Kaminsky. Liz was the Jewish Mae West. She had curly blond hair down to her shoulders, ice-blue eyes, and high-C breasts. She did four and a half miles on the StairMaster of New York Sports Club on Boerum Place every day and I had never seen her eat anything but salad. Her wardrobe was Britney Spears chic—low-cut scoopnecks, yeast infection pants, and white glittery eye makeup—and just to the left of her lip she had a small brown mole that, she admitted to me one drunken night in her apartment, was actually a tattoo she'd gotten at sixteen in an overzealous Cindy Crawford phase.

She had moved into the apartment above me in April, a few weeks before I left RCRJ, and immediately made her presence known to the building. Night after night I'd be awakened to her shouting, "That's right, honey! Fuck my hairy Lou Reed!" For weeks I tried to figure out why she called her vagina Lou Reed—Was she saying Lou's head hair looked pubic? Did she consider her genitalia the Velvet Underground?—but the reference was so obscure I was stumped.

One night I was writing a paper on Rashi's use of the grammatical plural as a way of emphasizing the principle of fairness when I heard her screaming extra loudly. I was so curious to find out once and for all what she was saying that I climbed on top of my bed, put a glass to the ceiling, and realized she was saying "Fuck my hairy Jew beav!"

I didn't mind her erotic use of a self-hating pejorative but I had to finish my paper, so after the shouting subsided I put on my slippers and knocked on her door. She opened it in a ratty white bathrobe. Her makeup was a mess, half on, half off, and her hair stuck out wildly.

"Hi," I said. "I live below you and I was wondering if your hairy Jew beav could *shtup* a little more quietly."

"Are you Jewish?" she said.

I nodded. "How'd you know?"

"You said *shtup*. I hope I didn't offend you with my language."

"On the contrary. I call my own vagina Miriam's Well."

"Who is det?" said an accented voice in the background.

"Go back to sleep, Bashir," she said. She stepped out into the hallway, propping the door open with her foot, and whispered, "He's Lebanese." I must have raised my eyebrows because she added, "Christian. The good kind, not the bad. He works at the Laundromat on the corner. I was trying to explain what 'gentle' meant and one thing led to another. Sorry about the noise. I used to only have sex with the lights out and come completely silently but now that I've worked through it in analysis I sometimes go overboard."

"Well, maybe you could put a rug under your bed, or some eggshell on the wall," I said.

"I'll look into it," she said, as I started down the stairs. "Hey! I didn't catch your name!"

"Rachel."

"Well, Rachel," she said. "Any girl who would ask me to quiet my fucking has got to be my new friend." And from that moment on I was.

We went out for coffee at Bagel World the next day and I asked her about Bashir. Before I knew it she was telling me all about her G-spot, her toy collection, her porno movies, and the joys of female ejaculation. I told her I'd never squirted and a few days after our conversation a messenger arrived with a brown package that had a San Francisco return address. When I opened it I found a video called *How to Female Ejaculate.* I watched it with a hand over my mouth, wincing, but even though the women in it were lesbianic and unattractive, they were inspiring, and afterward I spent an hour on the floor of the bathroom trying (unsuccessfully) to join the club. I went to bed frustrated by my own genital limitations but moved by Liz's gesture. She seemed to take an interest in educating a part of me that, despite my attendance at the Berkeley of the East, hadn't ever really gotten the schooling it deserved.

As soon as she got to our table she gave me a moist kiss on the cheek. I was about to introduce her to my parents when she extended her hand and said, "Liz Kaminsky. You two must be the parental extremities of this lovely creature."

"That we are," said my dad.

"You look familiar," said my mom. "Have I seen you in the neighborhood?"

"It's quite possible," said Liz. "After all, I walk the streets." My mom beckoned the waiter over and said she'd have a Chardonnay after all.

"Liz lives in the Martha Washington too," I said. I called my building that because out of twelve units, eleven were occupied by single women. The twelfth tenant was a guy named T. Russell who stayed inside all day smoking pot, judging by the fumes that regularly emerged from his door.

"Well, I hope you girls look out for each other," said my dad. Liz was standing at the head of the table, between my dad and me, and I noticed her breasts were about five inches from his eyes. She was wearing a light blue, deep v-necked cashmere shirt—the kind that leaves nothing to the imagination. My dad was leaning his head back all the way to avoid contact with the twin peaks, but I was pissed at her for standing so close. Liz was the kind of person who flirts with everyone, regardless of gender or age. She was the stink bomb of sex bombs. You couldn't run for cover.

"We certainly do look out for each other," said Liz. "I take very good care of Racheleh." She used the Yiddish derivation of my name a lot and I never knew if it was a maternal thing, a Jew-pride thing, or both.

"How did you two meet?" my dad asked.

"We had some noise issues," she said.

"You mean music?" my dad said.

"I'm afraid the noise was coming from *my* end," she said. "Literally." Before my parents could react she put her arm around me and her right boob bumped into my eye, which made my contact slide up into the lid. I'd been so worried about my dad being in the danger zone I hadn't realized *I* was.

I blinked hard and raised my hand to my eye. "Uh-oh," said Liz. "Did your contact pop out because of our contact?" My dad laughed way too loudly.

"Let me look," said my mom. She leaned across the table and stabbed at my eye like a deranged serial killer.

"Get away," I said, jerking my face back. "I'm going to the bathroom."

"I'll help you," said my mom.

"Why?" I said.

"It could be hard to find."

Inside the bathroom I stared in the mirror while my mom stood behind me and said helpfully, "Look under the lid." She had just switched from hard contacts to soft and considered herself an amateur ophthalmologist.

"Your friend is something else," she said as I hunted.

"Yeah, she's sort of a provocateur." I spotted the lens protruding near the corner. Just as it popped onto my finger I felt my underwear get wet. "Did you get it back in?" my mom said.

I placed the lens on my eyeball and blinked a few times until it settled. "Yeah, but I think I just got my period. Can I have a tampon?"

I reached for her bag but she held on to it like I was a mugger and said, "I don't have any."

"Why not?" My mom could manage a small Eastern European army with the contents of her pocketbook.

Her face got tight, delicate but determined. "Because . . . I don't need those anymore."

"*What?*" I said, feeling queasy. "When did this happen?"

"It's gradual, but it stopped for good about six months ago."

"Oh my God," I said.

"I'm not *dying*, Rachel," she said. "It's normal, you know."

I knew it was normal but it was still strange. I'd never thought of her as old before. She was only fifty-three. This wasn't supposed to happen till she was a grandmother. And God knew when that was going to be.

"You want me to go out there and ask your friend if she has any?"

"No, Liz is such a control freak I don't think she has a period. I'll just use some toilet paper." I opened the door and pushed her out.

When I got back to the table Liz was sitting in my seat, telling my parents about a synagogue scholarship she had created through Young Friends of the JCC–Manhattan. She was in a doctoral program in women's studies at Columbia but on the side she worked for many causes—cancer, the library, her people.

"So you donated the money for the scholarship yourself?" my dad was saying.

"No," said Liz. "I endowed it. I'm very good at raising things."

"I'm back," I said to Liz, hovering above the chair.

She didn't move. She just glanced up at me innocently and said, "Did you fish out the offending particle?"

"Yes," I said. "Can I have my seat back?"

"So how long have you lived in the neighborhood?" my dad asked.

"Three months," she said. "I was on Amsterdam Avenue before this and let me tell you, I'm never going back. These restaurants on Smith Street are as good as Manhattan, and so much cheaper too!" She often used a cadence that made her sound like a middle-aged Jewish mother. She was half yenta, half *korveh*.

"You should have seen this street five years ago," said my mom, warming up. No conversation topic excites middle-aged women more than gentrification. "When Rachel was little the only time we went to Smith Street was to buy kids' shoes at Johnnie's Bootery. It was all"—she lowered her voice—"Puerto Rican drug dealers. A lot of crack."

"Well, it's good the crack dealers are gone now," said Liz. "I certainly wouldn't want to live near any."

Before I could remind her she *was* a crack dealer she started waving frantically at the door. "I'm over here, Gordon!" she shouted. A tall, dark-skinned black guy was coming in. One other cause Liz worked very hard for was minority men. The whole two months I'd known her, every guy I'd seen coming or going from her apartment was Arab, Latin, or black. She was a hetero Mapplethorpe, a female De Niro.

The guy was Tyson Beckford material, with smooth cocoa skin and a shaved head, and he was wearing an Indian cotton long-sleeved shirt that only someone that attractive could get away with. Though I hadn't met him I knew he said "Fuck yeah!" when he ejaculated.

His name was Gordon Thompson III and they'd met at the Brooklyn Inn bar. She'd been drinking alone when he galloped up on horseback with some buddies and parked his horse outside. He was a member of the Black Cowboy Federation of America, this group of un-believably sexy black men who put on Stetsons and rode shiny horses throughout brownstone Brooklyn at night to call attention to the history of cowboys of color. He checked her out and she told the bartender to send him a black and tan. Instead of getting offended he laughed and drank it, and when his friends disappeared into the pool room he struck up a conversation. Since then they'd been inseparable and some nights I'd come home to find his horse tied to a lamppost.

She ran from our table, raced over to the door, gave him a long French kiss, and squeezed his ass hard with both hands. He removed them quickly and looked around, embarrassed.

"Is that her boyfriend?" said my dad.

"Liz doesn't have boyfriends."

"He looks just like Denzel Washington," my mom said.

"He doesn't look anything like Denzel Washington," I said.

Liz took him by the hand and led him to our table. "Gordon, this is my dear friend Rachel Block, and these are her parents Mr. and Mrs. Block."

"Call me Richard," said my dad. He's such a dork around black men.

"Nice to meet you," said Gordon. As they made small talk I found myself inadvertently glancing at the caricature on the wall behind Gordon's head. My mom, spotting me, turned to look, swallowed, and quickly turned back. My dad, not wanting to be left out of the game, glanced over too. Gordon spun around to see what the commotion was about and when he turned back he didn't look so good.

"*Vas? Vas?*" said Liz, craning her neck. "Oh," she said when she spotted it. "I asked the owner about that the last time I was here. It's some mascot for a French chocolate and banana drink. Isn't it adorable?"

"No, it's not adorable," said Gordon, regarding her as though he was not entirely sure how he wound up in this particular restaurant with this particular girl.

"It's meant in fun," she said. "It's cute, it's retro. It's so Uncle Ben's!" He stared at her in disbelief. "Minstrel's back!" she said. "Didn't you see *Bamboozled?*"

"Yes," he said, "but that movie was a total taking to task of—"

"Whoa there, cowboy," she said. "Calm your bad self down." He
opened his mouth to say something, then decided against it, shook
his head, and walked slowly to the door. "Gordon!" Liz called.
"Would you just—" She ran after him, calling over her shoulder, "Mr.
and Mrs. Block, delight to meet you!"

"It's *Richard!*" my dad called.

The door slammed behind her. We all turned to look as they
fought on the sidewalk without any sound. Liz put her hand on his
arm pleadingly, Gordon shook her off, and then he stormed off and
they both went out of view.

"So what did you guys think of her?" I asked.

"Quite a character," said my mom.

"Beautiful eyes," said my dad.

WHO KILLED MY WIFE?

T H E afternoon of Powell's play I couldn't do anything but pace around the apartment tearing at my hair. It wouldn't have been so bad if I had a bigger place, but it was a totally crapola one-bedroom about the size of a small studio. When you opened the door you came into a hallway that was long enough to foster the expectation of a decent-sized pad, but when you got to the end you found yourself on one side of a minuscule living room, off of which was a tiny bedroom that had a doorway but no door. For a sense of separation I had hung a bamboo shade from Pearl River on Canal but it blocked no sound and no light. The bedroom itself was so cramped the only things it fit were my queen bed and armoire. To get to the bathroom you had to walk through the bedroom in the tiny aisle between the bed and the armoire, and unless your girth was less than two feet you couldn't make it through at all.

What my apartment lacked in space it did not make up for in accoutrements. All the other women at RCRJ were really into home décor. They were dark-skinned and hairy but wanted to be Martha Stewart. They lived in the West Village in apartments paid for by their parents, decorated with the kind of generic Pottery Barn crap that made them all look alike. Despite my disdain for the conformity, I envied them their fresh flowers, throw rugs, and unstained slipcovers. My slipcover stains never came out and whenever I bought plants they died in a day.

Over the years I had done some minor improvements to my place, like caulking the holes in the floor, sweeping every six months, and hanging posters on the wall—*The Apartment, The Way*

We Were, an album cover from the Silver Jews. But no matter how cozy I tried to make it, I couldn't hide the views. The living room had two windows—one side faced the tennis bubble of New York Sports Club, and the other faced the Atlantic Avenue jail. I had rehabilitation in every direction. When I couldn't fall asleep at night, I looked out at the tennis bubble and tried to pretend my bed was a berth of a ship and the bubble was Moby-Dick, bobbing away.

An hour before I was supposed to leave for the play I opened the closet door. When I was at RCRJ I dressed weirder than most of my classmates—vintage dresses, knee-high combat boots, barrettes in my hair—but for the most part I didn't show cleavage. But now that I was going to a play written by a certified ass man, a whole new set of rules applied. You could watch for the asses in Powell's movies the way people looked for Ninas in Hirschfeld cartoons; each one featured an extraneous close-up butt shot that had nothing to do with the actual movie. I decided it would be to my advantage to highlight what I knew was his favorite feature, so I put on a tight knee-length pencil skirt that made me look like a secretary in the very best way. On top I wore a ribbed, beige wraparound that cut low but cost $120 at agnès b., and was therefore glam, not cheap.

When I got to the theater I scanned the wrinkled pusses in search of an authoritative man but didn't see anyone who paid more than a buck for the bus. Take away senior citizens and New York theater dies. You have to admire them for their loyalty but they make crappy audiences. They keep their coats on in the middle of summer and watch with morose expressions that say "I lived through Auschwitz. Now make me laugh."

My seat wasn't bad—about five rows from the front, audience left. I opened the *Playbill* and discovered that the star attraction was Mira Sorvino. I was excited for Joey because this seemed like a truly big break for him, but I wondered whether Powell was having an affair with Mira. How could any director not have sex with his leading lady? It was practically a job requirement.

As I was reading his credits, surprised to find that he'd included *Flash Flood* among them, I heard a loud male voice coming from the door. Like he was haloed in a fifty-thousand-watt spotlight, I saw him. His hair was curly and black, gray at the sideburns, and heavily receding, but he wore it slicked back and gelled like he wasn't ashamed to be a baldy. He was clean-shaven except for his bushy mustache and he walked in the brusque self-important style of someone who's made it big. Though his paunch wasn't huge by any means, he displayed it with pride, like he was from a country where stomach commanded stature. He was wearing a button-down white shirt tucked into expensive-looking gabardine slacks and his eyelashes curled out as long as a woman's.

As he spoke he gesticulated in a fey way that threw me for a loop. He was saying, "And that was when I realized that 'marriage' is just a pretty word for 'bankruptcy.'" At first I thought he was talking into a hands-free cell phone but as he moved I saw that trailing a bit behind him, just upstage, was a very attractive woman. She was blond, five-eleven, with white Carly Simon horse teeth and the blunt short cut that says *I don't need long hair to look hot.* The blonde threw me for a bigger loop than Powell's limp wrist. How could he write these ethnic fireplug women but enter on the arm of a shiksa?

As they walked up the center aisle he laughed with her and tilted his head back. I waited for him to notice me but he was turned toward her, listening overeagerly. They sat a few rows behind me, on the opposite side. I turned my head around and willed him to look my way. As though I had a God-given power of influence I'd failed to pick up on in rabbinical school, his head started to turn toward me just slightly. Joey had been right. Powell was psychic. He must have smelled my interest from across the room. I watched that aquiline nose begin to make its way toward my own fleshy beak and just as our eyes were about to meet the lights dimmed and he turned to the stage. Art always trumps love. It's so not fair.

When the lights came up Joey was standing center stage on a sparse living room set, holding a gun to his temple. "A man who can't work is worth nothing," he said. "It's like he's missing a leg. Since I'm already missing a leg I decided I'd rather have no head." He cocked the gun and just as he was about to pull the trigger there was a knock at the door. It turned out to be his maid Teresa (Mira Sorvino) coming to clean the house. He had to hide the gun so she wouldn't find it, which involved running all over the apartment and finally selecting the freezer as the appropriate spot. From then on the entire play went downhill.

It came off as an odd hybrid of screwball and melodrama—half the time people were chasing each other around the stage and the other half they were engaging in Powellsian monologues on the futility of living a happy life. By the time intermission came around, I could see why my parents had walked out.

As the house lights came up for intermission I craned my neck back at Powell to glean his reaction. He was smiling proudly, like it was a close-up on him right after his Oscar clip had been shown. There was something so incongruous about the failure of the play and the pride of its maker. I couldn't tell whether he was totally deluded or whether he knew he'd written a clunker and just didn't care. The blonde hugged him and whispered something in his ear that made him laugh. I would have projectile vomited but the seats were raked.

I pushed my way through the bluehairs, made my way to the lobby, and got on the concession stand line because I didn't have anyone to talk to. Powell was nowhere in sight. Maybe he was deliberately staying in his seat so as not to be forced to mingle with the hoi polloi. The line was long and moved slowly, and judging by their comments the seniors didn't like the play either. "This is no *Producers*," said a woman in Larry King glasses to her husband.

"*Producers?*" he said. "This is worse than *Sweet Smell.*"

When I got to the front I bought an oatmeal cookie. As I was unwrapping it I spotted Powell coming in, sans blonde. He was scanning the room nervously, like he didn't feel comfortable without his arm candy. Maybe he was going to buy some M&M's to compensate.

As his eyes cruised past me I gave him a huge Shirley Temple smile. He frowned in confusion, as though I was mistaking him for someone else, and I nodded my head up and down as slowly as I could. I felt like I was in a Molson commercial, but sometimes a girl can learn from beer.

Suddenly he broke away from the throng and strode toward me with great purpose and a huge scowl. In the bad teen movie of my brain his gait seemed to switch into slo-mo. He was the football-player thug and I was the scrawny nerd against the locker who doesn't know how to prepare.

As he got closer the slow motion switched to regular motion again and he was standing right in front of me, glaring. Before I could think of something to say he darted his head down and took a big sloppy bite of my cookie. I jumped. He chewed deliberately, unapologetically, never moving his eyes from me, and then without a word he turned and slipped back into the crowd.

My mouth was dry, my armpits dripping with sweat, my labia as swollen as the siliconed lips of a Hollywood has-been. I looked around to see if anyone else had noticed but they were all going on about the show, oblivious. I ran my finger along the U his mouth had left and touched my finger to my lips.

T H E second act had a little more energy than the first—there was a long scene where all the characters converged in Joey's apartment to convince him life was worth living—but it didn't add up. Mira and Joey eventually fell in love, and there were two dumb subplots involving her brother coming out as a gay man to his conservative Puerto Rican family, and Joey's ex-wife ordering a hit on him.

After the show Joey met me in the lobby. "You were amazing," I told him, which he was, despite the questionable material. His eyes were red and I could tell he'd already smoked something upstairs.

"We were totally off tonight," he said. "All the beats were different." Actors always had to give you TMI, too much information.

We walked over to the loft where they were throwing the party, which was a few blocks from the theater, and Joey smoked some weed on the way. It was an early September night, the kind that makes you love the city, and as we walked I breathed in deep, and looked up at the stars, hoping Joey wouldn't get arrested.

The loft was sparse and huge, with a DJ in one corner, a beautiful spread of food, a full bar, and a separate table laid out with plastic champagne flutes. There were already fifty people there—a mix of cast members, hangers-on, and celebs: Billy Crudup, Ed Burns,

Nathan Lane, and Ralph Fiennes. New York had so few parties compared to LA that celebrities all had to show up at the same ones. This was why they all ran the risk of becoming overexposed, not because they went out too much, but because there was so little to do.

The DJ was playing "You Can Make It If You Try." Powell was standing by the bar next to the blonde, deep in conversation with Ralph/Rafe/Raf. "So you want to meet Powell?" Joey asked.

"He's talking to Ralph Fiennes," I said, blushing. "I don't have to."

"Come on," he said, taking my arm. "Let me just—"

As he started to lead me over, a fey authoritarian raised a glass and tapped a knife against it. Saved by the nell. The DJ turned the music down, everyone got hushed, and a few caterers began distributing the glass trays. I took an extra-full glass. Joey didn't take any. Stoners have contempt for alcohol. It's an illogical but universal truth.

"I just want to say congratulations to everyone involved in the production," the fey guy said. "It was a great run and now we're going to *party till dawn!*"

Everyone raised their glasses and downed the champagne. I heard someone shout, "Say something, Hank!"

Powell shook his head no but after a few of the other actors called out "Yeah, Hank! Don't be shy!" he said, "All right already, if it'll quiet you children down" and moved to the front of the room. They laughed in an overamused, phony way, and then got reverentially quiet. You get sycophantic when you realize you're out of a job.

"I couldn't a done any a this without this stellar cast," Powell said. His accent was flat New York, but his *s* was affected, his lips pursed like a theater queen's. He was like Archie Bunker and Isaac Mizrahi rolled into one.

"You guys were rowdy and you could be tardy—*Robby,*" he said, eyeing Mira's brother to another round of raucous laughter, "but your enthusiasm carried me through. It almost gave me a second ulcer"—more overeager laughter—"but it carried me through. You made my first foray into the theater a ride. Not necessarily a smooth one, but a ride. Now leamme the fuck alone and get drunk." He raised his glass to his lips and the whole cast cheered loudly.

Joey went off to get me a drink and I sat down on an empty couch in a corner. I noticed my wraparound had sunk a little and my bra was peeking out. As I yanked the shirt up, I felt a shadow over me and when I looked up I was face-to-face with the scribe. He was peering at me with a kind of animal interest. I couldn't believe he'd chosen me over all these stars.

Before I realized quite what I was saying, I told him, "I don't have anything else for you to bite."

"We'll see about that," he said, chuckling so deeply I almost couldn't hear it. He squinted at me and rubbed his cheek. His eyes were steely blue-gray and looked like they could kill someone with one quick gaze. "Who are you?"

"My name's Rachel. I'm a friend of Joey's."

He sat next to me on the couch, so close the side of his thigh touched mine. I felt a bead of sweat burst out of my upper lip, and then three more, like the test kernels when you're popping popcorn. I looked around to see if anyone else had noticed he was sitting next to a total nobody but they were all caught up in conversation, and I wondered whether all of this was the weird hallucination of a groupie. "Are you afraid of me?" he said.

"A little," I said, looking at him sideways.

"You *should* be. You should be very afraid." I couldn't tell if I was supposed to laugh. "Why did you come here?"

"To see the show, but also . . ." My eyes felt wide, like a girl in a Keane painting. "But also because I wanted to meet you."

"And why did you want to meet me?"

"Because I wanted to know if you were like your characters. I've seen all your movies." It was an inevitable but crucial cliché—I figured it was better to seem educated than obsequious without due cause.

"And what's the verdict?"

"It's too soon to tell. I haven't heard enough lines."

"You're a politician! You're very clever! What did you think of my play?" He reminded me of my biblical history professor at RCRJ, Ted Snyderman, who used to call on students randomly and ask us these incredibly specific questions about the reading, inevitably the one portion we hadn't actually read.

I wanted him to know I was smarter than the average groupie, but he seemed so proud of his work I was afraid to sink his ship. "It—it was a real departure from your films," I said.

"You didn't like it."

"Well—"

"I can handle it. Be honest. I can see the cogs turnin' in ya head."

"I guess it just, didn't quite hold up to what I had come to expect from Hank Powell."

"That's right!" he said exuberantly. "It wasn't meant to!"

"Then why did you write it?"

"I wanted to taste the fruit of something new." I did too. I just hoped he wasn't the new of something fruit.

"Are you happy with how it turned out?"

"Personally, yes. From an audience perspective, no. But I answered some questions about my own mortality that have been nagging me since birth. That's the whole point of art—to answer the soul's deepest questions."

"I guess it is," I said, agreeing with the sentiment if not his execution.

"I'll tell you one thing, though," he said. "I'm glad I mounted *some*thing."

"Me too," I said. "But I hope this doesn't mean you'll stop mounting things in the future." It was the oddest thing. Something about Hank Powell made me want to one-up him. He chuckled and narrowed his eyes, like he was intrigued. I wanted him to toss me to the floor and stomp on me like grapes.

Joey came over and grinned at us, like a stoner yenta. "I see you two met," he said, handing me a beer. He was with Mira Sorvino, and the blonde Powell had come in with. Powell rose to his feet and kissed them both, but on the cheek. Mira looked good, like she was aging well. She had the kind of naturally curvaceous figure that people pay a lot of money for, and a radiant, megawatt smile. I felt intimidated because she'd gone to Harvard and wasn't a run-of-the-mill actress. She wasn't just hotter than I was; she'd gone to a better school.

They pulled up a few chairs and sat across from us. Joey introduced Mira Sorvino, who said she was pleased to meet me. The blonde shook my hand and said her name was Kim. Anyone that good-looking had to be a Kim.

"I'll tell you my favorite thing about the play," I said to Powell. "I liked how operatic it was."

"It's funny you say that," he said. "I hear that comment all the time about my movies and it never makes any sense."

"Why's that?" Mira Sorvino asked. She was smiling at him like they had something going.

"Because I experience life on a *cosmic scale*," he said, pounding his chest with his fist. "Everyone else's opera is my everyday existence."

"You mean like in *Knock for Greenberg?*" said Joey. "That was definitely your most operatic movie."

"'Loving you isn't something I choose or don't choose, Constanza,'" I said, quoting Ron Silver's heartbreaking monologue to Rosanna Arquette after they first make love on his kitchen floor. "'It's a disease creeping through my blood, infecting each of my cells like a lethal, incurable virus that leaves me sweaty and struggling to breathe.'"

"He ad-libbed that," Powell said.

I looked at Joey for help but he just shot me a helpless glance. Everyone was quiet as though I had insulted Powell so egregiously that they were going to bounce me.

And then, as quickly as if there had been no silence at all, Powell's face exploded in a wicked grin and he shouted, *"Just fucking with you!"*

"You're out of your mind, Hank!" Kim trilled.

"You should have seen him after the final dress," Mira Sorvino said, shaking her head. "I'd never seen a director get so angry."

"That's because I needed you guys to push things one step further. You see, whenever one of my actors gave a real personal, soulful performance in rehearsal I wouldn't cry or be moved. I'd just think to myself, *You think* that's *heartache?* I'll *show you heartache.*"

"That's very Jewish," I said.

No one laughed. I was Catskills in a white-bread world. "I'm not Jewish," said Powell earnestly.

I couldn't believe he was so slow on the uptake. He couldn't be dumb enough to believe I thought he was a Yid. There was one other possibility, one I wasn't quite ready to entertain: that he got my joke but didn't laugh because it wasn't his own.

"You're not?" I said fake-incredulously. "With a name like Henry Powell?"

Again there was a moment of silence. Even Joey looked confused. It's never a wise move to bring a stoner as your wingman.

"I know you're not Jewish," I said. "I was saying it was Jewish of you to glorify your own pain."

"I got it," Mira Sorvino said encouragingly.

"Rachel was in school to be a rabbi," Joey said, as though it would explain everything. This was terrific. He was whipping out my Jew card right when I was feeling most out of place.

"I didn't know rabbis came like this," Powell said, with a smirk.

"Oh, they do," I said.

"So what happened? Why'd you drop out?"

They were all looking at me like I had inadvertently wandered into the wrong party. I was sitting with the nation's greatest indie director and an Academy Award–winning actress, talking about my crisis of faith. It was like they were begging me to be a conversation-stopper. "I realized I wasn't sure I believed in God."

"You got all the way to rabbinical school before you realized that?"

"It actually happens a lot," I said.

He nodded and ran his hand over his chin. "What line of work are you in now?"

"I'm a bartender."

"It sounds like the setup for a joke."

"I know," I said quickly, noticing the annoyed looks on the women's faces. "So you going to write another play after this, Hank?" I asked brightly.

"Nah, I don't think I could do this again. It took too much outta me. Films I can handle. They're protracted, yet somehow manageable."

"So are you working on a new script?" I asked.

"Yeah. I'm gonna start shooting this winter if everything goes according to plan with this gorgeous specimen of humanity to my left." He leered at Kim, who seemed to blush.

"Are you the star?" I said.

She laughed and shook her head. "I'm his *agent.*" I heard "Joy to the World" blasting in my head.

"She gets that all the time," Powell said. "That's the world we live in these days: the agents are beautiful; the models are ugly."

"What's your movie about?" I asked.

"It's a memory flick about a murder, very dark. My homage to Berryman."

"Who?" I said.

"Ingmar Berryman. The Swedish—"

"I know who Ingmar Bergman is. I just thought it was a hard *g.*"

"No!" he bellowed. "In Sweden, the *g*'s are soft!" I could never tell when he was kidding and I wasn't sure he could either.

"What's it going to be called?" Joey asked.

Powell put his face close to mine and said, *"Who Killed My Wife?"*

"Good title," I said.

"I know," he said. "Titles are very important. I start with the title and go from there. What's the name of your bar?"

"Roxy. It used to be a jewelry store. It's in Cobble Hill, in Broo—"

"No kidding," said Powell. "I live in Cobble Hill. I'm on Strong Place. I moved there a month ago."

"Really?" I practically screamed. "I grew up there. I'm on Pacific."

"Where's Pacific? Is that near Starbucks?"

"You go to Starbucks?" I asked in shock.

"Are you outta ya mind? I go to D'Amico." D'Amico was a coffee place on Court Street that had been around for fifty years and sold roast coffee and sandwiches. I'd gone in there a few times but the local Italians who patronized it smoked cigarettes in the back and sometimes the smell made me so sick I had to leave. "They make decent cappuccino there," he said, "which is all I drink. It's smoother on the stomach than coffee, which was the cause of my first ulcer."

"You don't mind all those crazy people?"

"I love it. Everyone there should be institutionalized or incarcerated!"

I cast a glance at Mira Sorvino. She was sipping her drink and glaring at me. I had to step off Powell's tip. You don't win a man's heart by alienating his friends. "I have to tell you, Mira," I said, "I think your choice to do nudity was very brave. I loved that moment in Act Two when you ripped your shirt open and said to Joey, 'You wanna know me? This is me!'"

"That was tough for me," she said, "but I felt it was central to the moment."

"Those knockers made me very happy," said Powell. "Put a naked girl in a show and it makes it a hell of a lot easier to show up for rehearsal."

"I loved that you weren't just naked, but angry naked," I said. "It was very sexy."

"Funny thing about nudity," he said. If it were a late-night public television talk show, this would have been the moment when he leaned back and took off his glasses. "A couple years after I graduated Queens College I got a job as a stage manager in a tiny off-off-Broadway theater on East Ninth Street. One of the shows was an experimental production and in the last scene everybody in the play was supposed to get naked and simulate an orgy. This was post-*Hair* and at that particular point in time nudity was da rigga."

"What?" I said.

"Da rigga," he said. "That's French."

"Oh!" I said. "De rigueur!"

"That's what I said," said Powell, frowning. "Da rigga. The actors were doing a lot of acid at the time, sometimes even while they acted, and during the final scene, a dinner party, which was supposed to develop slowly, I noticed one a the guys acting strange, forgetting his lines. I was watching this from up in the booth. At a certain point he begins casually removing his clothes, one item at a time. But you see, this wasn't the part when they were supposed to do it. The naked part wasn't till page seventy-six and we were only on fifty-one. So he keeps stripping until finally, as though it's written into the script, he moseys over to a corner of the stage, squats down, and takes the most enormous dump I ever seen in my life." He paused and grinned wickedly.

"Oh my God," said Mira Sorvino.

"Are you serious?" said Joey.

"Evidently he had taken some magic mushrooms before the show and lost control of his bowels along with his mind. The audience was shifting in their seats. The cast members didn't know what to do. Some were continuing with the scene, others broke character and gaped openly. I knew that if ever there was a time a stage manager was needed it was now. But my ass was like Fluffernutter on the chair. The lighting guy was screaming at me to do something. People were walking out. Finally something snapped inside me. I yanked off my headset and ran down."

"You cleaned up the shit?" I said.

"*No!* I ran out of the theater! It was one of those situations where there's *nothing you can do but run away!*"

His face was blank, poised like a freeze-frame, his eyes bright, his tongue glistening. He stayed in this tableau for three solid seconds, threw his head back, and laughed at the top of his lungs: *"Heh heh heh heh heh!"* Then he stopped just as abruptly, his mouth still frozen in a smile, and glanced at us eagerly like he was cueing us to join in. Immediately we let out affirming chuckles too, at which point Powell erupted in another louder, longer wave himself. It was as though he couldn't experience anything as funny unless he had company. He was boisterous but lonely, and something about that combination made me want to know more.

"When Sam Shepard taught playwriting at Davis," I said, "the class met in the scene shop and sometimes while he was lecturing he would just go over to a prop toilet in the corner and take a piss in front of the students." I nodded to emphasize that there was a scatological through line from his story to mine, but Powell just said, "Shepard's overrated," stood up, and walked out into the crowd. A few minutes later the women followed.

"Powell likes you," Joey said.

"I totally blew it with that Shepard line," I said.

"He gave you a lot of attention. He doesn't give people attention when he doesn't think they're worth his time."

"But what about Mira Sorvino? They seem to have some history."

"He tried to sleep with her at the beginning of rehearsal but she rejected him."

"Why?"

"She thought he was too sleazy." I wished he had chosen not to share that. No girl wants to know her heartthrob's another chick's table scrap—even if that chick is a celebrity.

As we sat there I kept eyeing Powell, waiting for him to come back, but people kept coming up to him to congratulate him and it became clear he wasn't going to return. Finally I told Joey I was leaving and went over to Powell, who was talking to Nathan Lane. "Reinvention is overrated," Powell was saying.

"Sorry to interrupt," I said, smiling wanly. "I just wanted to say I'm leaving, Mr. Powell. It was an honor to meet you."

"You as well," he said archly. He was so hot and cold—the kind of guy who could turn the asshole on and off in an instant.

"Feel free to stop by my bar," I said. "Bergen and Smith. Or maybe I'll see you at D'Amico someday."

"But you said everyone there was crazy," he said.

"Then I guess one more can't hurt," I said, and exited stage right.

MOMS WITH THONGS

WH E N I got home I found Liz on the stoop, smoking a cigarette. She didn't have any roommates but she only smoked outside. My secret theory was that she liked to scope the three Dominican guys next door who played dominos on the sidewalk. They were there every weeknight from April till whenever it got cold—they put a small card table out, smoked cigarettes, listened to Spanish radio, and laughed loudly at each other's jokes. I'd known them five years, since I moved onto the block. Virgilio was short and in his forties with a sweaty face and thick glasses, Levi was in his sixties and wore a white Kangol cap, and Mariano was a hot daddy with a gorgeous wife and baby girl.

"Hellooo!" Liz screamed when she saw me. "What a delight to see you, my sweet Racheleh!" I sat down next to her as she gave me a bear hug. "I'm so glad to bump into you. I've been wanting to talk to you about the other night."

"You have?" I said, incredulous at her uncharacteristic self-awareness.

"Of course! I'm mortified that Gordon had the nerve to throw a Black Power hissy in front of your parents." Perhaps I had overestimated her.

"Wouldn't you be mad," I said, "if it were some hook-nosed Jew?"

"That would never happen. Jewish mascots don't move product. But I'll tell you one thing: that's the last time I take a black guy to Banania. He got so mad he dumped me! It started out as an argument over the painting but then we got onto other crucial subjects such as my unwillingness to take him up to Chappaqua." Liz's parents had made a fortune in real estate and lived down the road from the Clintons, and judging by the family photos Liz had shown me, they were snooty, cold, and assimilated—*Ice Storm* Jews. "He accused me of being a closet racist," she said, "I accused him of being too PC, and he said he never wanted to see me again."

"I'm sorry," I said.

"He was so slammin' in bed," she sighed. "I mean, the man let me rim him for *hours*. He had literally the most delicious rectum I have ever tasted."

Liz was obsessed with men's butts, and more particularly their assholes. When she wanted to express admiration for a guy, she would say breathlessly, "I wanted to bury my face in his wrinkled anus." She also enjoyed having her own asshole violated, and said the reason she loved black guys was because they were more open to doing so.

"How am I going to survive without Gordon?" she moaned, looking up at the moon as though it should answer. "He made me feel so good about myself. He told me I had the perfect-sized tits. Do guys ever tell you that?"

I looked down at my rack. I can hold a pencil under each breast. I can hold *candles*. I've lost quarters in my bra only to find them weeks later, with receipts, and small pieces of black licorice. Men do not tell me, "You have the perfect-sized tits." They say, *"You have the biggest tits I've ever seen."*

"Actually, no," I said.

"I don't know what I am going to do without him," she said. "I already ordered four new vibes for the box but it saddens me too much to have to use them." She had told me once that she kept all her sex toys under the bed in a Sigerson Morrison shoe box. "I mean he was *so* good in bed. I came like half a dozen times each time we had sex."

"Half a dozen times?" I said.

"Yeah, spread out, but still. He was so into me being on top. I guess because he rode horses so often, when he was in bed he wanted cowgirl. It's my favorite position."

"Why?"

"Because of the clit stim."

"But if somebody's using their hand it really doesn't matter what position you're in, does it?" This was the way I'd always gotten off with David and I'd never really given it much thought. I'd only slept with two other guys before him—Sam Rubinstein, my boyfriend the first two years of Wesleyan, who usually made me come by going down on me, after which we'd have sex, and John Suk, the Korean guy who had devirginated me at a party senior year of Stuyvesant and didn't make me come at all.

Liz regarded me as though I had walked into a toga party wearing street clothes. "Oh, sweetie," she lamented gravely. "Get with the times. This is the hands-free generation. You don't know about CAT?"

"What's that?"

"Coital alignment technique." She glanced at the garbage cans behind the gate in front of the building and picked up a stained pin-striped pillow that was resting on the ground.

"That's disgusting."

"Calm down, it's mine. I threw it out this morning." She placed the pillow on the sidewalk, flicked her cigarette into the street, climbed aboard, and began gyrating in slow motion like a recently institutionalized lap dancer. Her hands were on either side of the pillow and her face was just a few inches from the sidewalk.

"You see?" she said. "Grind, grind. And around, and around and around."

After a few more thrusts the domino players started pointing and talking loudly in Spanish, egging her on. "Looking good, Leez!" Virgilio shouted.

"Cómo estás, Virgilio?" she said, waving cheerfully. The window to the apartment building opened. A fat teenager stuck his head out and flashed her a big thumbs-up.

"Okay. I got it," I said, lifting the pillow out from beneath her and depositing it back in the can. Liz was like an eccentric older uncle at a family gathering: you can't stand being around him for more than an hour but you can always count on him to make the night more entertaining.

"So what should I do about Gordon?" she said. "It's so rare to find a guy who doesn't have rimming issues, and rarer still to find one that's hung like his own horse."

"Go to that Caribbean restaurant on Atlantic and Hoyt," I said. "Brawta. They get a good bourgeois black crowd."

"Nah," she said. "I have to stop dating these shines. They're too high-maintenance."

"*Shines?* No wonder he dumped you!"

"I wouldn't have so many problems with men if I could figure out how to be more like you. You date the right kind of guys. Good boys."

"That's a horrible thing to say."

"It's true!" she said. "What about David?"

I'd met David in my first month of RCRJ and somehow he became my boyfriend before I had a chance to decide how I felt about him. I was in the cafeteria carrying my lunch tray, headed for my usual table by a poster of Chagall's *Music* in a dark corner where nobody else liked sitting, and when I got there I saw someone in my seat. He was a tall, lanky pale-faced guy with shoulder-length red hair, and before I could find another spot he said, "I'm sorry, was this table taken?" I didn't want to be a total asshole and I hadn't made that many friends, so I shook my head no and sat down across from him. He was a second-year cantorial student from Cambridge, the son of a concert violinist. Almost all the male cantorial students were gay, so my instinct was to dismiss him as a prospect. But he shook my hand without giving me a total dead fish and over the course of our conversation he mentioned the Red Sox, so I optimistically told myself there was a chance he was a breeder.

He was funny and thought I was too, which was good since almost all of my classmates regarded me as though I was some weird rabbinic freak of nature, beamed down from Frisbee U. They mocked the fact that I wore barrettes in my hair and 1940s dresses, instead of the typical Jansport knapsack, jeans, and T-shirts. David wasn't like that. He was actually wearing a Sebadoh shirt the day we met, and he wore oxblood Doc Martens.

He told me his mother was brought up Irish Catholic and later converted when she met his dad. He said, "So that makes me a McJew." He kept dropping Yiddishisms, with lines like, "The first couple weeks of classes it was such mishegoss I could hardly keep my head on I was so *fakakta*," but it came off more charming than Linda Richman–cheesy. He had warm blue eyes that twinkled when he laughed and his hair was shiny and thick. At the end of lunch when he asked if I was single I shot back with, "I'm not single. I'm unaffiliated," and he laughed and laughed.

We dated from Simchas Torah to Purim, which means about five months. At the beginning it was amazing—he'd go down on me for hours in his Park Slope apartment and when he was finished he'd practice trope and I'd do my reading. But sometimes when we were rolling around his hair would catch under my hand and he'd cry out "Ow!" in this high-pitched voice, and once when I was going at it especially vigorously on top, he said I was crushing him, which was totally embarrassing. (We weighed about the same—one forty-five, except he was six inches taller.)

Sometimes he'd wake me up in the middle of the night sobbing, saying he was afraid I was going to leave him, and I'd have to stroke his hair until he fell back asleep. And other times when we were out to dinner he'd just stare at me, his mouth hanging open, not saying anything, a look of suffocating love oozing from his eyes. It wasn't that I didn't want him to be human; I just didn't want him to be so overt about his need.

Yet despite all my doubts I felt I should give him a chance because he was Jewish and arty, he cared about me, and I knew he wanted to have children. It didn't hurt that my parents loved him and he was Sephardic, not Ashkenazic, which meant our kids wouldn't even get Tay-Sachs.

So I stayed. And suddenly the other students got nicer to me. They'd say, "You two look so cute together," or, "What an adorable couple." I tried not to put too much stock in them but when the whole world tells you you've won the lottery, your instinct is to agree. My parents kept making noises that we should marry, and I told myself they were right. He had all the trappings of correctness—cantorial, intelligent, witty, sensitive—but emotionally I couldn't get it up. He was the Emperor's New Boyfriend.

One uneventful night in March we went to *Bend It Like Beckham* at the Sunshine theater on Houston, and on our way out to the street something snapped. It might have been the erection problems he was having as a result of his Zoloft, or his constant tirades against the seemingly never-ending reign of the Yankees. Or it might simply have been that he loved the movie and I found it totally insipid and contrived, but when we got outside I was surprised to hear myself say, "I don't think we should go out anymore."

He cocked his head and said, "What are you talking about?"

"I don't think I should be so serious with someone so early on in school," I said.

"That doesn't make any sense," he said. "We have so much fun together." I looked at him silently and he said, "What? I'm not fun?"

"You are, you are," I said desperately. "I just think you need to be with someone who can appreciate you."

"And you don't?"

"Not the way I should."

"Well, then what's wrong with you?" he shouted angrily.

"I'm not sure," I said, as I stepped out into the street to hail a cab.

For the rest of school I ate lunch in a diner a couple blocks from campus so I wouldn't have to run into him, and when I passed him in the halls I averted my eyes. He hadn't called me once since then, even after I dropped out. Sometimes I felt guilty about doing it so abruptly but more than anything I had this lingering anger at myself for trying to believe someone wrong was right. When you're in your twenties, five months is a long time to waste.

"Why would you want to date a David," I asked Liz, "when he's not even my BF today?"

"He was the right type! Don't be ashamed of it. Embrace it. You have an uncanny ability to fall for men your parents would appreciate."

A part of me wanted to tell her about Powell, but something about the admiring look in her eye told me this was not the time to confide. I was Liz's pedestal girl, the one she looked to as an example of how she was supposed to be. Every girl needs a pedestal girl on which to pin her vision of her ideal self. Nine times out of ten the pedestal girl isn't really moral at all—she's just more discreet—but the worshiper clings to the fake vision or else she has no reason to try to be good.

What Liz didn't know was that she was my pedestal girl too. She was the one I looked to so I could learn how to be slutty and base. She was the one who'd been in the back of my mind when I said things to Powell like "I hope this doesn't mean you'll stop mounting things in the future." She was my motivator, my evil twin. I didn't want her to meet a nice Jewish guy; we'd never have anything to talk about.

"I haven't been able to introduce my parents to one of my own boyfriends," she announced, "since freshman year at Hampshire when I was dating Lenny Lichtenstein, who later turned out to be a flaming Mary. Now he runs Gayjews.com. You know what their motto is? 'When you need a little *tuchis.*'"

"So date some MOTs." That was what we called Members of the Tribe.

"But the Jews never notice me! The Yids rebuke me continually, while the working class and minorities flock to me! I'm like the Statue of Liberty!" Before Gordon she had dated a Bay Ridge refrigerator repairman she'd met at a bar on Smith Street called Angry Wade's.

"Why don't you go on JDate?"

Her eyes popped out in horror. "Have you seen the men's photos on those sites? They're myopic and zitty. They look like Robert Wuhl!"

"You're so self-hating."

"There's no 'self' in this hatred! The women are knockouts and the men are heinous and over forty with kids. I don't want to be a stepmother to a bunch of Ramaz brats. I have to find a hot mensch with a lot of money who is grateful to have me. I'm thirty-two years old! I just want a nice guy who is kind, treats me well, and lets me lick his asshole from time to time. Is that so much to ask?"

"No it's not, baby!" said Virgilio, standing up and shaking his butt at her. "I'll give you what you want right now!" The other three guys erupted in a chorus of laughter.

"Oh, for goodness sake," she muttered.

"Whassa matta, Leez? You no hear me? I got what you want right here!" He did a salsa dance up and down the sidewalk as his friends pointed and howled.

"Yours is the only asshole in New York City I *wouldn't* lick, Virgilio!"

"Why's that, baby?"

"Ask your girlfriend," she said, pointing to Mariano. The laughter stopped.

"You calleen me a woman?" said Mariano, getting up too.

"Uh-oh," she said. "We'd better get out of here." I put the key in the lock and we raced inside, giggling.

T H A T night as I fell asleep I replayed my conversation with Powell over and over again. I knew it was bad to be into someone semifamous and not Jewish but he had cast a spell over me and I didn't want anything to break it. I wanted to believe that his interest in me was more than just passing, that he'd seen something special, something worth knowing better. But it was stupid to think I had a chance. Joey had said it; he was a devil with women. He probably just got off on flirting with fresh meat and I'd played right into his hand. Right at this very second he was probably fucking Kim doggystyle on an expensive bed with a mirror on the ceiling. Just because she was his agent didn't mean she wasn't also his girl.

And yet despite all my worries, as I fell asleep I imagined him covering my mouth with his hand. I saw myself screaming with wide excited eyes as he suppressed my cries and instead of making me frightened I nestled in this vision like it was a beautiful dream of something about to begin.

When I woke up the next morning Joey called. "You missed a good night," he said. "We stayed a long time after you left. Nathan Lane was doing these disco moves with Mira Sorvino. Powell got drunk and told a lot of stories about when he was a Hollywood golden boy, after *Bassett Hound* won the Spirit Award. Did you know he used to date Demi Moore?"

"Did you have to tell me that?"

"I'm just saying you're in good company."

"He said he wants to date me?"

"No, but he said, 'That girl is very ambitious.'"

"I'm a bartender!"

"It doesn't matter. You made an impression. I'm telling you, he reads people."

"Does he have e-mail?" I said.

"Hold on a second, I think it's on the contact sheet." He came back and said, "Anima@aol.com."

"What does 'anima' mean?"

"Beats me."

After we hung up I went over to the dictionary. "Anima—in the doctrine of Carl Jung, the feminine presence in a man. See also *animus*." Animus turned out to be "the masculine presence in a woman." Maybe this explained the limp wrist.

I went to my computer and wrote an e-mail in one quick burst: "Dear Mr. Powell, I am Joey's friend Rachel who met you last night at the party. I haven't lived very long but it was one of the high points of my short life. You are exactly who I expected, which is a good thing. Those flat vowels and the eyes that take in everything, even when a person doesn't think they are at all. I would like to talk to you. I'm trying to figure out what I'm supposed to do in life and right now I don't have a whole lot of ideas. You seem to know. You seem to know your own myth. Anyway I would like to drink a cup of coffee with you, at D'Amico or somewhere else." I put my phone number and signed it, "Love, Rachel. P.S. If I asked you really nicely, would you give me an anima?"

As soon as I sent it I clicked Check Mail, as though he could have read the entire e-mail, responded, and sent it back to me in a nanosecond. E-mail makes people lose all sense of logic and rationality. I got up, made a cup of tea, logged on, and checked again. I showered and checked, naked. I dressed, walked to the door, went back to the desk, and checked one final time for posterity. Nada. I knew my mistake. Never end a mash note with a scatological joke.

— ◆ —

I **A L W A Y S** ate breakfast at a little deli next to Cobble Hill Park, on Clinton Street and Verandah Place, and ordered an everything bagel and a large coffee with milk. But today when I told the counter boy the coffee part I stopped myself and said, "Make that a cappuccino."

"A cappuccino?" he said.

"Much better for the stomach."

I brought the food outside and sat in my favorite wicker chair outside the door. Just as I was opening the paper a gaggle of mothers came down the street, wheeling strollers. The mommy brigade was one of the unfortunate consequences of drinking morning coffee by a playground. Two of the women had single strollers and one had a monstrous double. They had shoulder-length blunt cuts and wore bright-colored Nikes, sunglasses on their heads, exercise pants, and T-shirts that were ostentatiously tight, like they were desperate to prove to the world that they hadn't totally domesticated out, they still had tits, however drained.

The one with the double was a blonde and had two sickeningly angelic two-year-old twins. Her friends were a hippieish brunette with a dark-skinned black toddler boy, and an Asian woman with a fat biracial baby boy and a large greyhound.

"Jacob can't fall asleep unless he has my breast in his mouth," said the Asian woman. "It's so embarrassing, but what am I going to do? Yank it out so he can keep us up the whole night?"

"Nicky was the same way," said the blonde, pointing to one of the towheads. "Whenever he woke up I'd just stick the tit in. Mark always used to say, 'He's going to need therapy when he grows up!'" They laughed in a horrendous, nasal, upper-class chorus and parked their strollers right next to where I was sitting. "What do you guys want in your coffees?" the blonde asked. The other two gave their orders and tried to give her money but she waved them off and went inside.

I peered over at her kids. The boy was sleeping and the girl was staring into space and picking her nose. Suddenly she seemed to realize her mother was not in the two-foot proximity, pulled her finger out of her nostril, and started to bawl, *"Mommy!"*

"Mommy will be right back," said Adoptive Mom.

The kid only shrieked louder and a second later her brother woke up and started bawling too. Adoptive Mom squatted down and tried to distract them with a rattle attached to the stroller. As she knelt I saw a thong sticking all the way up out of her jogging pants, Monica-style. It was bright red mesh and it rose so high it boggled the mind. I tried not to look but I was transfixed. It was like a Bee Gees song: "How Deep Is Your Crack?" She had to be in pain. Was this a deliberate flash, an attempt to compensate for her malfunctioning womb? She couldn't conceive but she wanted the world to know she was a babe?

She seemed to sense me staring because she turned around abruptly. I tried to look away but it was too late. She blushed, yanked her shirt down, and went back to consoling the child.

Just as I was recovering from the Mom with Thong incident the blonde came out with three coffees and the babies stopped crying as if on cue. "Mommy's right here," she said. She doled out the coffees to her friends like they were juice boxes. They each took one sip and then deposited the cups into these black holders attached to the side of the strollers.

These women were Ubermoms, on a tear to make mothering seem like some glorious grand achievement, when all you had to do to become one was lie on your back. I felt like motherhood was this awful disease the baby passed on to you on its way down that eerie canal. How else to explain the way the moms' decibel levels soared as soon as the kid popped out? How come as soon as they had a baby they began talking about themselves in the third person—"Mommy has to get her hair cut," "Mommy's coming, sweetie," "Mommy's going to have a sesame bagel. What kind do you want?"

I wished there was a vaccine I could take now to insure I'd never become the way they were. I didn't know what to do with my life but I didn't want to wind up like them. But it seemed so inevitable. Maybe none of these women had been rabbis, but before they had kids they ran corporations or traded stocks. Now they all seemed so content to nurse and make small talk about diaper varieties, like that was what gave them true joy.

If I was still living in Cobble Hill at thirty, with a husband and a baby, I'd be an even more disgusting breed than they were—not just an Ubermom but a *holdover* Ubermom. I saw a few of those on Court Street from time to time—girls I'd gone to nursery school with, or Hebrew school, who were the same age as me and were now living in brownstones of their own with non-native-Brooklynite husbands, wheeling a baby down the same streets they'd been wheeled down, pushing a kid on the same swings we used to swing on. Sometimes they'd recognize me and say hi and as we made chitchat I'd stare at the kid, totally befuddled, trying to figure out how it could have been squeezed out of a vagina the same age as mine.

Their coffees upright in the holders, the children momentarily silent, the greyhound under control, the Ubermoms gripped the handles of the strollers in unison, tilted them up like there was some really complex art to it, and headed down Verandah Place. "This is where Walt Whitman used to live," I heard the blonde say. She was wrong—it was Thomas Wolfe—but I knew better than to interact. I tried to go back to the paper but I couldn't focus. I had to get out of this neighborhood.

A T three o'clock that afternoon, as I was getting ready for work, the phone rang. I checked the caller ID. Blocked. I let the machine pick up. "Hello, Rachel," said a distinct, flat voice into my answering machine. "This is Hank Powell. What is my myth?"

I skipped to the phone and picked it up. "Don't you know?" I said.

"I do, but I'd like to know your answer."

"Well," I said, desperately trying to get my brain to focus, "it seems like the story you tell over and over again in your movies is about men figuring out how to be men, how to maintain their independence but at the same time come to terms with the responsibilities of domesticity."

"That's wrong!"

"But what about that line in *Lydia's Chest Wound* when Scooter tells Lydia, 'Marriage is like an unjust war. A man hates every minute of it but doesn't go MIA because his ingrained sense of responsibility outweighs the crippling guilt he feels at having sold his soul to the devil'?"

"Yeah, but then he leaves her!"

"I know, but I always felt he wanted to go back."

"Are you crazy? He'd never go back. He wanted her but he couldn't stand to be a part of the greatest evil of the known world: the bourgeois ideal."

"What's that?"

"Why don't I tell you over dinner?" I couldn't believe it. He'd upsold from a coffee to a meal. "Are you free at eight o'clock tomorrow night?"

"Yes," I said, wishing I could rewind and pretend I had a life. "But—"

"But what?"

"A girl's not supposed to make plans with a man so quickly. She's supposed to make him wait. There's an entire book about it. It's called—"

"*The Rules.* I know all about that book." It was incongruous to think of Powell as having read *The Rules.* It seemed so after his time. Then again he was single. No single man, even one in his fifties, could escape the terrifying power of *The Rules.*

"Well, if you've read it then you know one of the Rules is that you're not supposed to take a date for Saturday after Wednesday."

"Fuck all a that. I once dated a girl who was doing that book. I could predict each move she made. Everything was tactical. She made me wait for dates, she withheld sex, she cut conversations short. Finally I figured out the game she was playing and I bought the book. Once I read it I realized I could pinpoint the exact moment I was going to get her into bed. Instead of keeping it going I immediately lost interest. Her scent no longer intrigued me. I was a dog whose erection had gone down. When it comes to me you gotta throw all that shit out the window."

I loved that he had said "you." I felt it indicated that I was a real, legitimate romantic interest. He was counseling me which games not to play, which at least meant he was sitting at the table.

"Do *you* do the Rules?"

"No, and maybe that's my downfall. "I'm always the left, never the leaver. This is because I have the open and ready heart of a virgin."

"Somehow I don't believe you," I said.

"I'm not kidding," he said. He yawned loudly. "I gotta get back to work. So dinner. There's a place I like called Saul. It's on—"

"I know where it is," I said. "I'm from the hood."

T H A T night Roxy was so slow that I kept checking the total on the cash register the way some people check their answering machines. I wished it had been busier, partly for the money but mainly so I would have had something to distract me from thoughts of Powell. My hands were shaking so much I kept screwing up the Guinness pour, which wouldn't have bothered me so much if it hadn't taken me my first two weeks to master.

By eight o'clock I only had a few customers besides Jasper—a Cosmo complaining about her hot-and-cold boyfriend to a Stoli Tonic; a Jack and Coke laughing loudly with his buddy, Red Bull–and–Absolut; a Turkey Rocks with a chaser, who always came in alone; and a Merlot on a date with a Jack Daniel's. Jasper, who was sporting two huge muttonchops and pulling on a Harp, had been whining to me about some woman who had given him his number. When he called it turned out to be the Rejection Line, this voice mail that had a recorded female voice saying, "The person who gave you this number does not wish to go out with you or see you ever again."

"Why would she do that?" he said. "I mean how could she be so cruel?"

"Some people have really evil senses of humor," I said, shrugging.

"I don't know what my problem is," he said. "I'm a loyal, upstanding guy with a huge heart and I haven't had a girlfriend in three years." On the one hand I felt sorry for him. He *was* loyal, and funny, and really smart. But he spent every night of the week in a bar and he had a twenty-pound beer gut. It's very hard to broach the subject of alcoholism when you're talking to the person in a bar.

"Maybe you gotta get out more," I said.

"I am out!" he said. "It's not like I'm sitting at home. I'm right here, in primo territory for meeting bee-yotches. You see me with the women. I'm nice, aren't I? I mean, I'm a good guy, right?"

"Sure you are," I said.

"I used to think it was my weight but do you have any idea how many women I've been with who say they love my belly?" He leaned in conspiratorially. "They say it's great for clit stim."

I was in an episode of *The Twilight Pussy*. Everyone knew about clit stim but me. "Is that so?" I said.

"I don't understand it," he said. "They like me, they'll fuck me, but they won't stay. They can't conceive of me as boyfriend material. I'm the one they talk to when they're bumming about some jerk, and then when they're finished crying on my shoulder they go home. I'm the shoulder man. I want to be the asshole."

"You definitely don't want to be the asshole," I said.

"You've only been working here a month and already you're swearing?" a voice said by the door.

A panic shot through me and I spun around to look. "What are you doing here?" I said.

"Mom and I had a fight and I had to get out of the house!"

"You can't just walk in here and buy a drink, Dad," I said, lowering my voice so Jasper wouldn't hear.

"I'm sorry, miss," he said, looking around at the décor, fake-confused. "Am I mistaken? Is this a bar? I was certain this was a bar."

"I'm trying to cultivate a tough attitude here," I hissed. "I can't have these people knowing I have a father."

"How can I stay away from the night spots when the neighborhood's in such a glorious state of transition?"

"All right, all right," I said. "Just sit down."

"And I am not just any geezer. I happen to be a very happening fifty-four-year-old."

"Fifty-five," I said.

"You got me," he said. "But am I not happening?"

His hair was matted and standing straight up, like he'd been touching it all day. Evidently he hadn't dyed it in some time because the roots were whitish-gray and the rest was orangey brown.

I always told him he should get it done professionally but he was
hooked on his Just for Men. His beard, which he didn't dye, was
grayish and overgrown and contrasted with his dyed hair. He was
wearing a pair of Birkenstocks with bulky white athletic socks that
bulged out from under the straps. One had a yellow stripe at the
top and the other had no stripe at all.

His T-shirt displayed a series of silhouettes—a monkey, a Neanderthal man, modern man, a modern man with a slouch, and a modern man sitting at a computer with horrible posture. The caption
below read, "Somehow, somewhere, something went terribly
wrong." The shirt was tucked into khaki shorts that were hiked up
to the middle of his belly, and he must have been in a rush when he
dressed, because the tail of his shirt was protruding straight out of
his partially unzipped fly.

I pointed to the shirt peenie. "Whoops," he said, pulling the zip-
per down a little and sticking it back in. I spotted Cosmopolitan staring at us and I shot her a death glance. It was one thing for me to
mock my father, it was another thing for anyone else to.

He sat down at the bar next to Jasper. I felt very conscious of how
I was dressed. I was in a tight white tank, dark blue jeans, and high
black platforms. I had blown my hair out straight and put on dark
red lipstick and thick mascara. I hated dressing like a whore but the
business was better.

"Jasper," I sighed. "This is my dad, Richard Block. Dad, this is
Jasper. My personal bodyguard."

"Pleasure to meet you, Mr. Block," said Jasper, extending his
hand.

"I'm very grateful to you," said my dad, a somber look on his face.
He was such a moron I felt ashamed we shared blood.

"I'd defend Rachel's life any day," said Jasper. Evidently my dad
wasn't the only moron in the establishment.

"What can I getcha, Dad? Dewar's and soda?"

"No. 'When in Rome.' What are you drinking, Jasper?" He peered
over like a child at a lunch table.

"Harp. It's pretty good."

"All right, then. Pour me wannadose, barkeep."

"What accent was that, Dad?"

"Italian."

"It sounded more Belgian."

I poured the drink and slid it over. He took a big swig and looked down into it morosely. My father can be so bipolar.

"What's the matter?" I said.

"Your mother's impossible to be around these days. She dropped a plate on the floor when she was loading the dishwasher and started to cry. I told her it was just a plate and she said, 'Corelle's not supposed to break!', ran into the bedroom, and slammed the door."

"Are you sure you're talking about Mom?" My mom had her moments but for the most part she was very even-keeled.

"No, your other mother," he said. "Your real mother, the one who lives in a trailer park in Tallahassee. Of course I'm talking about Mom. It's been like this since she started—"

"I know. She told me." Jasper raised an eyebrow. This was all I needed—to have my customers know the intimate details of my mother's menopause.

"It's a very difficult change! I don't know why the medical establishment hasn't looked into mood stabilizers as a solution."

"They have. They're telling women to take Effex—"

"Not for the women, for the men! It's like a war zone in there! Yesterday in the middle of *Frasier* she ripped open her shirt like Tarzan. I asked if she had a thing for Kelsey Grammer and she said it was a hot flash."

"A lot of guys would be grateful to have their wives rip off their shirts spontaneously," Jasper said.

"Are you kidding? It was terrifying!" he whimpered. "She's moody all the time. She never used to yell and now she yells. *I'm* used to being the yeller. She'll snap at me for no reason, like if I leave my jacket on the sofa or don't hang up the bath mat. And she leaves the thermostat so low I'm freezing my ass off all the time."

Though I was glad my dad was reaching out I wasn't used to the notion of playing his confidante. I could handle it with the guy patrons, but with him it was too much information. "Why are you telling me this?" I said.

"You're my daughter!" he said, like that explained it. "And it's just not something I feel comfortable talking to Mom about. I told her to go on hormone replacement, but since that study she's convinced it leads to breast cancer. I don't know how bad it can be if Lauren Hutton's on it."

"Yeah, I saw that commercial. 'Knowledge is power. Information is how you get it.'"

"That's what I tell Mom, but every time I suggest HRT she calls me 'menophobic.' She's on this soy kick now, but as far as I can smell all it's doing is improving her bowels."

"OK! Stop right there!" I made the "beep-beep-beep" noise of a truck backing up.

"Ever since her 'change' she's never home. She's either away folk dancing or at a book group meeting or—"

"So? She can't leave the house?"

"She should be taking care of Number One! Do I look like the kind of guy who can take care of myself? My fly was unzipped when I came in!"

Red Bull–and–Absolut was waving at me from down the bar. I jerked to attention and shimmied over. I had to be more on the ball. I'm awful at multitasking and it's pretty much the only skill a bartender has to have.

"Could we get another round?" he said.

I fixed their drinks and lay down the change. Caitlin had taught me to give singles because otherwise they'd never tip, but half the time they didn't tip anyway.

Someone had put "Just Like a Woman" on and my dad started singing along. "'Nobody has to guess that baby can't be blessed/Till she finds out that she's like all the rest—'"

"Nice voice, Mr. B.," said Jasper.

"How kind of you, Jasper," he said. "My daughter thinks I have a terrible voice."

"You do have a terrible voice," I said.

"I think it's melodic," said Jasper. The gay prom was killing me.

There was some motion by the door and then my mom walked in. She was wearing a royal blue polo shirt and mom jeans, and her cheeks were flushed, I wasn't sure why. She waved at me cheerily and came all the way over to the bar before she spotted my dad and scowled.

"What are *you* doing here?" he asked.

"I came to talk to Rach."

"But that's what *I'm* doing!"

"So?" she said. "Who's stopping you?"

"You see what I mean?" he said, throwing his hands up. "She's lippy all the time."

Stoli Tonic was beckoning me for another round. I made the drinks and when I came back my dad was saying, "I can't be around you when you're acting like a crazy person!" Though they bickered occasionally, like when she threw something important out or he put the dishes in the refrigerator, they usually didn't do it in public. Usually they fought in their bedroom, with the door closed.

"The only reason I ever act like a crazy person is because you don't have any sympathy for what I'm going through!"

"Mom," I said, leaning over and touching her arm.

"This doesn't involve you, Rachel," she said.

"You're in my bar," I said. "I think it does."

"This isn't something I can control!" my mom spat. "It's a normal part of a woman's life but I can't get through it unless you show a little compassion. Joan Ibbotson says Peter's been very nurturing!"

"But she's on HRT!" he yelled.

"I'm not going to give myself cancer just because the patriarchal medical establishment tells me to." It's a dangerous day when your own mother starts using the word "patriarchal."

"OK," he said, "but there have got to be other solutions besides Rice Dream!"

"What—like testosterone? Fine! I'll try testosterone! I can't wait to see the look on your face when I sprout a *penis!* You can have DruPaul as your wife!"

"Mom," I said. "It's *Ru*Paul."

"Whoever!" My dad snickered as though *he* had half a clue who RuPaul was. "Do you see how he patronizes me?" she said.

"You're not around enough to patronize," he said. "You're gallivanting about town all the time."

"Am I not allowed to have a life? Am I not allowed to have interests outside of you?" I noticed some motion at the end of the bar. Cosmopolitan and Stoli Tonic were getting up from their seats. My parents were driving out my clientele.

"Did you see what you just did?" I said. "You guys are affecting my income! Would you please take this outside?"

"I'm not going anywhere," said my dad. "I want to finish my Harp."

"You're turning into a lush," my mom sighed, taking the seat next to him.

"There are no Jewish alcoholics!" he said.

"What about Sammy Davis Jr.?"

"He doesn't count!"

"Dad thinks I'm crazy because of my change but *he's* the one taking to the bottle."

"That's it!" he said, lumbering to his feet. "If you're going to stay, I'm outta here." He strode out, muttering something under his breath. I didn't know which was worse: that he'd driven out my customers or forgotten to leave a tip.

My mom leaned forward and said, "Why don't you pour me a glass of your best white wine?"

I felt a little manipulative but Mike had been encouraging me to push the new Pinot. "We got a good Pinot Blanc in. You want that?"

"Gimme a taste." I poured and she took a big sip. "Oh, that's good. Fill it up." My upper-middle-class Jewish parents were morphing into the cast of *Barfly*.

She drank it like she'd been stranded in the desert without water. "Are you all right?" I said. "Dad says you're having mood swings—"

She waved her hand. "He's projecting his own anxieties onto me. Did he tell you he's decided to be cremated? We're supposed to put in our reservations for the plots in Flatbush"—my mom grew up in Flatbush and her whole side of the family was buried in a Jewish cemetery there—"but he thinks coffins are too expensive. Only your father could be thrifty in death."

She let out a short but audible fart as though to punctuate her point. "Pardon me," she said to no one in particular. "It's the soy." She reached into her handbag and took out a Lactaid pill.

"Isn't that for milk?" I said.

"It's all I have," she shrugged, unwrapping the pill and swallow-
ing it with wine. "I almost forgot," she said. "My book group's reading Gail Sheehy's *The Silent Passage* Thursday night and I was
thinking you might want to come."

The thought of my mom sitting around with a bunch of her girlfriends discussing menopause was less appealing than the thought
of smashing a martini glass into my own face.

"I don't know," I said.

"It would mean a lot to me, Rach. I'm leading. I want you to know
what's going on with me so you're not afraid when it happens to
you. Sheehy says it's very important to bring the big M into public
conversation so people aren't afraid of it."

"Do you think calling it 'the big M' is going to help achieve that
goal?"

"I'm just trying to have fun with it," she said. "Please come." I
didn't want to but I felt guilty for being such a lousy daughter.
Sometimes when I was lying awake at night going over my credit
card charges I thought about how seldom we talked, and felt guilty
for not being more interested in her life.

"All right," I said.

"I'm so happy!" she said. "I brought you a copy so you can prepare." She whipped it out of her purse. It was paperback with some
sort of green leaflike figure on the front and looked vaguely like
feminist erotica. "There's something else," she said. She rummaged
around in her purse and produced a clear Ziploc bag filled with tam-
pons and maxi pads.

"*Mom!*" I said, shoving it under the bar so Jasper couldn't see,
though by the smirk on his face I could tell it was too late.

"It's everything I had left," she said, like it was inheritance money
and not a bag of blood rags. "I figured *some*one might as well get
some use out of them if not me."

"Was there any other time you could have given these to me?" I
said.

"What's the big deal?" she said. "Having a period is nothing to be
ashamed of." Jasper suppressed a giggle.

As I watched my mom sip from her glass I felt like I was watching
a Lifetime movie: *A Mother in Crisis*. I didn't understand why she

and my dad felt the need to get so Oprah about everything all of a sudden. When you pass your problems on to your parents they're supposed to know how to cope. It comes with the job description. But when they pass theirs on to you the problems double in weight. The kids aren't man enough to handle it.

I wished they'd never set foot in my bar and the fact that they were cracked enough to do it made me worried. My mom was tossing down Lactaid with wine, my dad was going to get cremated, and I was wearing slutty tank tops while enabling. The Blocks were going to pieces.

THE BOURGEOIS IDEAL

F o R my date with Powell I decided to wear a pink and orange Marimekko dress. It was outrageous but had a high waist that made my breasts look even bigger than they were and big bell sleeves that gave the overall effect of a pink confection. There didn't seem to be much point in going on a date with an older man if you didn't dress like arm candy.

Saul had a warm, wintry feeling and was the kind of place that was so expensive you could imagine being proposed to there. When I walked in I saw some other couples, mostly middle-aged, but no Powell. I looked at my watch. It was exactly eight. I considered the option of leaving, walking around the block, and coming back to insure that I would keep him waiting, but he had told me to throw all that shit out the window.

A cute brunette waitress with thick but perfectly shaped eyebrows came up to me. I held up two fingers. I love being able to hold up two fingers; it's a privilege I don't often have. She ushered me to a table in the back and as I was taking my seat I saw Powell coming through the door. He was wearing a loose linen white shirt that looked expensive and hid his paunch. He scanned the room with an expression devoid of any first-date anxiety and when he spotted me he nodded formally and headed over. As he bent down to sit I got a clear view of the top of his head. He had a comb-back like my dad, but less loss.

"You're on time," he said.

"I usually never am," I said. "I overestimated the length of the walk." He shot me a questioning look and I felt like an idiot for posturing. The top three buttons of his shirt were undone and I noticed some curly black-and-gray hairs protruding from his upper chest. I wanted to rub my face in that gray lawn.

The waitress came over and set down some menus. "Good to see you," he told her congenially.

"You too," she said.

Here I was thinking I was the mayor of Cobble Hill when he was the big guy on campus. I wondered how often he came here, if he was in the habit of eating alone. New York was the only city in the world that attached no shame to solitary dining. I once saw Diane Sawyer eating a pastrami sandwich alone at a diner on Forty-third Street and it made my entire month.

"Can I get you two anything to drink?" said the waitress.

"I was maybe going to order a glass of wine," I said hesitantly.

"Why don't we get a bottle?" asked Powell. Again with the up-sell. Either he was into me or he was a lush.

"That would be fine," I said, trying not to sound too excited. He looked at the wine list, reached into his shoulder bag, and pulled out a pair of bifocals.

"Do you prefer red or white?" he asked, perching them low on his nose. I wanted to yank them off and straddle his face.

"Red."

"Hmmm. How 'bout the Côtes du Rhône?"

"Great," I said, pretending I had a clue about wine when we barely served any at the bar.

When the waitress left he rested both arms on the table and said, "Have you been a victim of the Merlot crime?"

"What's that?"

"Most bartenders force it on women," he said. "Say you walk into a bar alone, you're waiting for an inordinately attractive gentleman friend to meet you, champing at the bit to see his dashing silhouette"—he flashed his eyes—"and the bartender says, 'Can I get you anything to drink?' You say, 'Yes, what kind of red wine do you have?' Nine times out of ten he says, 'We've got a *very* nice Merlot,' and you wind up ordering it."

"I *have* noticed that," I said.

"There's this assumption that women want a light wine, a smooth one, instead of something more complex and heavy. And often the Merlot is the more expensive. So they push it on the broads. And I think it's a *crime against humanity!*" His eyes were wide and deranged. I wondered whether he felt this passionate about all things or just red wine injustice.

The waitress came back with the bottle, presented it, and poured some in his glass. He took a sip, cocked his head, and said, "Lovely." I loved that "lovely." Powell came across cultured but not stuck up. The waitress filled my glass, then his, and disappeared. He raised his glass and said, "To the death of Merlot."

"To the death of Merlot," I said. We clinked and I took a sip. It was rich. "That tastes good."

"What did I tell ya?" he said. He put his down and moved the base around in a circle on the table before taking his next sip. As I watched him swirl that base I felt as though I was on a bona fide date with a bona fide man, not a boy, not a pansy, not a pushover. I wanted to be his trophy wife.

I imagined him taking me to the theater and introducing me as his little rabbi. We could go to art galleries and independent film awards and whenever we went out he'd know the right wine to order. As soon as he became my boyfriend he'd start sending a black limo to pick me up from Roxy and take me to his place. When he opened the door I'd fall into his arms and tell him the horrible stories of the married men and yuppie snobs. "There, there," he'd cluck as he kissed away my tears and carried me onto the bed for some CAT.

One night as I was telling him about the evil Italian guy who liked the way I shook, he'd get a look on his face that I knew meant inspiration was about to strike. He'd race to his Herman Miller chair, stick a sheet into the typer (he'd be too much of a purist to use a computer), and write the opening scene of his most brilliant film, about a rabbinical-school dropout bartender who kept crying on the job. *Chai-ote Ugly.* It would be sad and funny, true yet surreal, a really good cartography of the unique concerns of My Generation.

He would write one scene a night, as I sat on the bed and

watched his back, and when he reached the last page he would yawn, "I'm a genius," and throw me to the bed, where I'd joyfully let him violate me. When he finished he'd send it to his agency, Undertake, the hottest in Hollywood (I knew it was his because I'd seen his name mentioned in a recent *New York Times* article about them), and they'd set it up immediately.

Within an hour Kirsten Dunst would sign on to play the lead role of Reva the bartender, and the producers would insist she wear a prosthetic ski-jump Jewish nose, even though mine isn't ski-jump at all. Penny Marshall, the world's most raging quasi-Jew, would sign on to direct, and it would wind up getting nominated for three Oscars—one for Penny, one for Kirsten, and one for the makeup woman who did the ski-jump nose.

The night of the awards they'd haul a TV into Roxy and all the morons who hit on me would stare slack-jawed as I came down the red carpet with Powell on my arm, wondering why I never took them up on their offers when clearly I had a fetish for old ugly men. I'd return from LA to a huge parade on Smith Street, so elaborate it would rival the opening ceremony for the Gowanus Canal, and I'd be hailed as the Neighborhood Gal That Inspired an Oscar-Winning Film.

Powell was inspecting his menu. Even though he had on his glasses he was holding it a foot away, which seemed to defeat the point of wearing glasses. As he read he reached his hand up and stroked the ends of his mustache with his index and middle finger. I wondered if he knew he'd made the Universal Sign for Cunnilingus. He closed the menu with a loud contented sigh and said, "I'm ready."

"What are you getting?"

"The ribeye steak. You?" I inspected the fish choices. They all looked kind of bland. Except for the lobster.

The last time I had eaten shellfish was tenth grade, when as president of BReaSTY I arranged a lecture by a Staten Island professor who'd written a book on Judaism and vegetarianism. I was so inspired by his take on Judaism's mandate of kindness to animals I became a vegetarian the next day, which made me kosher by default. I never ate much shellfish anyway and I hated the smell of bacon, so going kosher was easy. By senior year of Wesleyan I had gone back to meat eating but I never went back to shellfish because it made me too uncomfortable. The thought of eating a fish that could walk made me ill, like a form of evil so gross I wouldn't be able to take one swallow.

But now it all seemed stupid and pointless. I hated the idea that what you ate made you a better or worse Jew. The point of *kashrut* was to make you think about being Jewish every time you put something in your mouth and tonight I wanted to put something in my mouth that wasn't Jewish at all.

The waitress came over. Powell ordered and I announced proudly, "I'm going to get the lobster."

"Lobster?" he said. "I thought you were a rabbi." The waitress raised a brow and then moved away.

"I told you, I dropped out. Besides, the motto of Reform Judaism is 'choice through knowledge.'"

"I like this branch," he nodded. "No kosher, and broads can preach. So tell me exactly what happened."

I took a big swig of wine and told him how awful and out of place I'd felt at school those first few months. I told him how drippy and nonartistic the other students were, and how most of them were Judaic studies majors with bad skin and huge, unjustified egos. I told him how even the gay students were by the book and obsequious and how all anyone seemed to care about that first year was jockeying for position with professors. Then I told him about my inadvertent murder at Memorial and how it had been the final straw.

He didn't say anything for a while and then he nodded and said, "Better you dropped out than lip-synched your way to leadership."

"I know," I said. "I just wish my parents weren't so disappointed."

"How old are you?"

"Twenty-six."

"What do you care what your parents think?"

"I shouldn't," I said. "But they live really close by and they're overinvested in what I do."

"Because ya letting them!" he cried. "You're drawn to the security and complacence of the well-traveled path! And now that you've stepped off I guarantee you will pay a price. When I told my mother I was going into the movie industry she came down with pneumonia she was so brokenhearted."

"And that's a good thing?"

"Of course it is! What a *thrilling time* this must be for you! How *lucky I am to meet you now!*" I nodded gingerly, not sure whether he acted like a lunatic with everybody or just with me. "Lemme tell you, it's no easy process to tear off the shackles of the bourgeois ideal."

"What exactly is the bourgeois ideal, Mr. Powell?"

"You gotta stop calling me that," he said. "It's annoying."

"Sorry. What exactly is the bourgeois ideal, Hank?"

"The bourgeois ideal is an inability to think for oneself. A commitment to a lifestyle of pointless, mind-numbing domesticity without any thought as to the implication of the choice. Look around the neighborhood at all these women selling their asses. Shacking up with rich men so they can be spared the process of having to work for a living. It's a dangerous new trend, this gentrified prostitution, and it frightens me."

"Does this have something to do with your divorce?"

"*Of course it has something to do with my divorce!* You know how much money I made last year? About a million dollars. You know how much money I have right now? *None!* Because my ex-wife got all my money in the settlement!"

"How'd you make a million dollars?"

"Uncredited rewrites."

My career curiosity had overtaken my romantic curiosity. "Really?" I said. "What did you rewrite?"

"I'd rather not say. But if the Writers Guild weren't run by a bunch of *smog-headed imbeciles* I'd have my toilet paper rolling off a platinum statuette. The point is my ex-wife was a feminist when I met her. She didn't shave her pits. But as soon as the marriage ended she played the damsel in distress. There is no telling what a scorned woman will do under the counsel of a good Jewish attorney. Money turns individuals into animals. My ex-wife is only one of them. The pursuit of bourgeois values corrupts the human soul." I imagined his wife as litigious and frightening, with humongous fake breasts, triceps of steel, and a fake Catherine Zeta-Jones–esque sheen.

"What does she do?" I asked.

"*She lives off her alimony!*" There were no illusions here; this man would never marry again. "I don't know why I'm even talking to you," he said, waving his hand. "You grew up in this neighborhood and liked it enough to stay. Which means you must have a very strong domestic urge yourself."

I felt totally attacked. Here I was trying to be a nice piece of ass and he was lumping me in with the Ubermoms. "Hey!" I said. "You live here too!"

"That's because I couldn't afford to buy in Manhattan. You know why? *Because my ex-wife got all my money in the settlement!*" He sighed, seeming to collect himself slightly. "Don't get me wrong. I'm not saying you're like those mother whores. You just have a strong bourgeois leaning. That's why you wanted to be a rabbi: to make your parents happy."

"That's not true!" I said, a little too loudly. "I became a rabbi because I thought Reform Judaism needed more women, that I could stand a chance of actually changing things."

"That's just white noise," he said. "You have the obedient mind of an only daughter mixed with the hyperambitious striving of an only son. You're torn between the feminine and the masculine. You have a real animus about you."

"You mean in the Jungian sense?"

"Yes. I, on the other hand, have a very strong anima, which is what continually *ruins* me in relationships. I have a maternal urge, an urge to take care, so I seek out women in turmoil. I'm drawn to violent women. Violent and crazy."

"I'm not violent *or* crazy," I said sadly.

"Who said I was drawn to you?" I jerked my head up, hurt. His face was deadpan and he gave no sign of reassurance. "Deep down you're a gullible innocent but on first meeting you project a very strong animus. That's why I bit into your cookie. So you knew that when it came to me, you could never be the bigger man."

"You think I want to be a man?"

He nodded solemnly like a shrink. "You're textbook if I ever saw one. You don't want to accept the things about you that make you female. You want to reject them. That's why you chose a male occupation. You can never progress until you stop being ruled by your animus. Women can never win. They must *be won.*"

"I thought you didn't believe in *The Rules.*"

"I don't. But I do believe in different sex roles. Twenty years ago I had this dream. I was working as a short-order cook, living in a walk-up in Astoria that overlooked an air shaft. I drank a quart of Jim Beam a day and fell asleep each night on the floor of the kitchen, my mouth pressed against the refrigerator grate. One morning I woke up, my head spinning. I had dreamed that a pigeon and an ant were having a fight, and then the pigeon flew away and shat on the ant's back, and the ant died, crushed by the weight of the crap. As I awoke I heard these words on my tongue, as clear and vibrant as if God was whispering them in my ear: 'Women are sin, men want sin. Men are soul, women want soul.' That's Aphorism Number One of Powell's Aphorisms."

He stared at me triumphantly as though he'd told me the meaning of life. "I'm not sure what it means," I said.

"It's men who have the connection to the spiritual world!" he exclaimed. "Women want to but they don't have it. They are anchored, they are sensual and earthy, but they resent it. Men have their heads in the clouds but seek out women so they can be vicariously anchored in the life of the body."

I got this image of Priya, my Indian resident advisor frosh year at Wes, staring down at me with disapproval. This was not the kind of stuff you could get away with saying at a left-wing college.

"Don't you have it backwards?" I said. "I think it's women who are more in touch with nature, more spiritual."

"*No!*" he shouted. "Women *think* they're in touch with nature but they're *not. They're not!*" His face was red and his eyes were gleaming.

"What does this have to do with the dream?"

"The ant was the woman, the pigeon the man."

"What does it mean that the pigeon killed the woman with his crap?"

"There was someone in my life at the time, someone I was angry with. Also, I was having a number of digestive problems as a result of my poor drinking habits."

"I think I'm beginning to get it," I said, grinning. "Women are fire, men are sand. Women are water, men are ice. Women are nature, men are nurture."

"Don't mock my aphorisms," he said. "That's Aphorism Number Two of Powell's Aphorisms."

"How many are there?"

"Five."

I wolf-whistled. "That's a lot."

"I've been alive a long time."

"What are the others?"

"I can never remember them all at once. That's one a the downsides of being alive a long time."

Though I wasn't sure how I felt about Powell's philosophy of the sexes, I loved listening to his stories. With guys my own age we got through all our stories early on because we hadn't lived long enough to fill more. That's why everything went downhill from there—once you tell all your stories there's nothing left to do but dissect movies, reference *Seinfeld* episodes, and complain about your friends behind their backs.

Powell was a raging narcissist and had read too much Jung but he was awake. Half of me wanted to tell him he was full of it and the other half wanted to keep listening because it was more fun to be with someone crazy than someone wrong.

So he wasn't a Jew but what did that matter? We could still make a go of it. At rabbinical school there was an unwritten policy that you couldn't be ordained if they knew you were living with a goy, but now that I had left, nobody was watching. I could sleep with an insane Gentile, marry him, even.

Maybe the entire reason Neil Roth had croaked before my eyes was so that I could stop having the wool pulled over them. Maybe he died so I could meet Powell and know not to turn the other way. I wasn't a flounderer; I was responding to a message from God, a different kind of God than the one I had always envisioned. He wasn't sitting in a throne but a plush leather armchair and he looked sort of like Hugh Hefner, with a burgundy robe hanging open over his fat naked frame. Instead of yelling at me for having walked out on my calling, he was saying in a complacent Yiddish accent, "Do vat you want. Hev a good time. Don't answer to anyone but yourself."

The waitress came over with the food and set it down in front of us. My lobster looked like it was suffering in that sea of sauce. I tore into a claw, the least sympathetic part.

"How you doin' over there?" said Powell.

"I'm having some trouble with it, actually."

He reached over. "You use the nutcracker like this. Then you ease out the flesh."

The meat released, I raised the fork to my mouth. As I bit in I felt nauseous, certain I was going to die or pass out as punishment for violating the Torah. But I kept chewing and the nausea passed, and . . . nothing happened. I didn't throw up or faint. I didn't even feel guilty. I took another bite, waiting again, and because I was not struck down I felt defiant. The meat was salty and rich and I felt like an idiot for not eating it all these years.

"So Hank," I said, chewing slowly, "how'd you get so perceptive about human nature?"

"I've always been that way. When I was a kid in Jackson Heights I got beat up every day because I would look at a thug and he would see that I could see him. It would scare the crap outta him. Though I didn't say it aloud he knew what I was thinking was *Why are you afraid?* or *How come you think you're ugly?* As a result I was a magnet for bullies. The constant blows are what made me decide to pursue the life a the mind and not the body."

"I could give you a lot of constant blows," I said.

He chuckled. I felt woozy and elated and leered at him, buzzed. It was one of those looks that feel sexy in your own head but if you could see it on a videotape you would howl in pained shame. I took my napkin off my lap, leaned forward, placed it on top of his hand, and squeezed his fingers.

"Are you a Hasid?" he said. "You can't touch me?"

"I'm Reform."

"Then what are you doing?"

"Swathing you."

"Why?" he said slyly. "Am I injured?"

"No," I said, "but even a healthy man can use a good nurse."

His mouth spread wide in deference to the line. He reached forward with his free hand and grabbed my upper arm. His grasp was firm but not violent, like a period at the end of a sentence, and as he held me he looked at me with mysterious intensity, as though communicating some telepathic message. We stayed like this for a few seconds and then, just as abruptly as he'd reached, he placed both hands in his lap, scooted his chair back, and said, "What do you want for dessert?"

We ordered two slices of Key lime pie. As he was licking the back of his fork he said, "You wanna get a drink somewhere?"

"There's a dive bar down by the expressway," I said. "It's called Montero. They have a pool table and it only costs seventy-five cents." I had gone there with David a few times, but opted not to mention that. You have to make every guy think he's the first to see the places you like, even if he's the twelfth.

"I like the sound a that place," Powell said.

"It used to be a sailor bar in the fifties. They would come and drink, get into a fight, go out on the street and maul each other, then come back in and have another beer. The owner told me about it. Pepe. I asked him once if anyone had been killed there and he said, 'The person didn't actually die *inside* the bar. He died in the hospital.'"

"I *really* like the sound a that place," Powell said, and raised his hand for the check.

W H E N we got outside we went to Pacific, turned, and headed up Court Street. As we were crossing Atlantic, I spotted my mom coming toward us, carrying a bunch of shopping bags.

"Uh-oh," I said.

"What is it?" he said.

"Nothing." Before I had time to hide she saw us, waved, and shouted, "Rachel!"

Feeling like a complete idiot for running from my own mother like she was an ex-boyfriend, I waited for her to come to our side. "Hi Mom," I said, as her eyes veered to Powell with confusion.

My mother is a conservative liberal, which means that she supports the library and votes Working Family but gets deeply disturbed if she gets a waitress at a restaurant who's pregnant or has visible brastraps. Before she could ask who he was, he said, "Hello, I'm Hank," and reached for her hand.

She transferred one of her grocery bags to the other side and raised her hand to meet his paw. "I'm Sue," she said. "Rachel's mom."

"I was certain you were her sister," he said.

"That won't work on me," she said. "But I love it anyway." No one said anything for a while, we all just smiled awkwardly, and then my mom asked how he knew me.

"She came to see a play I wrote. *The History of the Pencil.*"

"Oh," she said, playing it completely cool. You can't say you've seen a play when you've only seen the first half. It's setting yourself up for disaster.

"Hank's a screenwriter," I said deliberately. I turned to Powell. "The only one of your movies she's seen is *Flash Flood.*"

"My greatest fear is that when I die, that'll be the flick I'm remembered for," he said. I could tell this wasn't the first time he'd used the line.

"Then I guess I'll have to catch up on the others," she said, as I winced. "Well, I'd better get home before this ice cream gets cold. Nice to meet you, Hank."

I started walking as quickly as I could in the other direction as Powell skipped to catch up with me. "Ya mother's lovely," he said.

"You should have just gone on ahead," I said.

"Never! It's not often you meet a girl's mother on the first date."

"You don't understand! You give my parents an inch and they take a mile. Now she's going to tell my dad she saw me with an older man and they're going to ask me a million questions about you."

"You don't have to answer," he said.

"I know," I said, "but I wish I could have a little privacy sometimes."

"If you want more privacy," Powell said, as we turned and headed toward the water, "it's obvious what you gotta do."

"What's that?" I said.

"Move."

THE bar was a sad scene. Six sixtysomething Hispanic men were listening to Sinatra, with wounded eyes, drinking from shot glasses. As we walked in they eyed us with calm hostility. A hipster and a cradle robber; they had no respect for either.

"This is a dark place," said Powell, without lowering his voice. "It's like the Puerto Rican lonely hearts club here."

We ordered two Budweisers and went into the back room through an old ornate black wrought-iron gate. The pool table was in the center of the room and all over the walls were sailor paraphernalia—oars, lifesavers, paintings of seascapes, and huge framed photos of Latin social clubs from the fifties. A sign by the pool table said, "This is our OOL. Notice there is no P in it. Please keep it that way," and I wondered whether something had happened to make them feel the sign was necessary.

Powell put some quarters in the table. The balls tumbled out with a satisfying series of thwacks. "Are you gonna break?" I said, as he racked up.

"No, you." I had to kick Powell's ass. All the women in his movies were good at pool and I wanted to remind him of one of his protagonists.

I looked over at the rack. The order was crazy. "You don't do it like that," I said, coming around to his side of the table. "Haven't you ever heard of a New York rack?"

"What's that?"

I stuck out my chest and said, "You're looking at one."

"I liked that," he said. "That was good."

"In a New York rack you gotta put the yellow up front," I said. "That's 'cause it's the easiest to see. Then you alternate around the perimeter, stripe, solid, and so on."

"That's not how we used to play when I was a kid," he said. "All that matters is the eight in the middle. Everything else should be arbitrary."

"Well, this makes things more fair and trust me, when I whup your ass you're going to be grateful we started out even."

He sighed and fixed the balls, as I watched over his shoulder. "You happy now?" he said. I nodded. He lifted the triangle off but didn't do the flip. It was a thrill to be on a date with a guy mature enough to refrain from the triangle flip.

I put the cue an inch behind the dot, placed all my weight in the center of my body like I was taking a shit, because that's how you get power, and measured up eight times. "You look good," he said.

"Don't distract me," I said. I measured up another eight times and hit the sucker as hard as I could.

The balls separated OK but nothing sank. "You're all bark and no bite," said Powell.

"What are you talking? I'm very bite. It's just hard for women to break."

"Oh, so now ya pleading poverty? How quickly they turn." He sank a stripe, and then another.

"You're all right," I said. "How long have you been playing pool?"

"Let's see, since I was seventeen."

"Wow," I said. "You've been playing pool longer than I've been alive."

"That's right," he said, and missed his next shot.

"You're totally over the hill," I said as I lined up. "You're old enough to be my old man."

"I know I am," he said. "But you know what?" He came over to where I was standing and put his mouth by my ear. "I'm *not* your old man. And that's all that matters."

I giggled and sunk the three. "You're definitely in good shape for a geezer," I said. "You have excellent hair."

"I do have nice hair," he said, running his fingers through it. "I'm lucky. But I've had two ulcers and a herniated disk. So it all evens out."

I sunk four straight balls but then one went in that I wasn't going for. "Your turn," I said.

"Whaddaya mean? You got the six in."

"I didn't call it. If I didn't call it I don't deserve another shot."

"That's not how I play," he pronounced. "In my game, you sink you get another turn, regardless of intention. I prefer to leave as much to chance as possible."

"Why?"

"Because it makes life more interesting!"

As I chalked up he strode up to me and put his hand on the back of my neck. "C'mere," he said, and turned me toward him. He held my hair, and tongued me firmly like he already owned my mouth. As we kissed he took the cue out of my hand and leaned it against the wall. It toppled to the floor with a loud clatter. I opened my eyes and bent to retrieve it but he yanked me up and said, "Never mind that."

He lunged for my mouth again. He wasn't a biter but he seized me like a man. I felt like a shiny new puppy. I wanted him to lift me into the air by the nape. He pulled my body close and made a high-pitched moaning noise. The pitch of the moan, though high, was savage, a "Huh huh huh" first cousin to his "Heh heh heh" laugh.

With each pull I felt smaller and like more of a victim and Powell grew more menacing and big. He knew what he wanted and didn't need or care to ask my permission. He made me feel like a woman and I was too used to feeling like a man. I didn't know how much was his age and how much his hubris but I loved his outsized-ness, his running the show. With guys my age I felt like a movie director, exhausted by the ingénues who wanted to please. It wasn't their sensitivity I minded so much as their willingness to kowtow.

"I didn't expect this to happen," I said softly.

"Of course you did."

"I really wasn't sure," I said. "I wanted it to but I wasn't sure."

"Couldn't you tell in the restaurant when I grabbed you by the arm? It was a moment, an articulation. I was trying to tell you you'd been seen."

"You couldn't have just said it?"

"Getcha bag." My lips felt raw, like someone had just walked on my face.

"Where we going?" I said.

"Don't ask silly questions."

W H E N we stumbled out of the bar the streets were empty. It re-minded me of the scene in *Leon and Ruth* where Julia Roberts and Don Cheadle are walking together in Jackson Heights the night be-fore he's leaving for Vietnam and Julia turns to him and says, "I can't think of you going away, Leon. Without you I'm like an ant some-body stepped on but didn't kill, toddling around, half broken and afraid."

I looked at Powell and felt the instinct to quote but decided it was best not to overemphasize my fandom on my way to the boudoir. When we got to Baltic Street he went halfway down the block, looked around, confused, and said, "Where the hell is my street?"

"Which one do you live on again?"

"Strong."

"It begins at Kane," I said. "We gotta loop around. Don't you know your own neighborhood?"

"To you it's a neighborhood," he said. "To me it's a subway stop."

We did an about-face and as we made our way down the block we passed a middle-aged woman walking a dog. She was wearing a short-sleeved tight tee and had the thin tan arms of a woman who tries too hard to stay in shape. She took him in, and then me, and scowled.

"Did you see that?" I said.

"What?" he said.

"She gave me a dirty look. What did I do to her?"

"Isn't it obvious? She thinks you're taking me off her market."

"Am I?" I said.

"We're not even at my door," he said, "and already you're mov-ing in."

His block was a beautiful two-block street that stretched from Kane down to DeGraw. All the brownstones were pristine and well kept. It was one of the most bourgeois-ideal streets in Cobble Hill.

His apartment was a regal floor-through, one flight up. We entered in the kitchen and the rest of the apartment was laid out to the right—a huge dining area in the front, a spacious living room in the middle, then a pair of closed French doors with purple curtains. Powell bee-lined through the doors, saying something about "using the facility." The apartment was more feminine than I would have imagined from his movies, and more classily decorated, chic antique. Evidently what he'd saved from moving across the river he'd spent on interior design.

There were about twenty paintings on the walls, all 1950s-style pinups of women in various states of undress. Each painting fea-tured ass in a prominent and unapologetic way—in one a woman was bent over, standing, peering out between her legs; in another a librarian type was bending to retrieve a book from the floor.

There were no records, videos, CDs, or papers to be seen, and no clutter. I had always imagined he wrote in a separate office but on one wall of the living room was a black simple desk with an old Mac-intosh computer on it, and a plain wooden nonergonomic chair. I noticed his mouse was smudged with fingerprints, which made me less intimidated. Even superstars had trouble keeping their mice clean. He had three floor-to-ceiling bookshelves, which contained the complete diaries of Casanova, some Kafka, some Céline, the Klaus Kinski autobiography, and *Moby-Dick*. He also had three full shelves of *Scratchiti, The Stoop Sitter,* and *Powell: Six Screenplays.* I heard him coming so I scurried back to the couch and sat down.

"How ya doin'," he said, as he came in, yawning.

"Pretty good," I said.

He turned on a lamp. The light was warm, the kind I can never seem to accomplish in my own apartment, highbrow and soft. I don't even have a dimmer. He loped around the couch, opened his armoire (there was a stereo inside), and pressed a few buttons. A few seconds later this sad, familiar-sounding folk came on.

"What is this?" I said, as he sat next to me.

"Marc Cohn," he said.

"You listen to *Marc Cohn?*"

"What can I say? His music speaks to me."

"I just never expected someone as tough as you—"

"Marc Cohn has been through a lot of pain at the hands of evil women," he said, "as have I. You could tell he was about to lose his wife on this album. Every song speaks 'troubled marriage' but what

makes it so moving is that he didn't know it at the time. His subconscious did before he did. After this one came out she left him
and he went to pieces. The next one is considered the breakup
album but I prefer this one because he was anticipating his own demise. I find anticipation of demise far more interesting than demise
itself."

He blinked at me twice, pushed me down onto my stomach, and
got on top. As Marc Cohn crooned in the background he slid my
underwear down and put a couple fingers inside. The undies were
white and cotton and on the front they said "Brooklyn Rocks." I was
glad to be lying on my belly.

"You're so wet," he said.

"That's because of you," I said. Guys love it when you say that.

"I can't believe how ready you are," he said. "Oh Rachel, my
sweet little hoo-ah."

Was Al Pacino in the room? I flipped my head around to look at
him. "What's a hoo-ah?"

"You know, a hooker."

"A whore?"

"That's what I said: a hoo-ah." I was lying on a couch getting dry-
humped by my idol but I couldn't help laughing.

"What?" he said. "That's how we grew up saying it. I lost my accent in the rest of my speech but that word still comes out Queens.
Are you laughing at me, you little hoo-ah?"

"Yes I am," I said.

He put his face by my ear, his mouth right into the hole and
purred, "The laughing part is over now, Rachel. You are going to do
as I say."

He pushed my bra up without unhooking it and kneaded my
breasts perfunctorily before sliding his hands down to my ass. He
sighed loudly and openly and for once I felt good that I had something down there to grab. "Hank," I said, over my shoulder. "Are you
an ass man, a pussy man, a tit man, or a leg man?"

He turned his head to the side a second and said, "Ass, with pussy
rising."

There was some movement and it seemed like he was fingering

me, a bunch of fingers all pushed together. Then he moved it in deeper and I realized it wasn't a hand. I jerked my body away and turned over to face him.

"What are you doing?" I said.

"What do you think?"

"You're supposed to ask before you put it in."

"I wasn't aware that was necessary."

"Don't you have a condom?"

He looked at me like I'd asked the dumbest question in the book, and said, "Pfff."

"What?"

"I don't use condoms. I believe men should take women the way they were meant to be taken. The natural way. Flesh to flesh and skin to skin. That's the whole point of making love. I believe people should feel that every time they have sex they could die from it." I stared at him dumbly, thinking of this safe sex pamphlet I read in high school that had comebacks for all the anticondom lines.

"A crying baby isn't the kind of natural I need," I mumbled.

"What?"

"You sure you don't have any condoms?"

"I'm not gonna come in you," he said, "so you don't have to worry. I'm very good at not coming in women."

Before I could calculate the comfort quotient of the comment he turned me back onto my stomach. I did some math in my head. My period was over. I'd be all right. If this was the way he operated on all first dates, God only knew where his dick had been, but I tried not to think about that. If one thing was clear about Hank Powell it was that when it came to sex, things weren't really about a conversation. This was a lame rationale for risky behavior but an accurate appraisal, I felt.

He pushed up the dress again, looped his fingers against the waistband of my panties, and lowered them with one quick pull. Within a second he was in. I felt my body resisting, too nervous to open up. One thing I had loved about David was his never-ending supply of LifeStyles. It's a big load off your chest when the guy does as he's supposed to.

"You gotta put something on," I said, flipping over.

"Why?"

"Because . . . I'm from a different generation than you are."

"I know," he said, sighing, "and this is exactly why I don't have a lotta love for your generation."

He stood up and headed toward the bedroom. His pants were off and he walked like a woman, his head pushed forward like a bird's, his legs long and lean, his hand resting on his paunch. I watched him disappear through the doors and then I looked down at my own body. My dress was hiked up to my chin, my bra pushed halfway up my breasts, the underwire bisecting them so it looked like I had four. I lowered it and placed my boobs in, then fixed my dress so it was normal.

"The sheath is ready!" he called. I took a deep breath and went in. The lighting was soft and Powell was lying on his bed sporting wood.

I climbed up next to him. He put his hand on my face, and kissed me, open-mouthed and rough. I felt his erection bang against my thigh. He reached over to the nightstand and unwrapped a condom. I took the wrapper. Spermicided Trojan. "Is this all you have?" I said.

"What do you think this is, an all-you-can-eat buffet?"

He started to unroll it onto himself but an inch of the way down he stopped, flustered, and said, "I don't know which way is up."

"Lemme do it."

I climbed on top of him, inspected it, flipped it the other way, and unrolled it in about two seconds. "How'd you get so good at that?" he said.

"Eighth grade health ed."

"You wicked child!" he said. He tackled me and tossed my clothes onto the floor.

As he entered he started to growl. It wasn't rhythmic along with the thrusting. It came out at odd intervals, from deep inside him like he was becoming someone else. His face was turned to the side, his eyes wild and strange, his hair messy with sweat. I felt like he was murdering me and I heard myself say, "It's so wonderful and so terrible."

"Grrrrmmm," he said loudly, taking me with more venom. Half of me wanted to cry and the other half wanted to etch it all in my brain because I knew no other guy would wreck me this well.

When he came twenty minutes later, his face drenched, his armpits dripping, his hair wild and wet, he growled extra loudly and clawed at my shoulders with his hands. My eyes went wide and I watched him like a science experiment. He clawed, growled, and spasmed, clawed, growled, and spasmed, and then went heavy on top of me, his heart pounding against my own, his face resting in the crook of my neck.

I gingerly put my hand on his back and he spasmed again with a grunt. I eased him out. He lay next to me on his back and I watched his chest rise and fall. I turned over and inspected myself in the closet mirror to see what I was feeling. I looked violated but exhilarated. Suddenly he was in the reflection too, propped up on his elbow.

"You've completely transformed," he said, his hand on my hip, the light so soft on my old-school body that I felt like that violin girl in the painting.

"How do you mean?"

"Look how soft your eyes are. You look so feminine, and tender."

My contacts were kind of sticking so it was hard to see the expression on my face but even from a distance I saw what he meant. I was tranquil and liquid, my cheeks glowing.

"You calmed me down," I said.

I got up and went into the bathroom. His toilet was standard-issue, but the shower curtain was cream-colored and gauzy and looked as expensive as everything else. As I was peeing I noticed something colorful behind the curtain so I opened it. In the center of the tub was a blue basin filled with dozens of Barbie dolls in various states of undress, their heads turned backwards like little Linda Blairs, many with missing limbs. Their little shirts and dresses were littered on top, along with buckets and bath toys, boats and Tupperware cups. As I went to wash my hands I noticed that by the side of the sink there was a colorful wooden step stool with the name NORA spelled out by a series of acrobatic clowns.

I padded back into the bedroom. He was lying in the same position, his eyes closed.

"How old is your daughter?" I asked.

"Five."

"Is her name Nora?"

"No, it's Tuwanda. I bought her the step stool just to confuse her. Of course her name is Nora."

"How come you didn't tell me about her before?"

"It didn't come up."

"Are you ashamed to be a father?"

"I'm a multifaceted man. I don't show all a my facets at every moment. I'm like a diamond that way."

Clearly this was not the whole story. There had been half a dozen occasions when he could have said something about her but he'd chosen not to. Naturally, his reluctance to reveal her only made me want to meet her a thousand times more. "Where does she sleep?" I asked. He pointed to a door that I presumed led to a guest room. "How often do you see her?"

"Three times a week."

"What's she like?"

"She's smart and she likes to raise hell. She's impish. She loves dolls but she hates skirts. She's a tomboy."

"You better watch out," I said, "because when tomboys grow up they turn into sluts."

"Believe me, I know. I'm glad she's only five."

I wanted to ask if I could meet her but I decided his reticence was a sign I'd best not bombard. I felt Nora could be the answer to my own bourgeois predicament: it was a million times cooler to be a stepmom than a mom. You could deal with the good stuff without any of the bad. Nora wouldn't be my responsibility so there was no danger I'd transform into an Ubermom, which meant I could maintain my piece-of-ass status. It could allow me to sample at the table of motherhood without actually taking a plate.

The gleaming thought of child meeting made me horny and warm. I put my hand on his head and smoothed down his hair. I snuggled my nose into his armpit and took a deep, loving whiff.

"Hmm," I said dreamily, resting my head on his shoulder. "I wonder what I should do now."

"Whaddaya mean?"

"It's so late. Maybe I should sleep here."

He gazed at me intently and said, "For six months after my wife and I split up I would wake up in the middle of the night and feel around me on the bed. I was looking for her body. I would pat each portion of the sheets, on both sides of me, night after night until I realized I was totally alone, and then I would start to cry."

"That must have been very upsetting for you," I said, stroking his cheek.

"Are you kidding? I was crying from *relief.* It was a joyous, overwhelming flood of relief to finally be rid of that *castrating bitch!*"

"How long has it been?" I said, jerking my hand away.

"Three years. But I still have a hard time having anyone sleep over. I just can't do it. My nature won't allow it."

"What do you mean your nature?"

"I have a very strong connection with my nature and when it tells me not to do something I have to listen. Otherwise I become a trickster—the trickster for many years has been a very significant figure in my subconscious—and you don't want to be around when I'm him. Put on ya clothes. I'll walk ya home." He got out of bed and I leaned over the edge to look for my bra.

O N the way down my block we almost tripped over the PSB, the Pacific Street Bum. He was an enormous bearded Middle Eastern guy with a huge Buddhalike belly who lay on the sidewalk in front of the parking lot across from my apartment. He never asked for money, he just hung out horizontally, in varying degrees of consciousness. He used the green fence of the parking lot as shelves for all his stuff—I'd walk by and see shirts, shoes, individual socks resting in the nooks. Once I even saw a banana tottering but not falling.

I had asked the guy in the beverage center down the block from my building if he knew anything about him and he said rumor had it he used to be a millionaire but lost all his money gambling. It was hard to believe. He looked like a caricature of a bum, with grime all over his face, and he always showed a little bit of plumber's crack.

From the corner it looked like he was sleeping but as we passed he raised his hand to the cigarette in his mouth and took a drag. I jumped.

"You see what I mean about this being a bourgeois neighborhood?" said Powell. "Even the bums are spoiled."

When we got to my front door I said, "Thank you for dinner."

"Ya very welcome."

I wanted to race into his arms and kiss him a thousand times on the lips but I had a feeling it might not be the smoothest move. "I had a wonderful time," I said.

"And you," he said, "are one of the more intriguing Gyno Americans I've encountered."

I nodded and waited for him to kiss me but instead he just said, "Awright. I'll talk to you soon." And before I was safely inside, insulated and safe from the PSB, he walked down the street.

W H E N I got upstairs there was a note on my door from Liz that said, "Knock me up."

She opened the door in sweats and a T-shirt. Liz looks very different when she's not dressed up. Her face seems skinny and frail and her body way too tiny. Her face was all blotchy like she'd been crying. "Are you all right?" I said.

She shook her head no and led me in. Her place had the same layout as mine but it was sloppier. Every spare surface was covered with feminist textbooks, pop psychology, hard-rock CDs, and modern Jewish philosophy. Her desk was a beautiful glass Corbusier table and though it was a mess she had a fourteen-inch PowerBook right in the center, glowing regally. On the walls she had posters of the Smiths, Patti Smith, and the White Stripes, and her couch was draped with stoner Indian fabrics, the kind Deadheads had in college dorms. Her coffee table was bean-shaped with a projection of wood on it and her white Flokati rug was always filthy with pennies and pieces of dirt.

She had a vinyl vacuum cleaner box next to the TV and inside there were a hundred pornos she'd collected over the years—many on DVD. Her favorite director was a guy named Joey Silvera, who she liked for his ass fetish and love of transsexuals. Together we had watched ten minutes of a film called *A Clock Strikes Bizarre on Butt Row,* but after an unsettling portion in which a Mexican girl with a mustache ejaculated on the camera I insisted we watch *Double Indemnity* instead.

"So I met a cute Jew," Liz said, lying on her back on the rug and folding her hands over her stomach, as I sat on the couch.

"Isn't that a good thing?" I said.

"Noooo," she moaned. "Remember that JCC–Manhattan benefit I told you I was going to? Well, it was last night. I'm standing by the bar putting on my glasses so I could read the bar menu, when the sweetest-looking Jewboy came up to me. He had this flap of dark brown hair and the most amazing upper body, with a real old-fashioned Jew ass. You know when it kind of curves out in the Dockers?"

"Bubble butt?"

"Yes! He had the most incredible bubble butt! So he says to me, 'Someone with eyes as beautiful as yours should never wear glasses.'" I snorted. "I know," she said. "Then he said I looked like Daryl Hannah. Racheleh, do you have any idea how many times I have been told I look like Daryl Hannah? And they all think they're the first to say it."

She didn't look anything like Daryl Hannah, except that her hair was light and her eyes were blue. She always said she got her eyes from a slutty great-grandmother, who must have been raped by a Cossack.

"It's because men type us," I said. "They find it hard to distinguish, so they just see us in broad categories. Men look at women the way black people look at white people."

"Exactly. But I was trying to be open-minded and patriotic and take what I could get. I said, 'Yes, I'm the *Jewish* Daryl Hannah.' He said, 'The Daryl *Hannah and Her Sisters.'* So we keep talking and it turns out he's a lawyer for Skadden Arps. His name's Brian Ittner and he lives on the Upper West. He's into mountain climbing, dim sum, and this lymphoma charity. The male me. Could you die? We talk for like two hours, he asks me to his apartment for a nightcap, and all I can think in the cab over is, *This is some first-rate BM.*" That was Liz's slang for Boyfriend Material. I had told her several times to pick a better acronym but she refused.

"As we're riding over we're quoting *Annie Hall,* debating Middle East politics, and when we got to his place, on Sixty-seventh, he kind of lunged for me. We went to the bed, and he banged the shit out of me. I came three times—*in the position,* I might add,"—she looked at me imploringly—"and then he did, and when he pulled out I immediately felt The Shift."

"What's The Shift?" I said.

"You know. That cloud that hovers over them as soon as they jizz. The one that's like a mushroom cloud spelling out 'STAY AWAY.'"

"Oh, that one," I said. I had seen that look less than an hour before. Maybe this was a universal male quality I'd been lucky enough not to notice before because I'd always gone for men with the souls of women.

"So I stood up and put my dress back on and then I looked at him and said, 'Brian? I'm gonna go.' He's just lying there, under the covers, all postcoital and droopy-eyed, and he says, 'You don't mind if I stay in bed, do you?'"

"Whaaat?"

"Rachel, I have had men not walk me to a cab. I have had men not walk me to the lobby. But this man did not walk me to the *door.*" She sat upright and looked at me as though I had to know something she didn't. "If he didn't want a wife, why did he come to a JCC event? If he wanted a one-night stand why didn't he just fuck one of the girls in the Condé Nast building where he works, one of the shiksas, the blondes with the blowouts?"

"I don't know," I said.

She put her hands to her cheeks and moaned, "I let that Jewboy bang me and he wouldn't even walk me to the *door.* Racheleh!" She grabbed both of my hands with hers. "I have to stop fucking!"

"So why don't you?"

"Because I love fucking!" She started to tear up and pinched the bridge of her nose.

"I know what you mean," I said, putting my hand on her shoulder. "You want something more, something more ethereal and fulfilling, but men take one look at you and misunderstand. Women are sin, men want sin. Men are soul, women want soul."

"What the hell is that supposed to mean?" she said, scowling.

It had sounded so good when Powell had said it, but so stupid when I did. I had to work on my execution. "It's just something I heard somewhere."

She eyed me warily and said, "If I ever run into him again at another event I will die. I will literally drop dead of mortification. I never want to see that Brian Ittner again."

"Brian Shittner," I said.

She laughed. "Yeah. I hope I never see Shittner again."

She got up, pulled a Kleenex from the box on her desk, and sat back down. "Oh, Racheleh. I just can't stand that look! That look! Right after they've rolled off, and they turn to you with this disdain, and you know all they're thinking is, *How do I get her out of here?* When a man makes me come, I like him more. How come when we make them come, they like us less?"

"Maybe because every time they come they feel closer to death."

"What's that on your face?"

My hands flew up to my cheeks. "What do you mean?"

"It looks like a bruise or something, to the right of your mouth."

I jogged into the bathroom. She was right. I had a little shiner on my jaw, a one-inch circle of stubble scab that I must have gotten when Powell was kissing me.

I put my finger to it gingerly and spotted Liz in the mirror behind me. I jumped. "So what is it?" Her blue eyes pierced mine. She always got abrasive when she was seeking information.

"It must be a zit," I said.

"It doesn't look like a zit," she said. "It looks like a bruise."

She eyed me in the mirror like in a detective movie. She was trying to out-Columbo me but I wasn't going to let her. There was something about Powell that made me want to keep him secret.

I did an about-face and brushed past her into the living room. "Is something going on?" she said, following.

"No."

"Where were you when I knocked?"

"Having dinner with my parents," I said quickly.

"This late?"

"Then I stopped at Roxy and had a drink."

She eyed me suspiciously. "Really?" she said. "'Cause you look JBF."

"What's JBF?"

"Just been fucked."

Though I was tempted to spill, I wasn't sure I wanted to hear what Liz had to say. As out-there as she was about her own romantic choices, I was afraid that if I told her the truth she'd tell me I shouldn't have slept with him on the first date, or let him in without a condom, however briefly. And even if she'd be right I wasn't ready to have Powell looked at just yet. I wanted him to be mine and mine alone, not a pair of underwear to be hung out on a laundry line for the whole neighborhood to see. He might turn out to be the biggest mistake of my life but I wanted him to be *my* mistake.

"I'm just really tired," I said.

"I don't believe you," she said.

"I'm really sorry about Shittner," I said, rubbing my chin. "Not all guys are like that."

"Thanks," she said absently. But she was no longer thinking about her own problems, she was thinking about me. There's no quicker cure for misery than curiosity.

As soon as I got downstairs I went into my bathroom and flipped on the light. It looked like someone had punched me in the jaw. I ran my hand over the red spot and realized I was smiling.

THAT BROAD'S
LIKE VINEGAR

T H E next morning in bed I read a few chapters of *The Silent Passage:* "The Cheating Heart," "Embezzled Bone," and "Dangerous Breasts." It was written like gory pulp fiction, each page more eye-popping and horrific than the next. By the time I got to the part where it said Premarin was made from pregnant horse's urine, I had to put it down not to puke.

I decided to go to D'Amico in case Powell might be there. I had debated calling him as soon as I woke up but it was gauche to call a guy before twelve hours had passed, and besides, the trickster was active in him, which meant I couldn't act too romantic. For that I had to wait until the gentleman got active in him, although I wasn't sure if that was a codified Jungian archetype.

A buff young Italian guy was behind the counter. He had thick eyebrows and a 1940s face. There were a couple dozen big barrels of coffee on the right and an old deli counter on the left, with Italian meats and cheeses in the glass case. In the back were a few round tables. A mom with a toddler in a stroller was sitting at one and Powell was sitting at another, his back to the door.

"Think of the devil and the devil appears," I said. He turned around. But it wasn't Powell. It was an old Italian woman reading the *New York Post.* She had the exact same black curly hair. This was one of the disadvantages to dating an older man: you might wind up mistaking him for a woman.

"Can I help you?" she huffed in a nicotined voice.

"I'm sorry," I stuttered. "I thought you were someone else." I did a one-eighty and walked out.

As I emerged back on the street I spotted Powell coming down the sidewalk. He was carrying his shoulder bag and there was a *New York Times* tucked under his arm. When he got close I pretended to be surprised to see him. *"Hank?"* I said.

He put his hand on the side of my face and said, "So how *are* ya?"

"Look at the shiner you gave me when you kissed me," I said. "Isn't it beautiful?" I tilted my face so he could see.

"Nice," he said approvingly. "You wanna come in for a minute?"

We went up to the cappuccino bar in the back, which a skinny young guy with a hat turned backwards was wiping with a cloth. "What would you like?" Powell asked.

"A cappuccino," I said coolly.

"Ah, a fellow appreciater," he said.

We took the caps to a table in the corner, away from the hacking hag. "I got a question for you," Powell said, leaning forward in his chair. "In the English language, is there such a word as 'hoyle'?"

"Not that I know of. Why?"

"Then I'm inventing it."

"What does it mean?"

"It's whore and mohel put together."

"You're such a misogynist. What was your mother like?"

"Just like my ex-wife. A castrating bitch."

"Am I a castrating bitch?"

"I told you, you've got too much animus to be a castrator." I raised the cappuccino to my mouth and sipped through the hole. It burned my tongue. "Careful," he said, and eased off the lid.

I blew into it and looked up at him with a grin. "Last night was such an unanticipated surprise," he said. It was so strange to hear a guy put himself on the table like that. Maybe when they got older they got less tactical; there was less time and therefore less to lose.

"Didn't you know when I wrote that I had a crush on you?" I said.

"No. I thought you wanted someone to tell you what to do with your life."

"I do. I want that too." I thought for a second. "I want you to be my buru."

"What's that?"

"'Booty' and 'guru' put together."

"Very good," he said, grabbing the back of my neck. "What are you doing Thursday night?"

"I have to go to my mother's book group," I said.

"What's the book?"

"The Silent Passage."

"What's it about? Slavery?"

"Menopause."

"Mmm," he winced. "I don't know which is worse."

"Did you know that female babies are born with all the eggs they'll ever have, about seven hundred thousand of them? That means a tiny little baby girl already has all her capacities for reproduction."

"That explains why women are such materialists. They think they gotta hoard their wares. What time's the group?"

"Seven."

"Then I'd like you to come over in the late afternoon. Five o'-clock. And I'd like you to wear a dress or skirt, but no underwear. Will you do as I ask?" The question was like a hard cock fucking me. I felt my eyes glaze over like the dumbest blonde's.

"You know I will," I sighed.

"Something in you brings out the devil in me," he said. "You're so hard on the outside. I want to peel it away."

"I'm not hard."

"You are. The man in you is at war with the woman and it's the woman part I'm interested in, the recessive woman." He put his hand on the back of my head. I felt breathless and weightless like I'd just done a Whip-It. I wanted Powell to be my new career.

"If I bring out the devil in you," I said, "there's nothing I can do but *egg* you on."

"You're such a bad punner," he said. "You should be punished." He leaned forward, grabbed the side of my chair, and dragged it to his side so we were facing the same way.

"What are you doing?" I asked softly. I was wearing a black cotton tennis skirt and a T-shirt that said "West Side Pee-Wee League" in red letters. He put his hand under my skirt, nudged my panties to the side, and eased in a finger. "We're in D'Amico," I whispered.

As if on cue the counter boy came by with a box on his way to the supply room and said to the Italian woman, "Hey, Annie, how 'bout you and me get together tonight and I ram my big one up your ass?"

"You're disgusting," she said. "You got a filthy mout'."

"You see why I come here?" Powell said. He moved his head closer and raised his finger up onto my clit. I felt as though I was a stick shift and he was in the driver's seat wearing wraparound sunglasses. But instead of looking ahead he was staring right at me. His eyes were trained on my face like he had a medical interest in the moment-to-moment change in the tint of my skin and lips.

He held the hood up with his thumb and worked it. I opened my mouth and stared at him weakly. I saw a figure in the distance through the door and then it opened and Liz was striding toward us. "Hel-*lo!*" she cried.

"You're the mayor of Cobble Hill," he said, removing his hand. "Who is she?"

"Nobody," I said. I slid my chair away. Liz was wearing a low-cut pink sweater with what appeared to be a bullet bra, because her breasts stuck out straighter than June Cleaver's.

"Hello, Racheleh!" she said. She blinked at Powell placidly, waiting for me to make the intro.

"This is Hank," I sighed.

"Delightful to meet you," said Liz, extending her long bony fingers. Powell shook unceremoniously, with his nonpussy hand. "Elizabeth Kaminsky, Esquire."

"A lawyer, huh? What kind are you?"

"*Lay,*" she said. "I'm Rachel's very good friend. I live in her building. And you?"

"I live on Strong Place."

"No, I mean, how do you two . . . intersect?" She was squinting as though irked she didn't already know about this important person. She hated to be left in the dark about anything.

"Hank's a friend of mine from the neighborhood," I said quickly.

"How come I've never met you before?"

"He's new here."

"No kidding. How did you meet?"

"Rachel saw a play I wrote," he said.

"Wow," she said. "Have I heard of you?"

"Hank Powell," I said quickly, certain she wouldn't have. Powell had the kind of minor fame that meant the people who did know his name were cult fans and the rest were totally in the dark.

"Oh my God!" she exclaimed. "You're Hank Powell?" I wanted to throw myself across his body to prevent her from coming any nearer. "I loved *Leon and Ruth!*" she said, like she was telling him he had the largest, fattest dick she'd seen in her life. "I'm a huge fan of Don Cheadle's. 'When I kiss your mouth, Ruth, my heart explodes like Mount Vesuvius in my chest.'"

"Women love that line," Powell said. She was kissing his ass but he didn't exactly have to bend over.

"Who knew we had an auteur in our modest midst?" she cried. "A living landmark of the artistic craft?"

As Liz went on with her solo version of *Password* and Powell lapped it up, my heart got jumpy and irregular. I wanted to protect him from her wiles but it was hopeless. How could I measure up to a Vargas girl? I was going to get shafted for a skinnier witty Jew. He obviously had a fetish for banterers, and Liz was the bantering champ. I was menschier and way less fucked-up, but who wants Ralph Bellamy when you can have Cary Grant?

I shot her an imploring look. She cleared her throat and said, "I'd better get going. I have to go to the city to attend to some personal needs."

"What kinda needs?" asked Powell. I wished he'd stop interrogating. As long as you engaged the motormouth, it kept running.

"I have three appointments—my colorist, my analyst, and my gynecologist. It's a rainbow day. I'm attending to my gray, my blues, and then my pink. Ha ha ha ha ha!"

"You don't have gray hair," said Powell.

"Which is precisely why I continue to go to this fabulous colorist." She squeezed his arm and said, "Don't be naïve, Mr. Powell. It takes work to look the way I do."

"My name's *Hank*," he said.

"I'm sorry, Mr. Powell. I'm a nice Jewish girl. I take the Fifth Commandment very seriously."

"Which one's that?"

"'Honor thy father and mother,'" I sighed. She could outdo me in many ways but biblical literacy was not going to be one of them.

"But I'm not her father," he said.

"That's what they all say," she said.

"How long have you been in analysis?"

"Eight years. But I think I'm going to leave her. I had an appointment on September eleventh and tried to call to cancel but I couldn't reach her. I wound up going over anyway, right as it was happening—her office was in the Village. I sat down and said, 'Dr. Fromberg, these planes just hit the World Trade Center.' She said, 'What? What?' and I had to take her outside to show her. We wound up canceling the session but she charged me anyway."

"She *charged* you?" Powell howled.

"That's the way these people operate. Are you in therapy, Mr. Powell?"

"I was with a Jungian for four years," he said. "I never liked him. He sat just three feet opposite from me with his legs open so that I was always aware of his penis. When I told him stories about my mother and my wife, seeking solace, he would always take their side. He'd say, 'I can see why she might have felt that way,' or, 'Don't you think you're being a little unfair?' I started to convince myself that he was right, that all my pain at the hands of women was brought on by myself. I grew weaker and more depressed. I had trouble sleeping at night and dreamed of murderous brides. One morning in the waiting room I saw a woman with black hair and pale pancake makeup emerge from his office. She weighed no more than ninety pounds and resembled an anorexic version of Chrissie Hynde. I realized this was a sign that the man was a murderer, and it was only a matter of time before he would kill me. I walked out of the office and never came back."

He took a sip of his cappuccino. The young mom at the next table was gaping, and even her kid had gotten quiet. Powell could command any room, even the Romper Room.

"So you had no problem seeing a Jungian?" Liz said. "Even though Jung was a Nazi apologist?"

"He had a Jewish mistress!"

"Just because you fuck a Jew doesn't mean you love them," Liz said. Powell opened his mouth as though he was going to say something, then seemed to decide better of it and shut it again. Suddenly Powell's interest in Jung didn't seem so intriguing.

She stood up and arched her breasts forward. "Well, I'd better get going here or the day will escape me. I am so looking forward. First the chair, then the couch, then the stirrups." She put her hand on Powell's shoulder and lowered her mouth to his ear. "You know my favorite position, Mr. Powell?"

"What's that?" Powell asked.

"Prone."

With that the siren stood and headed out the door. "That girl *needs* analysis," said Powell.

"Tell me about it!" I exclaimed delightedly.

"Soon as she walked in she was lying down. She wasn't here five minutes and she was talking about the couch."

"I know," I said. "But admit it. Don't you think she's beautiful?"

"She's easy on the eyes, but all tied in knots. When you date a girl who's that tightly wound you always have to watch your own neck."

"I'll say," I said, eager to encourage any negative assessment. "She's filled with bile. And she's a nympho! She acts like she loves sex but she always uses words like 'banged' and 'stuffed' to describe it. And she loves anal sex. She particularly loves anal sex with black men." The toddler at the next table looked up and his mom shot me a dirty look. I lowered my voice. "But she's always saying she wants to meet a Jew."

Powell thought for a second and then he said, "She's all switched around, then."

"What?"

"She's having sex in the wrong hole with the wrong color. She's got it ass-backwards."

I giggled maliciously. "So you really don't have a thing for her?"

"Are you kidding?" he said. "That broad's like vinegar."

"What do you mean?"

"A few drops on your salad tastes good, but you don't wanna use the whole bottle."

"I think I love you," I said.

"Let's not be hasty," he said.

A F T E R our coffee I decided to take a walk up Court Street to see what was playing at the cinema. As I headed up the street I passed a parade of kindergartners in bright yellow vests, tied together on a long leash like prisoners, yammering as their teachers barked at them to stay in line. I wondered how these children were going to mature when their most evocative childhood memory would be the preschool chain gang.

The Cobble Hill cinema was the kind of small neighborhood theater that had really bad murals of Marilyn Monroe and James Dean on the walls, such lousy likenesses it took you a second to figure out who was who. When you called to find out the movie times it was the owner's voice on the answering machine and he said that in addition to cash they took "Visa rand Mastacard." He was like that shlub on the Men's Warehouse commercials—he had too much hubris to know when to delegate.

I bought a ticket for *Charlie's Angels: Full Throttle* and then I went to the concession stand. The saleswoman had a very elaborate set of painted nails with rhinestones embedded in them. I ordered a medium popcorn and soda and she said, "For a dollar more you could get a Combo Package, which is a large popcorn and an unlimited soda."

I took a deep breath. The Combo Package upgrade is the greatest evil in the known universe. The cheapnik in me wants to get the best deal but the rationalist knows there's no way I'll eat what they sell. "No," I said defiantly, like she was trying to sell me crack. "Just a medium and medium."

She nodded slowly, like she was personally disappointed in the choice, and turned for the bag. "Goddammit," I said. "Gimme the combo." When she rang it up it came to eight fifty-seven.

In the theater I found an aisle seat, jutted my feet out, and got to work on my popcorn. There were three other audience members that I could see—two old ladies, and a lone slender middle-aged man. The previews hadn't started and it was quiet except for the Muzak version of "My Heart Will Go On."

I heard the *pffff* of the heavy door opening and then a guy sat down across from me, a row ahead, and started munching on his popcorn. He was scarfing it down big time, scooping up big portions and chewing loudly. I got this weird feeling of déjà vu and slowly it dawned on me that there was only one person in the world who ate in such a vile, nasty way.

"Dad?"

He turned around, looking as though he had taken a shit in his pants. "What are you doing here?" I asked.

"Same thing you are."

"It's twelve o'clock. Shouldn't you be at work?"

He hesitated a second and then lifted his popcorn and drink (he'd gone for the combo too), climbed over me, and sat down in the next seat.

"There were some layoffs."

"I can't believe this," I said. "But you'd been there for, like, ten years."

"Times are tough, and old people are expendable."

"When did it happen?"

"Three months ago."

"Three months? Why didn't you tell me?"

"I didn't know how long it would last. I was hoping I could tell you when I got a new job." I knew the truth. He hadn't wanted to tell me because he was ashamed, and the fact that he was too ashamed to admit it made me all the more worried.

As concerned as I was for my father, I couldn't help thinking what it all meant for *me*. What if I was just like him? Maybe there was such a thing as Late-Onset Failure Syndrome. It was hereditary, just like high blood pressure or cancer, and mine was just kicking in. Sometimes when I watched the way he held his face in his hands or stroked his chin I realized I did the same thing and it always made me nervous, like he was in my blood. When he read the newspaper he sometimes said parts of sentences out loud—like "inverse relationship to fat consumption" or "war of words between the sides is abating"—as though he was trying to follow the train of thought. When I was a kid I used to make fun of him for it but in recent months I'd started doing the same thing. Whenever I caught myself I stopped immediately, terrified, like some evil alien baby was growing inside me.

Maybe he'd lost his job because he was so devastated by me dropping out. He was my biggest fan, in the worst way. When I was in Hebrew School, he sat in the front row every time I did anything special at services and came all the way to Wesleyan when I led my first Shabbat. And whenever anything bad happened, like the time I got rejected from a summer internship at the National Yiddish Book Center, he'd get this look on his face like he couldn't take it, like it had happened to him. Maybe I was the reason he was on skid row. And if that was true I was in worse straits than I thought. Not only did I have to worry about getting back on my feet for my own sake, I had to do it for his.

"So have you been going on interviews?" I asked.

"Yeah, yeah," he said. "I'm trying really hard to stay positive and Mom keeps telling me to keep an open mind. Yesterday I interviewed at a music company. A rap label."

"For a *computer* job?"

"Actually, it was administrative assistant," he said. "Have you heard of a band called Got 2 B Reel, spelled Got, two number sign, the letter B, and then R-e-e-l?"

"No."

"That's their main client. It may be their only client. I went to their Web site last night. The band members are posed with their fingers in this strange configuration."

"Oh my God," I said. "They're Bloods. Those signs spell out a gang name. You cannot go working at a rap label. You could get shot!"

"I wish I'd known this before I lowered my salary range."

The thought of him working as a secretary made me embarrassed, like *he* was the black sheep in the family instead of *me*. "Aren't you interviewing for any computer jobs?"

"Sure I am but the market is terrible. And it doesn't make it any easier that I'm twenty years older than most of the other applicants. Plus my skills are so outdated I don't know who could use me. Do you think I should shave my beard?"

He had worn his beard since I was one and a half, which meant I had no conscious memories of him without it. I had seen photos of him clean-shaven, wheeling me in a stroller over the Brooklyn Bridge, looking young and studly in tight bell-bottoms, but he always seemed like a different person. It was the same with the photos of him smoking cigarettes (he'd quit a few months after meeting my mom). Shaved or smoking, he didn't seem so much like my dad as his stand-in.

"Well, you'd definitely look younger," I said, trying to gauge his neck fat through the hair.

"But what if my bald spot looks more obvious without the beard to offset it?"

I had lobbied successfully for his switch from a comb-over to a comb-back a few years back and the improvement had been astounding. Right away he started carrying himself with more confidence, looking slick and Cary Grantish instead of dissembling and Rudy Giulianine.

But I didn't like the idea of him without his beard. I felt like I wouldn't recognize him. "The bald spot pitfall is an important consideration," I said. "You might wind up looking even more dorky and over-the-hill than you do already."

His shook his head wearily like he probably should have guessed my response in advance. "Thank you so much, sweetheart," he said.

"Why'd they lay you off?" I asked, eating some of his popcorn even though I had my own. "Was it personal?"

"It's hard to tell. But I must say, it buoys me that you and I are in the same position."

"What do you mean?" I said. "I have a job."

"Not a real one."

"It *is* real," I said, feeling the kind of insane anger that can only be brought on by a mother or a father. "And I didn't get fired. I left school because I wanted to. I don't have any problem with where I am right now. Why would you compare your situation to mine when they're not the same at all?"

"Misery loves company," he said.

"But Dad," I said. "I'm not miserable." He shrugged and turned to the screen with great interest, even though the only thing on it was a word jumble for Matt Damon.

"You were going to be a rabbi," he said, "the first in our family. And now you're mopping tables. Not to mention the fact that Mom told me she saw you with a man twice your age. It's like you've lost all common sense."

"Jesus Christ," I said. I could never count on either of them to keep anything secret. If I kept quiet about anything they acted like I was being a horrible child but whenever I told them things they turned right around and told the other. In Jewish families information is love. The more you tell your parents, the more it means you love them. This is true even if they take whatever precious, personal stories you have and repeat them at parties to their friends with no thought or care to the shame they might bring upon you.

"What are you doing cavorting with a middle-aged screenwriter?" he said. "Older men are only interested in one thing."

"What's that?"

"Do I have to spell it out for you? They're addicted to power! Only a young woman can give it to them. And the relationship never ever lasts. Look how the girl from Modesto ended up. Look at Bill and Monica."

"Are you calling your own daughter Monica Lewinsky? That is really low."

"It's not such a stretch! If you're in awe of his status, I beg you please to be more of an adult! Someone like this is just going to think of you as a flash in the pan."

"That's really generous of you. You don't think for a moment he might actually have some respect for my brain?"

"Of course not! You don't have anything in common! How old is he?"

"Fifty-one."

"What can you possibly have to talk about with a fifty-one-year-old?"

"Carl Jung."

"Carl Jung was a Nazi apologist."

"He had a Jewish mistress!"

"Listen to yourself," he said, like it was all getting way too surreal. "I can't believe you have no qualms about dating someone NJ, when just a few months ago you were on your way to the rabbinate."

NJ was our family's slang for Not Jewish, and the tone you used when saying it was similar to the one you might use for "convicted felon."

"Look," I said. "This isn't any of your business. The only reason you even know is because Mom saw us. If I want to date someone NJ nothing you say is going to stop me."

"You used to care about Jewish continuity! When you were fourteen you came back from that intermarriage shul-in and said you'd decided to marry a Jew."

"I was *fourteen!* And they threw those events to brainwash us!"

"All I can think is that you don't see yourself having anything long-lasting with this man, which I have trouble respecting, or that you're in complete denial and have totally lost your head!"

The hot dog and cheeseburger concession stand ad was coming on, the one where the hot dog looks like a hard dick and if there are teenagers in the theater they giggle loudly.

"I don't know what kind of hole you're sticking your head into, Rachel," he said, "but I wish you'd yank it out."

"Give me a little more credit," I said.

"Give yourself a little more credit. You used to be so ambitious and now it's like you don't even care!"

"I'm still ambitious. I'm just . . . repositioning. It's important to take stock once in a while. Madonna takes years in between albums!"

"Exactly," he said. "And when was the last time she had a hit?" He shoveled down some more popcorn, the corn spraying out from his hairy mouth.

———◆———

B Y the time the movie ended it was after two and the sky was bright and sunny. My dad was in high spirits, going on and on about the amazing action sequences and the chemistry between the actresses, like our whole argument never even happened.

When we got in front of my apartment building he looked down at the stack of supermarket giveaways that had accumulated on the stoop, scooped them up, and deposited them into the recycling bin. He did this every time he came over to visit. "Why do you do that?" I said.

"Don't you know about the broken window rule?"

"I don't think burglars are going to see my apartment building as a more appealing target just because they saw a stack of newspapers on the stoop."

"You can never be too careful." He put the lid on the bin and then his face brightened. "Hey, Rach. I have an idea. Why don't we go for a bike ride? There's a beautiful path by the Verrazano. We could pack a lunch and eat it under the bridge. I went there by myself the other day and watched the sun set."

It was a little bizarre: your own father's not supposed to sucker you into playing hooky. It was like his unemployment had opened him up to a whole new lazy worldview. "Dad," I said. "I have to get ready for work."

He sighed and gave me a grim look like he understood but wasn't happy. "How 'bout tomorrow, then?" He looked so eager and lonely. Whenever I was around him he made me want to say things like "I need a little space" or "Why don't we take things down a notch?" But you can't exactly request a trial separation from your own father. I told him I'd think about it and kissed him on the cheek good-bye.

THE NEED TO KNOW AND
THE FEAR OF KNOWING

I T was nine o'clock at work and for the past half hour a Greyhound and a Stella Artois had been dishing about men. In general women customers were less annoying than men but they drank more slowly and tipped worse. Still, given a choice, I liked women better because they left me alone and I didn't have to worry about fights.

I was pretty sure Greyhound's name was Alex, but not positive, so I always made a choice never to speak it aloud. I had mastered the art of the warm, seemingly intimate "He-ey!" when someone whose name I didn't know walked through the door. She had cat-eye glasses and bangs and lived on Dean, around the corner from the bar. She told me once that she was a grad student at NYU but I could never remember in what. Her friend had a hot figure and a butterface—great body, but her *face*—and they were talking about Greyhound's most recent dating fiasco. She had met this seemingly amazing guy on Nerve.com, a skinny Vespa-riding Web programmer, and after a great first date he completely flaked out. She kept calling him and he lost her cell phone number twice, and when they arranged their next date he showed up on Vicodin because he'd thrown his back out. He wound up passing out in her bed without so much as a kiss.

"So we didn't speak for the next two weeks," Greyhound said, "and just as I was thinking I was over him I ran into him at the theater. He was with a date."

"Oh, sweetie," said Stella.

"You know what's worse? She was totally mousy!"

"Generigirl," said Stella. "I hate those."

"Exactly," said Greyhound. "Empty smile, no soul. And then he had the nerve to come up to me and *introduce* me to her. We haven't spoken since and that was three, no four, days ago. So the question is," she said, drawing in her breath, "do I call him tonight or wait till tomorrow?"

Stella and I exchanged a grim look. The girl was a PhD candidate and when it came to love she had no IQ. There was zero awareness. It was as though she was so fixated on it working that she was willing to ignore every single red flag. I had never considered myself the luckiest girl in the world in the man department but now I was grateful that the guys I dated did one thing right: liked me.

Stella put her hand on top of Greyhound's. "I don't think you should call him at all."

"Why not?"

"The guy's a dick! And he has a girlfriend!"

"What if she's just a friend?"

"*Alex!!*" she shouted, with a withering look. "You gotta Palmolive." She rubbed her hands together under an imaginary faucet.

Greyhound's face fell as she seemed to accept, at least for a moment, that her friend might be right. "So you think I should just . . . forget about him?" she asked. Stella nodded somberly. "I guess it's over," Greyhound said, trying to look resolute and strong.

Suddenly her cell phone rang, piercing the relative quiet of the bar. She gave Stella a meaningful look as she fumbled for it and stared down at the indicator. "It's my mother," she said, sighing. "How do they always know when you're at your lowest?" She shut off the ringer and slurped the rest of her drink. "Could I get another?" she said, but I was already on my way to the bottle.

T H E next night around seven, I heard Liz having an orgasm. She wasn't saying "Fuck my Jew beav!" this time, though. She was moaning something muffled and unintelligible into her pillow. I craned my neck to hear the guy but he was a silent fucker.

I wondered if it was Shittner, which would have explained the lack of self-hating pejorative. When Liz came it was fast and soft, which was atypical for her: "Oh, oh, oh!" It was so quiet I concluded after some deliberation that it wasn't a man at all, but her vibrator, The Gun. She had shown it to me once. It was white and shaped like a big water pistol and you inserted it into yourself and turned it on by pressing the trigger. I always felt the symbolism was a little backwards, since she was a female ejaculator.

In the morning for my Powell rendezvous I opted for a white and red flowered silk dress I bought at the Village Scandal, a vintage store on East Seventh Street. It was cap-sleeved with a V-neck and high waist and it hung sleekly and smoothly around my body. It seemed designed for a sleazy secretary from the 1940s and every time I wore it people said, "That dress looks like it was made for you." I wore it with knee-high black boots with silver buckles to give it more of a modern feel.

As I was heading to my door I remembered Powell's caveat. I slipped my underpants off, feeling very afraid. Although it wasn't cold I felt that without underwear I needed added protection from any potential leerers, so I chose a 1970s tan trench coat, also high-waisted, with red trim, to wear on top. Whenever I wore it I felt like the Morton Salt girl.

On my way down the stairs I heard footsteps, high-heeled and aggressive, behind me. I waited at the landing below mine and when she saw me she screamed like she'd seen a ghost, then said, "Oh, hey, Rach."

"Are you OK?" I said.

"I didn't see you there."

"*You* sounded like you were having fun last night," I said.

"What?"

"Were you diddling the dai dai?"

"What are you talking about?"

"I heard you moaning but I couldn't hear a guy."

"Oh. Yeah. It was The Gun." She headed down the stairs to the foyer. She blinked rapidly like a squirrel on speed and held the door open for me.

Outside her eyes looked off balance and nervous. She was acting so moody. Maybe she'd blue-binned with Shittner and didn't want to tell me.

"Are you sure it wasn't Shittner?" I said.

"It wasn't Shittner!" she shrieked. "It was The Gun, OK?"

"All right, all right," I said. "Don't be a freakazoid."

"*You're* the freakazoid," she snarled, then brushed past me and walked briskly toward Boerum Place.

I looked down at my dress and party coat. I was annoyed at her for acting strange but I was also insulted that she hadn't noticed my outfit. I was all decked out and she hadn't said a thing. Something was fishy.

I headed left toward Court Street and as I passed CVS it occurred to me that it might be a wise idea to go Boy Scout. I walked through the electronic doors, went downstairs to the pharmacy section, and had just pulled a box of LifeStyles Ultra Sensitive off a hook when I heard a voice behind me say, "Rachel? Is that you?"

I would have dropped the box but it was already in my hand so I clamped it under my arm and turned around. "Stu Zaritsky," I said.

Stu Zaritsky was one of my former classmates and represented the worst that the Reform rabbinate had to offer. Though he was not the precise reason I had dropped out he definitely had something to do with my overall disillusionment with the program. He was thirty pounds overweight, wore tight chinos like Pat on *Saturday Night Live,* and breathed through his mouth. He came from Roslyn, Long Island, and had gone to Brandeis, and like many rabbinical students he had been president of his regional Reform Jewish youth group, which in our world was the equivalent of being homecoming king.

On the first day of classes, when we gathered in the sanctuary for the welcome speech by President Levine, Stu slipped into my pew and introduced himself. Within five minutes he had informed me that his father was a rabbi and his grandfather too.

He never asked me out—he had a young wife he'd known since freshman year of college, and a baby boy—but he got under my skin. What bugged me about Stu wasn't his pomposity, poor rhetorical skills, or tendency to kiss up to professors, but his irritating habit of Halachic one-upsmanship. He was the kind of guy who would ask me what I was doing for the weekend as a way of finding out if I rested on

Shabbat, which I didn't. So if I said, "Studying and going to a party,"
he'd raise his eyebrows like I was a bad Jew. I had always felt that ob-
servance was more about the spirit than the letter of the law but Stu
saw everything as an opportunity to prove his holiness.

"So how *are* you?" he asked weightily, like I had dropped out because I'd gone insane instead of because I'd chosen to. He was holding a jumbo bag of Pampers under one arm.

"Fine, fine," I said. "What are you doing in my neighborhood?"

"I was just visiting some residents over at the Cobble Hill nursing
home, for Prof Dev." Prof Dev was Professional Development, a
hands-on training course we had to take every year in order to graduate. "They're so brave, those old folks. They've got so much
ruach." *Ruach* meant spirit and it was one of those words that the
teacher's pets all loved to say with an exaggerated Hebrew accent.

"Really?" I said. "Every time I pass by and look down in the window they seem kind of catatonic."

"Oh no," he said. "They're filled with life." Stu was the kind of guy
who had to ennoble everything he did. He shifted the diapers from
one arm to the other and said, "Shoshanna just called to tell me to
pick these up. She's down to one diaper and she goes a little batty
when she gets so low."

"How *is* Zev anyway?" All the rabbis that had kids gave them biblical names even though they themselves had assimilationist ones
like Randy or Mitchell.

"Oh, he's a terror. Eighteen months and getting into everything.
What are *you* buying?"

"Cold medication," I said, shoving the box up into my armpit. He
nodded and then surveyed the wall, which, in addition to condoms,
held hemorrhoid ointment, suppositories, and diaphragm jelly.

He cleared his throat, swallowed, and said, "So is it true that
you're a bartender? Sharon Margolis thought she saw you through a
window but said you were dressed so provocatively she was convinced it was someone else."

I debated my options. I could tell him I was a contract killer or
Jew for Jesus but all I wanted to do was get the hell out of there.
"That was me," I said.

"That's a shift, huh?"

"What do you mean?"

"Well, you spend all your time with misfits."

"It's actually not that different from being a rabbi," I said tersely. "I mean, people ask for advice. I provide counseling."

"So why'd you drop out? I heard one of your patients died while you were sitting with him and you completely freaked out. Is that why?"

"I think my reasons for dropping out are between me and God, Stu."

He stared at me coldly—annoyed I wasn't giving him any good dish to report back to his friends, even though gossip was against Jewish law—and then he sighed and said, "You know, I should probably thank you."

"Why's that?"

"I won a hundred bucks because of you."

"I'm sorry?"

"A few of us had a pool going on how long you were going to last."

"Oh yeah?" I said, wanting to belt him.

"I had you leaving in the second semester, Sharon had you leaving second year, and Joe Slotnick must have had a lot of faith in you because he thought you were going to make it to ordination."

I wanted to take out one of the rubbers and slingshot it into his pimpled face. "And why are you telling me this?"

"I thought you'd get a kick out of it," he said.

"How sweet of you," I said. "It's nice to know my colleagues had faith in me."

"Rabbinical school really isn't about having faith in each other," he said. "It's about having faith in HaShem." He pointed to the sky. "It was obvious to me from day one that your faith was shaky."

"Oh yeah?"

"You were always looking out the window during services and you seemed to pray without *ruach*." There was that word again. "Plus you wear clothes that look like they're from flea markets." He eyed my tan trench coat and the bright print peeking out from underneath it.

"It's called vintage!" I snapped.

"You always struck me as more of an art school student. I knew you were hoping to revitalize the rabbinate but somehow I could never picture you on a pulpit."

I took in his oily hair and side part, his paunch riding over his high-hiked pants, his smudged glasses. He was the *putz* calling the kettle black. It was people like him who caused the declining rate of American Jewish affiliation. Who could entrust their soul to a rabbi who couldn't even take care of his own skin? I wanted to tell him it was better that I'd left than stayed on like morons like him, who were in it for the power and the narcissistic high, who had no creative thinking capacity whatsoever. I wanted to tell him that if he'd chosen the internship at Memorial instead of the cushy one up at Temple Shaaray Tefila working with nursery school kids, he might have had an opportunity to do some soul-searching himself. But Stu was a third-generation rabbi with a messiah complex. Arguing with him about anything was a waste of breath.

I was about to head out of the store when something strange happened. I thought about the way I'd let Stu walk all over me, and I imagined Powell being in this situation. What Would Powell Do? Before I was completely aware of what was happening, I pulled out the LifeStyles and said, "Great running into you, Stu, but I gotta get going. I have some fucking to do."

"What?" Stu gasped.

"I said, 'I have some fucking to do.'" He reddened and looked as though he was about to combust. "Great seeing you. Listen, come by the bar sometime. Roxy, on Bergen and Smith. Have you heard that Yiddish saying? 'If you're at odds with your rabbi make peace with your bartender.'" He gaped at me and I bounded up the stairs.

T H E first thing Powell said when I came in was, "Ya late."

I looked at my watch. "Only five minutes," I said.

"If I had been in a different mood," he said, "I wouldn't have let you up. I consider tardiness the worst of all sins. Ya lucky the trickster isn't more active in me right now."

"I thought the trickster *was* active in you," I said.

"I said the *devil*'s active. The devil and the trickster are two very different symbols. The devil seeks evil; the trickster seeks play."

This wasn't the most romantic opener. Then again, I had arrived without underwear; it wasn't exactly candles and incense to begin with.

"I brought you something," I said, and handed him the bag from the store. He looked inside, pulled out the condom box, regarded it as though it was a small dead animal, and deposited it on the mail table by the door.

"Let me take ya coat," he said. He hung it up in the closet and gave me a once-over. "You cut a fine swath," he said.

"They're different decades but I feel they work together."

He took the hem of the dress in both hands and lifted it slowly up above my waist. I felt like I was being unwrapped on Christmas morning. "Very good," he said when he saw. "You obeyed."

He kissed me and I went liquid in his arms. I imagined a war going on outside, explosions and catastrophes, and us still kissing with the world swirling around. I didn't think about his paunch or the flabbiness in his upper arms. He was a 1950s stud and I was a Tennessee Williams heroine who always had trouble breathing.

I felt him kicking the back of my leg. I wasn't sure what he was trying to do so I resisted and stood firm. He pushed his foot into the back of my knee and I realized he was cuing me to kneel. I wished he had just said it. I sunk down, banging my right knee against the floor as I did.

He stood in front of me and as though on pornographic autopilot I unbuckled his pants. It was terrifying and pale. I took it in my mouth and squeezed the base. He seemed to sense my inner blow slut. He patted the side of my face and said, "Good girl," and right away I got crazy inside. I sucked him deeper and then I reached up under my skirt and started playing with myself. I wasn't sure if he could see and I wasn't sure I wanted him to. I hoped he wouldn't think it was too Gen X.

When I looked up he was watching my hand. I stopped, ashamed. "Keep going," he said. He patted my hair and let me control the force. He kept saying "That's right" and "You're my little hoo-ah," and this time I didn't laugh.

He was gazing down at me so meanly, like one of those huge talking trees from *The Wizard of Oz*. I thought about his sternness, how he knew me, and how we were animus and anima, meant to be together. I felt that if I could just be with him like this every day, dress up and come over in the broad daylight, then it wouldn't matter what I did for a living or how long it took me to get a real job. He would be the most important thing and all the other stuff would be meaningless. His eyes were so knowing, so slanted. It was as though he understood everything about me even though he hardly knew me, and his cool knowledge made me so moved that I came.

"I came," I said. I am a very demure comer and if I don't make noise they just don't know.

"*That's* it," he said, like he was patting a good horse's flank.

He pushed me down onto the floor on my stomach and lifted my dress and after fumbling around for a few seconds, he was in.

"What about the box?" I asked lamely.

"We'll just do it like this for a minute," he said.

He moved in me and made his savage sigh. I found myself angling my pelvis up toward him. It was risky and stupid but we had passed the prophylactic point of no return, the point at which you feel that if you were going to get pregnant you already are, in which case all the other sex is icing.

The floor was cold against my face. I felt some drool trickle out of my mouth and form a small puddle by my lip and I moaned gutturally like a little retarded girl. I felt raw and weak and low-IQ. I noticed a coin on the floor under the couch and as I was trying to determine whether it was a penny or a nickel I heard a triumphant roar and felt a warm mess on my back.

"I'll be right back," he said, and went into the bathroom. I stood up, brushed myself off, and wandered over to the window. Three boys were playing hockey in the street and I wondered if they would grow up to be as ruthless as Powell.

He came in, picked up his pants, and started putting them on. I walked into the bathroom silently to wash my butt and then I went to the sink and threw some water on my face. My hair was a mess and my eyelids droopy and worn. As I dried my face I saw that the collar of my beautiful dress had ripped along the neck. I wondered what would be left of me when he was through, if I would just be a pile of scabs and ratty threads. He had kicked me out of his apartment on the first date and fucked me on the floor on the second. It wasn't exactly an upward curve.

I wanted to sleep over, to meet his kid. I wanted to have sex on the bed again, to move up in his life, not down.

When I came back Powell was sitting on the couch fully dressed, listening to bossa nova and sipping from a glass of wine. There was an empty glass on the table, and next to it an open bottle of red. "You all cleaned up?" he said.

"Yep," I said.

He pointed to the empty glass and said, "You want some?" I nodded and he poured me some. It was Côtes du Rhône, and there was a tag on it that said $17.99. It looked like a new bottle, that he'd opened just for us, not one he'd had lying around. Maybe I was making too big a deal of the floor thing. At least it was hardwood. It could have been parquet.

I drank the wine and we sat there quietly in the evening light. But as I watched him aerate it seemed like his face had turned frosty. I heard Liz saying, "How come when we make them come, they like us less?" and it was like a negative mantra hovering over us, mingling with the smell of our sex. Was Powell like those guys who hated women as soon as they had them, or was he old enough to know that a woman you could have was the best kind there was?

"Look what you did to my collar," I said. He held it by the corner and flopped it up and down like a child with a light switch. "What should I do about it?"

"What do you mean what should you do?"

"Do you have a needle and thread?"

"You should leave it like that. It looks good."

"But I'm going to my mother's book group."

"Exactly," he said. "You'll give 'em something to be nostalgic about."

M Y parents' brownstone was on Warren Street, between Clinton and Court. It was a modest building painted dark red and came off more *heimish* than stately. They'd been renting the ground and first floors since 1975. Even after the neighborhood got more gentrified, they continued to rent, and although they only paid a rent-stabilized grand a month, these days they kicked themselves for never having bought.

As I came up the stoop I saw my mom and her friends through the window. There were five of them scattered around, on the couch and on floor pillows, chatting and laughing in pastel Eileen Fisher, like the cast of a General Foods International Coffee ad. "I'm so glad you made it!" she said, greeting me in the entrance hallway. "Did you finish the book?"

"Uh—almost," I said. "So are you nervous about leading?"

"I'm used to it. I did *The Corrections* and *Things Fall Apart* and they were two of our most heated discussions."

"Where's Dad?" I said as we came in the door.

"In his office. I told him he was banished until I gave him the signal he could come up." We started to head into the living room but she pulled me back. "Listen. He told me he told you about his job situation. Don't mention anything about it in front of my friends. He's very self-conscious about the whole thing."

"I won't," I said. "How are *you* doing about it?"

"Fine," she shrugged. "I don't like having him around all the time, but I don't have much choice."

As soon as I walked into the living room I was greeted by a loud chorus of "Racheleh!" My mom had been friends with the same group of women for the past thirty years. They all had kids around the same age—in the early seventies they had a rotating playgroup at different women's houses—and since then they'd stayed close, getting together regularly to gossip and kvell, and starting the book group a couple years back, when they became empty-nesters.

There was Nina Halberstam, a tall go-getter corporate attorney

and our across-the-street neighbor; Carol Landsman, a curly-haired
social worker; Joan Ibbotson, an ESL teacher with a bad red-hair dye
job; and Shelly Katz, a hot divorcée and the only smoker. Nina was
pouring red wine into their glasses and I could tell by the tint in
their Semitic faces that this wasn't the first bottle.

"How's the waitressing going?" Nina asked, getting up to embrace me.

"Bartending," I said.

"I thought you were a waitress."

"Nope, not that classy," I said. My mom gave me a dirty look as
she headed into the kitchen.

"I bet you get picked up all the time," Carol said. "I was a waitress
at the Caffe Cino in the early seventies and I went home with a different man every night." She looked out the window nostalgically.
"Of course, there wasn't any AIDS back then."

My mom came in from the kitchen with two baskets, one filled with
French bread, the other with grapefruits. As she set them down on the
table she spotted my collar. "Oh my God," she said. "What happened?"

"It must have ripped when I was putting it on this morning," I
said, holding it up. "That's the problem with vintage. It just doesn't
wear well."

"That's a bad rip," Carol said, running her finger over it and giving me a dubious look.

"Why are you serving grapefruit and bread?" I asked.

"It's not grapefruit," my mom said. "It's blood oranges. And day-
old bread." We all looked at her blankly. "In honor of menopause,"
she said, giggling like a mischievous schoolgirl.

"You are too much, Sue," said Joan.

"What? I'm just trying to be theme-driven. We had New England
clam chowder for *The Perfect Storm,* why can't we have day-old
bread for *The Silent Passage?*"

"That chowder was delicious," said Joan. "More memorable than
the book."

"We're all here," my mom said, "so why don't we get started?"
She grabbed a copy of the book from the coffee table, and a page of
typed notes. They all got exuberant eager faces, like this was the

highlight of their week, and pulled copies of the book out of their totes. Carol sat on the couch and patted the space next to her. I didn't want to be in her proximity because she always leered at me like a lez but there weren't any other seats so I did.

As I sat down I felt my dress against my ass and remembered I wasn't wearing underwear. I crossed my legs tightly so I couldn't flash and held my collar up with my hand to cover the bra. I felt like a trailer-trash ho who'd accidentally wandered into an Anti-Defamation League benefit.

"Why don't we start with general comments?" said my mom, leaning back to survey the group. "Gail Sheehy says menopause is about the need to know and the fear of knowing. Reactions?"

"This goddamn Gail Sheehy made me want to put a hole in my head," said Nina. "It's the most depressing thing I've ever read in my life. If we go on HRT we'll die of breast cancer and if we don't we'll die of osteoporosis. What are we supposed to do?"

"I have a problem with the way you categorized HRT, Nina," Joan jumped in. "I've started talking about it with my ob-gyn and he says that given a history of osteoporosis I should stay on the hormones. I know it's politicized but it's a personal choice."

"You gotta be out of your mind!" Nina snapped. "When the Women's Health Initiative study came out I knew I would never do it. For years the male medical establishment told us hormones were safe and now we know they were lying to us! Why am I going to take something that could give me not just breast cancer, but heart attacks, strokes, blood clots?" Joan answered back, and then they both started talking at once. They were the middle-aged Jets and the Sharks.

"*Hey!*" my mom bellowed. Usually her voice was pretty soft but she had these power-lungs from teaching and once in a while she'd show them off. "No interrupting during Open Comments!"

"She's such a good leader," Carol clucked.

My mom blushed and looked down at her notes. "I think Sheehy's best point is that what's right for one woman isn't necessarily right for another. And it seems the reason these discussions get so polarized"—Polarized? Had she been taking correspondence courses at Brown?—"is because any discussion of menopause, at bottom, is a discussion of mortality." They all got hushed and nod-ded reverentially like black ladies in church.

"What gets my goat," my mom went on, "is how little research there is about it. The medical world has done so little to look into what it means and ways to treat it and as a result women are left completely at bay." I'd never heard her speak so strongly about any-thing. When she presented me with a tallis made by blind Israelis at my bat mitzvah she was so nervous I could hear the spit crackling in her mouth. "We need to feel free to talk to our ob-gyns, and not be ashamed, because menopause is a normal part of life."

"If it's normal then why is it so harrowing?" Nina said. "Gail Sheehy says women report the best sex of their lives between forty-five and fifty-five! *Where on God's green earth did she get that from?* If I can stop barking at Larry long enough for us to try, then I'm too hot to be in the mood, and other times it's so painful I have to make him stop."

"Maybe I should go," I said.

"This is important," my mom said. "You should listen."

"It's like my body won't pay attention to my brain," Nina said.

"You're like a man!" Joan shouted, and they all broke up in laughter.

"You see, this is why I'm glad to be divorced," Shelly said. "I don't have to worry about any of that."

"Nina," Carol jumped in. "Didn't your doctor tell you about the Estring?"

"I've never even heard of that."

"It's an estrogen ring that sits inside the vagina right below the cervix. You put it in for three months and it very slowly releases a small amount of estrogen directly into the canal . . ." I tuned them out. My deafness was instinctive and adaptive. The thought of Carol Landsman with a little cock ring inside her made my stomach weak. I didn't have any need to know; I just had a fear of knowing.

Suddenly I felt a spoonful of discharge slide out. My twenty-something vagina must have felt the need to make itself heard. I jumped a little and inched forward. If I wasn't careful I'd stain the couch.

"Are you all right?" Carol asked, slipping an arm around my shoulder. Another blob came out.

I leapt to my feet. "Can you excuse me?"

"Where you going?" my mom called after me.

"To the bathroom."

"Wait till you get older!" Nina called. "You'll have to go every ten minutes!"

A s soon as I got down to my bedroom I beelined for the dresser. All my teenage posters were still on the walls—Johnny Depp from *21 Jump Street,* Sean Penn in *Fast Times.* My old particleboard Workbench desk was in the corner and the Kelly green wall-to-wall carpeting still had the huge bleach stain I'd made when I tipped over a tray of Jolen I mixed for my mustache in ninth grade.

I opened the top drawer of the dresser and after rummaging through about a dozen stretched and malformed nightshirts that said things like "Jenny Stein's Bat Mitzvah—10/20/87," I came to the unsettling conclusion that there were no spare pairs of undies. I couldn't go back upstairs pantiless when I might leak all over again and if I left the meeting my mother would think I wasn't being supportive. There was only one recourse.

My parents' bedroom was adjacent to mine, and my dad's office was next to their bedroom. A thin stream of light was coming out of his office door. If he was working on his computer I didn't have to worry about him coming out; even a nuclear war couldn't pull my dad from the screen of a PC.

I pushed open the bedroom door. Their room had a dark homey feel and always smelled the same. My dad's mystery books and computer stuff were strewn all over the place and his dresser was littered with nails, bolts, and eyeglasses with lenses missing. My mom's dresser was opposite the bed and her underwear drawer was the top one, to the right. There was a divider in the middle and her bras were stacked on one side and the panties folded on the other. She'd worn the same kind since I was a kid—white satin three-panel control-top with total coverage in the ass—Full Dorsal Fashion. I lifted the top pair out and inspected the cotton patch to see if they were clean.

The patch was dingy but unstained. Trying very hard not to breathe through my nose, I stepped in and hiked them up. They were baggy and slipped down to my hips but the leg holes were tight, which was kind of a downer: it meant my thighs were as wide as hers.

As I walked out I noticed something on my mom's nightstand. It was something completely incongruous, more frightening than a glow-in-the-dark dildo or transsexual porn. Wedged between her glasses case and tub of Clinique anti-aging cream, sitting there as nonchalantly as if it had been there forever, was *Mars and Venus in the Bedroom* by John Gray, PhD. I opened it up and read the first line: "He wants sex. She wants romance. Sometimes it seems as if our partners are from different planets . . ." I dropped it to the floor with a horrified gasp.

Menopause brought on slight insanity, I knew, but this meant my mom was truly far gone. She was doing the middle-aged equivalent of *The Rules*, taking love advice from a sexist idiot. It was so unlike her. The only other book she owned that was even slightly self-help was *Fat Is a Feminist Issue* and she'd had it thirty years.

Why was she reading John Gray in plain sight of her husband? Was it a signal to my dad to lay off, and stop hitting on her? Maybe *he* was the one having sexual problems. Was he too depressed about his unemployment to get it up? I shuddered, unsettled by every possible visual.

As I replaced the book on her nightstand I heard a noise coming from his bedroom. It sounded like panting and it was rhythmic and determined. I walked out and stood outside his office. Beneath the panting was the faint sound of Terri Gross, interviewing Paul Auster about his newest book. I turned the knob and pushed the door open. He was on his back on the floor, his feet wedged under the couch. My fat father was doing sit-ups.

He was in a white V-neck undershirt and snot-green sweats, and he was counting, "Thirty-six, thirty-seven, thirty-eight . . . ," loudly, over the interview. When he saw me he jumped for a second in surprise but instead of stopping he held up a finger and made me wait till he got to fifty.

"Arrghhh!" he said, collapsing back onto the floor.

"What's going on?" I shouted.

"What do you mean what's going on?" he said, panting. "I'm getting in shape."

"Since when have you cared about exercise?"

"I figure it could help with my search. Didn't you see the article in the Job Market section about how men are taking personal grooming more seriously now that so many of us are unemployed?"

"I don't read that section. I'm not looking for a job."

"I've got to do everything I can to tip the scales in my favor!"

The plot thickened. Maybe my mom was reading *Mars and Venus* because she was the Mars in the relationship. Maybe he was the one trying to woo her back, by getting in shape. She was the one who was more masculine on the surface—she never cried like he did at movies, and she was totally unsentimental. Maybe he was afraid she'd leave him unless he cleaned up his act.

"This is so unlike you," I said. "You've never cared about looking good before."

"You see?" he said. "This is why I need to do it! Because people like you say things like that."

"That's not what I—"

"It's all right, Rach! I've let myself go and I don't have much time to make up for it!" There was a loud laugh from upstairs and he pointed to the ceiling. "How's the hen party?"

"They're talking about estrogen rings," I said.

"Ugh," he said. "I don't even want to know."

"You should take an interest," I said. "Gail Sheehy says that after menopause there's this thing called postmenopausal zest. It was named by Margaret Mead. Postmenopausal women have a love of life and a vim and vigor stronger than any they've felt before."

"She's right! The vim is killing me!"

"Why are you so insensitive? Maybe you should go upstairs and eavesdrop. You might learn something."

"You know what, Rach? I think I have enough on my plate right now." There was something new in his face: contempt. I'd only seen flashes of it before when I was young and they fought over stupid things like my mom throwing things away. He'd say, "Why would you throw out something labeled *taxes? Are you retarded? Are you a six-year-old?*" and she'd yell back, "You shouldn't be such a slob!" and then he'd yell some more and eventually she'd run into the bathroom and close the door.

But since then it had seemed like things had leveled out. He'd been placid, kind, even, and it frightened me to see the coldness in his eyes.

"I just don't see why your abs are so important," I said.

"I've told you before," he said. "It's a horrible market. I'm twice the age of my competition and I have to do something that gives me an edge. You should be happy for me. Feel how much harder my gut has gotten." He took my wrist in his hand and lowered it to his belly.

"I don't want to feel your gut," I said, jerking it away.

"Come on," he said. "Hit me."

"I don't want to touch your stomach!"

"Suit yourself," he said. "But don't come begging to touch it three months from now, when I can bounce a dime off my six-pack."

He grimaced and started his next set. I stepped over him like he was a dead body with chalk around it.

W H E N I got home from the meeting the phone was ringing. "So how was the passage?" Powell murmured.

"Dark and depressing," I said, slithering out of my mother's panties. I tried to chuck the underwear into the wastebasket by my desk but they missed. "How are you?"

"Exhausted," he said. "I just put Nora down. She was wired. Her class went on a field trip to the Tenement Museum. Since when did poverty become educational?"

"Where does she go to school?"

"Montessori."

"Am I going to meet her someday?"

"I dunno. I prefer to keep my private life separate. I'm very protective over what she sees."

"What's so scary about me? I'm good with kids. I used to babysit a lot."

"Exactly. You were the naughty babysitter. I don't need her under your influence."

"Do you like me?" I asked suddenly.

"Jesus," he said. "Now why would you go and ask a question like that?"

"I just meant, the way you insult me. I said I wanted to meet your daughter. I'm aware that day might not come. But why wouldn't you just say yes? Don't you have any social graces?"

"I want you to listen to me, Rachel," he said softly, "and I want you to listen very carefully. I understand you, maybe better than you understand yasself. I understand that instinct to ask these questions, these ugly and predictable questions—'Do you like me?' 'Can I meet the child?'" He put on a whiny high-pitched voice, the kind women cringe at when they learn that's how a man thinks they sound. "I am deeply aware of your animus problem so I know how hard it must be for you to wait to see me. I know how instinctive it is for you to keep saying and doing the *wrong thing*. But if you keep down this road, and I say this not as a threat but as a neutral statement of fact, we will have no further interaction."

I saw the whole thrilling future of Powell and me burning to my oak floor. There was an ugly intruder into whatever was beginning between us and I didn't know if it was my anxiety or his callousness. Whatever it was I wanted it out and so I did something I had never done before: I kowtowed.

"I understand," I said. I hated how high my voice sounded in my throat.

"Good," he said. "Can you come over Tuesday at four?"

"Yes."

"I'd like you to wear your hair up off ya neck."

"Why?"

"So I can see the veins." I was dating Dracula. At least he liked my veins, though. Most guys got weirded out when they saw them. I have a perfect W across my chest that stretches from my left shoulder all the way to my right. "I'd also like you to wear shoes with a little more heel than the last time. Shoes that raise the back of your foot and reveal the shape of your calf."

"Those boots were my highest pair!"

"So ya cancelling?"

"I'll see what I can do," I said, and hung up.

W H E N I got in bed I put the covers up to my chin but couldn't sleep. I kept thinking about my first date with David. He had taken me to an expensive Asian fusion restaurant on Mott Street but the service was really slow and the waitress was incredibly tall and hot, with this weird hard-to-place accent, and we joked about the inverse relationship between server attractiveness and quality of service. We called it the hot ratio and said *Zagat* should include it as its own category, and even though the whole thing was stupid, at the time I thought it was really funny. In the middle of dinner he put his hand under the table and held mine and I spent the rest of the meal struggling with my chopsticks because I didn't want to let his hand go.

I wasn't sure why I'd given up on him so fast. He was a good person and he was funny and he cared about me. If David had been a dad when we met he would have introduced me to his kid right away.

Maybe I should have given him a chance, and gotten married to him so we could have worked at the same congregation, him as a cantor and me as a rabbi. We had fantasized about that a little when we lay awake at night after sex, the way some people fantasize about building a home or moving to Paris. We both wanted to live someplace rural and liberal, so we always imagined Burlington or Montpelier, both of which had big Jewish populations. We'd live in a farmhouse with a cast-iron stove, drive pickup trucks to the synagogue, and raise kids that could chant Torah and milk cows.

In those moments, lying on my bed with David, cuddled up under the comforter, I never felt aimless or confused about anything. I didn't mind the fact that I spent half my day learning modern Hebrew because the program was so pro-Israel. I didn't care that I hated most of my classmates, or that sometimes I got really bored during services, or that some of the professors were drones.

I felt like I was on my way to doing what I wanted and spending my life with someone I loved.

Now I was a professional Rheingold girl and Stu Zaritsky was right at this very moment probably gabbing to all my former classmates that he'd run into me in a drugstore buying condoms. I wanted to feel like I'd done the right thing by telling him I had fucking to do but instead I just felt ashamed.

Deep down despite what I said to my parents, to my customers, to Powell, I felt pathetic. Maybe my dad was right and I really was losing all common sense. I was something I had never imagined I'd become in a million years: a screwup. Screwups were children of my parents' friends, the ones who were spoken about in hushed tones. They were the ones who got into drugs and tattoos, smoked cigarettes, the ones who had learning disabilities and trouble with authority. They weren't smart Jewish girls from Cobble Hill.

I felt stranded, and stagnant. It wasn't the lack of direction I minded so much as how hard it was for me to romanticize it. That was something that was very hard to learn. I'd been bad at being good but so far I wasn't very good at being bad. Maybe I just needed a little more time.

T H E best—and worst—thing about working in a bar is that you are constantly reminded you're not the only one in the world who is lonely. Around eight o'clock on my next shift a regular named Matt came in, went right to the jukebox, typed in some numbers listlessly, and came back. "What'd you put on?" I asked cheerily, hoping his dismay might make him drink more.

"Badly Drawn Boy," he said. "Can I get a Corona?"

We'd chatted a little before. He played in a band called The Changing Subject and usually came in with his girlfriend Sidecar, who worked as a waitress at Patois. This was the first time he'd come in alone.

As soon as I put his drink in front of him his song came on and he let out a long, laborious sigh. I looked straight ahead. The potentially dangerous consequence of striking up conversations with customers is that if you're not careful you inadvertently wind up stroking them the rest of the night.

"A few days ago I was shopping at the ABC Carpet in DUMBO with Jenny," he said.

"Uh-huh," I said, standing up straight so he wouldn't think I was too comfortable.

"And I saw her see someone across the store. It was this good-looking guy—built, tall, whatever. Jenny looks like she's seen a ghost and right away she's like, 'Let's get out of here.' I'm like, 'Why?' and she's like, 'I don't want to go into it. It's just some guy I went to high school with and I don't want to see him so let's go.'"

I washed a glass unnecessarily so I wouldn't seem too engaged. "So as we left," he said, "I was trying to get a good look at the dude from across the store and I could see he had this shaggy brown hair. The next day I'm at yoga and this shaggy-haired guy takes the spot next to me and I realize it's the same guy. I wasn't sure at first but he kept staring at me the whole class, and at the end as I'm on my way out he comes up to me and says, 'You look really familiar.' I said, 'Sorry. I don't think I know you.' He says, 'Wait a second, you know Jenny Ross, right?' I said, 'Yeah, I do. I'm going out with her. How do *you* know her?' He says, 'I used to date her. We broke up about six months ago.'"

"So? She probably didn't want you to know this guy was in her life."

"You don't understand," he said. "Jenny and I have been going out for *two years!*"

"Oh my God," I said.

"Yeah," he sighed. "So I started asking him all these questions and it turned out she started sleeping with him like a year into our relationship. She had both of us thinking we were the only one." It was beginning to seem like if I wanted to maintain even a smidgen of romantic idealism, I was in the wrong profession. "You know what the worst part is?" he said, pulling at his beer. "After I told her the whole story and had totally given it to her for lying to me, she said, 'It looks like you need space. Maybe we should take some time apart.' *She* cheated on me and then *she* dumped *me!*"

He started to sob right there in the bar. If I hadn't been so shocked I would have marveled at the beauty of a cute guy crying. I put my hand on his back and handed him a bev nap. He sniffled noisily into it. "Fuck, this is embarrassing," he said.

"It's OK," I said. "My dad cries a lot, actually." He wiped his nose and smiled faintly, like a kid who's momentarily forgotten both knees are gushing blood.

"Look," I said, "sounds like she wasn't cut out for you. Sounds like she was psychotic."

"I don't know if I'd go that far," he said, frowning. Insulting a guy's ex-girlfriend was like insulting his mother—it's one thing for him to do it, it's another thing for anyone else to.

"I know it's hard right now," I said, "but time will make it better. The only part that sucks is that you can't rush it. Just try to be active. Watch bad TV. Get out and do things."

"Like what?"

"We have three-dollar drafts every Tuesday."

"Thanks," he said dryly. He took a swig and set it down, fingering the label. "I guess part of the reason I'm so mad is that I was so blindsided. I wish I'd had some inkling. But even when she was two-timing me there weren't any signs."

"Come on—you didn't find any gifts? She never came home smelling funny?"

"No. The only thing that ever made me wonder was, right around the time she started seeing Shaggy, she got really into working out."

The bar started to feel a little stuffy and it wasn't because it was crowded. "What do you mean?"

"She was going to the gym all the time and working on her obliques. She'd never been into any of that stuff—she was always curvy but I liked her that way. And suddenly she started losing all this weight. She dropped like ten pounds in a month, and then she got a six-pack."

"Jesus," I said.

"I was such an idiot," he said. "I told myself it was a good thing that she was starting to care about her health. She even quit smoking. I thought it meant she was growing, not cheating on me."

His Corona was finished and he asked for another. I bent into the cooler, glad to get away so I could slow my thumping heart. I had to think logically. None of this could apply to my father. He'd told me why he was doing his sit-ups: for the job market. And despite the fact that he had never taken any interest in exercise beyond bicycling and squash, I couldn't jump to any conclusions.

But what other logical explanation was there for his newfound interest in his abdominals? Maybe he was getting something on the side. But with who? A person could only cheat if they could find someone to cheat *with* and there was no woman in all of New York City besides my mom who could possibly find my dad attractive. The woman would have to be a hag and a half. She'd have to be old, and desperate, and very very lonely.

Maybe it was Shelly Katz. She never talked to me as much as the other women did and when I really thought back on it, she'd been distant the whole meeting. He'd bumped into her in some local bar and gone out to join her for a smoke when he suddenly realized just how firm her tits were. If she was tipsy enough, and lonely enough, and my dad was turning into the most active bar crawler in Cobble Hill, then it wasn't totally inconceivable. Maybe this was why he'd stayed downstairs during the meeting—so he wouldn't act suspicious in front of my mom.

But no matter how hard I tried I couldn't make the image of a scoundrel mesh with the image of my father. As long as I'd known him the only things he'd gotten really orgasmic about were *New Yorker* cartoons and spackle. He had forty pairs of nonprescription drugstore reading glasses. He wore extra-wide shoes.

And men who cheated had to at least have a modicum of confidence. When I ran into him at the movies he'd seemed more down in the doldrums than he ever had before. I had to keep my head on straight and think about just who I was dealing with here. If I identified with every story my alcoholic customers told me I'd go insane. I had to compartmentalize, just like Bill Clinton.

I slipped my badly dumped boy a new bottle. "I shouldn't even be drinking anyway," he sighed. "It's really bad for my kidneys."

"You can make an exception," I said. "Look, just think of her rejection as a favor."

"How's it a favor?"

"She was letting you know she was wrong for you. Why would you want to be with someone who never loved you?"

"You think she never loved me?" he asked, panicked. I was trying to make him feel better but instead I was making him feel worse.

"Not if she could cheat!"

"I was harboring hope that she might come around."

"What are you—outta your mind?"

He stared at me for a moment, incredulous, like he'd suddenly seen the light. I was about to pat myself on the back for being such a good motivational speaker when his look of shock collapsed into one of total pain. "How long have you been a bartender?" he said.

"Two months," I said.

"That explains it." He plopped down a buck and left.

"Come back!" I shouted. "The next one's on me!" But he was already gone. I fucked the washer with a glass and set it upside down on the rack.

O N my way over to the deli for coffee on Tuesday, as I was crossing Court Street, I almost got run over. *"Hey!"* I shouted, leaping back onto the sidewalk.

"Sorry!" the driver shouted, as the car squealed to a halt and then pulled over. It was white and small and on the side it said US AUTO SCHOOL—WE HELP YOU PASS in bright blue letters. As I leaned down and looked through the passenger side I saw my dad sitting next to a bearded black man. "Hey, Rach!" my dad cried, waving.

This made no sense. He had resisted even getting a learner's permit for twenty-five years. My mom, who hated the burden of driving him to the country all the time, would nag and nag but he always said, "At a certain point it's just too late to learn something new."

Now, suddenly, he was snapping into action. He was showing enough drive to learn how to drive. I didn't want to believe it but maybe he really was kicking it to Shelly Katz. When you had an affair you had to be able to go for secret weekend getaways, so maybe he'd decided he had to step up.

I went to the driver's-side window unsteadily. "Rachel," my dad said, "this is my instructor, Mr. Goddard."

"Pleasure to meet you," he said, with a hint of a southern drawl, sticking his hand out the window.

I shook it fake-warmly, wondering whether my dad had told him things he hadn't told me. I figured driver's-ed guys got to hear everybody's stories.

"Since when have you been learning to drive?" I asked.

"This is my second lesson. I got my learner's permit last week." He opened his wallet and passed me a card with a photo of him on it smiling as happily as if it was the first day of first grade. I broke out in a cold sweat.

"Why are you doing this?"

"I don't know. I just decided there was no day like today."

"Dad," I said. "Are you quoting *Rent?*"

"I have all this time on my hands now with my unemployment, so I went over to the DMV, stood on line, and passed the written test on my first try! I missed the one about what to do when your front wheels skid in the rain."

"Ease into the skid," I said.

"How'd you know?" he said, like it was some sort of million-dollar game show question.

"I took the same test," I said. "When I was *fifteen.*"

"So? Don't I look good? I'm driving!" he said, jutting his elbow out through the door. "I feel like Harrison Ford in *American Graffiti.*"

"Try Charles Martin Smith."

"Who?"

"Never mind."

He looked at Mr. Goddard and put his palms up. "Is your daughter like this to you?"

"Daughters are difficult," said Mr. Goddard.

"You see? You see?" my dad said. "This is a wise man here. We give our children all the love in the world and what do they give us in return?"

"Bubkes," said Mr. Goddard.

"You know Yiddish?" I said.

"Sure I do. I've taught driver's education for twenty-one years."

"How can you even afford these lessons, Dad? Given your circumstances?"

"Mr. Goddard says half of his students are unemployed. It's the only thing that makes people finally decide to do it. Mom is in full support of this and I thought you'd be too."

"I think you're making a big mistake. You're not only a liability to yourself but to innocent people. Some people just aren't meant to get behind a wheel. I thought you were afraid you were going to kill someone."

"Mr. Goddard is teaching me to let the mind go."

"You're going to hurt someone. Tell me the truth, Mr. Goddard. Is he the worst student you ever had?"

"There was one worse," Mr. Goddard said.

"You see? You see?" my dad cried.

"She was blind in one eye."

I turned and made a wide circle in front of the car so he wouldn't run me over. When I got across the street I heard someone shout, *"Watch it!"* and I turned around to see the car about six inches from a woman with a stroller. My dad was waving his hands sheepishly through the rearview as Mr. Goddard sank into his seat.

I D R A N K two cups of coffee that morning and spent the afternoon feeling like I was going to bounce off the walls of the apartment. He had to be getting something on the side. Nothing else could make him care so much about his own well-being. People didn't just change on their own, for no reason. Something was going on; I just had to find out what. But what could I do? Call Shelly Katz and ask her point-blank? I wanted to bring it up with my mom but how do you casually bring up your suspicions of your own father's philandering? There's just no way to do it. Powell would have a solution. I just had to wait till I saw him.

At three forty-five on the dot I left for the date so he wouldn't complain that I was late. He had said to wear high heels and at the last minute I'd found these white vinyl stripper-style shoes with a three-inch platform that I'd bought online a few years before for a Halloween party. For attire I selected a polyester blue-and-white polka-dotted dress that pressed tightly against my boobs.

It took me five minutes just to get down the stairs of my building because I was so worried I was going to fall in the heels and break my neck. As I passed the Korean grocery at Kane and Court I saw a bouquet of mixed flowers in a vase out front. I knew that my job was to free myself from my animus, not burrow in it, but I felt an instinct to buy them for Powell. I wanted to bring him something beautiful, something the woman in him would appreciate.

On my way down Strong Place I passed a strange-looking man, a kind of man who didn't look like he lived in the neighborhood. He had gaunt cheeks and messy grayish-brown hair that hung down over his face, a denim jacket, and a cigarette hanging out of his mouth. He looked like the kind of guy who, if he wasn't a murderer, should have made a lot of money playing murderers in movies. As we passed he gave me a once-over, cool and even. When I was on the other side I turned around and looked at him over the shoulder and he was still looking at me.

Powell opened the door in a long turquoise blue robe. His hair was messy and he had a crazed though not drunk look in his eye. I had the flowers hidden behind my back.

"I saw a weird guy on your street," I said.

"That was Abel Ferrara," Powell said. "He directed *The Bad Lieutenant.*"

"What was he doing here? You working on something with him?"

"No, he left his heroin."

His eyes were even and I couldn't tell if he was kidding. "Do *you* do heroin?" I said.

"No! It fell outta his pocket the last time he was here! I been bugging him for weeks to pick it up."

He opened the door. "For you," I said, proffering the bouquet. He backed off like he was a vampire and it was garlic. "What's the matter?"

"You brought me flowers."

"It doesn't mean anything," I said softly. "I just thought they'd look nice." He yanked them out of my hand and strode into the kitchen. I followed unsteadily in the shoes.

He ripped off the paper and the cellophane and lay the flowers out on his cutting board like they were a nice loaf of bread, pulled a large knife from the knife rack, and began chopping off the heads. "Hey!" I said. He moved the heads to the side with the knife and then chopped what remained into one-inch pieces, shoved everything into a pile, and began cutting the other way. "What are you doing?" I said.

He kept chopping and chopping, the sweat glistening on his forehead, like some sort of psychopathic Food Network chef, until the beautiful bouquet was nothing but a big pile of color. He opened his Cuisinart, dropped the entire pile in, slid the top closed, and hit the On switch. I watched with horror as they turned into a vomit-green mush. It was thick so he added some water until it was liquid, and then he poured it into a glass, drank it down, and wiped his mouth, panting.

"You just drank my bouquet," I said.

"That's right!" he screamed. "I'm a *criminal!* You bring me any a that crap and I'll *eat it up! I'll eatchoo up!*"

His eyes were blazing and insane. I cowered against the wall. "Now take off ya jacket and lay it down on the floor," he said. His gaze was steady but not angry. It was as though telling me what to do calmed *him* down.

I did what he said. "Ya so much talla in those shoes," he said. He walked toward me and ran his hand down the side of my smooth dress and then he cupped my chin in his hand very sweetly. He stared at my tits, which were pressing up against the material and then he lifted one out and bent his head down to suck it, kneading my ass with the other hand. It was too much too fast. Instead of relaxing I kept wondering how the bouquet would affect his bowels. "I wish my ass was fatter," I said.

"It'll do."

"But you're like an ass purist—"

"Don't ruin this. The flowers were bad enough." He moved his finger into me as my lips parted and my head went back. I started to get hot and then he lifted me up in his arms and carried me to the couch. I'd had no idea he was so strong.

He tossed me onto the couch casually, and threw the big pillows on the floor. He unzipped my dress, pulled it off and lay it on a chair. Then he squeezed next to me, on my right, waving his hand so I could see why he wanted to be on that side. I started to take off my shoes so they wouldn't get the couch dirty and he said, "Leave them on. Why do you think I wanted you to wear them?" and moved my leg so it was splayed over the side. As he worked me with his hand he put his face very close and smoothed the hair on my head. From time to time he would put his mouth on my nipple and suck, moaning softly while he did it.

When I came it was long and intense, the kind that hurts your ovaries. This time I cried out and as soon as I did he pulled me close like he had female O envy. "Oh my God," I said, putting my arm over my forehead. "You're good at that."

"I know."

I leaned in to kiss him but he was getting up. He took off my bra, pushed my legs up so I was in pelvic exam position and kneeled on the couch, facing me. He unbuttoned his pants, took it out, and began stroking like it was some sort of magical wand. From time to time he said "Mmmm!" and "Ahhhh!" like he was listening to a very serious lecture that I couldn't hear, and agreeing with various important points. After about fifteen minutes he cried out "Uhhhhh! Uhhhhhhh! Unnnnnhhhhhh!" and shot it onto my chest.

I looked down at the puddle of white that had formed above my breasts and as he massaged it into my nipples I said, "Do you think sometime we could go to Manhattan?"

He scowled like I had suggested something completely perverse. "Why would you want to do that?"

"I thought you might have some events to go to from time to time."

"What kind of events?"

"Benefits. Like with Abel Ferrara."

"You think I got the kind a money to be going to benefits? My friends should throw a benefit for *me!*"

"I just thought you might want to show up somewhere with me on your arm."

He raised his eyebrows and nodded cynically. "Is that why you're interested in me? You want to rub elbows with Abel and Harvey?"

"You know Harvey Keitel?"

"I guess that's your answer."

"No! It's not that I want to meet famous people! I—I just want to meet your friends. I don't know why we always have to hide. It makes me feel like you're ashamed of me."

"*Do I look like the kind a person that cares what anyone else thinks?*"

"No," I said. "But why can't we hang out in any other borough?"

"I am not hiding you," he said. "I am a private person. I don't feel the need to showcase what I do like I'm filing some kind a romantic status report. If you don't like my rules I respect it and you are free to go find some otha cat. But if you want to be with me, I'm doing you the favor of telling you how it's gotta be." I was between a rock and a hard place. I could have him like this or not at all. I figured the former was better than the latter because he made me laugh and gave me a lot to think about but I had a strange dread in my stomach like it didn't sit completely right.

He rose to his feet and headed for the bathroom. I watched his wide back, afraid he was going to tell me to get out right now, and I'd have to walk home alone in slutgear, toddling in my strappy stripper shoes in the broad daylight, the smell of his spooge on my skin. He came back with a warm wet washcloth, and as he scrubbed off his come he said, "You wanna come get something to eat?"

"Really?" I squealed.

"Hold the waterworks," he said. "We're not crossing the river."

W E ate at a Mediterranean place called Sam's that had opened up in a greasy spoon on Henry. They didn't have a liquor license so on the way over we bought a bottle of Chilean Merlot (he said Chilean was different from other Merlots) and as we ate he was tender and not elusive. He told me he was struggling a lot with *Who Killed My*

Wife? and I realized that not all his writing came as easily as I'd thought. When we finished he said he'd walk me home, which I thought boded well for our future, and as we headed up Clinton he put his arm around my waist.

As we passed Cobble Hill Park he said, "You wanna sit for a while?"

"OK," I said.

The sky was glowing and blue and the trees were dark against it. In the day the park was like the town square but it quieted down early in the evenings, it was mostly couples and dog walkers. We sat on a bench under a tree, overlooking this huge grassy oval in the center, decorated with hedges and flower clusters, that kids played hide-and-seek on during the day. He put his arm around me and said, "You wanna sit on my lap?"

I hopped on perpendicularly and draped my arm around his neck. He rubbed my lips with his thumb and I sucked it. "Were you a thumb-sucker when you were a child?" he said.

"How did you know?"

"It's written all over you. You're very oral."

"What were you?" I said. "A bedwetter?"

"An insomniac," he said. "Even as a kid I held the weight of the world on my shoulders."

"If I'd been your girlfriend when you were young," I said, "you would have slept like a baby every night."

"Because your presence is so calming to the male species?"

"Nope," I said. "Because I'd deplete you of so much semen you'd never have any energy." I couldn't believe I was talking like this but with Powell it all came so naturally, like he'd turned some switch in me that no one else even knew was there.

He smooched me softly and when we broke for air we both stared up at the sky. "Isn't that your friend over there?" I heard him say. I looked across the way at the bench on the other side of the park, and saw Liz sitting in another guy's lap, kissing him intently and blocking his face.

"Yeah, it is," I said.

She was perpendicular too, facing the same way I was. I felt that if I lifted a foot hers would magically rise too. She broke off and stared not at the guy, but off toward the side, as though contemplating some grand truth. His face was still blocked but I could tell by his hands that he was white.

"Is that her boyfriend?" said Powell.

"Liz doesn't have boyfriends."

The guy stroked the back of her hair and leaned forward into the moonlight to kiss her again. As I saw his face a wave of nausea rose from my belly to my tongue and I clamped my hand hard over my mouth.

"What's the matter?" Powell asked.

"It's my dad," I said. "Without his beard."

ABANDONMENT'S
A TWO-LANE HIGHWAY

Do you wanna go over and say hello?" said Powell.

"Are you kidding?" I hissed. "We gotta get outta here before they see us."

"Shouldn't that be what *they're* thinking?"

I grabbed his hand and steered him out of the park briskly, like we were exiting a play before the curtain call to get our car out of the lot. He peeked over his shoulder to get another look but I yanked him down behind the oval mound of grass, and we squat-walked till we were out of their view.

As soon as we got on the street I started sobbing. Hard and loud and mucusy. We walked up Clinton and he leaned me against the Tripoli, the Lebanese restaurant on the corner, as I snotted into his shirt.

"Lemme buy you a soda pop," he said. We headed west on Atlantic toward the water and as I watched the cars zoom down the expressway I felt relieved by the motion, like if the world could go on oblivious to my problem maybe it wasn't so big.

When we got to the Long Island Restaurant at the corner of Henry, I pulled him in. The place was frozen in its original décor, which was late forties. All the bars on the block used to be sailor bars and this one had four booths, one table, a bar, and no menus. The owner, a hostile Irish woman in her sixties, made different specials every night like lasagna and cheeseburgers, depending on her mood. The official closing time was nine but she locked the doors at eight-thirty and closed the kitchen whenever she felt like it. It was the only restaurant in the neighborhood where the customer came second.

"How do you know about all these places?" he said, looking at the black-and-white wedding picture behind the bar. "You're too young to be nostalgic."

"Not anymore," I sniffled. "From this moment on I'll be old."

He led me to a booth in the back. The owner was standing behind the bar, watching a movie on the TV above the door, along with a teenaged girl, who was overweight and unhappy. I craned my neck to see what it was and was disturbed to spot Sally Field in a burka. *Not Without My Daughter.* She was getting lost in a big group of Arabs and calling out her kid's name. Her husband had a slick mysterious look on his face so you knew he had something to do with it. She was such an idiot. If Alfred Molina were my husband I would definitely know he was evil.

After they cut to a commercial the owner came over. "How ya doing?" she asked.

"OK," I said quietly.

"What can I getcha?"

"A root beer float," I said.

"And a coffee," said Powell.

She nodded, grinned at him, and then me, and said, "This your father?"

I collapsed into a fit of sobs so loud and pathetic even the truckers on the expressway could hear it. "Could we get a couple extra napkins?" Powell asked.

"I'm going to kill the bitch," I said, blowing my nose into the napkin on the table. I knew I sounded like Michael Douglas in *Fatal Attraction* but dire circumstances turn a girl misogynist.

"What are you going to use as the murder weapon?" he asked.

"What is this, *Clue?*"

"I'm just trying to inject some levity into an otherwise gravitas-filled situation."

"I had a feeling he might be cheating," I said, "but I never expected it to be with someone so attractive. I thought if anyone it would be one of my mother's friends!"

"Why would a man cheat with an unattractive woman?"

"If he didn't think he deserved any better. I just can't understand what Liz could possibly see in him. My dad's fifty-five, fat, and balding. Any girl who goes for a guy like that is doing charity."

"I see," he said archly. "You consider me a trip to the Salvation Army. I understand completely."

"Of course not! You're different! You're an alpha male! My dad's like . . . a *zeta* male. He doesn't have enough cojones to initiate."

"Maybe your father's got a trickster active in him that you don't even know about."

The woman brought our drinks and laid my straw down on the table. I banged it up and down on the table a few times to break the paper but it wouldn't give. "Gimme," said Powell, like I was his kid. I took a deep sip but the straw was wedged against the ice cream and all I got was air.

"Jewish men don't cheat," I said, stirring my root beer. "It's not in their blood."

"What about Eddie Fisher?"

"Celebrities are different. Jewish men cheat by reading, not by fucking. They're a people of the book. The closest my dad's ever gotten to something like infidelity was a few years ago when he got really into that *V.I. Warshawski* series."

"At the risk of stating the obvious," Powell said, "maybe all we saw is all that's happened. Maybe it's not going to go any further."

I told him about the silent sounds from Liz's apartment the other night. "With every other guy she's made noise," I said. "Why on that night would it be so quiet?" It was like the fifth Passover question.

I sighed and shook my head. "I just don't know why he would do something like this at a time when he needs my mom the most."

"What do you mean?"

I told him how he was out of a job and right away Powell said, "It makes perfect sense now! A man's like an amphibian. He needs both air and water to live. His air and water are work and sex and your pop's not getting either."

"What makes you so sure?"

"Your mother's reading *The Silent Passage.*"

"So?"

"She's drying up!"

"Women report the best sex of their lives between forty-five and fifty-five!"

"That's a load of crap. She's not giving him anything to be home for. Your pop can't solve both problems at once, so he's doing what he can to solve one."

"So you think he'll end the affair if he gets a job?"

"Not necessarily, but let's hope the market takes an upturn soon."

I spooned out some ice cream and swallowed it down. "Do you think I should tell my mom?"

He turned to me and took my face in both of his hands. "Absolutely not. I understand the instinct to tell. You're a truth seeker, like me. *We like the truth.* But just because you seek it for yasself doesn't mean you gotta share it. It's like tossing a stone into a pond. Eventually the stone'll sink but you never know how far the ripples will go."

"That's very poetic," I said, rolling my eyes.

"Good," he said, "'cause I think I'm gonna use it in this diner scene for *Who Killed My Wife?*" I gritted my teeth. Here I was having the biggest familial crisis of my life and he was testing out his latest draft. It was so not the time.

"If ya fatha's gonna do this, he's gonna do it," he said. "Like it says in the Bible, 'And this too shall pass.'"

"The Torah says, 'An eye for an eye, a tooth for a tooth.'"

"That's why you got so many problems in the Middle East," he said. He took a napkin and wiped some ice cream off my mouth. "Even if it doesn't," he said, "and ya parents split up, what do you care?"

"They're my parents! I don't want them divorcing!"

"You're acting the way a child would and you're an adult. The fact that you're so invested is proof that you're shackled to the parental chains."

"Just because I want them to stay together doesn't mean I'm shackled."

"It does. I've never met anyone so stagnant."

He was like a reverse motivational speaker. "I just don't understand how he could *do this to her.* I mean I knew they were struggling; I just didn't know how much."

"Abandonment's a two-lane highway. That's Aphorism Number Three of Powell's Aphorisms. I once dated a girl who had psoriasis. She had scales all over her body but she wore skintight sleeveless dresses and made no attempt to hide her lesions. I found this brave and exciting instead of repulsive. To soothe her itching, she liked to take oatmeal baths and together every night we would bathe together. Afterwards our lovemaking would be scored by the sound of my stomach growling as I recalled being a child in Jackson Heights and my castrating mother forcing me to eat Irish oatmeal every morn—"

"Get to the point!"

"After I'd been dating this girl a couple months her skin began to heal for the first time in twenty years. She told me it was because I loved her for who she was. I became so entranced with this change in her that I began to watch her less closely. When she came home late from work and said the trains had been delayed I believed her. One day I woke up and on the pillow there was a box of oatmeal with a note stuck to it that said, 'An ugly girl can be happy in the company of just one man, but a beautiful girl needs diversification.' I realized then that I had orchestrated her abandonment. I had made her beautiful because I hated myself too much to believe I deserved her. So you see, abandonment's a two-lane highway." He smiled and raised his head as though expecting me to applaud.

"I don't think my mom brought this on," I said.

"She had to! You said your mother is involved in many causes. Maybe that was her way of indicating that it was time for him to sniff other fish." I didn't agree but one thing I was learning with Powell was that it was futile to argue on the subject of men and women.

"Did you ever cheat on your wife?"

"That's a conversation we should have another time."

I couldn't count on anybody. "Oh my God! How many women did you cheat with?" He looked straight ahead and didn't say anything. "Was it less than a dozen?"

"Baker's?"

"I thought you said you had anima. I thought you were like a woman. Women don't cheat."

"Number one, *wrong!* Number two, if you must know, I was not the first member of my marriage to violate the matrimony." Every man in the world was a dog, even the one I was with. "But even if I hadn't strayed the marriage was a mistake to begin with. When Nora was two my wife and I would wake up every morning and begin fighting, like we had scheduled it. We would fight in the bed, then as we dressed, then in the bathroom as we bathed, and in the kitchen as we ate. Each morning ended the same way: she would throw appliances at me and I would cower in the corner. Eventually she would leave for work and I would go to my desk and write movies that critics dubbed woman-hating but which to me were just reflections of my reality."

"What did she do?"

"She was a nurse." I laughed. "It's not a coincidence. She worked in the caregiving industry because she had a craving for blood but was so ashamed of this she had to devote her life to saving people. She wanted me dead and I realized it was only a matter of time before she killed me. One morning I came home to find her whacking a mouse with a broom and it hit me that I had married a murderess. That was when I came up with Aphorism Number Four of Powell's Aphorisms: 'Never marry death.'"

"I'm not death," I said. "I'm life."

"The story wasn't about you," he said. "Why are you always trying to paint yasself into the picture?"

If there was any part of me that believed Powell might be a comfort in this strange time given his age and married past, that part died a quick and painless death. "It's been a rough day," I said.

"You gotta stop these histrionics," he said. "Jung would tell you to look at the symbols in the story. Who is your mother and how does this event make you feel about your relationship to her? Who is Liz—a part of you that you're afraid of? Who is your father? Is he me?"

"No!" I cried. "There's nothing to read into here! There aren't any symbols! My family's fucked." I started to snot up again. "Oh God," I said. "What if he comes over to her apartment again? Can I stay at your place tonight?"

"I know these are extenuating circumstances," he said, looking at his watch, "but Nora's mother's dropping her off at my place in half an hour. And I don't usually have ladies stay over when she's—"

"Please?" I said.

"I told you from the get-go," he said. "The mother figure in me is dead right now. You got two choices with me—the devil or the trickster—and the last time I checked neither one of those guys was running a boardinghouse."

"Have fun with your kid," I said, and raced out.

A s I walked down Atlantic Avenue I kept replaying the park scene in my head, wishing it had all been a dream. It was one thing for me to take the downward path, but why did *he* have to? I wanted to flip backwards in my own personal Choose Your Own Adventure to the moment of me hearing Liz fucking the Laundromat guy that very first time. Instead of knocking on her door I would know instinctively that she was the devil in the form of a Chappaqua JAP and I wouldn't have gone upstairs to complain. Then she never would have met him and it never would have happened.

But since I knew I couldn't rewind, instead I started thinking about how Liz could die. I pictured her crossing Atlantic Avenue and getting flattened by an eighteen-wheeler. I knew if she croaked my dad would only be a little sad, not a lot. Once he identified her black and bruised body he'd see her death as a necessary God intervention, not *When Bad Things Happen to Good People,* but *When Bad Things Happen to Bad People.* As he nodded to the coroner and Liz got shoved back in the body drawer he'd realize how much he really loved my mom and go back to her with a conviction and purpose he hadn't felt in twenty years.

How had all this started? Was all his common sense inside his shaved-off beard? As much as I wanted to believe this had been Liz's idea, was it possible he'd initiated this—my nebbishy, bad-posture, total failure of a father? It wasn't the moral corruption I had trouble comprehending; it was the drive. He was passive when it came to everything, content to be mediocre as long as I wasn't. It was like that joke about why there are so few Jewish drug addicts: they just can't trust feeling that good.

It had to have been Liz's doing. He'd come by my apartment to wrangle me into a bike ride and when he accidentally rang her buzzer she buzzed him up. After hearing his pounding on the floor below she came down one landing to inspect. "Mr. Block," she said. "I thought you were Special Delivery. Rachel's not here."

"Oh," he replied dorkily, checking out her measurements. "Well, I guess I'd better get going."

Taking in his Homer Simpsonesque gut, yet sensing an opportunity to ruin my life completely, she cooed, "Why don't you come in for a bit, and I'll fix you a cup of Darjeeling."

Confused, lost, and stunned by his recent job loss, he went up, and while he was sitting on her couch waiting for the water to boil, she noticed him eyeing *A Clock Strikes Bizarre on Butt Row* sitting on top of the TV. "Have you ever heard of Joey Silvera?" she trilled, and when he shook his head no she gave him bedroom eyes and popped it in. As he watched, open-mouthed, she got down on her knees, waddled across the Flokati, and unzipped him with the cool authority of that Oval Office Jew.

This must have been why she moved from Manhattan to Brooklyn, because she knew how settled and placid we all were. She messed with me because she knew I had a family.

I felt sick for my mom and sick for the lying. She was no rube but she was trusting. I snuck out of the house at five AM when I was sixteen to go make out with a guy in my French class, Johno Lederer, who lived in the Village and left the door open for me. It was easy. I left a note that said, "Had an early meeting." She never raised it with me again. Lying to my mom was like taking candy from a baby.

But the thing that got me going, that tore me apart about the affair, didn't really have anything to do with her. What riled me up and made me queasy inside, more than my anger at him and fear for her, was this: somewhere in the far reaches of my mind, in the places you don't like to think about or pretend exist, I had always imagined that if he ever picked another woman over my mom, it would be me.

The two of them always struck me as an odd couple, my father the hyperintelligent one who was always forgetting his keys, my mom the childlike innocent who knew how to put the food on the table. Sometimes she'd ask a silly question or misunderstand some crucial line in a story, and I'd feel like I was the ingénue and my mom was the one the hero's in love with at the beginning, but the one you know will never stay. It kind of messes up your head when you believe that you are the Hepburn to your own father's Tracy, but there were times it felt like he agreed.

If he was sleeping with Liz it had to mean he'd finally realized that somewhere in him he knew that he and I were meant to be together. But since he hated himself for wanting it he'd chosen my evil twin instead. My surrogate. It was worse than if he'd cheated with Shelly or Joan. The fact that it was Liz cut right to my quick, made me feel like I didn't have legs. He hadn't fallen out of love with my mother; he'd fallen out of love with me.

W H E N I got home I put the pillows over my head and tried to sleep but it was no use. Not long ago I'd had a stable family, a guy that loved me, and a career path. Now my dad was two-timing my mom with the ho of the hood, and I was dating an antimarriage activist while slinging drinks in the slowest-traffic bar on Smith Street.

I could pinpoint the exact birth of my father's insanity to me dropping out. Maybe if I'd stayed in rabbinical school this never would have happened. What if God was sending me some kind of message? What if the only way to get my dad to stop fucking Liz was to go back to RCRJ? It didn't seem fair. For the first time in my life I'd done something completely right and now everything was falling to pieces.

I needed someone to talk to, about all of it, but talking to Powell about infidelity was like going to Hitler for grief counseling. Before I was completely aware of what I was doing I got up and dialed the number that was still number one on my memory.

It rang twice and then a woman answered, with a slight foreign accent I couldn't place. "H-hi," I stammered. "Is David there?"

"Just a moment." I heard her hand muffle the phone and then he came on.

"It's Rachel," I said. He was silent and I added, "Please don't hang up."

"I wasn't going to," he said. "Are you OK? You don't sound so good."

"Yeah, I'm fine. Who was that?"

"That," he said proudly, "was my girlfriend Yael."

"She lives with you?"

"Yep."

"That's—amazing," I said, trying to sound generous and not in-flamed. "Where'd you meet her?"

"In Israel this summer. We were both counselors at this music camp for deaf children in Tzvat. I was going to move to Israel to be with her but she was thinking of moving to New York anyway so it all kind of worked out."

"Th-that's amazing," I said.

"Are you sure you're all right?" he said. "You sound funny."

And as quickly as I had felt the instinct to call him I realized that I couldn't tell him. It was humiliating enough that he had an altru-istic Israeli live-in; he didn't also need to know I'd just learned my father was a philanderer.

"I didn't think you'd answer the phone," I said.

"Why wouldn't I answer?"

"I thought you hated me."

"Well," he said, "I spent a long time being angry at you but I'm not anymore. It took me a while but when I looked back on things it seemed pretty obvious that you were wrong for me."

"Wrong for you? Don't you mean we were wrong for each other?"

"Sure. But what I learned was that you had so much anger toward me, when I hadn't done anything wrong. I kept tolerating it, telling myself it would change, but it never did. And I finally realized that I didn't want to be with someone who hated me."

"Is Yael in the room?" I said.

"She can't hear anything when she's got the loom on."

"She's a loomer?"

"Yeah." She was not only musical but good with her hands. It couldn't get much worse.

"Do you think I'm a bad person for what I did to you?"

"No I don't. I'm just glad you dumped me so that I could finally get a good look at what was going on. If you hadn't I think I would have kept lying to myself. And I never would have met Yael. So what's going on with you? There's all these rumors going around about why you left. One was that I broke your heart and you couldn't stand to see me, which I thought was pretty funny."

"This guy at Memorial died when I was sitting with him and his last words to me were, 'You are the worst rabbi I ever met.'"

"Are you serious?"

"Yeah," I said. "So I decided to believe him."

He was quiet for a while and then he said, "I'm sure you weren't the worst. Maybe he didn't even know what he was saying. Maybe he was going senile."

"He was thirty-nine. And totally lucid."

"You sure you're not putting too much stock in what a stranger had to say? What about what *you* wanted?"

"It wasn't right for me. I mean, I know I did the right thing by leaving."

"So what's the problem then?"

I wanted to tell him how awful everything was, how I'd seen my father in the park, but I was so ashamed. I'd never aired my family's dirty laundry in public but that was because up until now we didn't have any. It was too embarrassing to tell him what was happening. He wasn't my boyfriend anymore; he was barely even my friend. He had someone new now—a hot Israeli loomer. I had to leave him alone.

I felt my chest begin to tighten into a knot. "You know what?" I said. "I should go."

"Is something the matter, Rachel?" he said. "I'm here for you if you want to—"

"Bye, David," I said, and started sobbing as soon as I hit the button.

———◆———

W H E N I woke up it was eight-thirty in the morning and the buzzer was ringing. When I said "Who is it?" into the intercom I heard my mom say "Me-e." *Oh God.* Maybe she was onto my dad and was coming here with a loaded gun to kill Liz.

I ran downstairs and opened the door. "How you doing?" she said.

"Good," I said. "Don't you have school?"

"We have meetings this morning and I don't have to be in for an hour. Can I come upstairs?" I nodded reluctantly and watched her stomp up the stairs, holding the banister. "I love the new paint job," she said, running her hand along the wall. "The glossy really sets off the—"

"Mom. Can you examine the décor another time?"

"How's your friend?" she said when she got to my door, jerking her head up toward the ceiling.

"Who?"

"The one who lives upstairs. Liz." I examined her face for signs of connivance but she didn't exhibit it. I didn't think she was acting; she truly didn't seem to know. And though it chagrined me I understood it. It was enough of a leap of faith for me to accept that my father was capable of snagging thirtysomething ass; it had to be a bigger leap for her. She was the one who saw him naked.

"She's fine," I said.

"What's she up to these days?"

"This and that."

"Did she work things out with her boyfriend? It looked pretty—"

"Yeah," I said. "He was just over the other night." I shoved her in the door like I was Mrs. Van Daan yanking Anne Frank into the apartment.

"So what's up?" I said, as she took a seat at the kitchen table.

"Well, firstly I wanted to thank you for showing up the other night. It meant a lot to me. I know menopause might seem like a long way away but there's no medicine better than education."

"I'm with you on that one."

"After you left we all got to talking," she said. "Everyone was telling me what a great job I did leading and then we started talking

about how few intellectual opportunities there are in the neighborhood, and we got the idea to start a group." She reached into her
pocketbook and pulled out a cotton candy–pink flyer.

KOFFEE KLATSCH
Feeling a lack of intellectual stimulation in your life?
Think arguing is more fun than agreeing?
Come to a new weekly discussion group
at the home of Sue Block
191 Warren Street
Beginning Thursday, September 18 at 8
Bring a few ideas for topics!

Beneath it, printed neatly and nonchalantly, next to the word QUES-
TIONS? was our home phone number. I felt like I'd just seen my own
face on a wanted ad.

"So what do you think of the name?"

"It's certainly alliterative."

"Are you being sarcastic or not sarcastic? I can never tell with you."

"Why are you having it at the house?"

"Why not?" Leave it to a Jew to answer a question with another
question.

"Why can't you just have it in a coffee shop if it's Koffee Klatsch?
Why do you have to let strangers into our house?"

"A home environment's much more intimate. I want to create
meaningful relationships." She was the only one in the family who
wasn't drowning in meaningful relationships. "And since it was my
idea I volunteered the place. Nina and I are going to spend the afternoon postering."

"Crazy people could see these," I said. "Anyone could come! Like
Typhoid Mary."

"Who's Typhoid Mary?"

"That bag lady with the really red cheeks who always used to
crash Shabbat at synagogue for the free challah! What are you going
to do if she shows up? Did it ever occur to you that there might be
such a thing as too open?"

"That's the whole point of what we're doing! To facilitate conversation. We almost called it Open Lines but Nina thought it would sound like a heroin support group."

"This is a mistake," I said. "Someone could bring a gun. You live just blocks from the largest Al Qaeda cell in the country. Block is a Jewish name! They'll know from the sign that you're the enemy and come over to gun you down. At Passover we never open the door for Elijah because you never know who might wander in, but *this* is OK?"

She looked at me like I was not her own child but some evil kid that had been switched at birth. Then she shook her head morosely and said, "*What*ever."

She had started using this expression about a year before, and it irked me to no end. I didn't know if she used it with her friends too, or just with me, but lately she'd started saying it all the time. She would use it whenever we couldn't agree on something, or she felt I was shirking my familial responsibilities. There'd be a long pause and then she'd sigh it out, long and defeatist. It didn't seem right for a mother to have this much hostility toward her kid. It was like I had done something long ago that she was mad about, broken some cookie jar before I was conscious and was still paying for it now.

"Look," I said, through my teeth. "It's just—do you think it's a good idea to be doing this in the house when Dad's going through such a rough time?"

"What do you mean?"

"About the job hunt. I mean this could be a time to pay more attention to him, not less."

"What are you talking about?" she asked accusingly. It's not easy to tell your own mother what kind of wife to be.

"I just mean, maybe he needs a little support from you. Some TLC. Maybe you could buy him a present from time to time, so he knows you care. What about a book? Why don't you buy him the Koufax biography?"

"He shouldn't be reading biographies. He should be hitting the pavement. He shows up at his interviews late and then complains when he doesn't get the job!"

"Look," I said, "just try to be a little caring. I think he's really down in the doldrums."

"You don't know what you're talking about," she said. "He shaved his beard last week and since then he's been a new man."

"W-what do you mean?"

"He's even learning to drive! I don't like him out of work but if that's what it takes to get him to change his life around I gotta tell you, I'm all in favor. If you ask me, losing his job's the best thing that ever happened to him."

What could I say? It wasn't like I was going to tell her and as far as she was concerned he was doing great. Why did it take an extra-marital affair to catapult someone into positive life change? What did it say about the value of marriage?

As I walked her to the door she snapped her fingers and said, "I almost forgot. Mark your calendar for Rosh Hashanah dinner Friday night."

I couldn't believe the new year had crept up on me so fast. Without the RCRJ calendar to remind me, without any kind of regular relationship to a synagogue, the High Holidays had arrived. Usually I had them marked on my calendar in big block letters bigger than the ones I used for my birthday, but for the first time, they'd come without warning.

"OK," I said. "Do you want me to bring anything?"

"Maybe a bottle of red, whatever kind you want."

"Are you making brisket?"

"I was planning on it," she said. "With string beans from the farmer's market, and I was going to make *tsimmes.*"

"Do you have to?" I said. *Tsimmes* was one of those weird Jewish foods, a mix of carrots, cinnamon, and other halitosis-inducing dreck that I not only couldn't stand, but couldn't understand how anyone could.

"What's wrong with *tsimmes?*" she said. We had this discussion every year. It was a ritual more ingrained than the banging on the chest during the recitation of sins.

"It's the most disgusting of all Jewish foods," I said, "and that's saying a lot."

"You don't have to eat any. Anyway, I was thinking we'd eat around six-thirty since services are at eight."

"I don't know if I want to go to services," I said.

"What? Why not?"

"I don't think I'm in the mood this year."

She gave me a shocked look, as though she'd misheard. "But you love Rosh Hashanah."

It was true. I'd been a bigger nerd about the High Holidays than any other kid in my class. Since my bat mitzvah I'd gone Rosh Hashanah eve, Rosh Hashanah morning, and second day, which most Reform Jews don't even do. I'd get there early to get a front seat up by all the *alter kockers*. I always told my parents it was just for the seat but in truth I liked being there when it was practically empty, and I could just sit and reflect.

But the thought of sitting in temple next to my parents, listening to the new young rabbi, Rabbi Rob, spin on the value of knowing right from wrong, seemed too much to bear. How could I sit next to my lying, cheating father and watch him beat his chest while he felt no remorse? I didn't want to be near him and I didn't want to be in a house of God when I was increasingly sure there wasn't one. What was the point of going to synagogue with my parents, all dressed up like a show pony, when everything inside our family was totally *fakakta*?

"Rachel," my mom said, "I know you're going through a difficult time right now but—"

"This isn't up for discussion," I said.

"But everyone's going to ask where you—"

"I'm sorry," I said, "but that's not really my problem."

"You shouldn't be so rude to your mother," she said. "Or you won't be inscribed in the Book of Life." I wanted to tell her I wasn't really the one she should be worried about but instead I said I'd see her at dinner.

As soon as she left I got dressed and went up to Liz's. I pounded and screamed *"Liz!"* like I was Brando in *Streetcar.* I put my head to

the door. It was silent. I pounded one more time. T. Russell, the fat
fortysomething stoner across the hall, stuck his head out. "Could you
stop banging, please?" he said as the scent of cannabis rushed out.

"Sorry," I said, and skulked down the stairs.

The bitch had eluded me; she must have been onto the fact that
I might suspect, and she was keeping new hours to avoid a run-in.
If that was the case then maybe I stood a chance. Maybe her guilt
mechanism wasn't completely on the fritz, just running at really low
power. I'd nail her soon, before he could. Even if it meant a twenty-
four-hour stakeout. Block vs. Kaminsky was on.

I T was midnight on Thursday, when the only people in a bar on a
weeknight are the insomniacs, the alkies, and the lonely. A married
regular named Randy had been chatting up a very young-looking
twentysomething who wore her hair in two long blond braids. I
knew he was married because one night he'd gone on a long dia-
tribe about how little intimacy he had with his wife despite the fact
that they had an eight-year-old son and had been together ten years.
I'd noticed he wasn't wearing a wedding band and when I asked him
why, he pulled out his keys and showed it to me, on the key ring.

"That's how I remember to put it back on when I come home,"
he said.

But lately he'd stopped complaining about his wife—and a few
weeks ago he'd told me she was expecting their second child—so it
irked me to see him flirting so shamelessly. Still, it wasn't the first
time I'd seen a married guy act in unmarried ways. The blonde had
a petite curvy figure, amplified by her pink T-shirt that said in white
letters, "Take a picture. It'll last longer." About ten minutes after she
came in Randy went over to her and started chatting. Now they were
on their fourth round of kamikaze shots and she was looking so
sloppy I was worried.

Her cheeks were bright red and a few times when he'd touched
her arm emphatically she hadn't done anything to stop him. As she
finished explaining why the first season of *Survivor* was better than
all the rest, he leaned in for a kiss. She didn't resist and he went at

it recklessly, pawing at her hair. They sucked face for about ten more minutes as I cleared a few drinks and brought a Harp to Jasper, who'd been uncharacteristically quiet. I heard Randy murmur, "I'll be right back, OK? And then we'll go," before standing up and heading unsteadily for the john.

The girl was smiling but there was a sadness behind it as though there was a darker reason someone this attractive was about to go home with such a letch. I had spent two months trying to stay out of my customers' business but something about the doubt in her eyes made me really feel some responsibility. I scooted over to her, leaned in close, and said, "He's married, you know."

"What?" she asked absently, like she'd misheard.

"He's got a wife, and an eight-year-old son, and she's expecting the second." She squinted and peered down into her empty shot glass. "Look," I said quickly, knowing he was going to come out soon, "I'm not trying to tell you what to do. I just thought you should know."

She nodded and was quiet for a second and then she stood up and yelled, "What the fuck do I care if he's married? Maybe I'm married too!" People spun around to look. I wished I could disappear; now no one would want to tell me their secrets.

"I'm sorry," I said. "I just thought—"

"Maybe my boyfriend's been cheating on me with my upstairs neighbor for the past year and doesn't think I know! What about that? How about *that?*" I had made the biggest mistake a bartender could: assumed a customer's innocence.

Randy came out of the bathroom and strode up to her. "You ready to go?"

"The bartender says you're married and that your wife is pregnant," she said. "Is that true?"

"Now where'd she get an idea like that?" he said smoothly, flashing me a dirty look.

"So I told her I don't give a fuck if you're married. I told her I got a boyfriend anyway."

"Do you live with him?" Randy said, cutting right to the chase.

"*No!*"

She stood up, having trouble on her feet, and pointed her finger at me. "This girl should mind her own goddamn business," she said. "I don't like busybodies!"

"I couldn't agree with you more," Randy said.

I knew I'd done the right thing but I didn't know why it felt so awful. I wanted to tell them about Hillel's philosophy, "If not me, who?" but it would have sounded hollow and ridiculous. In school we'd learned that the Jews had a moral obligation to stand up against injustice but at a bar if you did that you'd just lose tips.

"Let's get outta here," the girl said, as Randy whipped his jacket on and grabbed her arm. At the door she threw her head over her shoulder and said, "You know what? From now on I'm going to Boat." Boat was on Smith and Wyckoff, a few blocks down, and they had hipper clients, pinball, and pulled in twice the receipts that we did.

"Please don't do that," I said.

They headed out into the night, arm in arm. The only sound in the bar was some really dumb Oasis song on the jukebox. The customers who'd overheard everything were giving me the evil eye. I grabbed a rag and wiped down the bar. I had thought my father's infidelity might make me a better bartender, not a worse one, but instead I was driving out my customers.

Jasper was gaping at me, aghast. "Cockblocker," he said.

"That's it," I said. "I'm cutting you off."

"Exactly," he said, nodding smugly.

THE next day after breakfast I found myself getting antsy. It had been three days since I'd seen Powell and I missed him. Despite everything he had told me, I decided it was OK for me to make a move. He liked the truth. He'd said he didn't believe in the Rules. We had the kind of relationship where I could go over unexpected.

I opened up the closet and pulled out a magenta scoopneck racerback slinky dress so low cut that if I leaned over my boobs popped out. To go with it I picked a pair of knee-high suede black boots that looked like instruments of torture, since I knew he'd appreciate them.

When I got to Powell's I pushed open the front door and went upstairs. I took out a mirror from my bag and looked at my teeth to make sure there was nothing there and then I looked down at my boobs. The top of one nipple was peeking out of the dress so I lowered it. I fluffed my hair out like a diva and sniffed my pits. My left was kind of rank so I wiped it with the back of my hand. But I didn't know where to wipe my hand. It was the dance of infinite sweat transference. I opted for the wall, then jutted my hip out and knocked.

As the door opened I put on a Jessica Rabbit voice and said, "Take me now, you evil man!"

A little girl with blond bangs was staring up at me, deadpan. She had pale blue eyes like his with circles under them, and sallow pink skin, and she was holding a very slutty-looking doll in her hand.

"I'm not evil," she said.

"You must be Nora," I said, lowering my hand from the jamb.

She nodded and squinted at me suspiciously. "Are you Jennifer?" she said.

The plot thickened. "I'm not Jennifer," I said. "Who's Jennifer?"

"Daddy's friend." He was seeing someone else. I knew it.

"My name's Rachel," I said, bending down to shake her hand. As I did it my right boob popped out of the dress. Though I managed to shove it back in it was too late. She spun on her heel and ran away as fast as she could, screaming, "*Daddy!* I saw Rachel's boobie!" It wasn't the best introduction.

I heard the toilet flush and then Powell emerged, Nora clinging to his leg so he walked like a gimp. "What are you doing here?" he said. His voice was cold and devoid of anything resembling affection.

"I—I thought I'd stop by," I said, eyeing Nora, unsure just how perceptive she was. He kissed me on the cheek coldly and eyed my outfit, which suddenly felt obscene in front of the kid.

"I was going to call you," he said. "I've had Nora the last two nights because my ex-wife got food poisoning. How are you doing?"

"I'm losing my head. My mom doesn't seem to know. I knocked on Liz's door but she wasn't home. I think she's avoiding me."

"You got to stay out of it," he said.

"Can Rachel have dinner with us?" Nora asked.

"Sure she can," he said grumpily, like he wished she hadn't asked.

"Could I put on *my* dress, Daddy?" said Nora.

"Which one?" he said. She pulled on his hand and he bent down, his ear near her mouth. "Oh," he said. "That's a good idea. You want Rachel to help you?"

"*No.*" She turned and headed off to her room.

"She'll warm up eventually," he said. "She's like me with new people. Very feline. She needs to know you before she opts to like you."

I planted my hands on his shoulders like at a prom. "I'm sorry I dropped in like this. I just wanted to see you so badly," I whispered in his ear, nuzzling his mouth with my own.

"She could walk in any second," he said, recoiling.

"So?"

"So I don't know what kind of household you grew up in but I don't want her to be in psychotherapy the rest of her life. I got enough money trouble."

"Why are you in such a crappy mood?" I said.

"You want to know why? I think my ex-wife faked this food poisoning thing because she wasn't in the mood to take Nora. It infuriates me but there's nothing I can do. I got outta the marriage partly because I couldn't hack the lifestyle a being a full-time father, so I feel very put upon when I have to take her at the last minute."

Nora emerged from the back in a blue-and-white striped dress with a boatneck collar. She looked shy and thrilled, like she wanted attention and didn't at the very same time.

"You look incredible," I said. "What a beautiful sailor girl."

"I'm not a sailor," she said with hostility. "I'm a flapper." She was definitely Powell's child.

She was still holding her doll in her hand. "What's your doll's name?" I said.

"Jade. She's a Bratz doll," she said.

"You don't know about this?" Powell said. "They got a whole line a them and each one's more of a hoo-ah than the rest."

"Do you think we should put Jade in a dress too," I said, "so we can all look fancy for dinner?" She nodded, took my hand, and led me through Powell's bedroom to hers. As we went through I checked the bed for signs of another woman but it was clean and pristine.

Nora's room was like a war zone. There were dolls, pink cars, and clothes strewn on the bed and carpet, and picture books littering every corner. I sat down next to her and splayed my legs out in front of me since I couldn't exactly go Indian-style given my attire. She took out a big plastic bin. Inside were dozens of Barbies, Kens, and doll clothes, everything from sparkly halter tops to jeans to hot pink undies. She handed me a doll that looked like the first cousin of the one in her hand. "That's Diana," she said.

She pulled out a 1970s halter dress, all glittery, and put Jade in it. She had a little trouble with the Velcro at the halter so I held the hair up while she did it. When the doll was dressed Nora posed her on her knee, one leg crossed over the other. How did she know about leg crossing?

"What do you think?" she said.

"She's a real disco lady."

"What's disco?" said Nora.

"It's like Britney Spears," I said.

She rummaged around in her doll box and pulled out a miniature barbeque and two chairs. She set her doll, Jade, in one chair, and Diana in the other.

"Hey, Jade," I said, bouncing Diana up and down. "Do you want another hot dog?"

"Definitely," said Jade. "I love hot dogs!"

We mimed eating and then I got an idea. "Jade," Diana said. "You're so lucky. You have two houses and I only have one."

"Yeah," she said. "Daddy's and Mommy's."

"Where does your Mommy live?"

"The Upper East Side." Of course. Home of rich divorcées. I imagined her as leggy and modelesque, a Madison Avenue hottie, with an immaculate wardrobe, Botoxed face, and shining white teeth.

"Does Mommy have a boyfriend?"

She nodded. "Robert. Robert's her boyfriend. We stay at Robert's in East Hampton."

"Does Daddy have a girlfriend?" She cocked her head and frowned at me like the first question was simple, the second wasn't. "Who's Jennifer?"

"I told you," she said, throwing down the doll. "Daddy's friend."

"How long has Daddy known her?"

"Seven years." The problem with kids was they had no sense of time. She could be parroting something she'd heard or just making it up.

"Is Jennifer Daddy's girlfriend?"

She shrugged. "Does Daddy play with Bratz dolls a lot?" I asked.

She frowned. "Daddy's a boy! He doesn't have dolls."

"But does Daddy have girls that *look* like Bratz girls come over a lot?"

"Who are you, Nancy Drew?" said Powell from the doorway. I felt my face go pinker than my polish.

"Who's Nancy Drew?" said Nora.

"She's the nosiest girl in the world," he said, pursing his lips.

I stood up, holding my chest to avoid another accidental free boob. "Are you seeing someone else?" I said quietly.

"I don't think this is the time to discuss it," he said, eyeing Nora, who had begun tearing off Jade's clothes.

"Why don't I set the table?" I said, and rushed out of the room, shoving the doll in Powell's hand.

DINNER was better than I might have anticipated. Powell made penne rigate, and we drank from goblets of Chilean Merlot while Nora had a juice box. He sat at the head and Nora and I faced each other. As for the conversation, I was a little nervous about what common ground the three of us could possibly have but we did all right. The two of them discussed the declining quality of *Rugrats*, the different attributes of the Powerpuff Girls, and the latest Mary-Kate and Ashley movie and how gross it was when Mary-Kate kissed the guy. This led to a discussion of the disgusting nature of kissing in general, followed by my own underappreciated offering that Mary-Kate and Ashley got their start as infants on a television show that neither Nora nor her father had ever watched, followed by a group discussion as to whether Nora wanted to be an actress when she grew up (yes) despite the fact that her father thought it was a bad idea.

After dinner Powell pushed out his chair, wiped his mouth with the corner of his cloth beige napkin, and told Nora she needed to take a bath. I sat on the couch as they went in. I heard the slapping noises of water and their voices in low muted tones. I felt jealous of their quiet intimacy. There was something about that small echo, the way you could only make out vowels, and not actual words, that made bath-giving exclusionary, a private duo act not to be trespassed on by a third.

The water gurgled down the drain and a couple minutes later I heard little feet pattering in. She came right up to me in a white robe with a hood on her head.

"Good night, Rachel," she said softly.

"Good night," I said. She hesitated a second and then climbed up onto the couch, kissed my cheek fast, and scampered away. I could see right then how a kid could break your heart.

She raced into her room. There was some shuffling around and talk about pajamas and then through the bedroom I heard Powell begin reading in a singsongy melodic voice.

"Interior," I heard him say. "Dive bar by the overpass. Lenny and Artie are drinking Scotch at a table with a red-and-white tablecloth. 'Lenny: Just because you hate your wife don't mean you should kill her.' 'Artie: She's eating my soul. When I married her I was six two. I swear to God, Lenny, I'm five eleven now.'"

Nora giggled. Powell went on, in an almost expressionless monotone. "'Lenny: The problem isn't her. It's you.' 'Artie: I know but how's that supposed to help? I'm between a rock and the hard face of my miserable wife.' 'Lenny: There are other options besides murder.' 'Artie: Like?' 'Lenny: I'm just saying, there's options.' Right at that moment a beautiful woman with legs like crème caramel meanders into the bar."

"Daddy?" Nora asked. "What's crème caramel?"

"You'll find out when you're older."

"She sits on a stool, looks at Artie and Lenny. 'Beautiful Woman: Gimme a shotta ya strongest bourbon, barkeep.' 'Lenny (smacking his lips): The Lord works in mysterious ways.'"

There was a pause and then Powell said, "You think that last line works? It's not too flat?"

"It wasn't flat."

"Is your Daddy a genius? Is your Daddy the smartest man alive? Who's the smartest mick this side a the Gowanus? *I am!* Who gives you your silly juices? Huh? Huh?"

She squealed, "Stop it stop it stop it!" and giggled insanely.

"What's the magic word?"

"Heel! Heel, Daddy, heel!"

I lay back on the couch and buried my head in a pillow. What did he need me for? She was a decent critic and there weren't any strings. I knew it was wrong to envy someone who had only recently learned to tie her own shoes but I couldn't help it. She had him all the way and I only had him half.

A little while later Powell padded in. He sat next to me and put my legs on his lap. "Does she ever give you good feedback?"

"All the time! Once she told me I needed to put in a ghost, another time she said a female character should be male. I made both changes. You shouldn't a grilled her about my love life."

"Well, can I ask *you,* then? Are we monogamous?"

"That's none a ya business," he said, like it was the most outrageous question he'd ever heard.

"I think it is," I said. "Especially since you don't like condoms."

"*Fine!* We'll use a rubber the next time!"

Talking to Powell was like approaching an oracle; it was impossible to get a useful answer out of him. "I just want to know where I stand with you. Remember that scene in *Queensboro Blues* where Yvette and Henry are standing on the bridge in the middle of the night and she tells him she's got choices she's got to make?"

His eyes bugged out. "Please do not tell me you're knocked up."

"No! I just mean—I don't know anything about you. I don't know what you do when you don't see me or if you think about me when I'm not there."

"How can I put this any more clearly?" he said, like he was talking to a child. "I am not in any state to be shackling myself to a woman right now."

"If you use the word 'shackle' I guess you must be right." I lifted my legs off of him and lowered them onto the floor. "Fuck the whole neighborhood for all I care. Fuck Liz."

"I think she's already got her hands full."

"That was uncalled for," I said. I looked down at my feet. I was wearing suede high-heeled boots, he was a shoe guy and he wasn't taking any interest. "Do you think I could suck you a little?"

He put his hands up in the air like Tevye talking to God. "Am I mistaken or were we just in the middle of a conversation?"

"We were, but can I suck you?"

"I got a child in the next room!"

"She's asleep."

"She might not be. What if she saw something? She'd be scarred for life." A loud snore sailed out.

"OK?" I said, gesturing in her direction. "Is that enough for you? That's the Lord working in mysterious ways."

"Don't appropriate my lines," he said, and put a finger up.

"I just want to feel it," I said, getting down on my knees and reaching for his buckle. "I won't even put the whole thing in. I'll just . . . pick."

"Maybe I want to connect with you," he said, putting his hands on my shoulders and pushing me back. "A man can't live through his pud every minute of every day."

"Sure he can!" I cried. I knew I was making a fool of myself but the less he wanted it the more I wanted to convince him. I was try-ing to apply the rules of doing well in school to my love life, like for-mulating a clear argument, showing real stick-to-itiveness, and focusing hard on a task at hand, yet it didn't work as well for Powell as it did for my grades.

"Rachel," Powell said. "It's good not to do it sometimes. It means I respect you."

"Couldn't you respect me just a little bit *less?*" I wailed.

"What's going on with you?" he said, lifting me up and plopping me down next to him. He had a hint of bite to his voice, which I didn't like.

"Don't you think I look good? Didn't you like my boots?"

"I love them," he said. "I wasn't prepared for you tonight. We'll have a rain check."

"I don't want a rain check," I whined.

"You can't get everything you want all a the time."

"You're the only thing in my life that's good. I don't see why I can't have you when I want you."

"I'm not a mollusk," he said. "I'm an octopus." I realized in a way it would be good if it didn't work out between Powell and me; I wouldn't have to figure out what to put on his grave. "What I mean is, I got obligations that predate you."

"I don't want you to predate me. I want you to date me."

"I should a seen that one coming," he said. I rose to my feet. A girl can only take so much humiliation before she rings her own gong.

He stood with the exaggerated effort of an exhausted fat old man and walked me to the door. "I'll call you, OK?" he said, with a sigh.

I nodded but my throat was tight and spastic. It was a dangerous sign, the sigh. The sighs are the beginning of the end. I wished I could inhale it out of the air but it had already flitted away.

THE ELANA COMPLEX

A COUPLE days later my mom left me a message to remind me about her first Koffee Klatsch. I wasn't going to go because I thought it would be too torturous, but by eight o'clock my guilt mechanism kicked in and I decided to go. In the living room I found a group that resembled the cast of *Mixed Nuts*. There was a fat Latino guy who looked about thirty, a short, nervous-seeming Semitic woman in her fifties wearing a *shmatte,* a couple of spacey-looking folkie men—slightly paunchy but oblivious to their decline, and Nina, who seemed delighted to be one of the coolest people around.

The only semi-cute guy was a biker-style guy in his thirties with long greasy hair in a ponytail, the kind who felt the need to touch it way too often. They were all holding decorative paper coffee cups in their hands, the kind with attached handles that fold up from the cup. The Latino guy had an electric-blue barbell in his hand and he was saying, "The author of *Flatland* proposed that time was the fourth dimension. If the first dimension is a line, the second a plane, and the third a cube, then the fourth is a hypercube, or time."

"What does that look like?" said Shmatte Woman.

"That's the thing," he said. "We don't have the framework to conceptualize it."

He passed her the barbell. "I think the meaning of time changes over time," she said. "When you're a child it passes very slowly and then when you get older it passes more quickly."

She passed the barbell to Greasy Hair. "What about the notion that time is cyclical?" he asked. "Why do we say 'I feel like I've known you forever' when we meet someone we could love?"

"That's such an interesting question, Ray," my mom said.

"Is it possible that we have met that person in another life? When I was fifteen a girl was transferred into my school whom I was convinced I'd known before. We gravitated toward each other at recess, like there was a magnet between us, and she told me that she was the reincarnated spirit of a thirteenth-century Egyptian princess and that I was the spirit of her first love, a soldier who had died on the battlefield." Everyone giggled. "I know it sounds strange but I believed her. We stayed friends for the rest of our lives and we still keep in touch."

The room got hushed and they all glanced at each other nervously, waiting to see the others' reactions. The Spanish guy put his hands by his face and moved them in waves like in *Wayne's World,* and everyone burst out laughing.

"Before we go on," my mom said, "I want to introduce you all to my daughter, Rachel." Her face was glowing and excited, like she was proud that I had come, that I had taken an interest in what she was doing.

Then there were a few utterances of "*I* didn't know you had a daughter" and "You two look so much alike," which was the worst thing anyone could say to a mother-daughter combination.

"Did you want to add anything?" my mom asked.

"I just want to know what the barbell's for," I said.

"You missed the beginning," she said with a hint of annoyance. "It's the talking stick. It's a Native American tradition, to insure that everyone gets equal speaking time."

Greasy Hair passed it along to Nina, who launched into a monologue about her love for Madeleine L'Engle's *A Wrinkle in Time.* The meeting went on another forty-five minutes but for some reason time seemed to move much more slowly.

At the end of the meeting everyone milled around and chatted, coming up to my mom and telling her how great she was and how glad they were that she'd started the group. She ate it up, throwing her head back and laughing too hard at their jokes, nodding so vigorously it was like she was teaching six-year-olds. She was trading my father in for a bunch of loony tunes.

Shmatte Woman spotted me staring and said, "That's so great that Sue's your mom."

"Yeah," I nodded.

"I was just thinking how much the neighborhood needed something like this and then I saw your mom's sign in Cobble Hill Park. She's a real visionary."

"I don't know if I'd go that far." She frowned as though not sure how someone as nice as my mother could have possibly birthed a bitch like me, and moved away.

You don't get it! I wanted to shout. *She's keeping my father out of the house by doing all this and he started boning my former best friend! Normally I'd be much more supportive but in light of what's going on it's a little hard to root for her newfound interests!* but instead I just went into the kitchen to see what was in the fridge.

By the time all the guests had gone it was nine-thirty. I helped my mom clear up the cups and food. She was so high from it all it seemed like she was on speed. She kept clucking and replaying the highlights of the conversation, like she'd just had some amazing first date. When we finally collapsed on the couch she clapped her hands together and said, "I can't believe how well it went!"

"Me neither," I said.

"I had no idea we'd get that kind of turnout. It's so strange, all those people in the living room. It reminded me of when Dad and I used to entertain more. I like this house full." She got a sentimental, nostalgic face.

"Are you having a hot flash?" I said.

"No," she said, annoyed. "I was just thinking about what different choices you and I made in our lives."

"What do you mean?" I said, waiting for her to lay in on me for dropping out of school.

"When you graduated college you worked, you supported yourself. You applied to rabbinical school. I got married at twenty-one and by the time I was your age I'd already had you."

"Yeah, but then you went back to teaching. It's not like you were a housewife."

"It's just that sometimes I feel like I have to make up for lost time.

I wish I'd done more. Sometimes I even wish I'd stayed single longer."

This was not what I needed to hear. "No you don't," I said. "Singlehood is overrated."

"But look what a wonderful time you're having! You're dating a celebrity!"

"He's not a—"

"Sure he is. I never dated anyone important. Dad was the only guy I ever—you know."

"Why did you just tell me that?" I asked belligerently.

"So you know how lucky you are."

"Are you thinking of leaving Dad?"

"No!"

"Did you ever *want* to leave him," I said, "like when I was a teenager and you guys used to fight all the time?"

"Those were not good days," she said, and her eyes clouded over. When I was fourteen I came home from a friend's birthday party in the Village to find my dad fuming in the living room about some computer problem, and my mom in the bathroom, sitting on the toilet with a Kleenex in her hand. She had obviously been sobbing from the fight but when I asked if she was OK she tried to pretend nothing was wrong, just wiped her face and said, "Yeah, I'm fine."

"What did he do to you?" I had asked.

"It's really not your concern," she had said gruffly, and I had walked out feeling doubly slapped. You can't stick your nose into the business of your parents' marriage because neither one will be grateful for your assistance. Their bond trumps yours with each, their privacy trumps their need to cry on someone's shoulder.

"Did you ever think of cheating on him?"

"Rachel!"

"It's a fair question."

"It's not my style," she said, wrinkling her nose. "I'm in it for the long haul." She said it with such resign I didn't know whether to be happy or sad.

"Have you ever worried that *he* might?"

"Dad?" She laughed so hard and threw her head back so violently

I thought she was going to topple the couch. "He'd have to find someone to cheat *with.*" Just as I'd feared. My mother's lack of faith in my dad's prowess would be her own undoing.

"Where is he anyway?" I said, looking for signs of suspicion in her eyes.

"Fixing somebody's computer. I told him he's going to have to start hauling in some more income so all the financial responsibility doesn't fall on me. This week alone he got three jobs on different PCs in the neighborhood." He was definitely working a few PCs all right, but not the ones she was thinking about.

As much as I felt like she deserved to know the truth, how could I tell her? If my mom found out it would all fall apart. You can't mess around on your wife when she's in a conversation group; she's too amenable to change. They'd have a Koffee Klatsch on infidelity and with the help of Fat Spanish Guy and Shmatte Woman she'd weigh the pros and cons of divorce, and once she left him she'd change their Koffee Klatsch into group therapy so she could cry on their shoulders week after week.

Right around this time the Pacific Street Bum would die and my dad would replace him as the bearded fattie on the corner smoking cigs and begging for change. I'd try to forget he was ever related to me as Powell and I stepped over him each night on the way to my apartment. To cope with the strain on my soul I'd resort to spending more and more time with Powell, and sink into an S&M thing with him so dark and evil it would be a miracle if he didn't kill me.

"Why all these questions all of a sudden?" she asked, squinting at me.

"No reason."

"Are you having problems with Hank?"

"No." I hadn't confided in her about my love life since I was a teenager. Somewhere along the way I just stopped trusting her, needing her, and though I sensed her hurt at this, there was nothing I could do.

"So when can we meet him?" she asked perkily. "I mean officially? Do you want to invite him for Rosh Hashanah dinner?"

How could I tell her I wasn't even sure *I'd* see him again? Or that even if I did, the chance of Hank Powell being up for a family sit-down on the Jewish New Year was about as great as him writing a screenplay about a happy marriage?

I wanted Powell to be the kind of guy who was interested in where I came from but I also knew that the whole reason I'd been drawn to him in the first place was because he wasn't.

"He's NJ," I said.

"So? He can still eat with us. What—is he allergic to brisket?"

"I'll ask him if he's free," I said, but as we looked at each other we both knew I wouldn't.

O n my way back home I bumped into my father. I didn't recognize him at first even though he was coming right toward me, so when he stopped in front of me with a big grin I leapt back like he was a mugger.

"That's right!" he sang, touching his face. "You haven't seen my beard! Whaddaya think?"

"I dunno," I said. He probably did it as soon as he got home from Shtup Number One. Liz put her hand on his mildly retarded post-coital face and said, "You'd look so much better clean-shaven, Mr. B." He went home like some sort of brainwashed Stepford Wife and took out the clipper, the stench of Liz all over his hands.

He was wearing a batik T-shirt with a print of an empty squash court and two racquets in the air and he had on headphones, his CD player tucked into his shorts. I could hear something thrumming softly from inside them.

The music was energetic and enormously catchy and as it continued I realized it sounded familiar. "What are you listening to?" I said, as he slipped his headphones over my head.

The vocalist had a hoarse voice and poor diction, and he was singing through a filter something about walking out a door. I yanked the headphones off and threw them back at him. "You're listening to *the Strokes?*"

"I love them," he said. "I've been playing this nonstop."

They had to be fucking. There was no other way.

"How do you know about the Strokes?" I said.

"Ira played a sample last week on *TAL*," he said. Ira was Ira Glass, my father's idol, and *TAL* was *This American Life,* a show my father could not listen to five minutes of without crying. "Did you know their lead singer is John Cassavetes's son?"

"Casablancas," I sighed. Some things never changed.

This was horrific. Liz was far more dangerous than I deemed possible. Up until now my dad was totally uneducable in matters of popular culture. He thought Courtney Love was an actress on *Friends* and was convinced Marilyn Manson was a woman.

I smelled something funny in the air. It was vodka. She was turning him into an indie alkie. My father was morphing into Jack White. "Have you been drinking?" I asked.

"No," he said, shaking his head. Whenever he lied he did this thing my mom and I had dubbed GHM: Gratuitous Head Motion. Usually it was over something dumb—he'd exaggerate a story someone had told him at work, or say my mom had said something she hadn't said at all. Usually we got a big laugh out of it—we'd say, "Are you making that up?" and he'd say, "Well, maybe just a little." But now that he was doing GHM over something grave I wanted to choke him.

"Then why do you reek of vodka?"

"OK, you got me," he said. "I had a drink at Brawta."

Liz was using my restaurant suggestions for the purpose of wooing my dad. It didn't get any more evil. "Mom said you were fixing a PC."

"I was. This was afterwards. It was the first paying job I'd gotten in weeks so I decided to reward myself. Is that all right with you? Is that OK?"

His eyes were so hostile, and mean. I wanted to shake him by the shoulders and tell him to stop using career advancement as his foil. I wanted to scream at him to get a blow-up doll or better lube, that my mom was a good person even if she was welcoming strangers into our living room, that he should wait it out and think long-term the way he did with his mutual funds.

But when I opened my mouth I just shut it again. They said cheating men never admitted until the wife had concrete evidence.

If I confronted him he'd just deny it till the end, like the husband in *Gaslight*, and try to convince me it was all a hallucination. Or what if he said he was glad I knew, he was going to tell me anyway, he was planning to leave my mom and run off with Liz? What if she was already pregnant? It could all be her sick Hurleyesque plot to get herself knocked up before thirty-five.

I tried sending him a subliminal message, *"Stop the affair, stop the affair,"* because I'd read in Laura Day's *Practical Intuition* that that kind of thing could work, but he didn't seem to be getting my brainwaves.

"What does Mom think about your new look?" I asked.

"She says she doesn't recognize me but I think that means she likes it."

"I wouldn't be so sure."

"I can't believe this," he said. "You're the only one that's had anything negative to say about it. Everyone else has been telling me what an improvement it is!"

"It's not an improvement," I said. "I barely recognize you."

"That's perfectly understandable," he said, pinching my ear. "But once you get used to it, you won't remember me the old way at all."

AT quarter to six on Erev Rosh Hashanah, I was changing into my clothes when I heard Liz blasting Nico's version of "These Days." Those horrible triplets that sounded like the goose-stepping anthem of an injured cow.

It was one thing to listen to Nico when you'd been dumped but another when you were tearing apart a family. I knocked on her door but the Nico was so loud she didn't hear me. I pounded my fist hard several times and then I tried shouting her name. There wasn't any answer. I went down to the end of the hallway where the window to the fire escape was and wrested it open. Above her fire escape she'd hung a clothesline, with a bunch of bras hanging on it, plus a few Cosabella thongs. This was the contradictory essence of my former New Best Friend: she was an environmentalist JAP.

"Liz!" I hollered, sticking my head out. A few seconds later, her

emaciated mug popped out. She looked flushed and bothered. "What?" she said.

"I need to talk to you. Could you open the door, please?" She hesitated a second—I wasn't sure what she was going to do—then disappeared. When she opened the door her face was even and hard. She was wearing sweats and a Juicy T-shirt, no bra, and no makeup. She turned around and I followed. From *her* living room window you could only see the top of the tennis bubble and I envied her for getting sky. I scanned the room for signs of my father but the only possible one was a shiny black shoehorn sitting on her desk, which was plausible but not enough to build a case on.

Her blow-dryer was sitting on her kitchen table. She picked it up and began blowing out her hair with enormous expertise. The plot thickened as her hair thinned.

"I thought you didn't believe in blowouts," I said.

"I'm opposed to the *regular* blowout," she said over the noise. "The occasional one I have no problem with."

There was a gay porno called *Honcho* lying on top of her magazine rack. I thumbed through it, staring at the bulging cocks. I was stalling but I had to.

"I saw you," I finally said, putting the magazine down.

"Yeah?" she replied dully.

"In the park the other night. I saw you with him."

She met my gaze, picked a few spare hairs out of the brush, and said, "I know."

I hadn't exactly been prepared for her to trump me in the information department. "What?" I gasped.

"How could I not have? You guys were so obvious when you left, with your little crouch walks." She made a scrunched, mock-nerdy face and moved her two fingers like a bug. Leave it to Liz to mock me at the most dramatic moment of our so-called friendship. "It's a good thing he didn't, though. He would have had a conniption."

"*Why are you doing this?*" I said, striding over to her and leveling my eyes with hers.

"I'm not *doing anything*," she said sullenly, like I was the crazy one and not her.

"You mean that was it—you just kissed—but nothing else?"

"Oh, no," she said. "We've been fucking for the last two weeks. I mean I didn't set out to *do* anything. It just kind of happened."

"*Liz!*" I yelled. "You don't start an affair with your girlfriend's father because it *happened.*"

"Sure you do! It's actually a really funny story. I was on my way home from the subway, and I stopped in Boat for a drink when—" I stuck both fingers in my ear and sang the first few lines of "If I Were a Rich Man." I was not sure why I chose that tune.

When I finally unplugged she was saying, ". . . your dad sure knows how to eat quiche!" I didn't know which was more upsetting: what she'd just said or the fact that she'd used the word "quiche" to describe it.

"That's disgusting!" I said.

"No it's not. I think what surprised me most about our sex together is how vibrant and modern it is. He's a very open-minded guy, and way less judgmental than some of the other guys I've dated. Such an eager learner. He already knows the name of every vibe in my box—"

"Stop right there!" I said. "Just tell me how long you've been seeing him. Since before Banania?"

"Banan*ia*," she said. "That was when I met him."

"And how many times has it been since then?"

"That depends," she said, setting the brush down on the desk. "Are we talking *occasions* or—"

"You know what? Forget I asked. I don't care how many times. I just want it to end." I knew I sounded like a mother telling her kids to stop fighting but you resort to inane maternal logic when you're in the midst of stopping sin.

"Why?" she asked blankly, going into the bathroom.

"'*Why*'?" I repeated, following her in. "Are you seriously asking me why? Did you happen to notice the other night that he had a wife?"

"Of course I did," she said, as she began to pluck her brows. "But how could I let that stop me when he didn't let it stop him? Your dad can be very aggressive when he sees something he wants."

"Are you sure we're talking about the same person?"

"*Oh yeah,*" she said, plucking a big one.

I massaged my temple with my hand and sat down on the edge of her bed. There was a V-shaped stain on one of the pillows and I really wanted to believe it was saliva.

"Look, are you mad at me about something?" I asked pleadingly. "You're jealous about Powell so you want to punish me somehow?"

"I find it very interesting that you think this has something to do with you."

"Of course it has something to do with me! He's my father!"

"I feel no anger, Rach," she said. She pulled a purplish Missoni V-neck from her closet and set it on the bed.

"But you've got to," I said. "Otherwise you wouldn't be doing this! If you want to put me through pain, I could give you about fifty other really horrible things you could do that would make me equally miserable and wouldn't involve him. You could slap me in the face." I grabbed her hand and hit myself with it across the cheek. "Come on! Go to it! Tell me what you're pissed about. Let's get it out right now. Let's tussle."

"Rachel," she said, peeling my fingers off her hand. "I do not want to tussle."

"I don't understand why you won't break it off!"

"Because I'm not entirely convinced that that's what he wants."

"It *is* what he wants!" I brayed. "I know him very well and trust me, it's what he wants. I'll help you join a white-women-who-love-black-men support group. I'll post a JDate ad for you. Just don't keep seeing him."

"I'm sorry," she said. "I can't do that."

"How can you even be attracted to him? He dyes his hair."

"So do I." She got some deodorant off her dresser by the window and rubbed it up and down her armpit.

"And he has unbelievably bad seborrheic dermatitis. Have you noticed it? On his face? It's like *all over.* And it's really contagious."

"It's not contagious," she said. "Do you think I'm an idiot?"

"I thought you wanted someone with money! My dad's out of a job!"

"I know," she said. "I told him he should consider suing for ageism."

"He *told* you?"

"We talk, Rachel. We don't just—"

"All right!" I said, forcing her to talk to the hand. I hated the fact that he'd told her. It made me feel like he was letting her in. And he hadn't even told *me* right away.

"I'm not entirely convinced he should stick with programming anyway," she said coolly. "He's always wanted to write the great American novel and—"

"My father has *not* always wanted to write the great American novel. Where did you get this?"

"Yes he has. When he was at Columbia he took this English class he really liked. His professor told him he had real promise but when he married your mom he had to get a real job and give up on his dreams." She said "dreams" like she was one of them. "I think this could be an opportunity for him to regroup, take stock of his options."

"My father can't even write a coherent email!" I said. "He uses all these parentheticals and double-dashes. I have to read them three times in a row just to figure out he's telling me to tape *The Sopranos.*"

She nodded slowly like she had years of wisdom on me. "He says it's your family's lack of support that's one of the main reasons he's put off his novel-writing for so long."

"How often do you see him anyway?"

"As often as we can. He only comes over here when you're working so sometimes we go to the Brooklyn Marriott. I figure we might as well revitalize the Brooklyn economy while we're being illicit."

"*Ugh!*" I said. "I don't even see what you see in him! He's like thirty pounds overweight! How can you even—"

"Why don't *you* tell *me*?" she said. "Hank Powell's fat."

"No he's not!"

"Sure he is. He's got a bigger gut than your dad."

"He does not!" I was a terrible negotiator. You can't reason with someone who's insane to begin with. I could sneak into Liz's bedroom in the middle of the night, slip her a Mickey, then do a secret vagina stitch. It was the only way to stop her. And I did have an extra set of keys.

As she slithered out of her sweats I saw that she had an enormous thatch of dark curly hair, twice the volume of my own. But it tapered to a perfect V above her clit, like the arrow a computer mouse made when you moved it. It was a hairy Jew beav, with a pair of perfectly waxed labia underneath—a perverse mix of modern and retro.

She pulled off her shirt, fluffed out her hair behind her head, and turned to me, exposing her pert pink buds. My dad was dating the Jewish Uma Thurman. How could he ever go back to my mom? You can't eat at White Castle once you've tried four-star.

I tried compassion. "You know, my mom is going through a tough time right now. She's really not on stable ground at all. If she finds out I could see her doing something very irrational."

"From what Richard says she's got a really solid support network." I shuddered. His name sounded weird in Liz's mouth, like it didn't belong.

"Where's your decency?" I said. "Don't you have any respect for the sanctity of marriage? My parents have been married thirty-one years!"

"Thirty-two."

"How do you know how long they've been—"

"It came up," she shrugged. I did some quick mental calculations. I was terrible with dates. Every year I went into a crazy tailspin trying to remember if my parents' anniversary was May 17 or May 18.

"All right," I conceded. "Thirty-two!" She was showing me up in the arena of my own parental expertise. Her trumping me as a daughter infuriated me far more than her trumping my mom as a wife. She opened her dresser, drew out a white Cosabella thong, and stepped into it. The front patch was tiny, much thinner than her pubic hair, which emerged from all sides, like a bearded man eating a Dorito.

"You can't go messing with a thirty-two-year-old marriage," I told her. "It's Rosh Hashanah. How can you live with yourself?"

"What do you mean?"

"You're breaking three commandments."

"Oh yeah? What are they?"

"Let's start with the Seventh."

"Ah ah ah," she said, wagging her finger. "It's only adultery if the woman cheats, not the man."

"Reform Judaism doesn't believe in literal interpretation of the law!"

"That's why no one takes it seriously."

I wanted to lift her by her skinny arms and hurl her into the tennis bubble. "OK, fine. You're coveting something that belongs to your neighbor."

"He doesn't belong to you," she said, slithering into a tan pencil skirt.

"Of course he does!"

"I find this very intriguing," she said. "You experience this as a slight to *you*, not your mother."

"It's a slight to everybody!" I said. "If my mom were in the room right now I'd gladly have *her* take this up with you."

"You obviously have unresolved issues. You see him like a husband. It's the Electra complex. Classic Jewish daughter."

"Electra wasn't Jewish."

"The Elana complex, then," she said. "I seriously think you should try to work this out because it's going to be a real problem for you in your relationships. I know a really good Buddhist psychologist in Tribeca who might be able—"

"You think *I* need therapy?"

"*I* get help, Rach." She shrugged. "You don't."

"Liz," I said, getting down on my knees and gazing up at her pleadingly. I was stooping low but I was stooping to conquer. "Please dump him. I'm begging you." She regarded me as though I was a Vietnam vet with no legs riding a dolly through a subway car asking for change.

"This is not a one-way street," she said. "I need to see where this is going to go. And to tell you the truth, Rach, I think he does too."

I felt like Stella McCartney. But at least she could take solace in her wicked stepmom's gimphood. Liz was *mobile*. Maybe if I chopped off one of her legs I could take it but this way it was too much. My chest felt more constricted than Liz's bulimic waist. I was only twenty-six but suddenly a heart attack seemed plausible. I'd drop dead in Liz's apartment then and there. Then again, the grief might bring my parents together. They'd be forced to get over their differences in the interest of mourning their most prized possession. I wouldn't be alive to appreciate it but what did it matter? Even death was a small price to pay to stop a divorce.

Liz drew a pair of alligator-skin fuck-mes from the closet and stepped into them one by one. "Where are you going?" I said.

"Rosh Hashanah dinner at my parents'," she said. She lifted me up off the ground, spun me around, and ushered me through the doorway and out to the front door. "Have a great Rosh."

"What's going on?" I said.

"Nothing," she said. "Just—don't you have to be at your parents' soon? Richard told me you guys were having dinner."

"I have a few more minutes," I said. "Why are you in such a rush to get rid of me?"

"It's no rush. We just seem to be at a standstill."

"Are you expecting someone?"

She paused for a second, then let out a long sigh and said, "I cannot tell a lie. I did chop down that cherry tree."

I looked at my watch. It was six-oh-two. My dad was right at this moment showering for dinner listening to *All Things Considered* on the waterproof radio. "Do not tell me he's coming over," I said.

"I didn't say it was your father."

"What?"

"If you must know," she said, rolling her eyes, "it's our waiter, from that night."

"From Banania."

"Ban*ani*a."

"What's his name?" I said to test her.

"Sebastian. He's French-Algerian. I went in a couple nights ago for a drink and we started talking."

"You're two-timing a two-timer?"

"Whose side are you on?"

"I don't know!" My dad was cheating on my mom with a girl so promiscuous she couldn't even commit to an extramarital affair. I felt seriously worried for the state of his pubes. What if she gave him herpes? It would be the irony to beat all ironies: my dad had managed to survive the seventies without it, only to contract it during the naughts.

"What kind of protection are you using?" I said, as she nudged me out into the hallway.

"Happy New Year," she said, and shut the door in my face.

I TRUDGED down the steps to my apartment, feeling like a wounded soldier coming home from battle. I was going to be late for Rosh because I was trying to get someone else to atone. It was the Neil Roth scenario all over again. I was totally lacking in oratory power.

I went into the bedroom to change my clothes and as I was slipping on my skirt I heard the downstairs door open and shut. A pair of feet jogged up—fast and two at a time. My father was more of a clodder than a hopper. There was some murmuring from Liz's apartment—I was almost certain I could make out a French accent—and a couple minutes later that Coldplay song came on, the sappy one.

As Chris Martin wailed about the stars, and how they shine for you, and all the things you do, I went into the bathroom and ran a brush through my hair, since my mom was always telling me it wouldn't hurt me to run a brush through my hair. I put on a vintage silk button-down blouse with a knee-length tweed skirt to make my mom happy; even if I wasn't going to services with them I knew it wouldn't hurt to dress like I was.

I looked at myself in the mirror and put on a little lipstick and foundation and then I tossed some Roberto Cavalli on my neck. The Coldplay was droning on sappily and I wondered how any guy, even a frog, could keep it up in the face of such treacle. I jogged down the stairs and continued down the street and when I got a few steps away I stopped in my tracks.

The supermarket giveaways were gone.

My father picked up those goddamn giveaways every single time he passed my place. No other man could be micromanagerial enough to deposit a bunch of papers in the recycling bin on the way to visit his chippie. My dad was the Bette Midler of Cobble Hill. Even if he had no problem violating the Seventh Commandment he'd surely heed his own personal number one: "Do not litter."

Liz had concocted the frog just to get me out of her pad. And it had almost worked. But it wouldn't work again. I had to put an end to it once and for all.

I could hear the Coldplay getting louder and louder as I climbed. As I arrived at her door I made my hand into a fist and was about to bang it against the door when over Chris Martin's insipid whine I heard another, older male moan over the falsetto.

The tone was vaguely familiar, close to the yelp he made when he stubbed his toe tripping over his own toolbox, or lowered himself to his knees to weed in the garden, but it was more elongated and slightly surreal. I stood there with my hand frozen inches from the peephole, unsure whether to pound or run. And then, before I could decide what to do, my father, as he so often did, decided for me. Through the door he exploded with the most disturbing two-word phrase that had ever emerged from his mouth: *"Oh brooother!"*

I spun around and took the stairs so fast I tripped and almost fell on my ass. I clung to the banister and swung myself around it like in a dream where you're flying, coasting on the air, and I didn't stop until I was all the way to Court Street.

How could he have the gall to sleep with his mistress on Erev Rosh Hashanah? How could he have the gall to say "Oh brother!" when he came?

They were definitely doing it; there was no more denial. He had stopped over at his sweetie's for an end-of-year bang. What did he think this was—the Jewish millennium? He'd arranged to see her when he knew I'd be out of the building, on time for the one thing per year I was on time for. And now he was going to be late and I'd have to cover. He would arrive at his Rosh Hashanah hearth, stinking of poot. This wasn't just adultery. It was sacrilege.

———•———

T H E inside of my parents' house smelled sickeningly sweet. My mom was in the kitchen mixing the *tsimmes*, wearing a black-and-white plaid belted dress, stockings, and heels. "What's in the oven?" I said.

"Honey cake," she said.

"Happy New Year," I said, trying to sound normal.

"Shanah Tovah to you too." She took in my face, frowned, and put the back of her hand on my forehead. "Are you all right?"

"Yeah. Why?"

"You look a little pale."

"I'm wearing base." I snuck a peek at the kitchen clock. Twenty to seven. I hoped he came soon, which meant I *really* hoped Liz did.

"So where's Dad?"

"He said he was going to be a little late. He wanted to stop off at the bookstore and pick up some programming books. He's trying to update his skills to meet the needs of the new technology market."

What a snake. Then again, knowing him, there was a good chance he really *had* stopped off at the bookstore on the way over to Liz's. He'd pried *Adobe for Dummies* from the stack when he spotted *Adultery for Dummies* and decided to buy that instead.

I glanced at the door, willing him to come through. I severely doubted he'd do a postcoital linger; he knew how important this dinner was to my mom. Then again, he was right at this very moment kicking it to an anorexic chippie; it wasn't fair to say I knew much about anything anymore.

"Did you bring the wine?" my mom asked.

I did a V8 smack to the head. The one time I had a decent excuse for forgetting something I couldn't even share it. It was just my luck. What was I supposed to say? "No, I didn't. See, I heard Dad ejaculating and kind of lost my head"?

"I'm so sorry," I said. "I forgot. You want me to run out now?"

"Never mind," she said, with the hint of exuberance she always showed when I let her down. She might never be a rabbi or even a star student but she could always beat me when it came to practical matters, to matters of the home. "I'll call Dad."

"I don't think you should do that," I said quickly, running over to her as she went to the phone.

"Why not?"

"Because—I'll just go out, OK?"

"He's on his way," she said, picking up the phone. "Lemme tell him."

I heard his keys in the door. "I'm ho-ome!" he shouted, like a mental Ward Cleaver. He strode in with a huge shit-eating grin, which I hoped was just metaphorical, given Liz's predilections.

"You look beautiful," he told me, planting a big one on my cheek.

"She's wearing base," my mother said.

He ran up to my mom and wrapped his arms around her waist from behind. "Shanah tovah, my precious," he said.

She spun around and gave him a funny look like she wasn't used to such attentiveness. He took a brown bag from under his arm and withdrew a bottle of red. "I thought we might be out," he said.

It was totally unthinkable: his affair was making him a better husband, not a worse one. He was acting like a more honorable family member than me.

He sidled up next to me, as I began setting the table, and said, "I mean you really look lovely. I don't know whether it's this new man in your life"—I flashed him a look to see if he was being sarcastic but he just smiled like our whole fight in the movie theater had never happened—"or what, but you really seem like you're glowing. You're so radiant, so alive." He stood behind me and massaged my shoulders. I flinched like Ted Danson's daughter in the Very First Prime-Time Movie on incest.

He retrieved a bottle opener from the top drawer and uncorked the wine ceremoniously. "I cannot tell you how happy I am at this moment," he said, pouring a glass and filling one for her and one for me. "To be here, on this perfect night, with the two most beautiful women in the world." They held their glasses in the air and sipped.

"That's really good," said my mom.

As I laid out the challah I spotted something very strange on the floor under the table. It was a big white box that said "iBook."

"What is this?" I said.

"Dad bought it the other day," my mom said, spinning around.

"You bought a *Mac?*" My father had been a PC guy since the days when PCs were the only computers that existed. He learned how to program on a computer the size of a wall. His favorite pastime was taking apart old Compaqs and putting the hard drives in new ones. At any given moment he had thirty half-dismantled computers strewn all over his office.

"I figured it was time to make the switch," he said. "I want to get into Web site designing and the graphics programs work so much better on Macs." He raised the box and ran his finger over the picture. "Isn't it gorgeous?"

"But you hate Macs!" I said. "When I told you I was using one in the computer lab at Wesleyan you didn't speak to me for a week."

"And *you* told *me* I was antiquated and stubborn, which I have now realized was completely true. Macs are the way of the future." Liz's influence was stronger than a million "Switch" commercials. One pussy hair could pull an entire ship.

Couldn't my mother see how unusual he was acting? A PC-to-Mac transfer was better proof of infidelity than lipstick on the collar.

"The food smells so delicious!" he pronounced, running up to her again. "Do you know who this woman is? This is the Ringling Brothers of Women. The greatest wife on earth!"

"Let me vomit," I said.

"Give your mother a little credit!" he said, frowning. "Look how hard she's working, slaving over this meal! You shouldn't take your mother for granted, especially on this of all nights! Wake up and smell the *tsimmes!*" He lifted two pot lids from the counter and clanged the two of them together like a dork.

My mom giggled and grabbed the lids from him. He put his mouth on her neck and gave her a big sloppy kiss.

I wanted to bolt for the door. I always thought if a guy cheated he'd be tormented by it, racked with guilt, but the strangest thing about my father's infidelity was that it was turning him into a generous person.

"Would you cut that out?" I said.

"Can't I show your mother a little affection? Come on, Rach. Get in the spirit of the holiday."

"She's not going to services," my mom announced triumphantly, as she set the brisket on a trivet in the center of the table.

"What do you mean you're not going?" my dad said, losing his faux chipper tone for the first time all night.

"I just don't see the point in going through the motions," I replied dully.

"Going through the motions?" he said, his voice rising. "You're going to abandon synagogue the same way you abandoned rabbinical school? Just like that?"

"Yep."

"This doesn't make any sense! I know you're doing some soul-searching but not to go to synagogue with your parents on the holiest night of the year?"

"Second holiest. Kol Nidre's the holiest."

"Why are you doing this? To hurt your mother?"

"*No!* I just—I can't go through with it. Nobody feels guilty for the bad things they've done." I gave him an even, steady gaze but he acted like he didn't know what I was talking about. "Nobody actually keeps any of their resolutions."

"That's not true," he said. "I vowed last year to control my temper better and I have. Right, Sue?" She nodded emphatically. Of course he was controlling his temper; he had nothing to be mad about anymore.

"Look, I'm not going to services and I'm never getting ordained. And the sooner you both realize that, the better it'll be for everyone."

They silently exchanged the kind of worried, fed-up glances they'd exchanged for most of my teenage years, and then my mother set some glasses on the table and my father kneaded his forehead self-pityingly. "Well," he said. "I just hope Mom can get a refund on the ticket."

After we sat down he tapped his glass with his fork and said, "I'd like to propose a toast." My mom raised her glass happily and I lifted mine too.

"To the two most beautiful women in the world," he said regally. "And a new year filled with love, happiness, and prosperity."

"That's a laugh," I snorted as they clinked. "We're totally poor."

"We're not poor," my mom said.

"Yes we are," I said. "Four months on one income is a long time."

"Three and a half," he said.

"Maybe you should just throw in the towel, Dad, and retire early. I mean what are the chances of a fifty-five-year-old getting a job out there in this economy? You're banging your head against a brick wall."

"I can't believe the way your daughter talks to me," he said.

"She's not my daughter," my mom said. "She's yours."

"That was really mean," I said.

"If you're not honoring your parents," my mom chimed in, "why should your parents honor you?" He put up his hand and the two of them jubilantly high-fived.

She asked him to serve the brisket and as he speared a few pieces onto her plate, he had a weird twinkle in his double-crossing eyes.

"So how was your interview today?" she asked.

"Very promising," he said.

"A computer job?" I asked.

"Nope," he said, lowering his head slightly.

"What, then?"

"Personal assistant," he said.

"For who?"

"Susan Sarandon."

"What? Why are you interviewing for a job like that?"

"Gosh ding it, Rach! You don't even ask the important questions! I waited for her under a Warhol. An original. I am telling you, this woman is as beautiful now as she was in *Atlantic City*. More. I had to hold myself back from jumping across the table." My mom rolled her eyes the way she always did when he made jokes about other women, but this time it didn't seem so funny to me.

"How'd you find out about this anyway?"

"She put a classified in *The Nation*. She felt it was important the person share her politics."

"What are the responsibilities?"

"I'm supposed to help her with scheduling, light grocery shopping, and some computer work."

"But you can't take orders."

"I could take orders from Susan Sarandon!" he said. He was going down the tubes in every department. Kissing Liz's ass on a nightly basis was enough to make him kiss the world's.

"Why would you want to do something like this?"

"Advancement."

"But you're middle-aged. By the time you're ready to advance you'll be dead."

"Try to be more charitable," my mom said. "There's nothing wrong with him keeping an open mind."

"You should listen to your mother," he said.

"Why are you acting so schizo, Dad?"

"What do you mean, schizo?" he Haskelled.

"You treat her like shit ninety-nine percent of the time and then you come in here acting all *Father Knows Best.*"

"He doesn't treat me like shit!" my mom said.

"You said he was being a total jerk about your menopause! You said he was making you feel lousy about it!" Her face turned red.

"You think I'm being a jerk about your menopause?" he asked, wounded.

"That's not what I meant—"

"It's OK," he said genteelly. "I know I have been less than pleasant to be around these last few months. But in the interest of making reparations on this holy night, inasmuch as that is possible, let me make a resolution." He took her hand. "I am going to work really hard not to be a lousy sonuvabitch in any way this year."

"And me too," she said. "I will try really hard to control my emotions, and accept that my Change can be a good thing." I eyed the challah, wondering whether I could fit the entire loaf into my mouth. He reached for her palm and kissed it. "Get a room," I muttered.

My mom yanked her hand out of his and grabbed my arm. "You know what?" she spat. "I wanted us all to be together tonight but if you're going to keep this up for the rest of dinner, I'd rather you just went home."

"*Fine!*" I yelled, hurling my napkin onto the table and running to the door. My life had sunk to a sad new low. I was the only child in the history of the Jewish people to get booted from Rosh Hashanah dinner with the fam.

Outside I started running. I ran and ran and ran toward Smith Street. I thought about Jeremiah as I raced and how he hated being a prophet, hated knowing what he'd known. But even he never had to hear his father ejaculating through a cheap door.

I kept running, trying to block it all out, but I was so out of shape that I had to stop after just a few blocks to rest. I put my hands on my knees, panting, right in front of the Serenity Hair Plus Salon, and as I did I saw something small and furry scamper right toward me. I yelped and jumped back. It stopped in the middle of the sidewalk, disoriented, then disappeared down into the subway grate. Just my luck. It was the year of the rat.

WHEN I got home I lay on the bed and thought about Powell. I felt certain that if he loved me everything else would fall into place. I had to try not to panic, not to assume it was over. He was finishing *Who Killed My Wife?* He didn't have time to spend with a psycho twentysomething bartender. He wasn't blowing me off. He was just a Very Important Person.

I went to the closet, took out my racerback dress, and smelled it. There was a faint whiff of Powell on it, masculine and musky. I threw myself on the bed, held it over my face, and sniffed in deeply. I didn't want to be lying alone in my bed thinking about him. I wanted him near me, whispering horrible things into my ear.

The phone rang. I jumped and raced. "Hello?"

"I was wondering if you could meet me at this party," he said. There was a loud ambulance noise and I couldn't hear anything he said. "Sorry about that," he said. "I'm at a pay phone."

"Don't you have a cell phone?"

"No."

"What do you do when you go to LA?"

"I try not to go to LA."

"Where's the party?"

"Julian Schnabel's."

"On Rosh Hashanah? Shouldn't he be at services?"

"He's not that kind of Jew."

"I can't believe this!" I said. "Who's going to be there?"

"A lotta people."

"Who?"

"I dunno. De Niro, maybe. Willem Dafoe."

"This is incredible," I said. "I used to be a rabbi and now I'm going to a party with Jesus!"

"If you're gonna be like this maybe I should ask someone else."

"Just give me the address."

When I hung up I jumped up and down into the air a couple times and then opened my closet. I had to look like I wasn't trying to be famous but I also had to look good. Powell was going to be walking me around on his arm and I had to come off as the kind of original, non-cookie-cutter eye candy that other men would approve of but at the same time respect. I put on a pink, yellow, and orange wraparound dress with split Oriental sleeves. It had a miraculous way of making my tits and ass look huge while keeping my waist slim. I put my hair in two low braids for originality and instead of lipstick I put on a little gloss.

On the train ride over I stared up at the ads feeling intoxicated and antsy. The new year might turn out all right after all. He had invited me to Manhattan—and not only that but to a celeb-packed party. He couldn't think I was a *total* whore.

Schnabel lived in a converted factory in the meatpacking district. There was a coat check in the entryway, tended to by two women way too good looking to be checking coats.

I climbed a set of concrete stairs and entered into a huge gaping space that was dimly lit, with paintings all over the walls and minimalist Renaissance décor. I felt a blinding flash of light on my face and then a photographer, an affable guy with greasy long hair, came up to me and said in a raspy voice, "I need to get your name."

"Rachel Block." He frowned and gave me a look as though wondering whether it should ring a bell. "I'm not a boldname," I said.

"Oh," he said, then walked away like I'd wasted his time.

I looked around the room and saw Laurie Anderson and Lou Reed making their way around with a little dog that everyone was pretending to be interested in as a way of not seeming interested in the two of them. I felt someone bump into me and when I turned around I saw Vince Vaughn and Jon Favreau coming in. Vince was getting fatter and Jon was getting skinnier. I wondered how their friendship was changing, if the power dynamic was the same as it had been at the beginning, how they felt about each other's successes and failures. "Sorry," Vince said. "Didn't mean to *bang* you there."

"Don't be an ass," Jon Favreau said, and they moved away.

I made my way into a side room and saw Jim Jarmusch lying on a chaise chatting with Harvey Keitel. "You gotta go there in the winter," Harvey was saying.

Trying to act casual and normal in the presence of two living monuments to cinematic greatness, I sat down on a couch opposite them, dipped some olive bread into some ambiguous-looking sauce, and took a bite. "Whaddaya think?" Jim asked in his deep baritone.

I almost choked. Jarmusch was the only filmmaker I respected as much as Powell and meeting him felt like meeting a president. "I-I'm not sure what it is," I said. "I don't even know if it's a vegetable."

"Me neither," he said. "And I don't eat anything when I don't know the food group." I giggled a bit overzealously and they looked at me with tired eyes. Everyone here was a star or an onlooker and there was no doubt as to which group I fell in.

"I like that dress," Harvey Keitel said to me. I felt like asking if he wanted to rip it off me.

"Thank you," I said. "It's used. I mean, it's vintage. But that's really just a nice word for used. It was one of those dresses that you try on and then instantly have to have, you know? I've had to stitch the side and the underarm like three times because the thread is so corroded and old but—"

"I see you've made yourself comfortable," Powell said, coming up next to me. I stood up and kissed him but he turned his face to the side and made it a cheek.

"You're here with this good-for-nothing prick?" Harvey said, standing up. Powell embraced him fondly and they held each other's shoulders like Mafiosi. It's not a good thing when your guy embraces another guy more warmly than you.

I waited for Powell to introduce me but he didn't so I said, "How do you guys know each other?"

"I almost cast him in my first short, *Death Comes Too Slow*," said Powell, "but I went with Ben Gazzara instead."

"And he's been regretting it ever since!" Keitel said, and they both burst into an exaggerated round of overmasculine laughter.

Jim Jarmusch hadn't said anything, he was just lying with his hand over his forehead like he was sunning on a beach. "Is that *Jimmy* hiding under there?" Powell said. Jarmusch removed his arm and nodded slowly. "How you doin', man?"

Jarmusch yawned and strode out, his carriage long and erect. I wondered whether they had a rivalry going, because Jarmusch was so much more famous when Powell came up and now Powell was more prolific.

"What's with him?" Powell asked Harvey. "Bad mood?"

"He's in preproduction on a Noh version of *The Bride of Frankenstein* and his backers want him to cast Britney Spears," Harvey said.

"Sleeping with the devil won't buy you a ticket out of hell," Powell said.

"You're a wise man," Harvey said, wagging his finger.

I cleared my throat and gave Powell an imploring look. Why wasn't he introducing me? I didn't look like a model but I was cute and smart and he had *asked* me here. I felt like cracked and stale arm candy. "Oh," Powell said. "Harvey, this is Rachel."

"You an actress?" Harvey said, shaking my hand.

"Bartender," I said. His eyes lingered on me for a second, as he seemed to weigh whether it was worth his time to ask a follow-up question, and he must have concluded it wasn't because he turned to Powell, said, "Great seeing you," clapped him on the back, and left.

"That wasn't very nice," I said.

"He's got a lot of people to say hi to." Powell's look was even and mean and it made me want to walk right down the concrete stairs.

"Are you OK?" I asked.

"Not really. I dropped Nora off at her mother's today and my ex-wife and I had a horrible fight. She wants me to take Nora for all of Christmas vacation so she can go to St. Vincent with her new boyfriend but I wanted to go visit friends in Rome. She's a toxic individual and impossible to tolerate."

"Why can't you split it up?"

"I don't want to *talk about this*."

I decided it was my job to cheer him up, to be as friendly and light as possible. "So where's Schnabel?" I asked brightly. He led me into the outer room and pointed to a corner where the painter was holding court with a swanlike woman of ambiguous ethnicity. He looked like a happy Buddha. "You see that? Whenever he throws a party he stands there in that exact corner, and he doesn't move." As I watched I saw that Powell was right. As guest after guest made their way over to say hi, Schnabel stayed rooted to his spot, not budging an inch. They all had to come to him. Maybe this was how famous people got famous—by making everyone come to them.

"You see?" Powell said. "It's a work of genius, pure psychological genius. I've been working ten years on getting him to move but so far no luck." He raised his hand in the air and said, *"Julian!"* Schnabel raised his glass like Powell was making a toast. "Happy New Year!" Schnabel smiled and nodded. Powell beckoned him over. Schnabel smiled again, pretended not to notice, and went back to talking to the woman. "You see?" Powell said, shaking his head. "The guy's unbeatable."

Powell spotted a short guy in a suit across the room and said, "I gotta talk to that guy. He owes me money." Then he ran off. I was beginning to feel like I should have stayed home. I went into a study off the main room and saw a small white cat making its way around the perimeter. It looked solitary but happy. An anorexic server came by with a plate of cucumber sandwiches and I grabbed one. As I was biting into it a throng of fame came in, flashbulbs going off wildly behind them: Harvey Weinstein, Chelsea Clinton, Nicole Kidman, Chloë Sevigny, and Robert De Niro.

"Could I get a shot?" I heard the photographer say. Before I knew quite what was happening they were ramming themselves in a line next to me, turning their heads to their good sides. He raised his camera, and I waited for the light, but instead of taking a shot he lowered it. "Could you move a little?" he said to me, waving his arm.

Harvey Weinstein, Chelsea Clinton, Nicole Kidman, Chloë Sevigny, and Robert De Niro all glared at me for holding them up and I skulked miserably out of the room.

I found Powell deep in conversation with Willem Dafoe. Dafoe was wearing a gauzy halfway unbuttoned shirt and he looked as beautifully ugly as ever. I went over and put my arm around Powell's neck protectively. "I'm Rachel Block," I said, shaking Dafoe's hand.

"I'm Willem," he said, as though it was necessary. He grinned through his messy teeth. I was certain his penis reached to his knee.

"Willem's been having some trouble with a female costar and I've been telling him she's just envious of his talent," Powell said, disentangling himself from me.

"Who's the actress?" I said.

They stared at me like I had asked a totally verboten question. "Can't say," Dafoe said, "but she's been taking cheap shots at me every day on the set so I've asked the king of women for advice."

"It seems obvious what you gotta do," Powell said. "There's something about you she can't tolerate and you have to confront her so she stops being angry for the wrong reasons. Twenty years ago I had this dream. I was working as a short-order cook, living in a walk-up in Astoria that overlooked an air shaft . . ."

Something strange happened as he continued. It became clear to me that Powell was more interested in having the floor than in communicating with any particular person. He was repeating what he'd told me on our date, word for word, with the same intonation, facial expression, and cadence, as though it was a pivotal monologue he was performing eight shows a week. The story mattered more to him than I did, or the reason he'd told it to me, and this enraged me because it made me feel irrelevant.

Before I knew quite what I was doing I jumped in with, "Yeah yeah yeah. Women are sin, men want sin. Men are soul, women want soul."

Powell glared as though he wanted to incinerate me. "Thanks a lot," he said.

"What?" Dafoe said, not understanding. "I didn't hear because you were talking at the same time. What was the dream?"

"It doesn't matter now," Powell said, with a wave of his hand. I had done the single worst thing you could do to an attention-hog narcissist: stolen his punch line.

"I'm sorry, Hank. I—I wasn't thinking."

"You never do," he spat.

Dafoe looked from Powell to me, swallowed like he didn't have the mental energy to be witness to a lovers' quarrel, said, "Is that John Waters over there?" and dashed away.

"I can't believe you!" Powell said. "Does someone *pay* you to ruin things?"

"No, I—I do it pro bono, actually," I said.

"I never should have invited you here."

"Maybe you shouldn't have," I said. The huge room felt tiny and airless. I was the lowest form of life on earth: a civilian. "I'm really sorry, Hank. I'm not usually in situations like this. I just got carried away. Plus I haven't really eaten because I got kicked out of Rosh Hashanah dinner with my parents for being a bitch. It hasn't been the greatest night."

He paused for a second, as though the jerk and the nice guy inside him were having a fight. I wasn't sure why, but the nice guy must have won because he put his hand on my shoulder, sighed, and said, "Let's get outta here."

We took a cab to Raoul's, on Prince Street, because Powell said he hadn't been there in a while. The restaurant was dim and romantic and everyone there looked like they'd lived a long time and suffered.

The hostess led us to a booth in the back. A waiter came over with a chalkboard that was all in French. Powell said he already knew what he wanted, the steak frites, and I said I'd get the same. I waited for him to order a bottle of wine but he said he just wanted a glass of Syrah so I said I'd have one too.

"I didn't mean to be rude at the party," Powell said wearily, as though even apologizing was exhausting. "It's been a rough day because of my ex-wife."

"That's OK," I said softly.

"So what happened with your parents?"

I told him about my ruined intervention, and the "Oh brother" moment, and how duplicitous and phony my dad been with my mom, and by the time I finished I was close to crying. "If I knew it was going to end soon it would be one thing," I said, "but it doesn't look like it. Liz is encouraging him to write the great American novel."

"It all makes sense," he said, fingering his chin.

"What does?"

"The affair is your father's attempt to resolve his anima problem."

"I thought it had to do with him being out of work."

"It's both! This girl, the flip-flop, represents your father's anima. She's the symbol of his untapped creative potential. She's the veiled figure in his dream. When she appeared to him in life he had to be with her, to work it out. And she's got a very masculine jaw, which only makes it easier for him to see himself as her."

"Why does he need her to work it out?"

"He thinks she's him. He's distraught, in need of validation. I was like this once with a woman."

"Who?"

"I'm not naming names. I met her at a party. I was watching her listen to a man and I could tell she was bored by what he was saying. I eyed her from across the room and two seconds later we were out on the street. The first words she spoke were, 'It's a pleasure to meet me.' She knew she was my projection. We were together for two years. We would walk around and she would see someone she knew and as they conversed I would feel that the person was talking to me. I felt I was she. Eventually she left me because she knew my love was all projection, and I realized I was only dating her because I thought she could solve a plot point in Act Two of *Roberto Bites His Tongue*."

"I never heard of that one," I said.

"That's because it never got made. Once we broke up I was thrown into a frenzy over a different plot point in Act Three, one that I'm still trying to solve. The point is, it's better to be alone than to date your own face."

"Aphorism Five?"

He nodded solemnly. "Your father will stay with this girl until he can integrate his own anima. When he realizes she just represents a part of him, he'll be able to move on." I was beginning to wonder whether all his aphorisms were just different ways of saying, "Women suck."

The waiter brought the wineglasses and said he'd come back for our order. Powell took a sip but no pleasure in the taste. "Listen," he said. "This might be the wrong time given your histrionic state but would it be all right if I read you something?"

"Sure," I said. "What?"

"I got a pitch meeting tomorrow," he said, taking some papers out of his bag, "and since I haven't done one in a long time I was hoping I could do a dry run."

"Definitely! Who's your meeting with?"

"Joe Roth. Revolution Studios."

I was a former rabbinical student but like every New Yorker I read the business pages of *The New York Times.* "That's amazing!" I said. "What's the movie about?"

"A guy who falls in love with his wife's sister," he said. It was an arena I might be able to assist with. He laid the papers out on the table. There were about ten of them but as I leaned over I saw that they were single-spaced. I prayed he wasn't going to read the whole thing.

"I'd like to read the whole thing to you," he said. "It might take a little while but it'll be good practice for me." Though I hadn't really thought about it before, Powell was at a crossroads in his career. He hadn't made a movie in three years and I realized that he might be struggling, flailing, just like I was.

"So did you pitch yourself for *Flash Flood?*" I asked.

"Of course."

"What was your 'take' on that?"

"Two hundred thousand dollars." He put on his glasses and began to read. "*The Brother-in-Law.* Act One. Nick Clay, our hero, is standing face to face in an ornate church with his beautiful bride-to-be, Alessandra."

"Is she Italian?"

"What?" He looked up from his pages, his glasses cockeyed on his nose.

"I thought names are symbolic. That's why Rose of Sharon is called Rose of Sharon in *The Grapes of Wrath*. She represents sexuality and life."

"I never subscribed to that particular school of dictatorship," he said. "To me it's arbitrary. I change half the names of my characters at the last minute. I like the name Alessandra because I was thinking about the limited amount of time I had to prepare this pitch and I pictured *sand* running through an hourglass. May I continue?"

"Sure," I said.

"The expression on Nick's face is not one of joy but of terror. In fact, he is not even looking at Alessandra—"

"Sorry," I said, raising my hand like I was in school. "But if they want to go in a mainstream direction with this maybe you should pick a name that's a little less ethnic. Hollywood's very self-hating. That's why Diane Lane got cast as a Jewish mother in—"

"Don't interrupt me," he said. He regarded me as though I was a special-ed McDonald's worker who had just screwed up his order.

"I thought you wanted feedback," I said.

"When did I say that? I never said the word 'feedback.' I said I wanted practice."

"OK," I said. "I'll be quiet." It was such a downer. I was on the verge of critiquing a living icon only to find out I had to stay Helen Keller.

He cleared his throat again. "In fact, he is not even looking at Alessandra. He is looking up at the statue of Jesus on the wall above the altar and his expression mirrors that of the pained savior. As he stammers his way through the vows, he looks up at Jesus' hands, bloody and nailed to the cross, and begins to weep. Alessandra mistakes his tears for tears of joy and embraces him as we pan up to the real Jesus, who now appears to be crying for real."

"Does it need to be that specific?" I said.

He put down the papers. "What?"

"I mean with the camera direction and all. Isn't a treatment just supposed to give a general idea of the scenes more so than a shot-by-shot—"

"You know what? Forget it," he said, shoving the papers back in the folder.

"No!" I said. "It's OK! I can keep listening."

"I don't think this is going to work."

"Come on! I really want to help you."

"I mean I don't want to see you anymore." My heart lurched to my throat and bounced up and down inside my mouth like a pink rubber ball.

"Is this all because I gave you unwanted feedback?"

"No. It's because of a lotta things. I feel put-upon in general right now and you only put upon me more."

"But I don't mean to."

"It doesn't matter what a person means to do. It's what he does. I saw it the second night we were together. You want things I can't give you. I feel no ill will toward you but I can't do this."

"You invited me out tonight!"

"And I shouldn't have," he said gravely. "As I was on the phone with you I saw a black cat crossing the street. I had the instinct to hang up on you then but I fought it and I always get in trouble when I fight my own instinct."

"I think you're making a big mistake," I said.

"I know you do but we want different things. I can't have a relationship."

"But I don't *want* a relationship!" I yelled.

"You do," he said. "You don't want a criminal. You want a bourgeois boy, a Jew your own age."

"I don't!" I said, fighting hard not to cry. "I'm not even going to synagogue tonight and it's the second-holiest of the year!"

"This isn't a debate. If we keep at this it will lead to more pain for you, and I don't want to cause anyone else pain. I need to conserve my energy." He was the Keyspan of breakups. Dumping me as an environmental act.

The waiter brought over our food and asked if I wanted ground pepper. I shook my head. Powell took out some twenties and laid them on the table, put his papers into his shoulder bag, and stood up. "I'm sorry to do this when things are so rough for you, but this is the right thing. I know it."

"What makes you so sure?"

"I've lived longer."

I nodded numbly and watched his back as he walked out. If only I'd just stayed home and gone to bed, or even to shul. At least then I wouldn't be single.

Suddenly the door opened. He was coming back, walking just as briskly as before, with a look of enormous purpose. He had changed his mind, realized what an ass he'd been, realized he not only loved me but wanted to be with me forever.

"I'm all turned around," he said.

I started to weep but I smiled through the tears and said, "I know you are."

"I don't know the right subway to take. How do I get home?"

My hope plummeted down to the floor of Raoul's like a Slinky and toddled out onto Prince Street. "Oh," I said. "Make a left on Sullivan till you get to Spring and then turn right till you get to the A. You can switch to the F at Jay."

"Thanks," he said. He turned again and disappeared out the door. I took a sip of his wine and stared at the place where he'd been.

W H E N I was thirteen I had to go to a junior youth-group party at a temple on the Upper West Side. I wasn't allowed to ride the subway myself so my dad said he'd take me, but I was going through an overly self-conscious phase and when he offered I said, "I don't want to show up with you! I don't want anyone to see me with you because you don't know how to dress."

He didn't say anything. He just got a face of pure rage and walked away from the table. My mother offered to take me instead, and wait around until the event was over. When we got home and my mother put the key in the door it turned back. I thought it was a ghost. She turned again and it turned back. She realized, before I did, what was happening. "Richard!" she said, pounding on the door. "Don't be ridiculous!"

"She's not coming in until she learns to stop being a spoiled brat!" he said.

"Come on," my mom said wearily. "It's late. Just let us in." Again she tried the lock and again he turned it back.

"I'm not kidding!" he shouted. "No one's coming in!" This went on for about five minutes and then my mom took me by the hand and walked me across the street to Nina and Larry's.

She explained to Nina what was going on, in hushed urgent tones, and then told me she'd come and get me. I sat at Nina's kitchen table and began to cry at the shame of it, at the shame of being child to someone insane. "It's so embarrassing," I said.

"All parents go a little crazy sometimes," she said, squeezing my hand, but I didn't believe her.

A little while later my mom came over and picked me up. She made a comment to Nina like it was a big joke when we all knew it wasn't, and then we walked over. The house was quiet and he wasn't in sight and when I went downstairs the bedroom door was closed. I went into my bedroom and lay down on the bed. My mom came in and I asked what he was so upset about. She said, "He was hurt by what you said about his clothes. You know how he gets."

"What should I do?" I said. "Does he want me to say I'm sorry?"

"I don't think he's in the mood right now," she said. "But if you wanted to write something down you could."

And so I wrote a long letter of apology about how spoiled and awful I was and how sorry I was for hurting him and how I'd never do it again. I slipped it under the door and in the morning he came in and said, "I overreacted," got all choked up, and walked out. We never spoke about it again and from time to time when I would remind my mother of the story she'd swear it never happened.

A s soon as I got home from Raoul's I went to the bookshelf and pulled out *Powell: Six Screenplays.* If I could just find one tiny piece of evidence in one of his movies that he and Rachel Block were meant to be together, then I could present it to him like evidence and he'd have no choice but to take me back. I knew I could make him happy. All I had to do was make him agree.

I opened to *Knock for Greenberg,* the one about the ailing landlord who got nursed back to health by his home health care worker. The climactic scene was the one right before Rosanna Arquette and Ron Silver made love for the first time.

GREENBERG
(waving Constanza away)
I can get into bed fine on my own. Go home to your husband.

CONSTANZA
I live with my mother. Lemme help you with that shirt.

He eyes her hungrily as she approaches. She opens his first button, then his second, and runs her finger over the scar from his heart surgery.

CONSTANZA
Does it hurt when I do this?

GREENBERG
(without irony)
I can barely feel it.

CONSTANZA
(massaging more intently)
What about now, Mr. Greenberg?

As Constanza strokes Greenberg's chest, he opens himself to the possibility of love. This feeling hits him like a lightning bolt and he reexperiences the pain of being alone for so long. He sobs hysterically, like a woman on the rag, but then locates the man in him. He seizes her and kisses her with enormous power and an erection that could tear the roof off a building.

CONSTANZA

I been waiting for this moment my whole life. You
got the biggest heart of all the guys I've known,
and trust me, I known a lotta guys. What I'm trying to say is, you kiss good, Mr. Greenberg.

GREENBERG

Call me Izzy.

I wiped the tears from my eyes. Powell was a romantic; I knew it
from his words. He didn't really want to cut me off. He'd just done
it because he was afraid. All he needed was for me to be tender, the
way Constanza had been to Izzy Greenberg, and then he'd soften up
and tell me what a huge mistake he'd made.

His phone rang three times and the machine picked up. "The
chill of fall is upon us, easing summer into the far reaches of our
memory, forcing us to look toward the inevitable onslaught of the
winter holidays with a mix of optimism and dread."

I cleared my throat. "Hank? You there?"

Nothing. He was probably screening but I'd already said his name
so he knew who I was; I couldn't just hang up. "I just—wanted to
say I'm sorry. I was definitely overcritical with you about the pitch.
It's my family. They're driving me crazy." I hated my tone, the need
in it. I should have practiced what I was going to say, written some
talking points.

"Anyway, I'm sorry you're having such a tough time with your ex-
wife. I just wanted you to know you can call me. I mean, we don't
have to stop being friends."

What was I saying? We were never friends. We'd had sex on the
first date. This was revisionist history, the kind that made a person
come off as completely deranged. I had to hang up before it got
worse. "So do you want to have coffee tomorrow? I was thinking I'd
go over around nine. Anyway, give me a call."

I hung up and hung my head. I was the dumb-dumb of dumb-
dumbs, the imbecile of imbeciles. I'd called to smooth everything
over and wound up asking him out. I didn't sound like a sweet

Puerto Rican nurse. I sounded like an insane neurotic Jew. Maybe right at this very moment he had another girl over, this mysterious Jennifer, and they were laughing their asses off at the deranged groupie filling up his digital tape. I shoved the book back on the shelf and pushed it as far back as I could so I wouldn't be tempted to open it again.

E v e r y morning for the next week or so I went past D'Amico, looked for Powell, and walked out when I didn't see him. I went back to drinking my coffee by the park even though it was turning colder and I had to sit outside at the table, holding my newspaper down with two gloved hands.

Liz's apartment that week was eerily quiet, even though the supermarket giveaways never returned. I told myself the silence meant they'd stopped, that Rosh Hashanah had miraculously given them a conscience, and the next day they'd ended it. Unfortunately, as with all pipe dreams, it was only a matter of time before the ugly truth came out.

One night on my way home with some takeout from my favorite restaurant, the Fountain Café on Atlantic, I saw Liz coming out of our building. She was wearing a black form-fitting blazer with high black boots and a miniskirt. I ducked around Boerum and waited till she crossed.

When she was halfway down Pacific, I followed, keeping my eyes on her round perfect ass like it was a compass. She walked down Pacific to Hoyt past the community garden, which in a lifetime growing up in Cobble Hill I had never seen open. At Atlantic Avenue she turned right toward the Williamsburg Savings Bank. As we kept walking the neighborhood started to get blacker; the antique shops and women's clothing stores, high-end furniture places and galleries started to shift into seedy bodegas and charity clothing shops.

We passed the strip of antique stores, the flower place with my absolute favorite name, Flowas, the chic women's clothing shop that sold overpriced T-shirts. Halfway between Nevins and Third she opened a door and disappeared. I ducked into an entryway so she wouldn't see me as she turned, then waited to see where she had gone.

It was a seedy bar I'd never gone to before, with a sign that said "Studio Tavern," which sounded to me like a compromise after an argument over the name. There were neon beer lights in the window, with Christmas lights around the perimeter. If I hadn't been so concerned about finding out whether he was in there I would have paused for a moment to appreciate the grungy beauty. I squatted down and duckwalked over to the window, my nose just barely above the ledge. There weren't many customers, just a few Hispanic men in their sixties sitting together by the window.

My dad was on a barstool, and his arms were wrapped around Liz's skinny waist. Her hands were tight around his neck and he was scooted forward so his groin was pressed right against hers. They were kissing, his mouth opening and closing rhythmically like Maggie Simpson sucking her pacifier. When Liz pulled away she put her thumb on his mouth to wipe off the lipstick.

He patted the stool next to her and she sat down and crossed her legs toward his. He grabbed the seat part of her stool and dragged it closer to him. I could hear the scraping noise of the chair all the way through the window like a horrifying broadcast of his love.

He gestured to the bartender, a stout Spanish woman, who smiled cordially and went to mix their drinks. She must have had May-Decembers come in here all the time, to escape their wives. It was a Hernando's Hideaway right in the middle of Boerum Hill.

Inside Liz was lighting a cigarette for my dad. The bar was so remote they could ignore the ban. "I thought you quit," I said. My dad's head spun around like Linda Blair's as I walked up and stubbed his cigarette out in the tray. It was one thing for her to be fucking him, another for her to be killing him.

His face turned so white the red spots of his razor burn stood out like zits. I really hoped he didn't keel over onto the floor. He had such high cholesterol he was on Lipitor. The last thing I needed was a dead adulterer on my hands.

He stared at me terrified, his mouth hanging slightly open like Neil Roth's, and said softly, "How?"

"She saw us in the park," Liz said.

"And you didn't tell me?" he said angrily.

"I didn't feel you needed to carry any more guilt around than you were already carrying."

The bartender brought their drinks and set them down. "Grey Goose grapefruit and an extra-dry Grey Goose martini," she said as Liz shelled out some dough.

"You're drinking Grey Goose?" I said. "And smoking? Are you in the cast of *Swingers?*"

"It's the smoothest vodka," he wailed. "And I only smoke when I drink." He sounded like some bimbiotic fuckslut who carried a pack of Parliament Ultra Lights in her party purse.

"*Why are you doing this?*" He didn't say anything for about a minute and then he started to sob—full, open-throated, and gobble-like, his head bobbing up and down.

He'd always had a problem with tears. When I was ten he took my best friend from Packer, Ruthie Levinson-Rudowsky, and me to see *Splash* at Cobble Hill Cinemas. At the end when Daryl Hannah leaves Tom Hanks to go back into the ocean where she really belongs I heard this quiet rhythmic noise right by me. "Is your dad crying?" Ruthie said, as I nodded mortified.

"I'm so sorry," he choked into his sleeve. "I hope someday you can forgive me."

"I don't want to forgive you. I want you to end it."

"I didn't want you to find out! That very first night I said to Elizabeth, 'Please do not tell Rachel.' I didn't want my problems to become yours." The snot was streaming down his face. When he had his beard it used to trickle into his mustache and harden there but now his shelf was gone. Liz grabbed a bev nap and passed it to him. "I know this must be rather unpleasant for you," he went on. "I can't think of many moments in my own life that have been more unpleasant for *me.*"

"Hey," said Liz, swatting him in the arm. I stifled a giggle. Blocks: One. Blockwreckers: Zip.

"I know you must be questioning a lot of things right now," he said. "You're probably thinking I'm a terrible husband."

"Check," I said.

"That I'm a bad father."

"Check!"

"And you're probably right. I'm not on the most stable ground right now or I wouldn't be doing something like this in the first place."

"Hey," Liz said. Maybe I didn't have to say a thing. Maybe my dad's big mouth would do the work for me.

"Not because of you," he said, putting his hands on her shoulders. "You're wonderful. You're beautiful." I'd never understood Catherine Zeta-Jones's appeal to Michael Douglas but now I saw their relationship in a new light. How could I sway him when all we shared was history? Liz was like Scientology in a slip. I wanted to believe my bond with him was stronger, but she had an ace in the hole in her hole.

She nuzzled his nose and said, *"You're* the wonderful one."

I made a vomit noise in my throat. "Bitch," Liz murmured over his shoulder.

"Do you really want to get into a 'Who's the bigger bitch' contest with me?" I said, "'cause I think we both know who would win." I had to admit I was shocked at how fearless I sounded. I had the kind of crazed adrenaline high that makes you run extra fast when you're being chased in the woods by a bear that smelled your period.

"I hate to be the bearer of bad news," I said, turning to face the Evil One, "but my dad's breaking up with you. He thinks you were a great lay while it lasted but now he's gotten a grip and reevaluated his priorities." I grabbed his arm and started to pull him out of the seat. Maybe the tough-love thing would work. Once he came back to our family, I could start a wilderness camp for parents who'd screwed their families over: Outward Scoundrel.

"Come on, Dad," I said. "It could be so easy. Think about it. You could pretend she's just a car wreck you were passing in the road. You've seen the devastation, the flattened near-dead corpse. Now it's time to keep driving."

"Rachel," my dad said. "Don't talk about Elizabeth that way."

"*Elizabeth?*" I spun around to her in shock. "Who are you— Sybil?"

"I don't get it," said Liz.

"You see, Dad?" I cried. "Mom would have gotten that. She didn't. You might think lack of generational connection is a small thing but it's not. This girl has never seen *Bonanza* and she doesn't think of Opie when she goes to a Ron Howard movie. Think how close you feel to Mom when she hums the theme to *The Dick Van Dyke Show*. You could never have those moments with Liz."

"We have other moments," she sniffed.

This wasn't working at all. If I couldn't turn him against her maybe I stood a chance of turning her against him. "He's just using you, Liz! Don't you get it? He doesn't respect you." She looked a little pale. Then again she might not have eaten since ten in the morning.

"Nice try," she said. "But I know Richard cares about me. Just because *your* relationship is all about sex doesn't mean ours is."

"What are you talking about?" I said. "My relationship isn't all about sex!"

"Then what *is* it about?"

"It's more . . . mentor-mentee."

"Oh yeah," said Liz sarcastically. "Right."

"You don't know anything about it!"

"She has a point," my dad chipped in. "I don't think you should be telling us what to do when you're involved with an older man yourself."

"It's not the same! He's not married!"

"But obviously you understand the appeal of a May-December affair," my dad said. "If you're going to take issue with me, I think you're going to have to look in your own backyard first."

"My backyard is spic-and-span!" I hollered. "You want to know why? Because he dumped me."

My father got a look of intense concern and put his arm around my shoulder. "Oh, honey," he said pityingly. "I'm so sorry. Why'd he do it?"

"He thinks we're incompatible!"

"How could he not see how special you are?" It was a pretty good question.

Then Liz's face softened too. She squeezed my hand and said, "You must be in a lot of pain."

I shook both of them off. "Look, this isn't about me and Hank anyway! It's about you and Mom. Don't you care about her at all?"

For the first time I saw a glimmer of chagrin on his face. "Rachel," he said, "what's going on between Mom and me is complicated. There's—there's stuff you don't know."

"Like what? You seemed pretty cozy on Rosh."

I looked at Liz for some sign of hurt but instead she said, "It doesn't bother me that they still sleep together. He cares deeply about both of us." It was my worst nightmare; my dad had laid two women in the space of one day.

"Dad, don't you have any taste? This girl is evil. 'Happy is the man who does not walk in the counsel of the wicked.' Psalm One, OK? That means it's the most basic one." They were gaping at me with white eyes but I didn't care. "She's a waste of airspace, which she must herself be aware of, since she does her damnedest to occupy as little of it as possible. She has major body issues, she's probably carrying more than one STD, and she's going to leave you for someone working-class. It's like a parade in her apartment, one after the other after the other!" I spun around to face her. "Didn't you tell me a couple months ago that you almost slept with the refrigerator man? Or was he the plumber? You're the cunt that ate Cobble Hill!"

It got very quiet in the bar. My cheeks were hot and the room was very small. "You're the cunt," Liz said.

"Stop using that word," he said to both of us. Then he turned to me and said, "You can be angry at me, but please try to temper your rage at your friend. I'm the one to blame here."

"Friend? Oh my God! I think she relinquished the *friend* privilege as soon as she let you in her apartment."

His eyebrows were meeting at the center of his forehead like Woody Allen's. He looked like a poor shmo who's just pulled his two buddies apart in a bar brawl. He took a sip of his martini, then set it down and said, "Elizabeth, do you think you could give the two of us a minute?"

"Why? So she can bad-mouth me behind my back?"

"Please? I'll make it up to you."

"Oh yeah?" she said, raising one eyebrow in such a mischievous way I felt sick to my stomach.

The back room had a pool table in it. All the tables were red Formica and my dad and I sat at one, out of view from the bar. A young Hispanic guy was shooting balls in a seemingly random order.

"Rach," my dad said, placing his hand on mine. "I feel so ashamed—"

"Then dump her," I said, yanking it away.

"It's not that easy. Look, I know this is wrong. I know that deceiving Mom is—but it's just that—" He put his head in his hand and kneaded his brow. "I'm struggling here. I'm suffering and I'm working on—fixing this—but I can't do it right away." He sighed slowly, like he had the weight of the world on his shoulders instead of the weight of an anorexic ho on his tip. "I'm floundering. But I won't be forever. So if you can keep quiet for a little while, I promise this will all work itself out."

"What do you mean 'work itself out'? Are you going to leave Mom for Liz?"

"I don't know. I'm trying to figure it out."

"Oh my God! What if she winds up my stepmother?"

"There's a lot about Liz that you don't know."

"Not really," I said. "She pretty much lays it all out there for the world to see."

"Please just give me a little time."

"How long are we talking?"

"A few weeks. I promise you it won't be like this forever." I stared at him morosely. "Come on, Rach. For me." I sighed and shook my head. "Thank you," he said, but I didn't feel very generous.

At the bar Liz was on her second Grey Goose grapefruit, and her cheeks were red. "How was the summit?" she said.

"None of your business," I said.

"That's a really sophisticated comeback, Racheleh," she said. "I'm awed by the power of your discourse."

"I'm awed by the power of your discharge."

"Girls," my dad said. I stared at her angular profile, that jaw jutting forward like a Neanderthal's, the fake mole next to her lip. I wanted to reach inside and yank the ink out with my fingernails.

I headed for the door and my dad said, "I'm going to walk Rachel home. I'll be right back, OK?"

"I don't want to be near you," I said.

"Come on, Rach," he said, coming over. "I want to make sure you're OK."

"I'm not OK!" I yelled. "So just leave me alone!"

He hung his head and said, "Just a little while longer, all right?" I wasn't sure I believed him but I nodded like I did and pushed the door open against the wind.

I MADE it to my apartment building but when I got there I found myself propelled toward Court. I went down a couple blocks, hung a right on Kane, and stood in front of the Kane Street Synagogue, the oldest one in all of Brooklyn. Every time I passed I got a warm feeling even though it was Conservative and not Reform and I'd only been there once, for the funeral of an elementary school friend's mother. Reform Jews feel about as comfortable in Conservative temples as black people do in Vermont.

I went up the stairs and into the lobby and pushed open the double doors to the sanctuary. A comforting musty smell, more New England than Cobble Hill, rushed into my nostrils as I raised my head to take it all in. The ceiling was breathtakingly high and there were narrow stained-glass windows in all the walls. I went up the aisle and took a pew about halfway in. I sat quietly for a while and stared up at the Ark, the pulpit, the Eternal Light.

I hadn't been inside a synagogue since services at school the week I dropped out, but I figured maybe it was time God and I had a talk. Pleading with my dad hadn't worked so maybe I had to go one level higher. Maybe this whole affair had happened not because my dad went crazy but because God was trying to punish me for dropping out of school. He was sending me a message by ruining my life: I had done the wrong thing by leaving.

But if that was true then God was even dumber and more misguided than I'd thought. Dropping out of rabbinical school was the single best thing I had ever done for the Jews. I had spared thousands of sick and dying people from early expiration. With me at a pulpit generations of young people would grow up morally bereft. Doubting religious school students would drop out before they even had their bar and bat mitzvahs. Synagogue membership would plummet and the national affiliation rate would sink even lower than it already was. If God was making my dad shtup Liz as some sort of cosmic symbol to me to return to the rabbinate, then the best thing I could do was ignore Him.

Maybe He wasn't punishing me so much as trying to get my attention. He was feeling jilted after he'd heard the things I said to Neil Roth, the way I was feeling jilted by Powell, and He needed to know I still cared. Keeping my fingers over my eyes, I davened. As I moved I said in a quiet voice, "God, I'm really sorry I've been so down on you lately. A number of factors transpired to cause this but let me be clear. I'm not angry with you. You don't cause these horrible things. I know that you are weeping with me as I am witnessing the *complete wreck my father is making of his life.*"

"Despite the fact that the last few weeks have been the worst of my life, I should have counted my blessings more often and in general acted with a spirit of thankfulness. Thank you for providing me with a job even though it's as a barmaid. Thank you for letting my family and me survive September eleventh. Though I don't often stop to think about it, I am lucky. I could be some Iraqi child with no parents living on a steady diet of sewage water and gravel but instead I work in a bar in a neighborhood with an affluent clientele and I live in a fine although cramped one-bedroom apartment."

I started to feel a little better, like maybe I'd laid the groundwork. God was like anyone else; you had to pump Him up before you asked for His help. "But I need some things from you, God, and I think it's important you not forsake me. I beg you: Please make my dad stop fucking Liz, please make my dad stop fucking Liz, please make my dad stop fucking Liz." After I said it a few times I decided it might be a bad idea to swear, even if I wasn't using God's name in vain. So I did something the Jews are very good at: modified. "Please make him see that this is not the way. Please make him come back to my mother. Make him get his sanity back. If you do that I will be a better daughter to my mom, I will never again make friends with evil vixens like Liz, and I will look into the roots of my masochistic problem, go into therapy, and find a nice Jewish boy to marry."

I kept davening for a while without saying anything. I tried to feel the presence of God in the room, and I thought about my mom and how much I loved her, and how happy we'd all once been. Then I said the Shehecheyanu, the prayer for special occasions, because I figured it was a special occasion that I had stepped inside a shul, and opened my eyes. I started to go but as I turned I noticed something funny by the Ark. The Eternal Light had gone out.

At first I thought I should just leave it but as a quasi-rabbi I felt it was my duty to right something so patently wrong. I went up onto the bimah and stood under the light. They were all electric nowadays; just a bulb in some fancy Magen David casing, plugged into the wall. I followed the trail of the wire to an extension cord in the back, but it was plugged in. I took it out, plugged it in again. Somewhere during my prayers God had decided to take five. He couldn't be counted on. My people were masters of implausible miracles but even I couldn't fix a bummy cord. I got off the bimah and hurried down the aisle.

THE next night at work, I found myself checking out my clientele. It's an embarrassing thing when you find yourself scoping your own customers. It's like stealing a homeless guy's change.

A thin guy by the door had been sitting there for an hour, drinking Guinnesses. He had a shaved head and he kept running out of the bar every ten minutes to smoke hand-rolled American Spirits, which I could smell on him from twenty feet away. But his eyes were sweet, with long, delicate lashes.

I was remoting "Pale Blue Eyes" onto the jukebox for the third time that night when he leaned in and said, "That's some thousand-yard stare. Are you OK?"

"I'm fine," I said. "Another Guinness?"

He nodded and I loaded one up. As I set it before him he said, "So what's the matter?" I wasn't sure I wanted to open this door but I had four and a half more hours on my shift.

"Have you ever loved someone who didn't want to be with you?" His eyes turned black and filled with doom. "You know what?" I said, backing up. "Forget I said anything."

"No," he said. "As a matter of fact I have some expertise in this area. My wife and I were together for twelve years and then I found out she'd been cheating on me."

Twelve years? How old was this guy anyway? I'd had him pegged for early thirties but he had to be late, which made it even more pathetic that he was sitting in a bar alone. "How'd you find out?"

"We were going through this rough patch where we never had sex and never spoke to each other. I knew something was wrong but I thought it was just one of those distant phases that's part of a marriage. We were doing Dr. Phil's *Relationship Rescue Workbook* at the time, this self-analysis thing to go with his seven-step strategy." He must have seen the look on my face because he added, "He's actually really good on male-female stuff. Anyway, you're supposed to record a lot of different things you're going through and for weeks she left her workbook right out on the kitchen table, open. Every day I walked past it and didn't look—"

A fat black guy from the projects named Blimp came in and raised his head to order. I moved to his stool. I always felt bad when I had to cut people off in the middle of their stories but I was working; they couldn't expect me to just drop everything.

"How you doing, Blimp?"

"Crazy. Last night my girlfriend and I were fighting and this picture of the two of us fell off the wall." He made a heebie-jeebies face. "I think it's a sign."

"A sign of what?"

"I gotta cut the bitch loose." Guinness nodded encouragingly even though they'd just met.

"What are you having?"

"A Henny and a Heiny," Blimp said. All the PJ guys ordered this, a shot of Hennessey and a Heineken. I always got excited when someone ordered one because the shots were expensive, eight dollars, which meant better tips.

When I came back to Guinness his eyes were needy and wild like he was going to die if he didn't finish the story. "So anyway, she used to leave her workbook out all the time and one day I was feeling so alone that I looked. Under the part where you had to list your regrets she had written, 'I regret my affairs.' Plural."

"Jesus," I said. Every time I started thinking my situation was worse than anyone else's I found out I was wrong. "What did you do?"

"I locked myself in the closet, curled into a fetal position and cried for three hours." I wondered what therapists did between seeing patients, how they refrained from shooting themselves in the brain. "When she came home I told her I'd read it. I said, *'Affairs? Affairs?'* She said it was only one affair, she'd written 'affairs' because she wanted to make me angry, but later in the conversation she broke down and said it was two. She had one about seven years into the marriage, and another one that had ended a year before."

"So did you kick her out?"

"I didn't have to. She slept on the couch that night and packed the next day."

His gaunt cheeks seemed to sink even deeper. He tossed down the rest of his beer and started rolling another cigarette. "I'm Buddhist," he said, "and they say it's really bad to hold on to any kind of baggage, so I try not to be angry, but it's hard."

Every man I met was dying over some terrible woman. I had always assumed men were the original sadists but maybe it was the other way around. Maybe I was a man inside and that was the reason I could never put any man under the bridge. "Do you wish you'd never married her?" I asked.

"No," he said, like he was offended by the question. "We had a lot of good years. But I wish I wasn't thirty-eight and single. The chances of me ever falling in love again are very slim."

"Don't be so pessimistic," I said.

"I know what I'm talking about," he said. "I do databases for big corporations. Did you know that if you stand outside any Seven-Eleven in the country from eight o'clock on a Friday night till eight o'clock on Sunday night, there's a seventy percent chance that a male customer in his twenties will come out with a bag of Pampers and a six-pack of Bud?"

"Could you excuse me?" I said, and went to the phone. I turned my back and dialed my machine. This was the fourth time I had done it this shift. The phone rang, rang again, and rang a third time, which meant no Powell. In the mirror I could see Guinness watching me from the bar. If I hung up quickly he'd know I had no messages so I put on a fake listening face, pressed a few buttons on the phone, listened for about thirty seconds, and hung up.

"So who's the guy who doesn't want to be with you?" he said.

Immediately I regretted opening my trap. "I probably shouldn't have brought it up."

"Any guy who doesn't see how wonderful you are is an idiot."

"But you don't even know me," I said.

"I'm very intuitive." Jasper was sitting a few seats down in his usual spot and he raised his eyebrows like I needed his protection.

"Thanks for the advice," I said, moving away to check on Blimp. He'd burned through his drinks already. "One more?" He nodded.

"That guy bothering you?" he said. "'Cause I'll whup him."

"No, that's really OK."

When I finished with Blimp Guinness beckoned me over. I moved, reluctantly. "Do you want to get dinner with me sometime?" Guinness said. "It wouldn't be a date, it's just—you seem like a really bright girl."

"That's nice of you," I said, my standard line, "but no."

"If you're pining over some jerk who doesn't love you, I just—wish you wouldn't."

"I'm really sorry I opened my mouth about it."

"It's just that the way the light's falling on your hair, and your top lip, the way it hangs over your . . ." He trailed off and hung his head.

"Leave her alone, man," Jasper said.

"It's cool, man," he said, waving him off. "I'm just chilling. I'm all right." They always got macho when they got called on their act.

I checked on the other customers, refilled a few beers. Guinness left me alone for the rest of the shift but he stayed, which was a sign. By Last Call the only customers left were Jasper, Guinness, and a hipster couple that had started sucking face on the chairs by the pool table. I had to give the guy credit for one thing: longevity. He was skinny and pathetic but I felt like maybe if I hooked up with him it would help me forget.

I went over and told the couple I was closing. They walked out, glued to each other. Jasper helped me carry beer up from the basement for the cooler, and liquor that needed to be restocked. On the way up he said in a low voice, "You need a walk home?"

"No, I'm all right," I said.

"Are you going to go home with him?"

"Why is everybody in this goddamn bar so nosy?"

"Suit yourself," he said, "But remember, he knows where you work."

He was right. I had to think this through a little. I wiped down the bar and took down the trash. Then I locked the door, and cashed out. Jasper gave me a look of warning and left. I locked the door behind him and when I turned around Guinness was grinning like he'd just won a lottery.

He smoked a cigarette on the way over and when we got to my building he leaned in and went for it. His breath reeked of nicotine and I missed Powell's clean adult smell. "You're so beautiful," Guinness said.

"What's your name?" I said.

"Tony." It could have been worse. He could have been a Rick, or a Gary. "What's yours?"

"Rachel." This was terrific. Now he could call it when he came to the bar.

"I really want to be with you," he said, kissing me again. "I just want to be with you tonight." And despite the fact that he had used the word "be," despite the fact that I had a suspicion this was a big mistake, I turned the key and took him up.

We went right to the bed and Tony ground around on top of me, with our clothes on. "You're so beautiful," he moaned. "You're soooo beautiful." They were the right words from the wrong mouth.

I undid his belt buckle and took his dick in my hand. It was small and slender like a musician's finger. I pumped it for a while, got up, and said, "I'll be right back." I went into the bathroom and brought out a LifeStyle from under my sink, left over from David.

"Good brand," Tony said when I handed it to him. It meant something that he didn't have a problem with condoms, made me think Powell's aversion was totally unfair. He rolled it on and I took off some clothes. He put his finger in me but I wasn't very wet so he started squiggling down my body.

"What are you doing?" I said.

"Can I taste her?"

I had never been with a guy who felt the need to use the third person to describe it. I wanted to call Powell and tell him so we could laugh about it, but the whole reason this guy was here was because I couldn't call Powell at all.

"No, that's really OK," I said, looping my fingers under his armpits.

"But I want to," he said. "I want to make her happy. Please?"

"She's in kind of a weird mood right now," I said, lifting him up and kissing him firmly on the mouth. We rolled around a little more and then I tried to angle it in. It didn't go easily so I had to hold my legs out with my hands. When he was finally in he said "Ahhhh!" with such jubilation it made me nervous.

He moved in and out of me for what felt like a very long while— probably because of all the Guinnesses. If I ever slept with another customer I'd have to cut him off sooner. "Is this OK for you?" he finally said.

"Great!" I said.

"'Cause you don't seem that into it," he said, "and a woman's pleasure is very important to me." It was funny the way some guys felt the need to announce this, like it was a special citation on their résumé instead of just the norm.

"Don't worry about me," I said. "Just think about yourself." I could fuck a stranger but I couldn't come with one. It was illogical but irrefutable.

He gave it a few more strokes, then stopped and said, "I think I drank too much. And I'm kind of nervous. I find you very intimidating."

I nodded sadly. He pulled out and said, "You sure you don't want me to kiss her a little?"

"Yeah," I said.

He didn't say anything for a while and then he pulled the condom off slowly. Then he went out to the fire escape and smoked a cigarette.

When he came back to bed he said, "I'm really sorry."

"So am I," I said.

He gave the kind of pitying look that meant he was disappointed too. I was probably the first bartender in the history of female bartending this had ever happened to. We were supposed to be easy happy-go-lucky sluts but I couldn't even get my one-night stand to come. He gave me a halfhearted kiss on the mouth and we turned back-to-back, facing different walls.

DIFFICULT WOMEN

I N the morning, after Guinness left, I took a shower and tried to scrub the smell of him off. Then I changed the sheets. There is nothing worse than bad substifuck sex; it makes you feel worse than you did before. I didn't want a barfly; I wanted Powell, even with his insanity, his coldness, his narcissism. He knew what to do to me, how to rev me up, and he was never, ever boring. Maybe the key with Powell was to come on as strong as he did. He needed to know I wasn't scared of him, that I could be a big-enough woman for the man in him.

It was a chilly Sunday and the streets were crowded with yuppie couples that were way too attractive for anyone's good. They wore rugged autumn colors and toted babies that wore more fashionable outfits than any I could ever hope to own.

I ate breakfast in the park and afterward I found myself meandering over to Strong. When I got to Powell's window I looked up at it. There was this great scene in *Difficult Women* where Lola (Lena Olin), a Latvian cocktail waitress in Brighton Beach, was trying to win back the heart of Shmuel (Michael Imperioli), the small-time Russian Jewish Mafioso who frequented her bar. He had broken up with her because some thugs were after him for money and he didn't want her to get mixed up in his problems. She cried for a week straight but then one night she had a vision of her dead grandmother Rushka saying, "Tell Shmuel you love him."

She snapped into action, ran to his apartment, made a pulley out of stockings, and airlifted a bottle of Chivas up to his bedroom window. Shmuel was sitting at his desk composing a suicide note be-

cause he knew he couldn't come up with the money, when he saw
the bottle swaying in the wind outside. Right then it started to snow.
He opened the window to find a tray with two glasses filled with ice
and the Chivas, looked down, and saw her standing in the street,
holding the stocking pulley.

"Lola!" he cried.

"What is it, Shmuel?"

"I was gonna kill myself but now it's all different!"

"Whaddayou mean, Shmuel?"

"I thought death was the answer but really it's love!"

"Of course it is," Lola called in an accent that sounded more
Swedish than Latvian. "You've always been dumb."

He started crying with joy, suddenly recognizing the value in life,
grabbed the bottle and glasses, and clambered down his fire escape
onto the snow-glistening street. He ran up to her and kissed her all
over and she wept beautiful tears that mixed with the snowflakes.
Then she said, "It's happy hour," and they sat on a hood of a car and
drank to their future.

I wondered what Powell would do if I airlifted him a bottle of
Chivas. If I somehow managed to get a pulley rigged up to the roof,
I'd probably smash his neighbor's window in and wind up getting
arrested. Plus it was a mistake to be that derivative; he might consider it plagiarist. I had to come up with a variant, a shining declara-
tion of my love, like Lola's for Shmuel, that nonetheless took into
account the Powell of Powell and the me of me.

I walked back to Court Street and down to Winn Discount. I
roamed through the aisles, among the tools and screws and nails,
the garden hoes and hoses, until I finally saw what I needed: a big
spool of white clothesline rope. I kept meandering through the
aisles and found a pile of bandannas, so I bought one for ninety-nine
cents.

D'Amico was closed so I went to Starbucks and ordered a large
cappuccino with a travel lid and stuck it into one of those four-cup
Styrofoam trays with a couple sugar packets since I couldn't remember how he took it. As I walked briskly back toward his house
I put the clothesline in the second cup, and the bandanna in the

third. When I got to Strong I stopped on the stoop next to his and
took out a piece of paper from my bag.

> Dear Powell—
> Want to have a cup of morning coffee, or are you all tied up?
>   —Block

That sucked. I crumpled it up and tried again.

> Dear Mr. Powell—
> Can I rope you in for morning coffee?
>   —Lola

That was worse. Something was missing and not just in the note. I
looked down at my chest, and within twenty seconds I had wriggled
out of my bra, a Wacoal minimizer. I stuck it in the tray, next to the
cappuccino, the rope, and the bandanna, and tried the note again.

> Dear Mr. Powell—
> Now that I know your cup size I felt it was time you knew
> mine.
>   Love,
>   Your Cock Tail Waitress

I folded the note into a square, nestled it next to the bra, and
opened the door to Powell's building. I set my tray of love on the
foyer floor like an offering and pressed the buzzer. "Who is it?" I
heard him say.

I ran outside in search of a place to wait. Some kid had drawn a
pink hopscotch board in chalk right in front of the stoop and I lay
down on it, my head between the one and two. I crossed my hands
over my chest like I was dead and closed my eyes. After a few minutes the door creaked open and slammed shut. I flinched and felt
my blood coursing through me. A pair of feet jogged down the stairs
and then stopped right by my head.

I could feel the cold pavement against my back. Through my eyelids I saw something block the sunlight. I felt a hand on my neck and prayed it was Powell's; you're asking for trouble when you lie down braless on a sidewalk. I kept my eyes closed and gasped from the thrill. "I don't take sugar," he grunted, as the two paper packets ricocheted off of my boobs like bullets of love.

I opened my eyes and smiled openly as though he had just given me a piece of beautiful jewelry. He put his hand under my head and pried it up like I was in a war hospital with an amputated arm and he was feeding me brandy from a bottle. I felt the cool cotton of the bandanna over my mouth as he tied it behind my head. He grabbed me by the arm and raised me roughly to my feet. "Whr w gng?" I said through the gag.

"Don't talk."

He steered me up the stairs and through the door. We walked down the hallway and he opened the door to the basement. I had a momentary flash of him cutting me into a million pieces. As we started down the stairs I noticed there wasn't a banister or a light. He gripped my arm tightly as we went down, then steered me around a corner. A few bikes were chained to the pillars and barbeques and old exercise equipment were scattered around the room.

We came to an open door and he nudged me in ahead of him. I heard a loud humming and felt a sudden rush of dust. I sneezed into the gag and wiped my nose with the back of my hand. "Gesundheit," he said.

There was some rustling behind me and then the light came on and I was face-to-face with a boiler. It was huge and terrifying and reminded me of a locomotive. Powell came around and looked at me like I was an exhibit in a museum he wasn't sure he liked. Then he smoothed my hair. I was reminded of the game where you put your hands on someone else's and then they try to slap you when you don't expect it.

"Take off your shirt," he said.

"What if your landlord finds us?" I said.

"This is a co-op!"

I turned my back, lifted my shirt, and deposited it delicately on the filthy floor. He came around with the rope and gazed at me

calmly, like a surgeon about to begin a complex operation. He tied
both my wrists with some sort of fancy sailor's knot and maneuvered the rope up over a pipe, then pulled until I rose onto my toes.
He lifted me just enough that my heels were hovering off the floor,
the balls of my feet still touching down. Then he tied the rope to the
pipe and threw the spool to the floor. It bounced a few times on the
concrete below and he walked out of the room.

"Whr y gng?" I called lamely. I heard his feet disappear up the
stairs. A minute went by and then another. I began to worry that
he'd never come back, that this would be my punishment for messing with a maniac.

On Sunday mornings when I was little, my dad would take me on
the back of his bike to the Lower East Side and we'd shop for cheese
and coffee for my mom. Before we went back he'd always stop in
the Chinatown branch of the library to check out books. Inevitably
when we got there it would be right before closing, and as he went
through the aisles grabbing books they'd suddenly start shutting off
the lights. "The library is closing in fifteen minutes!" a male guard
would call out in a sonorous voice, a jarring violation of the whisper
code.

"Dad!" I'd cry. "We're going to get locked in."

"I just need a few more things," he'd say. "Why don't you pick out
some books for yourself?" Reluctantly I'd wander the aisles, as more
and more lights went out in huge sections at a time, until I was
standing totally in the dark. Finally I'd find him in the mystery books
section and tug on his shirt, telling him to hurry. "I'm almost there,"
he'd say.

I'd start to sweat because something about libraries always made
me have to shit, but I wouldn't ask to go because I was too afraid I'd
get locked in the bathroom. More lights would go off, and the room
would feel airless and bleak.

"Dad!" I'd cry. "I'm scared. They're going to lock us in!"

"I promise they won't," he'd say.

"The library is now closed," the voice would call, and even then
he'd take more books before finally making his way to the checkout
counter, forcing them all to wait till he got what he wanted.

Out on the street I would cry at the stress of it all, and he would say, "It's all right, we didn't get locked in, everything's fine," but still I'd clutch his back the whole ride home.

I hung from the rope, feeling my calves getting more tired, trembling from the strain. What had I been thinking coming over with rope? It was like walking into a bar brawl and then handing one of the guys a gun.

I heard footsteps on the stairs and Powell came through the door, a folding chair in one hand and the Sunday *New York Times* in the other. He sat in the chair a few inches from where I hung, crossed his legs woman-style, and opened up SundayStyles. He flipped forward to the weddings section and held it up for me to see. "You see this?" he said, "This is porn for single women."

He pointed to a photo of a shifty-eyed frat type and his generic-looking bride. "He's gonna cheat," he said.

"He doesn't love her," he said of an Asian couple.

"Something's funny about him. She's marrying for money. These two'll last because they're Indian. This guy hates her guts. This one's a *pooftah*. She's already pregnant but he doesn't know."

As I hung there wobbling on my feet, my calves losing all sensitivity, the feeling beginning to leave my ankles, my wrists raw and weak, he went through every single photo and gave his prognosis. Then he read for a while, calmly, going through Real Estate, optimistically crowing about the property values in the neighborhood; Arts and Leisure, mocking a profile of a young ingénue he didn't find intelligent; working himself into a frenzy over a "manipulative and thoroughly false" Banana Republic ad spread in the magazine showing a woman, man, and baby happily sleeping in bed.

"Hnk!" I cried. "Pls tk m down!"

"You have no stamina." He was right. It took courage to be a masochist, way more courage than it took to be a rabbi. You had to have the focus and the will. I wanted desperately to be good at suffering but I was too much of a coward.

"I cnt fl m ft!"

He sighed, shook his head, stood up, and put both hands on my breasts. He ran his fingers over the nipples. I closed my eyes, trying to get into it but afraid I was going to pass out from the exhaustion.

He knelt down on the floor, unbuttoned my corduroy Levis, and eased them off. He pulled down my underpants—black bikini Jockey for Hers, laundry panties I only wore when I hadn't done a wash in a while—and set them on the floor with no comment. Then he knelt, placed one hand squarely on each of my buttocks, and arranged my legs on either side of his head.

Slowly he rose and as he supported my ass with his hands, he began to eat me with the sound of a man who has not had a meal in many months. His technique was all right but I was struck with a wave of performance anxiety. Sometimes when I'm with a guy I feel like a painter with a disobedient model. Every time I get a decent stroke the goddamn girl moves and I have to put down my brush, walk across the room and reposition her, then struggle to get back into my groove. It would not be good if this didn't go anywhere. You come all the way down into a boiler room to be illicit, you expect it to lead to an O.

He moved his mouth around like a wild animal devouring its prey and I grimaced and jerked my pelvis back. He raised his head like a bull, his eyes red and angry, and said, "You have a problem accepting pleasure."

He raised the hood with his hand, like he'd taken a course, and did a series of magical tongue flicks. I wondered if he was spelling out his best lines. There was something so commanding and nonchalant about the way he maneuvered, so proprietary and matter-of-fact, that after a while I let him take over. I went limp and threw my head back. As he lapped he eased in a finger and I started to tighten and sweat. There was an advantage to being with a guy who had sampled from the cooze buffet. He knew just what to do. This was why young women liked older men. It had nothing to do with status or money. It was much, much simpler.

I moaned and he grunted, a cunnilingus call and response, and then he moved his finger in a particular way and I came, my body warm and electric, my thighs quivering, my throat forming the hollow bleat of a dying lamb.

He lowered my feet to the floor and wiped his mouth with the back of his hand. He untied the knots so I was standing again, and untied the rope. I undid the bandanna, bolted toward him, and kissed him, trying hard not to cry.

Instead of kissing back he fumbled with his own pants and pushed me down onto the floor. He flailed around demonically, his hand reaching up every few seconds to claw at my breast or down to grab at my ass. I tried not to think about the fact that I had had sex with somebody else less than twenty-four hours before.

I wrapped my legs tightly around his waist, clenching my insides like a socket wrench, and after another twenty minutes he was out and I felt a puddle on my stomach. "We're going to have to find another contraceptive," I said.

"I know," he said, rising to his feet and brushing off his pant knees.

I sat up and looked at him. "Do you want to maybe go to brunch?"

He gazed down at me with an expression of utter contempt. "You're outta ya goddamn mind."

"Why?" I said, sitting up. "It's such a nice day. I thought we could go to Banania."

"If the wedding pages are porn for single women, then Sunday brunch is the money shot."

"They have free muffins," I tried, but he had already stormed out the door.

I stood up and grabbed a piece of the paper, and as I wiped the come off my stomach I saw that my wrists were red and raw. There was no blood but there were two big marks, and when I touched them they stung. This was a totally different level than stubble scab; I'd have to wear long sleeves at work or my customers would start to ask questions.

Upstairs the front door was propped open. Powell was sitting on the stoop, watching a young mother with a baby carriage pass. The only indication of our sex was the hopscotch board, which was smudged from where I had lain in it. The three looked like an eight. "Hank," I said, sitting down next to him. "I'm sorry I asked you to brunch. I didn't mean to offend you."

"Yeah, well don't do it again," he said.

We sat in silence and I said, "So did you like my gift? Did you like my little note?"

"Yeah, but stop asking. You gotta learn to quiet your mind. Every Jew I know is like you. You do the whole world's math homework in your head. What's the latest with ya pop?"

"I told him I knew and he says he needs a little time."

"Uh oh."

"What do you mean 'uh oh'?"

"It means the jury is out."

"I don't want to talk about him! I'm glad you came down," I said, taking his hand. "I really thought I'd lost you."

"I was gonna call you anyway."

"You were?"

"The pitch went well. I sold the film."

"That's amazing!"

"Not really," he said. "Now I gotta write it." Powell could find a way to complain about anything.

"I missed you so much," I said, lowering myself one step and resting my head on his knee. "I'd like to come here every day with a different present for you."

"Easy now," he said, but he didn't move his knee.

"I'd like to live underneath your desk," I said. "I'd like you to tie me up and leave me in your place and then go run some errands, maybe buy yourself a free-range chicken. If I lived with you, you wouldn't leave the house. You could order Chinese all the time, and I'd sit under the desk and blow you whenever you needed it. A maid could come once a week to clean. You could bring your friends over and watch them fuck me."

"I'm thinking of moving to Bologna," he said dreamily.

"What?" I said, coming up a step.

"Have you seen the asses in Italy? Things heat up a lot faster there."

His face was totally placid as though he was talking to a male friend and not a female. What was it about me that screamed *don't take her seriously?*

"Why would you say that at a time like this?" I wailed.

He jerked his head back, surprised, like I was getting offended without due cause. "I thought you liked the truth."

"I do, but not a reckless and obnoxious truth! I don't understand how you can be so mean! It's a beautiful day and I'm sitting here telling you I'd like to live under your desk, and you say you want to leave the country. That's just . . . malicious."

"You get too worked up over nothing."

"I don't want you to talk to me like I'm a guy," I said. "I want you to be sweet to me."

"You know what?" he said, standing up. "I got a lotta stuff to do."

"Don't just leave!" I said. "Let's talk about this."

"Why can't you let things be easy?"

"You're the one who can't be easy. You're the one who got in a bad mood all of a sudden. Sometimes you act so premenstrual."

"I did not *get* in a bad mood. You *pushed* me." He spun around and marched up the stairs. "Enjoy the day," he said, and gave me a mock salute.

I sat there for about fifteen minutes trying to think Zen. I kept seeing his behavior as a problem I could solve. If I reacted the right way then he wouldn't be a jerk. If I was easy and quiet and didn't ever challenge him then we could build a perfect life together.

I started to get up to go when I saw a middle-aged woman coming down the street, holding a small child's hand. Nora's. Judging by the woman's light hair and resemblance to Nora I realized this was Powell's ex-wife. As she got closer I saw that she was not at all Catherine Zeta-Jones–esque. Her hair was pulled back in two barrettes and she was wearing a tan coat that, though fitted, did not look particularly expensive. She wasn't as young as I had imagined either, she seemed to be in her early forties, and she definitely didn't look like someone who would throw heavy appliances.

When Nora saw me on the stoop she stopped and said coolly, "Hi, Rachel." I was impressed at her retention; she hadn't exhibited any the first time we'd met.

"Hi, Nora," I said. I extended my hand to the ex-wife. "I'm a friend of Hank's," I said.

"Oh," said his ex, with a penetrating yet not particularly hostile look. "I'm Annie."

He had made her out to be the most evil woman in the world and yet her name was Annie. How evil could an Annie be? A Diana, maybe, a Katerina, but an *Annie?*

"Are you going up?" she asked, gesturing toward the house with a look of slight trepidation.

"No, I was on my way out." Nora was wheeling a little Pokemon suitcase and she hoisted it up the stairs one at a time, grunting with each step. "She's good at that," I said. "She could be a stewardess."

"Yeah, well, that's always been my dream for her," Annie said, deadpan. She even had a sense of humor. It was hard to picture the two of them together. She didn't look like the kind of woman that would tolerate long-term insanity.

I wanted to ask her whether everything Powell had told me was a lie—whether she was the litigious bitch he made her out to be, whether he'd cheated first or she had, what it was like being married to a misanthrope, whether she had any advice about what to do when he said things like "I'm thinking of moving to Bologna." But if she really had any idea how to live with Powell they wouldn't be divorced in the first place.

"Come on, Nora," she said, nudging her up the stairs. "Daddy's waiting. Say good-bye to Rachel."

"Bye, Rachel." Annie nodded at me politely and said it was a pleasure to meet me. Nora rang the buzzer and when I heard Powell's voice over the intercom I jogged down the steps.

A T two in the morning on my next shift Powell came in. It had been a long night, a busy one, and I was exhausted and not looking very good. Bartenders get less attractive as the evening goes on, especially if they're too busy to dash into the bathroom and reapply lipstick. He walked right up to the bar where I was mixing a gimlet and said, "I'd like to grind you into a salami and eat you between two pieces of ciabatta."

"Are you drunk?" I said.

"No," he said, "just feeling romantic. Could I get a Chivas, water on the side, no ice?"

I served the gimlet to a Jewish girl with obvious Japanese hair straightening who was on a date with a dumb-looking hammerhead. Then I fixed Powell's drink. He took out his wallet but I shook him off.

"That was something else the other day," he said. "You read me right and gave me just what I needed."

"So why did you storm off?"

"I didn't storm," he said. "I had work to do."

"Why don't you just admit you were a jerk?"

He narrowed his eyes and appraised me. I was afraid he was going to yell at me again but instead he said, "You've changed. I could feel it the other day as I strung you up but I was afraid of it because it was unexpected." He searched my face as though there was something new and beautiful in it.

"Oh yeah?" I said skeptically. "What's different?"

"I'm not sure. You got a lotta fire. Fire I haven't seen before. And I *like* it." He nodded like he had just examined me with a stethoscope and heard the precise irregular heartbeat he had expected to. "You're filling up and coming into your own. Your voice is coming outta a different place in your body."

"Yes, it is," I said from my diaphragm.

"There's a hysteria that's gone, I can hear it in your timbre. You look different too. Your cheeks are red and your eyes aren't so frenzied. You're like a 1950s Italian movie star."

"You mean that psycho hooker from *Nights of Cabiria?*"

"I've never seen this power in you, this ease of being." I tilted my chin up and tried to arrange my jaw in a position of great strength. "Maybe this is all because of your family strife. You've been forced to show grace under fire. The same thing happened to me when my father died. I let go of all my anger and woke up each morning feeling alive to the world, renewed. I had a spring in my step. Everyone kept asking if I was in love."

"So you really think I'm different?" I said. Maybe he'd been testing me to see if I'd call him on his behavior and now that I had he'd finally seen that I was the ball-busting bitch he wanted all along.

"I do! It's *wondaful!*" he cried. "You're just aware! You see what's coming and you're ready for it. Seeing the truth has made you grow up." There was a fascination in his face, an openness that I hadn't seen since our first date. I knew it was dangerous to buy into the totally invented fantasy of a half-cocked maniac but if this meant he wanted to see more of me then I was happy to agree.

"It definitely has," I said.

"Listen," he said. "What time do you get off?"

Things couldn't get any better. He'd fucked me in his boiler room, he'd said I had changed, and now he wanted to come over. It was almost like a Real Relationship.

I had another hour on my shift but there were only seven customers so I cupped my hand around my mouth and bellowed *"Last call!"* There were a few groans but I didn't care. Hank Powell was worth closing early for.

When we got to the building I put the key in the lock but he didn't follow me up the stairs. "So you want to come inside?" I said.

"That doesn't interest me." Maybe I'd gotten too jubilant too soon.

"I thought you wanted to come home with me."

"I meant I'd walk you. I gotta get up early in the morning. I got a meeting."

"But you've known me like a month. Don't you think it's about time you saw it?"

"Soon as you see a woman's place there's problems. I once dated a woman who never let me come over. I would ask and ask but she wouldn't give in. After six months, she finally relented. Big mistake. She lived in a walk-up on West Forty-seventh and it was a sty. There were takeout containers, dozens of garbage bags filled with trash, magazines from the 1980s, exercise equipment that had been discontinued. She stood in the midst of this inferno, began to cry, and said, 'I hope you can love me anyway.' I said, 'Not a chance!' and ran out."

"But I'm not a slob."

"This is the way I want it."

There was a noise on the stairs, the front door opened and my dad came out. He flinched when he saw me but then he noticed

Powell and his expression changed to one of great interest. "Hank," I said wearily. "This is my father, Richard Block."

"I was wondering why she was hiding you from me," Powell said genially. They shook hands like old college buddies.

"I've heard so much about you," my dad said. If it wasn't three in the morning on the stoop of his mistress's building it could have been Sunday-morning brunch at Banania.

"I can honestly say the same," Powell said.

My dad's eyes flickered nervously. "It's OK," I said. "He's aware of your doggitude."

"Although I'd never use that term," Powell said. "Rachel told me you're going through some interesting and fruitful transitions."

"That I am," my dad said, like he'd been handed a compliment. This was all I needed: for Powell to romanticize my father's infidelity.

"What are you doing here so late?" I asked. "Isn't Mom going to—"

"She thinks I'm at Boat, drinking."

"At three in the morning?"

"She said she sleeps better when I'm not in the bed. She's been having insomnia because of her meno."

Powell nodded grimly like my mom had it coming if she told him not to sleep in her bed. I didn't like the idea that Powell was com- miserating. My dad was supposed to be struggling, processing, but instead he was currying sympathy.

"I must say, Hank," my dad said, turning to Powell, "when Rachel said she was dating a fifty-one-year-old, I was a little nervous, but you could pass for early forties easy!"

"I'm not fifty-one," Powell said, scowling. "I'm forty-eight."

"But I IMDB'd you," I said. "And it said you were born in—"

"Don't believe everything you read!"

"Well, you look younger than forty-eight too," my dad said quickly. "I'd put you at forty, tops!" He always did this, came on to my paramours like he was trying to seduce them himself. "I hope this doesn't sound obsequious, but I thought *The History of the Pencil* was the best off-Broadway play of the season."

"Dad! You walked out!"

"What?" Powell exploded.

"We left at intermission, but only because of my wife. I loved it but she took issue with the language. I can never get her to stay for the second act of Mamet either."

"Women never like my work," Powell muttered.

"I thought it was insightful and provocative, the first act anyway. As a meditation on the tenuous hold the artist has on his own mind it was rivaled only by Ed Harris's *Pollock.*"

"If only you wrote for the *Times*." Ben Brantley's review of *The History of the Pencil* had begun, "There comes a time in every great artist's career when he makes a misstep so grave it makes you question all his prior achievements."

"But I don't really mind bad reviews," Powell said, resting his hand against the gate behind him. "It just fires me up more. *Ow.*"

"You OK?" my dad asked.

"Yeah. It's just tennis elbow. My doctor gave me an anti-inflammatory but all it's doing is making me excitable."

"I play tennis too," my dad said. A truck made its way around the corner and as it rattled on its wheels I had a sudden desire to throw myself beneath it.

"Where do you play?" my dad said.

"New York Sports," Powell said, pointing to the bubble down the block.

"Those courts are terrible," my dad said. "So over priced, and there's no backcourt! You gotta play at the courts down by the water. You register with the parks department for a hundred dollars a year."

"Ya kidding. I've never been down there. I'd love to play you some time." This was *My Two Dads* but gayer. "Can I give you my number?"

"Sure," my dad said, whipping out his cell phone and punching it in.

"Which way you walking?" Powell said. My dad pointed toward Court.

"You weren't on your way in?"

"No, I just walked Rachel home from work. I live on Strong. I'll walk you."

He wouldn't come upstairs but he was willing to walk my dad

home. They should have just fucked each other up the ass right there on Pacific Street. It would have created some new problems but it definitely would have solved some of the old ones.

I watched them head off side by side. "So I got this theory about your anima issue," Powell said, gesticulating effeminately.

"What's anima?" my dad said. I waited till they were halfway down the block but neither one turned to say good-bye.

T H E next night I called my mom and said I wanted to see her. She said she was folk dancing at Families First if I wanted to stop by. My mom had started folk dancing when she was a teenager at a left-wing summer camp but it was only in the past few years that she'd gotten back into it. It started as just a once-a-week thing but lately she'd been doing it the whole year round, all over the city. She often invited me to come with her but the thought of being alone in a room filled with aging hippies seemed as appealing to me as a Brazilian with the honey wax, not the gourmet.

But I figured she needed me now. I wanted to be kinder to my mom. It was something I had tried to do, longed to do, but been unable to do, since as long as I had an independent mind, and yet now it felt natural and right.

I walked over to Families First on Baltic and found the dancers all in a community room. There were about twenty of them, their arms around each other in a circle, and they were doing this fast elaborate kicking thing that looked more Scottish than Jewish. They were a different strain of geek than the Koffee Klatschers, older and more overtly nearsighted. The women looked like spin-offs of my mom, with loose skirts, and glasses, and the men were effeminate and graying.

My mom was shouting out "Slow, fast fast" and "Step, touch, touch" and "And now back to the first figure." Everyone was grinning wildly, like they were having the time of their lives. When the song ended they went over to this table where grape leaves, hummus, and baba were laid out. My mom was standing at the CD player trying to figure out what to put on next and when I came up to her she looked surprised I'd actually made it.

"Hi," she said. "To what do I owe this visit?"

"I just wanted to see you. I'm sorry I was such a jerk on Rosh Hashanah."

"What was with you that night? You were horrible."

"I—I was just in a really bad mood."

A tall, big-nosed guy in a red bandanna meandered up, pretending to be interested in the veggie dip. "Is this woman related to you, Sue?"

"She's my daughter," my mom said, and put on a fake smile. One-on-one we didn't work but when there was an audience we were a dream combination.

"She looks just like you," he said. He shook my hand and said, "I'm Yitz." He was cute but I couldn't exactly see him slapping my ass on a nightly basis.

"We're going to be doing 'Leftes' next," my mom called out to the group, "so gather in a circle." The music started up—Greek and frighteningly fast.

"There's no watching here," said Yitz, taking my hand.

"I don't have my mother's dance skills," I said. "I'm really bad."

"There's no bad here," he said. I rolled my eyes and before I knew exactly what was happening he had whisked me into the circle to learn.

I thought I could get the hang of it but when the music started it was way too fast, with a lot of skipping and hopping. Every time I thought I had a foot in the right place it would turn out to be the wrong one and I'd crash into Yitz. To make matters worse, my mom kept calling out, "No, Rach! *Left* foot, not *right!*" and everyone stared at me like it was cute that her dancing genes had skipped a generation.

At the end of the song everyone clapped and hooted, unstuck their peasant blouses and Mostly Mozart T-shirts from their sweaty chests, and wiped their brows.

"You weren't that bad," Yitz said. "You've got a great natural sense of rhythm." He placed a warm clammy hand on my arm.

A young woman with a black bob I hadn't noticed before was coming toward the table. She was in a suede skirt and 1940s high heels and by the hipness of her look I was convinced she'd wandered in by accident. But she barreled past me toward my mom and said, "Sue?"

"What is it?" my mom said. The girl murmured something into her ear in a low, hushed tone. My mom threw her arm around her and ushered her into a corner.

The woman started crying and my mom got her some Kleenex and gave her a deep, strong hug. I'd never seen her hug anyone that way, not even my dad. "Rebecca and her husband are separating," Yitz said quietly, "and she hasn't been coming to dance that often."

"Oh," I said. I had never thought of my mom as the nurturing type before but maybe she just hadn't gotten enough opportunity, since I never needed much care.

"Your mom's really amazing," he said. "Rebecca was just saying the other day she didn't think she'd be able to get through it if it weren't for her."

My mother was nodding and I heard her say something about men being like trolley cars. She seemed totally comfortable, like a television mom, Meredith Baxter-Birney. Rebecca blew her nose into a Kleenex, nodded and smiled, and made her way back to the table. It was illogical, unfair, and misguided but I couldn't help feeling like if my mom paid less attention to all these random losers and a little more attention to the one she lived with, he wouldn't have gotten together with Liz in the first place.

Before someone else could accost Florence Nightingale, I went over. "Who was that?"

"A friend."

"What was she talking to you about?"

"That's not really any of your business."

"Is it really your responsibility to be helping some random girl out with her personal problems?"

"When someone needs me, sure."

"I don't know," I said, sulking. "Sometimes it seems like you've forgotten you have a family."

"You're the one who seems to have forgotten she has a family," she spat. "I've never seen you act as ugly as you did on Rosh Hashanah. And you're always in a bad mood when I call. Every time

I ask you a question you make me feel like I'm prying even though you tell Dad things all the time. You make me feel like you wish I'd just crawl into a hole and leave you alone."

"You don't understand."

"What don't I understand?"

This was my opportunity, to spell it all out so she'd see why I'd been a bitch on Rosh Hashanah, why it was driving me crazy that she was never home. But the last time I had offered honesty someone had wound up dead. As much as I wanted to be exonerated I wasn't ready to spill my father's beans. I loved my mom and wanted her to know the truth, but it wasn't my choice to make.

"Forget it," I said.

She glared at me for a second like I had once again proven I was an awful daughter, and then she went to the CD player to start the next song. It was slow and moving, "Erev Ba," the easy one they always leave till the end. The dancers formed in a circle, chatting, hands around each other's shoulders, glad to have a break in the calisthenics. She went over and broke apart two hands to join.

She had a new life, one that didn't involve him, and it wasn't fair of me to try to yank her out of it when he was the real betrayer. I watched them go around in circles for a while and every time my mom's face came around she was smiling.

T H E next night at work I was off balance and short with all my customers. I knew things had gotten off to a bad start when Jasper informed me that Tony had stopped in the other night when I wasn't there. Thinking he was looking for me, Jasper told him I was off, and Tony said, "No, man, I came in because I knew she wasn't working. That was a big mistake the other night. The girl has some major issues with men." By twelve-thirty, I had a decent crowd, a dozen local middle-aged Italian guys shooting pool, a few scattered white hipster girls flirting eagerly with the PJ boys to show how liberated they were, and a couple single guys in their forties with moist lips and sad eyes.

I played a steady stream of Bob followed by some Costello and Bacharach and had just gotten enough of a break to wash some glasses when a bunch of preppy post-tennis assholes walked in with perfectly tousled hair and collared shirts, already buzzed. They all ordered Guinnesses except one—a hotshot black Irish guy with a good build. "I'll have a Cape Cod," he said.

I fixed it for him and when I plopped it down I couldn't help myself. "Just FYI," I said, as all his friends turned to listen. "In the future you might want to refer to it as a vodka cranberry. Nobody really calls them Cape Cods."

His friends burst out laughing, covering their mouths in the way men do when they know a woman's crossed a line. "Thanks," he said tightly. "How much for the round?"

"Twenty-one," I said. He gave me a twenty and a five. I laid down four singles. He took three.

Just as I was about to complain, Powell and my father dashed in the door and barreled up to the other side of the bar. "Rachel, Rachel!" my dad cried. "Your boyfriend is the toughest guy in the entire *world!*"

"Oh stop it," said Powell, swatting him on the arm. "It was nothing."

"It wasn't nothing!" my dad cried. Neither one seemed to feel the slightest need to explain what they were doing together. I wasn't sure which upset me more: that they were hanging out without my permission, or that they had just upped the median age of my clientele from twenty-three to forty-five.

"We were getting out of the taxi on Court," my dad said, "and it was dark because it was raining. Hank said he had to go to the bathroom really badly and I said he should wait because we were only a few blocks from the bar but he said he couldn't because—"

"Where were you coming from?"

"The theater! So Hank says to me, 'I gotta go. I'm gonna lose it if I don't go,' and I say, 'To tell you the truth I gotta go too,' so Hank turns against the Barnes & Noble. I said, 'You're comfortable whizzing on the wall of a superstore?' and he says, 'Last time I checked they didn't carry my books.'" Powell let out a low, satisfied chuckle.

"We're standing there letting it go when outta nowhere this black guy comes up behind us and says, 'I got a gun. Give me all your money.' Well, in two seconds flat my wallet's outta my pocket and in his hand, but instead of giving in, this Irish Schwarzenegger here, this Westie, grabs the guy by the collar, lifts him ten feet off the ground, and throws him into the gutter. No. *Hurls* him."

"It wasn't a hurl," Powell said. "It was more of a toss."

"So the guy's moaning and groaning," my dad continued, "and he didn't really have a gun, he was just using his finger, because he lies there looking like the sorriest piece of garbage you ever saw. As though Hank hasn't humiliated the poor guy enough, he kicks him in the stomach and says, *'Never jump a guy when he's urinating. It lacks class.'*"

He turned to Powell with a huge worshipful grin. Powell shrugged and said, "I used to be in gangs."

"You're lucky he didn't have a weapon," I said. "You could have been killed."

"I have good instincts," Powell said.

"You think he's OK?" I asked.

"He was moaning when we left," Powell said. "I'm sure he'll be mugging again in no time."

"So what show did you see?" I asked, trying to sound more casual than I felt.

"Take Me Out."

"You guys went to a gay play?"

"Don't pigeonhole," Powell said. "It's more about baseball and the American dream."

"It's about a gay baseball player!"

"It's the best new drama of the year!" my dad cried.

"Why didn't you ask *me?*"

"Because you were working, obv."

"'Obv?'" I cried. "Since when have you been saying 'obv'? Did you pick that up from Liz?"

"Obv," he said. "Rach, you have got to see this play. It is the most stunning work of new American theater I've seen since *K3.*" Powell cleared his throat. "Except for *The History of the Pencil,* but that goes without saying. Hank didn't like it as much as I did. He thought

it was a little talky but I said, 'What does that matter when it's got all that frontal nudity?'" I'd never seen my father act like such a queen. Maybe his late-life anima problem was about something else entirely. "I'll tell you one thing. It definitely gave credence to the stereotype about black male anatomy."

"They should have renamed it *Shvartzer Shvantzes*," Powell said. "They woulda sold a lot more tickets!"

"*Shvartzer Shvantzes!*" my dad roared. "I *love* it!"

I didn't understand how Powell could be such a jerk to me and so sweet to my dad. It seemed like he was doing this to hurt me. What if he'd realized he had more in common with my father than me, and decided to trade me in?

"Hey, what kind of a bar is this?" my dad called out. "Aren't you gonna ask what we want to drink?"

"Extra-dry Grey Goose martini and a Chivas and water," I said.

My dad turned to Powell, nodding slowly, like the man had once again proven he was the king of cool. "On second thought," my dad said. "I'll have a Chivas too." It was pathetic. He was stealing everything about Powell, even his drink.

I made them both, skimping on my dad's. "So did you have dinner too, or just the theater?" I asked as I set them down.

"We went to Joe Allen," Powell said. "That was our hangout joint when we were rehearsing *Pencil.* I know all the waiters."

"Al Pacino was at the next table," my dad said. "His hair is blond now and he looks much younger than his years."

"So what did you guys talk about at dinner?" I said, slitting my eyes at Powell.

"A lot of things," my dad said.

"Oh my God," I said to Powell. "Did you tell him to leave my mom?"

"Hey," my dad said. "Abandonment's a two-lane highway."

"You did!" I shouted. "You're trying your aphorisms out on him!"

"Rachel knows about the aphorisms?" my dad asked jealously, like he felt possessive over Powell's friendship when they'd only just met.

"Everybody knows about them! He spews them to whoever will

listen!" Powell glared and took a long pull of his Chivas but I was so bent on keeping my father away I didn't care about offending him. "You know what? I don't want the two of you spending any more time together. My dad needs good influences right now, not bad."

"Don't tell ya fatha what to do."

"He's right, Rach," my dad said. "I have to figure it out myself."

"What is there to figure out? I thought it was just a matter of time before you ended it."

"I never said that." I felt like he'd totally duped me at Studio Tavern, made me think he was struggling when all he was really doing was having his cake. Powell was only going to drive him further from my mom. He was like a reverse conflict mediator; instead of bringing people together he drove them apart.

"We didn't only talk about Mom," my dad said. "Hank told me about his life as the swordsman of independent film. Did you know he almost got together with Julia Roberts?"

"What?" I said.

"Julia and I were very close once," Powell said.

"I thought you'd told her," my dad said. "I'm sorry. Maybe this is inapprop—"

"No, I'd really like to know," I said. "Please. Tell me about the time you almost got together with Julia Roberts."

He hesitated and shook his head like he knew he was playing with fire but the chance to be the center of attention was too much for him. "Well," he said, laying his hands on the bar, "when we were shooting *Leon and Ruth* she was living in Hell's Kitchen with an undependable malingerer named Fritz, a performance artist who lived off her acting work and supported them both by shoplifting groceries. One morning she shows up to set with a duffel bag on her back, her hair matted, her eye makeup running down her face. She had a revelation about the guy, walked out on him, and spent the night sleeping on a park bench. I was living in a basement apartment in the East Village at the time and told her she could stay with me."

"Of course you did," I said.

"It was a truly innocent gesture. I saw nothing in her. She was an untouchable, sterile beauty, well constructed but sexless, like a

neutered Persian. There was no heat in my place and every night because it was so cold we would sleep naked, hugging each other for
warmth. One night during the last week of shooting she came to
bed in a pair a my pajamas. Right then I knew there would be trouble. I said, 'What's going on here?' and she says, 'I can't help it,
Hank. I'm falling in love. It's always been you. When I kiss Don I
close my eyes and pretend he's you.'"

"I don't understand," I said. "How could she pretend Don Cheadle was you?"

"She was very Method. I said, 'Julia, you do nothing for me.' She
said, 'How can you say that?' and ripped open her pajamas. Her nipples were brown and small and greeted me like two buttons sewed
on the head of a sock monkey. But I'm the kind a guy that just can't
do it if my heart's not in it. And I knew it would be good for the
movie if I rejected her. The three days of shooting we had left were
the ones after she finds out Leon's died in Vietnam and I needed her
raw as a freshly fucked cooze. So I said 'Get outta here,' and made
her sleep on the living room couch."

"The willpower!" my dad said.

"It worked like a charm. Every night after that she came in my room
begging but I refused. On set she was magic. When she's about to
jump out of her window, and says to God, 'Just answer me one question. When your man's away at war, what's the point of getting up in
the morning?' the tears were so real they froze on her face."

My dad was smiling openly with such unbridled awe I wouldn't
have been surprised if he'd leaned over to kiss him on the mouth.
"Julia Roberts," he said. "Can you believe it, Rach? He's the only man
in the world that passed up a night with Julia Roberts."

"I severely doubt that," I said.

My dad gave me one of those paternal, knowing looks that always
made me seethe. "You see this, Hank?" he said. "She can't even bear
the thought of you *almost* sleeping with Julia Roberts. This girl is
crazy about you." Powell looked like he had just made diarrhea in
his pants. I didn't know which upset me more—that he looked so
uncomfortable at the idea of me being crazy about him or that he
was making no attempt to hide it in front of my father.

They wound up staying another half hour and then my dad begged off, saying he had to get home to my mom or she'd ask questions. As soon as he stood up Powell did too, saying he had to work on *The Brother-in-Law.* I gave him a pleading look as he left but his face was hard and devoid of emotion. He'd said I had changed but it was beginning to seem like he hadn't.

A C O U P L E nights later Powell invited me to dinner at Sam's. I was supposed to work but because he was asking me out, and on street level—a plane that was elevated from the one we'd met on before, I felt it was a mark of progress. I called up Caitlin and asked if she'd switch and since it was a Saturday, a good night, she said OK.

Despite my good mood at dinner Powell spent most of the meal complaining—about how insane Annie was, how much trouble he was having with *The Brother-in-Law,* how anxious he was about money. I sat there nodding and agreeing, backing him up, figuring that was what he needed right now—to vent. At the end of the meal he leaned in close and said, "You're a good friend to me, Rachel."

"What's that supposed to mean?"

"Don't get up in arms," he said. "You're a good lay too. I just mean you do me a lotta favors. I don't know many people in this neighborhood and it's good to have someone I can talk to." It was the closest he had ever come to saying he cared and I was flattered he'd opened up, even a little.

After dinner I walked him to Kane and to my surprise instead of turning to his street he said, "I was thinking maybe I could come over."

"Do you mean walk me home or do you mean come over?"

"I mean come over," he said.

"I thought you didn't like to see a woman's place."

"I figure you wouldn't have asked me so many times if I had something to worry about." I giggled and threw my arms around him. "Watch it," he said, "or I'll change my mind."

———◆———

W H E N we got up to my place I made him wait in the hallway while I cleaned. As fast as I could I set about getting rid of every single element in my apartment that I deemed to be in the slightest way adolescent. This meant removing the Crosby, Stills and Nash album cover above my computer, and the still of Bob Dylan in *Don't Look Back,* and the *New York Times Magazine* photo of Sean Penn next to my bed. The last thing a middle-aged guy needed to see when he was fucking me was a picture of a 1980s teen idol.

I went to the door and threw it open, following Powell as he made his way in. "I dig your digs," he said. "They're minimalist but well utilized." He spotted something on the bookshelf across the room. "You have *The Stoop Sitter?*"

"You could tell from here?" I said.

"I know the binding," he said. He took it out and flipped open to the title page, which had a price of $1.00 scrawled in the upper right-hand corner. "Where'd you get this?"

"The Strand," I said.

"You bought me *used?*"

"No other bookstore even had it in stock."

His face hardened like he was going to lash out but instead he ran his hand over the cover, which was a really bad painting of a guy, from the waist down, in tight jeans, sitting on the steps of a decrepit brownstone. "I'll sign it," he said.

I grabbed a pen from my desk but he'd already whipped one out of his shirt pocket. He scrawled something down and handed me the book. I flipped to the title page.

> Love is romance without makeup.
> —Hank Powell

He was trying to communicate something deep and important. Maybe this was his way of saying he really cared—that he wasn't putting a pretty spin on his affection because it was so real. "What does it mean that you wrote that in my book?" I asked huskily.

"I write that in everyone's," he said.

He was hopeless beyond belief. But he was here. I went to the

stereo and inspected my vinyl before finally settling on Bread's
Baby I'm-A Want You. "You like David Gates?" he said as the music
came on.

"I think he's highly underrated as a lyricist," I said. I sat on the
couch and he sat by me. He leaned in very slowly and put his mouth
against mine. We made out a little and then I took his hand and led
him into the bedroom.

I pushed him down onto the bed, threw my shirt off, dropped my
bra onto the floor, and ground myself against him over our clothes.
There was nothing like an apartment visit to make a girl horny. He
pulled my jeans and undies down and slipped his hand up between
my legs.

"Just a second," I said. I scampered into the bathroom and got
the LifeStyles.

He was fully naked and stroking himself. "Oh no," he said when
he saw the rubbers.

"So you don't want to do it?" I said. Two could play this game.

He pulled me to him and said, "I guess I'll just hold my nose." I
unwrapped the condom and unrolled it.

I climbed on top and leaned myself forward, using CAT, just like
Liz had said to do, and roamed around. "Mmmmm," I said. Everything around my pelvis got warm so I pressed my face even closer.

"Ya suffocating me," he said.

I put one hand over his mouth and moved more vigorously.
"Shut up, you little hoo-ah," I said. Instead of getting angry he just
grinned and put his hands on my hips. I felt clear and hot, like a
body more than a brain. I thought about him coming through my
door. I remembered this quote I'd read somewhere, that the best
part of making love to a woman was climbing the steps to her apartment, and I wondered why if that was true so many guys didn't
make it that far.

But I felt like things *had* changed since he'd tied me up in the
boiler room, like I'd freed him to be a decent guy. We could do anything now. I could tie him up with rope and whip his fat middle-
aged ass.

I moved around like I was stirring soup, focusing all my energy on my clit. I tried not to think about anything except how good it felt. I closed my eyes and kept my hands planted by Powell's face. I imagined secretaries required to give blow jobs to their bosses, and women in forests making love to men with heads of wolves. I imagined important business conferences with each man assigned a personal female attendant, clothed only in expensive lingerie, there to wait on him hand and foot. I thought about the scene on *The Sopranos* where the guys did it with a huge group of Icelandic stewardesses. I remembered the part in *Candy* where Professor Mephesto grabs her breast and her sherry glass drops to the floor. These images warred it out in my mind, some lingering longer than others, some potent immediately while others flitted away. Twenty minutes later something miraculous happened: I came.

"Oh my God!" I said, less out of orgasmic delight than shock.

"Get a hold of yasself," Powell said.

"Oh my God ah my God ah ma gah I'm a guy! I'm a guy! I'm a guy!"

"Calm your animus down," Powell said, removing my hand from his mouth.

"So this is what it's like!" I said as the contractions subsided. "To just use someone for what they can give to you! You're nothing but a piece of abdomen rubbing against my clit! You're flesh attached to a body! A tool, a toy!" I raised my hands up in the air like an athlete who'd just won a game.

"Are you going to do this every time?"

"Leamme alone," I said. "This is a big moment for me. I see what all the fuss is about."

"What do you mean?"

"This is why so many men are jerks to women. When you fuck to come it changes everything. Women fall in love because they have to find a reason to fuck the guy without coming but men don't need a reason and that's why they're so blasé about commitment."

"You sound like me," he said, like that was the biggest compliment he could give.

I held on to the bottom of the condom and climbed off. He stared at his erection like I was a waiter who'd forgotten to clear the table.

"Sorry," I said. "I'm finished. Can't go any longer."

"Whaddaya mean you're finished?"

"I want to feel what it's like to be a guy. To fuck to come and nothing more."

He looked slightly stunned, but then the stunned look was replaced with something more resigned, like he was too exhausted to put up a fight. "You're not going to argue?" I said.

"You know I have the heart of a complacent woman."

I went to the bathroom and looked in the mirror. I was exuberant and alive, my cheeks flushed. I got back in bed and spooned him, resting my chin in that place between his head and his shoulder. He put his hand on my ass and pulled me closer, which surprised me so much I almost leaned over to check and be sure it was him. It was the best night of my year: I'd fucked to come and gotten Hank Powell to sleep over.

Just as I was drifting off I heard a strange whirring noise coming from up above. It sounded like an industrial fan or a vacuum cleaner. There was a moan—I couldn't tell who it was—followed by another, lower-pitched electronic hum. The lights flickered off for a second and then came back on. "Ohhhhh," said my dad. It was hard to tell if he was in pain or pleasure.

"Is that who I think it is?" Powell said.

"Uh-huh." I nodded, throwing a pillow over my face to muffle the noise.

"You like that?" Liz said.

"Do I *like* it?" my dad exclaimed. "That feels am*a*zing!"

I rolled over onto my side and groaned. There was a third humming noise, this one higher-pitched like a bee, and then a giggle and a yelp.

"Jesus H. Christ," said Powell. "Are they running a factory up there?"

"She's very into equipment," I said.

"It sounds like he is too."

"Turn it faster!" my dad said, like he was calling plays at a football game. "Oh yes! *Yes!*"

"Does he know you're here?" Powell said.

"I think he thinks I'm working. I switched my shift tonight to be with you."

"Oh, Elizabeth," my father cried. "This is *heavenly!*"

Six months ago I was a normal first-year rabbinical student, my greatest concerns being whether I'd finish my Mishnah reading in time for class and sitting far away from Stu Zaritsky so he wouldn't stare at my tits during modern Hebrew. Now I couldn't even have a guy over without being aurally accosted by my father and my upstairs neighbor's electronic sex show.

"Oh baby!" my dad said. "I'm gonna come!"

"I'm gonna go," I told Powell, getting up.

"Are you kidding?" he said, standing up on the bed so he could hear better. "This is action! This is primal shit right here."

"It's only primal if it's your parents!"

"It's postmodern primal, then!" he said. "Don't you see what an incredible opportunity this is for your psychic self? Your dad's having sex with a surrogate you while you're down here with a surrogate him!"

"What are you talking about?"

"He's fallen off the pedestal and launched himself into the Industrial Age with a woman young enough to be his kid! What's going through your brain right now? What are you thinking about?" He cocked his head at me and gave me a deep, searching look.

"About how I want to run out of the apartment!" I said. I bolted into the living room with my clothes and began to throw them on.

"You gotta get through this!" Powell cried, chasing after me and holding my arms. "Break free!"

My father said "Ahhh," and Liz said "Yes, baby!" I didn't know how many heads they were working with, and how many holes. And I didn't *want* to know. I hoped nobody got electrocuted. How would I explain it to my mother?

Just as I was dressed and almost out the door I heard my father's high-pitched "Oh brooooooooother!" sail through the floorboards, into my ears, right into the part of my brain that would form all of my future relationships with men.

"Why are you being so self-pitying?" Powell asked, jumping up and down like a crazy circus man. "This is *wonda*ful! It's you coming face-to-face with your animus problem! Your father image is breaking through the ceiling of your idealization. You have incontrovertible proof that the man's a cheater, and not only that but an energy sucker. You'll never be able to see him the same way again."

"*I know!*"

"You shouldn't lament it. It's the truth that's going to catapult you into your adulthood. You should have separated from your folks fifteen years ago but you've delayed it till now! Until you recognize your father as an entity separate from you, an entity capable of his own needs that is not stern or controlling or punitive, you will forever be married to your parents and unable to have a healthy relationship." He was eyeing me with a dangerous smile. His penis was perking up again, the condom still on.

"Now that is seriously sick," I said.

"I can't help it," he said. "When I overhear the shattering of the bourgeois ideal I get excited."

I leapt up and bolted backwards toward the wall. "I'm not going to have sex with you at a moment like this! I'm dealing with some serious shit here."

"You're too sanctimonious," he said, with a scowl.

"I don't think it's sanctimonious for a girl not to be in the mood given the circumstances."

"I thought you were different," he said, shaking his head angrily. "But you backpedal and lead with fear!"

"Not everyone has such an easy time breaking off the shackles of the bourgeois ideal! What if they decide to go for another round?"

He shook his head and pulled the condom off. "*Ow!*" he said, as a hair caught in it. "You see? This is why I never use them." He stormed into the bedroom and began putting on his pants.

"What are you doing?"

"Getting outta here."

"But I thought you'd spend the night," I said.

"I thought so too," he said. "But nothing is *ever simple.*" He put on the rest of his clothes and walked out, the door slamming loudly behind him.

I lay down on my bed and tried to block everything out. Every time I took one step forward the men in my life had to throw me back on the floor. My father was assaulting me with his sex and whether he knew it or not, it didn't matter. He had stopped caring about anyone but himself.

It was bad enough that I knew his vocalization of choice but now I'd have trouble just looking him in the eye. I had no idea he was so open-minded. These toys were the equivalent of high-speed cable access. Once you signed on there was no going back. Liz owned practically the entire Good Vibrations catalogue. She had undoubtedly introduced him to areas he'd never explored before, positions he didn't know existed. Before long she'd find a way to make him come from his nostrils. How could he go back to my mom now that he had a new bag of tricks?

Powell had been not just useless but actively detrimental to my sanity. I had invited him over with the hopes it would take our relationship to a new level and instead he had only proven that he was bona fide crazy. If he'd heard what he'd heard and it made him horny, what did it say about his ability to take care of me on a long-term basis?

I went into the bathroom and brushed my teeth. My face was haggard and sad and from the side my jawline looked just like my dad's. He always had to barge his way into my affairs even if it meant coming through the ceiling. How could I take any pleasure in my very first hands-free O when it was followed immediately by something like this?

I dropped out of school and he'd decided he liked being unemployed. I found an older man and immediately he grabbed for a younger woman. I came from fucking and he'd suddenly discovered perineal joy. It just wasn't fair. No matter what I did he had to upstage me.

A T five o'clock the next night there was a knock on my door. I hoped it was Powell coming to apologize for being such a jerk but when I looked through the peephole I saw my dad. He looked crazed and giddy. Maybe it was residual voltage from the night before. "What is it?" I said, opening up.

"Your mother found out." He didn't seem sad or even worried. He seemed happy.

I felt my heart plummet out of my chest down through the first three floors into the basement of the building. "What?" I said, holding my hand against the oven to steady myself. "How?"

"The details aren't important," he said. "What is important is that it was the best thing that ever happened to our marriage!"

I couldn't believe it. All my fantasies about her being capable of forgiveness had come true. Once he explained just how wrong he'd been my mom had seen a humanity in him he hadn't displayed in years, realized how much she really loved him, and decided to forgive and forget.

"So you're leaving Liz?" I asked, my voice cracking happily.

"*Leaving* her?" he said. "I'm moving in with her!"

RIGHTS ARE
LIKE TIGHTS

It turned out my mom had found out through her friend Carol Landsman, who had spotted my dad and Liz canoodling at Halcyon, the coffee shop on Smith, and deliberated for a week before breaking down and calling. When my dad arrived home from an interview in the city my mom began throwing computer books at him, screaming that she was a moron for thinking he was job hunting when clearly he was hunting for something else.

She said the woman had to be a whore because only a whore would ever sleep with him and my brilliant father cried out that she was a graduate student, at which point my mom put two and two together and realized it was Liz. My dad didn't deny it, sending my mom into another burst of fury, which involved her picking up one of the dining room chairs and getting it over her head before he wrenched it out of her hands and begged her to get a hold of herself. That was when she threatened to call the cops. Before she could, he went down to the bedroom for some clothes, ran out, called Nina Halberstam, and told her to go over quick to make sure my mom was OK.

When he finished the story my head felt thick like I had just taken a Tylenol PM. "So that's it?" I said, trying to find enough saliva in my mouth to get a sentence out. "It's all over, just like that? You're not going to go into couples therapy and try to work it out?"

"Are you out of your *mind?*" he said. "Did you think she was going to forgive me? Mom's practically *Sicilian* when it comes to forgiveness. She's still mad at me for the time I prank-called her the first year of our marriage pretending to be her Israeli ex-boyfriend

Yigal, wanting her back. Did you honestly think she'd forgive me for *sleeping with another woman?*"

"Maybe," I whispered hollowly. I wandered over to the kitchen table and sat down in a chair, feeling my heart throbbing in my chest. "I thought that was what you meant when you said you were in process. I thought it meant you were weighing the value of staying."

"I was," he said, "but if I was going to stay with her I wasn't going to confess!"

"So you didn't even try to argue with her?"

"She was going to call the cops—I had to get out of there! And she had those fierce eyes, the ones that mean she's not in the mood for a discussion." His passivity made him useless at a time like this; how could he argue when she was the strong-willed one?

"Why do you have to move in with Liz?" I said. "You could rent your own place. Just see how things go. Maybe with a little bit of time you'll feel better. You'll miss Mom."

"I don't see any point in postponing what I'm sure would be an eventual move-in anyway. Liz said she'd make room for me in her place and next month we could start looking for a place together."

I slid down from the chair onto the floor like a dead Glenn Close leaving a streak of blood on the bathroom tile wall. "I know it sounds strange," he said, heaving me up, "but once Mom told me she knew, it was like this huge weight was lifted off me. And then when I saw Elizabeth and she seemed so happy, well, everything became clear."

"I thought you loved Mom."

"Of course I love her. But we've been married thirty-two years and people change. It's a different kind of love. I'm just so glad everything's out in the open now, that Liz and I don't have to hide." He made it sound like they were some lesbian couple from the 1940s instead of an oversexed *alter kocker* and a nymphomaniacal trophy girl. "Elizabeth and I have to be able to be together without sneaking around. Without being ashamed of our love."

Hearing the words "love" and "Elizabeth" in the same sentence made me have to swallow hard not to upchuck. "Just look on the bright side," he said, squeezing my shoulders from behind me. "You and I could start spending a lot more time together."

"That's not a bright side."

"It's what I've always wanted! Now that Liz and I can be in the open you and I can go to lunch together every day!"

"I don't want to spend any time with you. Don't you get it? I want you to *go home.*"

"I can't do that now. And even if I could, I don't think it's what I want." I squinted, trying to see if there was anything recognizable about his face. But he was a different person—not just because he'd lost twenty pounds, but because he seemed totally unrepentant. He sat down next to me and rested his hand in his chin. "I know it's hard right now," he said, "but I think we'll both get used to this soon."

"I can't believe I was so *stupid* as to think you were being honest with me at the bar. When you told me to give you more time, that was all just a ploy because you were afraid I was going to tell Mom?"

"It wasn't a ploy. I was searching. I was lost."

"You sound like Billy Graham," I said. "The Jewish Billy Graham."

"Please don't do this," he said. "I know it's a strange situation but don't despair yet. It's all just a little too new." He brushed some crumbs off the table into his hand, walked over to the garbage can, and threw them in. Then he turned around brightly and said, "So Liz wanted to know if she could cook for the both of us tonight. Whaddaya say? You could invite Hank. It'll be a double date."

"That's not going to happen."

"It could be fun!" I stood up, walked him out the door, and closed it in his face. He kept knocking and knocking but I turned up NPR so I couldn't hear.

T H E first person I called was Powell. He didn't say anything for a while and then he sighed and said, "He wanted to be caught. Men cheat overtly because they don't believe they're entitled to happiness without strings."

"But if he wanted to be caught, then—you mean he wanted out of the marriage?"

"Of course."

"So you think it's over? I was hoping this could be the best thing for my parents." Even I didn't believe it as I said it. "Maybe now that they have everything out in the open they can finally be together again, in an honest way."

"Did you ever see a movie called *Bob & Carol & Ted & Alice?*"

"Why do you have to be so pessimistic?"

"I'm not. Look on the bright side. Divorce isn't the worst possible scenario."

"You think they're going to get *divorced?*"

"A woman who knows her husband is cheating but doesn't *know* is one thing. But one who knows in no uncertain terms is dangerous. As soon as she tells her friends the friends project their own reservations about staying with their lying, cheating, or unresponsive sonuvabitches. They say things like, 'You gotta leave him or you'll never be able to look at yourself in the mirror again.' By that point even if the wife has second thoughts she's gotta leave him, if only so she maintains the respect of her friends."

"So why didn't Hillary leave Bill?"

"Alphabitches play by different rules."

"Is there anything I can do to bring him back?"

"I can't be of any more assistance. He made his own bed."

I knew I might be pushing my luck but I couldn't help wondering whether he was just pissed about his lack of orgasm. "Why are you so grumpy?" I said. "Is this about last night?"

"What about it?"

"Are you mad you didn't—you know?"

"That would be infantile," he said. "I got work to do. I'm jumping off."

He hung up.

ON my way over to what I found myself reluctantly thinking of as my mom's, I tried to convince myself it was all going to work out. She'd be mad at first, but once she got over the initial rage and incomprehension she'd realize at the very least she should let him explain. After the week it took him to realize what a psychotic bitch Liz was he'd go back to my mom and devote the rest of his life to pleasing her in bed. Their first night together again, he'd show her the new cunnilingus technique he'd learned from the queen of quim. Aghast, impressed, and astounded, she'd have no choice but to take him back. He'd call up Good Vibrations, order all the toys he'd used with Liz, and have them sent to my mom, insuring an old age filled with hot sex, G-spot orgasms, and perennial perineal satisfaction. Grateful to Liz for having invigorated her middle-aged life, my mom would arrange a Cuckold Conversation to thank Liz for having given her a crash course in sexual technology.

My dad would smell a commercial idea and the three of them would start running sex-toy workshops for couples, where he and Liz would do live demonstrations on each other while my mom lectured on technique. They'd call it Cobble Hill Electric Company and they'd go on a world tour, teaching middle-aged men and women all about dual vibes, female ejaculation, and the pleasures of plugins. They'd build up a buyership of thousands, their seminars skyrocketing to Anthony Robbins–like attendance levels, as they restored vitality to the sex lives of menopausal women and menophobic men from Syracuse to Shanghai.

When I got home Nina was hugging my mom, who was rocking in tears on the couch. I hugged her but she didn't hug back. "So this girl was a friend of yours?" Nina said, as I sat down next to my mother.

I nodded. "But not anymore."

"How long have you known?" my mother said.

"I don't know. A month and a half."

Her face reddened in rage. "You knew for a month and a half? *How could you not have told me?*"

"I didn't want to hurt you! I didn't know what was going to happen and I thought it was up to him to decide."

"Apparently he was going to keep her in the dark as long as he could," Nina said. "Typical American male."

My mom blew her nose angrily into a Kleenex. "Don't you have any sense of family obligation?"

"It wasn't my business! It was between you and him!"

"You knew your father was going around behind my back and you didn't think this was information I deserved to know?"

"I thought about it a long time," I said, "but it's against Jewish law."

"Since when have you cared about Jewish law? You wouldn't even come to Rosh Hashanah services!"

"That doesn't mean I stopped thinking about it. You're not supposed to speak evil of others, even if it's true. You're not supposed to do anything that would cause pain. 'A tongue is like an arrow. Once an arrow is shot, it can never be called back, even if the archer has a change of mind.' I knew if I told you, things might happen that I didn't want to happen. I was trying to protect you!"

"That's not the real reason!" she hurled. "You were protecting *him.* You never support me in anything."

"This isn't fair," I said. "If I had told you, you'd have been furious at me and you're furious at me anyway. Nothing I do is right with you."

"It would have been right of you to tell me right away!"

"Don't be so hard on her," Nina said, rubbing my mother's back. "How was she supposed to know this girl would turn out to be a conniving little whore?"

"She should have had better instincts! You surround yourself with dangerous people and this is what happens!"

"I can't believe this," I said. "I couldn't help it that Liz walked into that restaurant that night."

"No, but afterwards you probably encouraged him. What, he came over to visit you and you invited her up?"

"Of course not! You're out of your mind. Why would I do that?"

"I don't know," my mother said, and covered her face with her hands. "I don't know what to think anymore." She collapsed into a fit of tears and Nina went to get more Kleenex from the bathroom. I looked around the room at the two bookshelves on either side of the fireplace, the framed photos of me getting picked up from summer camp, the three of us cross-country skiing in Vermont, me in a Laura Ashley dress standing in front of a bulletin board that said BAT

MITZVAH RACHEL BLOCK, me graduating Wesleyan and smiling in my cap and gown, flanked by my parents. We looked happy and intact. And now everything had gotten ugly so fast.

"Maybe he'll come to his senses," I said. "Maybe he'll find a way to make it all up to you."

"It's too late for that!" she said. "When I told him to get out I swear I saw glee in his eyes, like he knew this would happen eventually and was glad it finally did." Nina came out of the bathroom and passed her another tissue.

She blew her nose, collected herself, and took a deep breath. "I knew something wasn't right with him," she said. "He was never home. I kept thinking he was fixing computers, like he told me. I can't believe I was such an *idiot!*"

"Don't blame yourself for thinking he was a halfway-decent person," Nina said. "You thought he was a mensch because he never gave you any reason to think otherwise."

"I just can't believe he was so *stupid!* To be cavorting with this girl out in plain sight where anyone could see him! He must have wanted to be caught." She wiped her eyes, suddenly looking very old. I leaned over and hugged her tightly but she pulled back and glared at me, her eyes cold and devoid of love.

"You know what, Rachel?" she said calmly. "I appreciate you coming over but I don't think I want you here right now."

Nina got a strange, uncomfortable face and then coughed into her hand. "I don't understand," I said.

"I need to think things through," she said. "It's all too jumbled right now. I'm feeling really angry at you and I think the best thing is for you to leave."

"But Mom," I said. "You have to believe me when I say it wasn't my fault. I swear to God I tried to stop it!"

"Rach," Nina said, standing up and leading me to the door. "She'll be all right. I'm here. But I think you should listen to her. I've had three other friends go through this so I know how to handle her. She'll come around."

I looked over my shoulder at my mom. Her eyes displayed a steely rage and I was afraid something had changed in her, that she'd lost whatever residual love she had for me, even though I knew I hadn't done anything wrong. I didn't like seeing her there next to Nina, I wanted him back, I wanted him to fix things, I wanted it never to have happened.

I hated Carol for blabbing, however entitled she was. My mind went through a series of negative Dayenus. If only she hadn't seen them, it would have been enough. If she had seen them but hadn't told, it would have been enough. If she had seen them and told but my mom had been able to forgive, it would have been enough. But she'd set things into motion and now everything was falling apart, more quickly than I could have imagined.

When I got outside I peeked in the window. Nina and my mom were sitting side by side, their faces downcast and hard, like this was the beginning of the end.

O v e r the next week I was totally spacey at work. I kept mixing ingredients, putting gin in my vodka tonics, and mixing up the Harp and Brooklyn Lager. My tip total for the week came out to three hundred dollars, my lowest since I'd started working at Roxy. Jasper tried to comfort me by telling me how hard it was when his parents separated, but as an overweight celibate who spent all his free nights in a bar he didn't seem to be a raging example of good coping skills.

I left three different messages for my mom but she didn't call back and I figured the best thing I could do was give her space. When I called Nina she said I shouldn't worry, my mom would come around, and all the women in the book group were taking turns coming over to make sure she was all right.

Now that he lived above me, my father began treating my apartment like Kramer treated Jerry's. He'd knock at all hours of the day, wanting to chat, talk about job interviews, and go for bike rides. When I tried to explain that just because he was living upstairs it didn't mean I had to spend all my time with him, he'd pout and pad out, sulking, like I had a completely warped sense of parental obligation even though he was the one who had turned our family on its head.

Powell, meanwhile, stopped inviting me to his apartment altogether, and I was too demoralized by his walking out on me to try to invite him to mine. But instead of disappearing completely as any decent guy would have done, he would call me at all hours of the day to read me scenes of *The Brother-in-Law,* and invite me to breakfast every morning at D'Amico. And because it still flattered me that he wanted to be with me, even though he stopped touching me and commenting on my body, I took what I could get. We'd sit at a table in the back and I'd laugh appreciatively as he riffed on all the *New York Times* headlines, hoping that one day he'd have a change of heart and invite me over to his apartment.

One morning he strode into D'Amico with a wide smile. I was sitting at a table listening to two old Italian guys, both in fedoras, argue about which one of them did more for the country during the war. One was saying he was in the service and the other said his friend wouldn't have had any ammo if it wasn't "for the balls of tin foil we sent over."

Powell ordered his cappuccino and sat down across from me. The two old guys looked up, trying to figure out how we were connected.

"What is it?" I said.

"I got a call from someone at Jennifer Lopez's office saying she wants to meet with me. I'm having lunch with her on Thursday. Supposedly she's seen all my movies and says she's been dying to be in one of my films."

I found Jennifer Lopez to be the lowest level of talent on the block, a living testament to the unexplainable appeal of mediocrity. "Oh my God," I said distastefully.

"Yeah," he said. "I'm kind of nervous myself."

"Why?"

"Because I want it to go well."

"Hank!" I said. "Why on earth would you want to make a movie with Jennifer Lopez?"

His face contorted into a furious mess. "That individual knows how to act! Did you see the tour de force of *Selena?* What about *Out of Sight?*"

"Everyone's good under Soderbergh," I said. "You can't judge her by that. A decent director can get good work out of anybody."

His eyebrows flared and he flashed his teeth. *"So you don't think I'm a decent director?"*

"Of course I do," I said, realizing this was not going in the right direction. "I just—didn't think Jennifer Lopez would meet your idea of a decent actress."

"You know what you are?" he said, leaning back in his chair. "A racist."

"I'm not a racist!"

"You don't respect her because she's attractive, talented, successful, and Puerto Rican. She threatens you. You should try *opening your mind.*"

What was wrong with me? I had to learn to be more normal, more quiet. I had to learn not to say every thought that came to my mind. But wasn't that the point of being in a relationship, however dysfunctional it was? Was I testing him to bring him down off his high horse, or was I just being myself?

"I'm sorry," I said as daintily as I could. "But I have a right to an opinion."

"Rights are like tights," he said. "They make my balls itch."

"Look, if you want to work with her to make money that's one thing but don't pretend like you respect her. I mean I know you have a lot of money problems. I know these last few years haven't been easy for you."

I didn't think it was possible for him to get any angrier than he already was but he exploded and pushed his face up against mine. "You don't know when to shut up, do you?"

"I just—she can barely put lines together. To be honest, I thought Rosanna Arquette was a dubious choice for *Knock for Greenberg* but J.Lo? In a Hank Powell movie? Don't you have any respect for your own oeuvre?"

"Jennifer Lopez is the most dynamic female screen presence to come along since Judy Holliday," he said, "and if you can't see that I don't know why I even bother talking to you."

All I was doing was stating my opinion but Powell didn't seem interested in a two-way conversation. It was beginning to seem that if I committed to being around him I'd have to commit to being a stroker, and after a while all the stroking got tiresome. It was like the only leverage I had with him was my willingness to be polite and when it came down to it, that wasn't leverage to be proud of. I couldn't decide which I wanted more—to have him or to have him be nice.

"Can't we disagree?" I said.

"Not when it comes to incontrovertible facts, such as the talent of Ms. Lo." I had to chill out or he'd leave. I knew better than to defame a star that could pay Powell's alimony for two years straight. I had to learn to shut my mouth and be better company. The key was not to kiss his ass but to say just little enough not to piss him off.

"I'm sorry," I said. "I mean this could be great for you. If she was in one of your movies it could do good things for your career. Catapult you to high-level fame."

"What level of fame do you think I have now?"

"Mid."

"You think my fame is midlevel?" he hurled.

"All the best talents were marginal until they died! Look at van Gogh!"

"You're the queen of the sabotage," he said, looking at me as though he could no longer remember a single thing he liked about me.

"Hank," I said, suddenly terrified. "It came out wrong. I really didn't mean to say you were only marginally famous."

He was still glaring at me, like a pouting child. "Look, you're probably right. I probably don't like J.Lo just because she's so attractive. I guess I have a lot of competitive issues with women. That's probably why I spend all my time with men."

"You definitely leave issues."

This had ceased to be any fun at all but I was so afraid he was going to dump me that all I could think was to try to calm him down. "Why don't you read me some obituaries?" I said. "That always makes you happy." His face softened just slightly and he picked up the paper.

F O R   T H E   F I R S T   three hours of my shift the next night my
clientele was almost entirely single men. Jasper had gone out on
what he thought was a really good date with a girl who never returned his phone calls; Octavio, a gray-haired architect, was trying
to decide if he should dump his girlfriend; and these four drunk
guys who worked at VH1 and played tennis together once a week
were saying there were no good women left in the city.

"Do you know anyone who would go out with me?" Jasper said.
"Do you have someone to set me up with?"

"I'm not sure," I said. How was I supposed to tell him that even if I
did have a single friend, I wasn't sure how I would bill him? It would
be easy enough to say he was big, but how would I explain that I knew
him because he spent every night sitting opposite the spigots?

As I set his Harp down in front of him a cute girl with low pigtails
and a YMCA summer camp shirt sat down at the other end. She had
the kind of pubescent breasts guys like, and I felt certain her nipples
were the puffy kind. I angled my head toward her. "You want me to
make her sit over here?"

He glanced up and took her in. "She's not my type."

"What do you mean she's not your type? She's smokin'!"

"They have to be at least five-seven, big and strong, built like Midwestern girls, and blonde. I prefer them to weigh between one-forty
and one-sixty and they have to wear a double D or bigger. And they
have to have really high arches."

"You're incorrigible," I said.

"Come on, Rach, you're just down on men these days because of
your dad."

"Why don't you shut up?" I said.

"What happened with your dad?" one of the VH1 guys shouted.

I asked the girl what she wanted. "Um, an apple martini?" she up-
talked.

"I can do one," I said, "but you'll regret it." Our apple juice was disgusting and the apples we kept in stock weren't even the right kind.

"OK," she said. "How bout a Cosmo, then?"

Women never tired of Cosmopolitans. I didn't get it. It was a stereotype that I was quickly discovering to be apt: women didn't like the taste of alcohol so they had to turn it into candy.

I mixed it and passed it to her. She gave me nine dollars on seven. Not bad. Maybe I could make Jasper less picky.

"These guys are sitting around complaining about how they don't get any," I said. "I'm trying to explain that they need to lower their standards. Jasper over here wants a girl with high arches."

I pointed to him and he blushed a little even though he said he wasn't interested. "I have really high arches," she said. "I used to have to wear corrective shoes!"

"You do?" Jasper said. "I mean, you did?"

"Yeah," she said. "You want to see them?"

He walked over and she began untying her vintage Sauconys. She peeled off her sock and put her leg in his lap. She did have beautiful feet, shapely and long, and her arches were so high it almost looked uncomfortable.

"Oh my God," he gasped. Octavio came over more slowly and gave a wolf whistle when he saw. She gave a giggle and wiggled her toes around but even when the skinny boys came over she didn't take her eyes off Jasper. I couldn't believe she was so attracted to him but maybe she knew about fat guys and clit stim.

"It's too bad you like your girls to be at least a hundred forty pounds, Jasper," I said.

"He said that?" the girl said, shaking her pigtails.

"Yeah—they also have to be built like Midwestern girls, and wear a D cup or bigger."

"That was ballpark!" Jasper shouted.

"I can't believe you're so picky," she said.

"I'm not," he said. "I swear." He leaned over and kissed the back of her hand. "I'm Jasper."

"Delia," she said, and flipped his hand over to kiss the back. The peanut gallery let out a collective moan of jealousy.

"That's Octavio, Jim, Dave, Rob, and Matt," I said, pointing to the other guys. Between twenty-five and thirty-five they all had monosyllabic names.

"Have you thought about being a foot model?" Jasper said. "Because I have seen a number of high arches in my life and yours really rank up there."

"That's sweet of you," she said.

"What *do* you do?" Octavio said.

"I'm the activity director at a nursing home," she said.

"Lord Almighty," Jasper said. "That's so noble."

"Not really," she said. "They need help. Society is really cruel to older Americans."

"Another round," Matt called with a growl, as they made their way back to their seats.

As I went over to the tap I smiled. All it took was a little nudge and only the bartender had the power to do it. Maybe I wasn't meant to be a rabbi but a yenta. If my parents were about to divorce I could make up for it by bringing some more people together. Maybe it would all even out in the end. The best part was, there was no God necessary. Just a little faith.

A couple days later the phone rang at eleven. "I need to see you," my dad said. It was loud—there were a bunch of cars in the background—and I was worried something awful had happened.

"Are you OK?"

"Yeah, I'm fine," he said. "I want to talk to you about some things. I was hoping we could go for a bike ride."

"But I just woke up."

"Please, Rach," he said. "I know things aren't right between us and I want to fix them."

I sighed. If he wanted to try to patch things up I had to give him a chance. Maybe he was going to tell me he'd decided to get back together with my mom. "OK," I sighed.

"Oh, I'm so happy!" he said. "Wear sneakers and comfortable clothes."

"Did you think I was going to wear heels?"

"Meet me at the corner of Congress and Hicks," he said. "Where the playground is."

"You want to bike on the BQE?" I said. "You wanna kill us?"

"I have a route in mind. Can you be here in fifteen minutes?"

When I arrived at the playground, the seat of my rusty ten-year-old Columbia cutting into my ass, I didn't see anyone. It was just a bunch of tennis courts. Then I heard a whistle from the court and when I came around the gate I saw my father, Powell, and Liz, whacking practice balls back and forth. Liz tossed me a wave and said, "Hi honey!" and then slammed one across to Powell, who didn't get it.

"Nice one!" he called.

"Thank you, Mr. Powell!"

I hopped on my bike and started riding away but my dad chased after me and grabbed the seat. "*Rach!* Just let me explain!"

"There's nothing to explain. You tricked me."

"I knew if I told you I'd set up a doubles match you'd never play. Can't we all just get along?"

"Who are you, Ronald King?" I said.

"Just listen for a second," he said. "I'm going to be living with Elizabeth for the indefinite future. I think if you get accustomed to things being a little different it will make it easier for everyone." He was wearing a baggy T-shirt he'd bought at Shakespeare and Company in the Berkshires that said, "Theres many a man hath more hair than wit.—Act Two Scene Two, The Comedy of Errors." How could she live with him when he wore things like that?

Powell drove a ball long to Liz and as she panted and missed she called out, "You're something else, Mr. Powell!"

"I'm too old to fall for flattery!" he said.

I threw my hands up and pointed to the court. "Why would I want to do this?"

"To make me happy. Liz feels terrible about all of this. She wants the two of you to be able to be friends again."

"She does not feel terrible."

"She does! She told me so just the other day."

I eyed the court. I didn't like how flirtatious Powell was being; it made me think if things didn't work out between Liz and my dad she'd go right into Powell's arms.

"I barely even play," I said.

"Yes you do!" he said. "You got very good that summer at Camp Eisner."

"I was nine! There's no retention!"

Just then Powell jogged over, with Liz trailing behind. "You made it," Powell said.

"Could you excuse us?" I said, dragging him a few steps away.

"You let him trick me," I said.

"He knew you wouldn't come if he told you. I think this is a good idea."

"You thought having sex after we heard them having sex was a good idea."

"That's true."

"Why should I do this? Why did you even let him set this up?"

"You can't go on hating him forever. Eventually you're going to have to come to terms or it'll be more painful for you in the long run." He eyed me up and down. "You look good." I was wearing cargo pants, thick heather-gray socks, and a T-shirt that said "GI Joe" and had very gay-looking action figures standing in a row raising their fists.

I softened at the compliment. I was too easy. "How was your J.Lo meeting?"

"She's very interested. She may attach herself to *The Brother-in-Law* now that I'm writing it."

"That's great," I said, trying to put a little pep into it.

"Don't go," he said. "Try to have a sense of humor about this."

"How come you only want to see me when my father's around?"

"Are you guys in a fight?" Liz said. "Because the game could be really good for that. I think it could be really good for everyone. My analyst thinks that healthy channels for aggression are essential to harmonious relationships."

"You wouldn't know a harmonious relationship if it bit you in the—"

"Ladies," my dad said.

I wasn't exactly sure how it was possible but ten minutes later Powell and I were positioned on one side, the dog and the bitch on the other. Liz was serving and she looked out for blood, like a Jewish Venus Williams. She was in a white mini and a sleeveless black top that said HEAD. "I don't want to do this," I called over my shoulder to Powell.

But he wasn't paying attention; Liz had already slammed it viciously to his backhand, the ball whistling past my ear. Powell lunged to return. He and Liz hit it back and forth a few times and just as I was beginning to feel relieved the game was not involving me she drilled one right to me. I cringed and covered my body with my arms, whimpering like a boy who's soiled his pants, as the ball hit the edge of my racquet and bounced into the net.

"Fifteen–love," Liz called out.

"Good one, babe," my dad said, flashing her a thumbs-up. I couldn't believe he had the nerve to call her "babe" in front of his own daughter.

They won the next three points straight. My dad cried out, "That's my girl!" and sashayed over to give her a hug and a kiss.

"Who are you two?" I said. "Andre and Steffi?"

"I'm so much hotter than that German bitch," Liz said.

"You gotta try a little harder," Powell hissed as we moved to the net. "Put something into it! Pretend you care! Didn't you say you had lessons?"

"At a Jewish summer camp," I said. "The athletic department was pathetic. And I had no acuity. My dad doesn't like to admit it but there are some things I'm not any good at."

"That's not true!" my dad said. "You're a naturally gifted athlete! You've got perfect hand-eye! You just have to put your mind to it."

"I was thinking maybe we should switch it up a little later on," Powell said.

"Am I *that bad?*" I sputtered.

"It's a dog-eat-dog world," he said, "and I can't be shamed into getting trounced."

"I'm with Rachel," my dad said. "I mean, Hank's a much stronger player than I am. It's got to be interesting and if we switch the girls it's going to be too imbalanced." My own father was begging off having me on his team.

"I think it's a great idea," said Liz. "What fun is mixed doubles without a bit of . . . swapping?"

She bounced from foot to foot like a demonic boxer. I noticed my shoe was untied and as I was stooping to tie it Powell served up the middle to Liz's backhand. She returned it and Powell sent it back crosscourt. My dad stepped in and whacked it and before I was even fully aware it was coming it slammed into my thigh. "Jesus Christ!" I cried, rubbing it with my hand. "That's going to leave a bruise!"

"I'm really sorry, honey," he said. "Are you all right?" But there was a glint in his eye like he cared more about the point than his own daughter's welfare.

"She's fine!" Powell said. "Let's keep going."

"You're amazing, Richard," Liz said, skipping toward him and planting a soul kiss on his mouth.

"Could you cut it out?" I said.

"You're just bitter we're winning," Liz said.

"I'm just bitter you're fucking my father!" I said. One of the middle-aged guys on the next court looked over with a raised eyebrow.

"This could be a reality show," Powell said.

On the next serve Powell and Liz went at it for a while and just as I was getting comfortable she shot one near me. I was caught off guard and hit it way off at an angle so it bounced far into the next court, where one of the guys tossed it back.

"You gotta stay on your toes!" my dad said.

"It was your point! You should be happy!"

"You had enough time to get in position! Are you trying to lose because you're not having fun?"

"I wasn't trying to lose at all," I said, as my lower lip began to tremble.

"You don't have any discipline. You used to have a little competitive spirit! You used to be a fighter!"

"Is she crying?" Liz called from the other side.

"She's fine!" Powell said. "You gotta calm down," he whispered. "Make 'em nervous. Don't let 'em intimidate you."

"I won't," I said, feeling like maybe I stood a chance at influencing the outcome.

"Now cover the alley," Powell said from behind me. I turned around. He waved me over. I moved a few steps further.

"Shouldn't I play the whole square?"

"No."

Powell won the next three serves with no assistance from me at all. Forty–fifteen. He served the ball wide to Liz's forehand, and though she got her racquet on it, it blooped up high and short over the net and bounced right in front of me. There couldn't have been an easier shot. Liz was so far away I could barely make her out. In my peripheral vision I could see my father sliding toward me, looking very concerned. The ball was floating in the air like a scoop of lime sherbet, frozen in *Matrix*like suspended animation. I could hear Powell's sneakers behind me as he called, "I got it!"

My father was coming closer. I felt a rush of hatred well up in me as I saw the outline of his clean-shaven face. All this time I'd been reluctant to blame him but now it seemed so clear. He was the selfish one, not my mom. He was the one who had ruined everything. He had found Liz and *chosen* her. He didn't fall into this, he wasn't pushed. He'd thought it out and made a conscious choice to betray my mother, to betray me, to destroy the family. He'd given up everything that mattered for a piece of skinny ass.

I hated him for what he'd done and who he'd been. I hated him from long ago for making me stay in the library too long and locking us out of the house. For pushing me to run for youth group president when I was happy being just the secretary. I remembered all the times when I was little that he took me out and tried to teach me to throw a ball and the way he never gave up even though it was clear that I would always, always throw like a girl. I thought about the time we'd all gone skiing in Vermont and over dinner out at a restaurant he'd gotten in such a bad fight with me over something stupid that he walked home alone in the snow and my mom had to drive next to him at five miles an hour. I thought about the times he yelled at my mom for losing things that she didn't lose and made her feel inadequate and small when she had it together way more than he did.

I hated what a hard time he'd given me about being a bartender while neglecting to inform me that he was unemployed. How when

I'd confronted him about his affair, he'd had the gall to ask for my pity, when he was the two-timing lying asshole. How dismissive he'd been of my mom and all her groups, as though she was skirting her responsibilities when all she was doing was getting a life. I hated how he'd acted on Rosh Hashanah, and how he'd had the nerve to have sex right above my own apartment, how he'd stolen my boyfriend as his new best friend and acted generally in the last month and a half as though nobody else's needs mattered but his own. It all hit me square and clear like a glorious epiphany from an otherwise silent God: my father was a shmuck.

I raised my racquet above my head, like Judith about to slay Holofernes, and slammed the ball as hard as I could toward that bobbing bull's-eye called My Father's Head. Instead of bouncing crazily off the racquet, the ball shot out hard and clean like a bullet and nailed my father square in the eye.

"*Ahhh!*" he cried, falling to the ground like he was shot, his knees in the air, his hands covering his face. The court was silent. I could hear the cars rushing down the expressway and behind it the distant waves of the East River lapping at the Brooklyn shore.

It had taken me a quarter of my life but I had finally leveled my father.

Suddenly everything started moving again. "Stay back, every-one!" Liz shouted, racing to his side. "I know first aid."

Powell dropped his racquet and hopped over the net. The two guys on the side court jogged over as Powell and Liz crouched over my dad. He rolled back and forth and whimpered, "The pain! The pain!" and though one entire side of his face was covered I could swear I saw him glaring at me through his one good eye.

F I F T E E N minutes later, we were crossing the BQE on Union, my dad clutching a bag of frozen peas to his eye and insisting that despite his injury he was in good-enough shape to take us all to lunch.

It had only taken me a second to snap out of my stupor and re-alize what I'd done. As soon as I saw the swelling I wanted to puke, like I was the evil one and not him. While Liz ran to get the peas from a deli and Powell shot me dirty looks, I hovered over my dad, apologizing so many times he finally had to tell me to just shut up.

The restaurant was at the corner of Union and Hicks and looked like it hadn't been altered since 1944. We pushed open the door and though there were no bells as we entered, it seemed like there should have been. It was dark inside, more like a bar than a restaurant, and the floor had original octagonal tile, like a barbershop from World War II. The wooden tables were empty except for a few white-haired men eating pasta.

The woman behind the counter had a lot of black hair piled on her head and thin red lips. "Four for lunch," my dad told her.

"You all right?" she said, glancing at the peas. "We got some ice in the back."

"Oh, that's not necessary—"

"Ice would be wonderful," Liz said.

She led us to a table in the back, laid out the menus, and disappeared into the kitchen. I sat next to Powell, across from Liz and my dad. "So how'd that happen?" the waitress asked, returning with some ice stuffed in a cloth napkin.

"His daughter hit him with a ball," Liz said.

"By accident," I said.

She nodded, looked at me, and then at Liz, and pronounced, "This is so sweet."

"What is?"

"It's not often you see two grown girls out with their fathers for lunch."

Liz burst into a smile. "That's nice that you think that," she said, "but he's not my father." She draped her arm over my dad's shoulder and French-kissed him. I slumped in my seat.

"Oh," the waitress said, more confused than ever. "I just thought you and he—"

"Save yourself the energy," Powell said.

Everything on the menu was in Italian and though I expected the prices to be World War II prices they weren't. This was the nature of brownstone Brooklyn—you got a walk back in time, but you had to pay.

"I think I'm going to get a Caesar salad," Liz announced. "What about you, Richie?"

"Richie?" I said. "You hate it when people call you Richie."

"No I don't," he said, glaring through his good eye. He perused the menu and said, "I guess I'll get the spaghetti and meatballs without the spaghetti."

"He's on Atkins," Liz said.

"Since when are you on Atkins?"

"Since a few weeks ago. It's one of the reasons I've dropped so much weight."

"But you love pasta!"

"I know, and pasta's the reason I've been overweight for the past thirty years. Now I avoid the white devil."

"I think you're avoiding the wrong one," I said.

"Come on, Rach," he said. "Hitting me with the ball wasn't enough? You gotta keep hitting?"

"I swear to God it was an accident!" I said, but he pursed his lips like he didn't believe me.

Powell got the spaghetti puttanesca, and I ordered linguine marinara. "Did you know that 'puttanesca' means 'whore brew'?" Powell said. "It's because that's what the whores used to eat in Italy after they worked."

"Why didn't you order that, Liz?"

She shook her head at me solemnly. "So much bitterness. I saw it during the game, the way it chokes you up. Don't you think Rachel should go into therapy, Mr. Powell?"

"She doesn't need therapy," my dad said quickly. "Therapy is for people with really bad childhoods."

"What do you think I had?" I said.

"You think I was a lousy parent?" he gasped.

"You had a terrible temper. I was afraid to spill milk or you'd throw a fit! You were a completely reckless authoritarian."

"I wasn't authoritarian," said my dad. "I was just more mercurial. And you were not an easy teen."

"Don't take it too hard," Liz said, patting his hand. "The ideal parent wasn't perfect, as any therapy neophyte knows, but, in the words of the great Swiss psychoanalyst Alice Miller, simply 'good enough.' In therapy we learn to be accepting of good enough. You were good enough but she's obviously playing out some sort of incestuous attraction to you by dating Hank."

"What?" my dad sputtered.

"It shouldn't upset you. Obviously I have some father issues too or I wouldn't be with an over-the-hill Yid myself. Rachel has a serious persecution complex due to what she's just described as your authoritarian parenting. She's working it out through masochism."

"What do you mean masochism?" my dad said.

"Look at her wrists." They were still bruised from the rope, just slightly red, but Liz had amazing powers of perception. I grabbed my hoodie and slipped it over my arms but my dad leaned over and pulled them out to look. A look of concern crossed his face and then he glanced at Powell, nodded slowly, and said, "Well. As long as it's consensual."

I didn't know which was more upsetting: that I was eating post-tennis lunch with my father, his mistress, and my fifty-one-year-old lover or that in the process my dad had discovered my penchant for being strung up to the ceiling. There are things you don't want your parents to know, and there are things you *really* don't want your parents to know.

"So what's your safe word, Mr. Powell?" Liz asked.

"The phrase conjures visions of a sick house," he said, "but please. Enlighten."

"It's a word that lets you say *stop* unequivocally, that signals the game is over. Ours is Itzhak." She and my dad exchanged a glance and then giggled simultaneously. She leaned back in her chair like she was some anoractress on late-night television talking about her dog. "You see, Richie was working me with this pink vibe I have called the Mini Pearl and he was so good with it I started calling him the Pearl man and then he said, 'I'm such a Pearlman I'm *Itzhak* Perlman,' and now whenever one of us wants the other to stop we say, 'Itzhak.'"

"You're using the name of a patriarch as your safe word?" I said.

"What's wrong with that? All the men in the Bible were totally kinky promiscuous swingers." She was right. Abraham's first son was born to his concubine, and Solomon, David's son, had seven hundred wives. But it still grossed me out.

"So what's your word, Mr. Powell?" Liz asked.

Powell regarded Liz coolly, his head tilted slightly back, and then folded his hands and said, "You see, this to me is the essence of what is wrong with your generation."

"What?" Liz said.

"You're the first generation in history whose parents had more fun than you did, and you feel the need to punish yourselves for their sins, so you make sex as unpleasant and formulaic as possible. You can't allow yourselves any spontaneity or enjoyment of the act because if sex suddenly became fun then it would cease to be sex." Was that what he thought of me? Why was he saying this in front of my father? Did he think I was unspontaneous when I'd let him hang me from his pipe?

"*We* have fun!" she said. "Right, Richie? Just the other night Richie came over around nine and—"

"I'm not saying you kids are frigid," Powell said, extending his hand. "I'm saying you grew up so ververbalized, with the political correctness on college campuses and the sex education in the schools. The thing between men and women used to be about what *wasn't* said but with your generation it's all gotta be out on the table."

"You can't blame us for coming of age during AIDS," said Liz. "If we're vigilant about condoms, it's because we were taught to be. You guys all slept around in the seventies and now a whole bunch of people are dead. So we pay the price."

"Not really," Powell said, shaking his head. "We had to worry about herpes and pregnancy but most guys pulled out and for the most part it worked. Only the junkies and figs are dead. But your generation can't fathom the idea that casual sex could happen without punishment. In order to buy into the *raging fallacy* entitled Safe Sex Education you've been taught to sterilize sex so that there's nothing sexy about it anymore. Everybody's gotta ask permission." He made a goofy childlike face and raised his voice so it was high and wimpy. "'May I kiss your mouth?' 'May I put my hand on your breast?' It's ridiculous. Sex is about women *finally shutting up*. When I met a girl on a dance floor in the eighties I didn't ask permission to fuck her in the bathroom. Right, Richard?"

"Absolutely," my dad said, like he was the Steve Rubell of his day.

"You got married in 1971," I said. "How would you know?"

"I—dated a few women before Mom."

"She said you were a virgin when you met."

"Is my daughter the sweetest kid in the world?" my dad said.

"Maybe I'm seeking support from the wrong guy," Powell said.

"Who had the puttanesca?" the waitress said, arriving with the dishes.

"I worry about you children," Powell said, addressing Liz and me, after the waitress had set down the food. "I really do. You're so terrified of sex that you spend more time talking about it than having it. It's like a protracted adolescence."

"I've been fucking since I was thirteen!" Liz said.

"TMI!" I said.

"Why should she be ashamed of her sexuality?" my dad said, putting his hand on her back and rubbing up and down. "It's a beautiful thing."

"You know, Hank," I said, dabbing my mouth even though I'd only eaten a few bites of my linguini. "I think you were right about our generation."

"Yeah?"

"I think what distinguishes us from others is that we suffer from both too many boundaries and too few. We don't know how to be sexual without broadcasting it for the entire world to hear." Liz was eyeing me nervously but that only revved me up more. "We don't know a sexuality that can exist in private because our sexuality has been a part of the public discourse since we were adolescents. Sex has become such a disconnected act. The orgasm exists in total isolation from the individuals involved."

"Do you really feel that way?" Powell said.

"Absolutely. That's why we need so many crutches. But it's not just young people this affects. It's everyone. It's not enough for two people to be together. They always have to whip out a box of toys."

My dad was starting to look a little ill. "It really upsets me. It makes me crazy. I mean, when I think of what we do with all these machines as a sublimation of real sexual connection, when I think of the total lack of respect for personal privacy and the use of exhibitionism as a substitute for intimacy, all I can say is, 'Oh brooooooother!'"

They all got pale and frightened, like I'd suddenly whipped out a gun. My dad pawed at his eye with the ice napkin. Liz's eyes were as narrow as a pissed-off Bangkok whore and Powell was regarding me with something beneath contempt. It was quiet for a long time and then my dad looked down at his plate, peeled off some twenties, and put them on the table. He set down the napkin, replaced it with the bag of frozen peas, and rose to his feet. "I'm sorry," he said, and walked out.

"Nice one," Liz said. "He's never going to live that down."

"What about me?" I bellowed. *"I'm the one who's never going to live it down!"*

She leaned forward and clapped Powell on the shoulder. "Mr. Powell," she said, "I heartily enjoyed the match." And then she was gone too.

Powell spent a long time spinning his fork in his pasta and set it down on the plate. "What does the world need prophylactics for anyway," he finally said, "when it's got you?"

TABOULI
OR NOT TABOULI

P O W E L L walked my bike and me back to the neighborhood but when we got to his street he turned and said he needed to get home. "I don't understand what you're doing," I said. "I thought that night you came over that things had changed."

"Never take anything for granted."

"What happened? I know I made a fool of myself back there but it wasn't an easy situation."

"That's not why I'm going home," he said. "It's this work. I got a lot riding on *The Brother-in-Law* now that Lopez is interested. I don't have time to be your family therapist."

"I don't want a therapist! I just want to be a guy again. The way I was before. I want to ride you and have sex with condoms. I want to sleep over."

"My home is my haven. The only girl allowed to sleep over is the one I made."

"What—is that Aphorism Number Six?"

"No, I just made it up. But come to think of it—"

"I can't believe you've lived this long with all these idiotic expressions. I would have thought one might have killed you long ago."

"Have a good afternoon," he said, and turned down the street.

T H A T night I went over to my mom's. The house was empty. The living room was well kept but the pictures of my dad were gone and the one with the three of us skiing in Vermont had been relegated to the back, behind the five-by-seven framed photo of my mom with her folk dancing group.

Sitting on top of the coffee table, next to a pile of her papers, was a book called *Surviving Infidelity*, written by two psychotherapists. She had dog-eared one of the pages so I opened it up. The section was called "Poor-Risk Partners" and it began, "The poor-risk partner is most likely to have serial affairs or one-night stands. Many such partners have serious personality problems, often with a long history of poor interpersonal relationships starting in childhood. In fact, his history may be one of having erratic and stormy relationships with family members, bosses, friends, and members of the opposite sex." I should have known when I saw *Mars and Venus in the Bedroom* that soon she'd be reading *Surviving Infidelity*. John Gray was like the gateway drug to divorce.

I went into the kitchen and stepped on the garbage pedal. No Kleenex there. I wondered if she'd even been crying. Maybe her postmenopausal zest had made her take it with a kind of inhuman strength. She'd found a way to rise above it all and keep her head screwed on straight when no one else in our family could.

I checked the fridge to see if she had changed her diet but it was mostly green vegetables from her farmer's market and some focaccia, but nothing too out there like macrobiotics. I decided that was a good sign. A wife is exponentially more likely to end a marriage if she's eating nonprocessed food.

I looked at the calendar on the wall to find out where she was. The boxes were so crowded it was hard to read anything. Dinner with Carol, Koffee Klatsch, Women's League for Israel, Dutch Folk Dance teacher here, with an arrow over three days. Maybe her key to coping was never to be alone. I moved my finger along the activities until I got to Tuesday. "Knitting Hands," it said. "Introductory Meeting."

Knitting Hands was the knitting store on Atlantic Avenue and Bond, in Boerum Hill. It had opened a few years before and was one of the only businesses on the street that was doing well, maybe because so many young women were going retro. When I opened the door I saw a dozen women of all ages, sitting around a table at the back of the room moving their needles and knotting their brows. No one had gotten more than a few rows finished and they were all saying things like "Is it supposed to *grow?*" and "Which side should I hold the yarn on again?"

My mother was sitting near the instructor, a crew-cutted woman in her forties with a bony face. It was like I'd hallucinated the whole goddamn affair. I saw no tear streaks. She was so busy with her knitting that she didn't even look up when I came over until I tapped her on the shoulder.

Up close I could see that her eyes were bloodshot. There were lines extending out from her wrinkled lips. "How'd you know I was here?" she said.

"I saw it on the calendar." She frowned like she didn't like the idea of me going over there unbidden. "So are you doing OK?" I whispered.

She stood up, took my arm, and ushered me to the front of the store. "What am I supposed to do?" she said. "If I stay home I'll just cry more—" Her voice broke a little and she covered her mouth to stifle the sound. "I figured I might as well go to the class. Nina kept insisting I come over to her place instead but I told her, 'It's sixty-five dollars, I don't want the money to go to waste,' and finally she gave in."

"Maybe I should take you home," I said.

"I'm fine," she said. "I'm learning to knit." She blinked a few times and then she started crying. "We shouldn't be talking here," she said, eyeing the dreadlocked guy behind the counter, and pulled me out onto the street.

"Can we go get some dinner or something?" I asked. "I wanted to find out how you are."

"I already ate. And I'm fine. Really. These attacks come but then they pass. I've been seeing a psychotherapist who specializes in"— her voice cracked—"my kind of issues." My mother had started therapy before I did. It was such a role reversal. "Where's Dad staying? Is he living with that—"

I didn't know whether to lie but I wound up not having to say anything because she took one look at me and said, "He is." She shook her head bitterly. "I guess he has everything he wants now. Her, and you."

"That's not fair. You think I want him living above me?"

"I don't know what you want."

She was still angry, still putting it all on me. "I can't believe this," I said quietly. "You still think this is my fault."

"I didn't say that! But if you hadn't become friends with that—"

"Oh my God," I said. "You do. Is this how bad it's gotten? You're even going to blame me for his infidelity? I can never win with you."

My mom and I were like a miserable married couple—stuck together for the long haul but unsure exactly how we'd wound up related. She resented me for my bond with him and I resented her for punishing me for something that really wasn't my choice to begin with.

"Why do you hate me so much?" I said.

"I don't hate you."

"Then why do you act like you do?"

"Look," she said, crossing her arms over her chest, "I have a lot of thinking to do. I was angry the other night, which you should understand, and I'm still angry. I'm just beginning to sort everything out. I'm in process."

You know things are scary when both of your parents say they're in process in the same month. "I just want you to feel like you can talk to me about this," I said.

"I appreciate that."

I reached forward and gripped her wrist. "Please don't blame me. It's bad enough that the two of you hate each other. I don't want you to hate me."

"I'm trying not to blame you," she said.

"Is that the best you can do?"

"Right now it is." I lowered my hand. "It's all right, Rachel," she said wearily. "It'll all be all right."

But of course I didn't believe her. I didn't think my relationship with my mother could have possibly gotten worse than it was already but I have a really lousy habit of looking on the bright side.

O N Thursday night I had a good crowd—three yuppie guys drinking Bass at the end of the bar; a few hipster couples getting drunk enough to hit on each other; and some cute British soccer players, all in uniform, shooting pool and making noise. Jasper was by the spigots, in a good mood because he had gone on a date with Delia and at the end of the night she'd kissed him, though she didn't let him inside her place.

Powell hadn't called since the tennis game and I'd been too embarrassed to call him. If only I hadn't met him now, when I was so messed up. It was like going on a great first date when you were on the rag; you might be a much more agreeable person normally, but how was the guy supposed to know?

I checked my total on the cash register and then I checked my machine. No call. I had to right things with him. He picked up on the second ring. "Hi," I said.

The music in the bar was loud and he said, "Who is this?"

This wasn't good. "It's Rachel. I wanted to see you. I feel really embarrassed about the scene I made the other day. I think if we could just be together alone it would be different."

"But you get off so late."

"You can take a disco nap! It's only five more hours till I finish. We could—do what we were doing before. And in the morning I'll buy you breakfast."

He was quiet a while and then he said, "I'm not good for too many more hours anyway. Maybe I'll come by around one."

"Great!" I said.

I hung up. "You are so whipped," Jasper said.

"You can't be whipped when it's a guy. You can only be whipped when it's a girl."

"You are so tipped, then."

"Not tonight," I said. "I only have like a hundred fifty bucks."

That was when my dad came through the door. He did not look good. His hair was messier than usual and he was wearing a T-shirt that said "Tabouli or not Tabouli," with a pair of dark blue jeans, cuffed way too high, the kind you could get away with if you were James Dean or under thirty, but not if you were neither. His eye was looking better but there was a thin line below it like he'd gotten punched, and the overall effect was of a scruffy HIV-positive homeless guy. There was a shadow around his face, midway between a growth and a thin beard, and his face looked puffier than usual, like Alec Baldwin's.

He headed straight to the jukebox and put some money in. I didn't ask what he'd put on. I just waited for him to sit at the bar and then I said, "Chivas and water?"

"Nah, maybe just a Harp."

"Really?" I said. "You don't want a Chivas? Or a martini?"

"No, Harp's good."

I poured the drink, set the glass. He didn't seem to want to talk so I checked on one of the hipster couples and fixed them a second round.

"You remember Jasper, don't you?" I said when I came back.

He nodded at him. "Good to see you."

"You too, Mr. Block. How you holding up?"

My dad gave me an angry look like I shouldn't have blabbed. "I had to tell him," I said. "We spend like thirty hours a week together."

"It's cool, Mr. B.," Jasper said. "I'm a moral relativist anyway."

My dad nodded like it was all a little too deep for him and then he leaned in and said to me quietly, "I have to tell you something."

Liz was preggo. I knew it. She'd abandon the baby and I'd be left to raise it, like a surrogate Hester Prynne, forced to pretend it was my own illegitimate Powell-child, as my dad became the most doting and active grandpa the world had ever known.

"What is it?" I asked hollowly.

"I think I'm going to try to work things out with Mom."

I levitated a thousand feet up into the sky and bumped my head against the midnight moon before parachuting down to my feet. "Really?" I said, choking on a sob. "That's the best news I've heard in—"

"Get ahold of yourself," he said, handing me a napkin. "You don't want your customers to see you crying."

"It's nothing they haven't seen before," I said.

"She's right," Jasper said.

"I'm so happy for you! What brought on this sudden flash attack of wisdom?"

"I don't know," he said, his eyes darting back and forth nervously. "I guess I just realized Mom and I just have a lot more in common."

"You realized this all of a sudden?"

"Elizabeth and I were watching a *Saturday Night Live* rerun, I mentioned something about Jewess Jeans and she didn't know what I was talking about."

"You see?" I said. "You see? Shared reference points!"

"But it wasn't just that. We didn't find the same things funny. She would make cruel comments about women on the street, about their clothes, or bodies, and I found it disturbing. Not to mention her family issues, which would have taken Freud himself half his life to figure out."

I was such an idiot. His eyes were blazing and his lips pursed together tightly. It was all painfully obvious. "Dad," I said. "Liz dumped you, didn't she?"

"Last night," he nodded. His nose flared out further than Ali Mac-Graw's and his eyes brimmed over. "She thinks we're . . ." He bit his lip and cleared his throat so he wouldn't crack. "Incompatible." A fat tear trickled down his cheek. "She says she was deluding herself to think we had any long-term potential, that we just don't have enough in common and that the only reason she went for me was because of some unresolved issue with her father."

Jasper stood up and put his arm around him. "It's definitely cool to cry, Mr. B. In fact it's a sign of strength."

"I love her," my dad said, his voice breaking. "Loved her. I know you don't think I do but I do. She's so smart and not like how she seemed—on the outside. She made me feel—not young, but funny and handsome." He kneaded the spot between his eyebrows and looked remorsefully down into his beer.

I wanted to be sympathetic and concerned, but I couldn't help but see his sudden desire to be with my mom in a slightly less positive light. "So you only want Mom because she's better than no one?"

"*No!*" he said. "I think I could actually be a good husband to her now, now that—and especially in light of the time I have on my hands, I could help her out with some of her projects. Elizabeth says part of my reason for straying was jealousy of how active Mom's social life has gotten. I didn't want to believe it at first but there's some part of that that's right. I feel like now that I'm more self-aware I might actually be a decent mate to my wife."

The word "wife" coming out of my father's mouth sent a shiver of delight down my spine. But I was still nervous about his motives. My mom knew him better than anyone and if she suspected for a second that Liz had put him up to the reconciliation she'd freak. I had to help him out before he burned the only bridge he had left.

"I think you're right, Dad," I said. "This is the best decision you've made since—since having me."

My dad nodded, not too confidently. "It'll all be all right," I said, squeezing his shoulder. "You gotta have a little faith. You just have to convince her it was all a mistake. That you've changed."

"What if she doesn't believe me?"

It was a possibility I didn't want to entertain. But I had to sound hopeful or he wouldn't try at all. "She will," I said. "You *have* changed, haven't you?"

"Of course I have!" he said, with so much fire it was apparent he hadn't, or at least not yet. He wiped the tears from his eyes, stood up, pulled his T-shirt down, and headed for the door. I gave Jasper a look and he got up and dragged my dad back.

"Why don't you chill out here for a while, Mr. B.?"

"No, I think I should go. I've made my decision. I should go home and wait on the stoop until she comes home."

"That's a really bad idea," I said.

"Why?"

"Because—because you're wearing a shirt that says 'Tabouli or not Tabouli'."

"I think it's charming," Jasper said. "But Rachel's just saying you might want to plan your speech a little. It can't hurt to be prepared."

My dad looked down at his shirt, got a somber look, and said, "I guess you're right." He sat back on his stool and I fixed him a water with ice. He seemed so tormented, so off balance. Maybe he'd seen something in Liz that no one else could see: a heart.

"I'm sorry she dumped you," I said.

"No you're not," he said.

"OK, I'm not. But I'm sorry you're in pain."

"I guess I should try to think positively," he said sullenly. "If it had all worked out I would have gone through the rest of my life thinking there was nothing wrong with what I did."

I'd never seen him show such insight. Was this what it took for a person to have a wake-up call: running the risk of losing everything he had?

His eyes were turned down and he looked way too old to be sitting in a hipster bar. "It's all going to be OK, Dad," I said, placing my hand on top of his. "I promise."

"I forgot to ask you," he said. "Can I stay at your place tonight? Liz wants me out pronto. I've slept on the couch the last three nights and she says she can't take waking up and—seeing me there."

What could I do? I'd convinced Powell to come over, I didn't want to cancel. And if I asked to go to his place, he'd beg off, saying he needed his space.

"Can't you stay at the Brooklyn Marriott or something?"

"You'd make your own father stay at a hotel?" my dad moaned.

"You can stay with me, Mr. Block," Jasper said. "I have a futon. There are some pretty dubious stains on it but—"

"*Jasper!*" I said, and reached for the phone.

"Hello?" Powell said.

I turned my back so my dad wouldn't hear. "Liz dumped him," I said.

"That didn't take long."

"He needs a place to sleep tonight." There was silence. "So I was thinking maybe I could come over to your place and my dad could stay at mine."

"Oh no," he said. "I got stuff to do in the morning. I can't have you here."

"I'll leave early!" I hissed.

"No, we'll do it another night."

I couldn't say what I was thinking, that I didn't know if there would be another night. "I thought you might think it was good for me to leave him alone. I thought you said I had to separate from my parents."

"Not in a time of crisis. When things are rough you don't turn your back on family." It was incredible. My father was like a human condom.

I made my dad stay at the bar till he sobered up a little and then I made Jasper walk him back to my place. When I came home at four-thirty AM he opened the door in one of his old undershirts, a pair of black sweats, and his old 1970s glasses. His shirt was V-neck and frayed at the bottom and his stomach protruded out a little. It was strange but I found myself enormously buoyed by my father's belly. Maybe the old him was back.

"I'm sorry to wake you," I said.

"That's all right," he mumbled, and yawned.

"Go back to sleep."

"OK," he said, and turned his back. He had turned the couch to the side, away from the tennis window, so there was room for the bed to fold out, and I had to sidestep around it to get to my bedroom.

As he hauled himself onto the sofa bed it creaked. "Good night, Dad," I said through the archway.

"Good night, Rach," he said. I lowered the Pearl River shade until I couldn't see him anymore and then I went into the bathroom and brushed my teeth. I put on my Gowanus Canal Yacht Club T-shirt and got in bed.

I was tossing and turning, wondering whether he was asleep or not, when I heard the sofa bed creak again and the pitter-patter of his feet as they came up to my doorway. There was a knock. "You awake?" he said.

"Yeah."

"I'm so sorry to bother you," he said, "but I have to . . . visit the loo." If only I'd lived in a place where he didn't have to go through the bedroom to get to the bathroom.

"Go right ahead," I said. The shade went up and he walked past the bed to the bathroom. The bathroom door was cut unevenly and never closed all the way, so you could hear everything going on inside. The toilet lid went up and made a loud crash as it hit the side of the tank, and then my dad began to pee. My father had the loudest and most aggressive flow of any man I ever heard. He could be the Foley artist for drunken men's urination scenes. The flow halted and then came the shake. There were a few drops, the toilet flushed, and he emerged.

He started to move past me into the living room but then he stopped and sat down on the bed. He was quiet a second and then he said, "I—there's something I need to talk to you about."

"OK," I said. He was having second thoughts. He wanted to get back with Liz. He wanted to know if I'd serve as a character witness in divorce court so they could split their money equitably.

"What?"

"I just—I'm a little concerned about your relationship with Hank." So was I, but I wasn't going to share.

"What concerns you?" I asked, pulling the covers up to my neck even though I was in a T-shirt.

"Well, I consider myself a liberal individual but when I saw those marks on your wrists—"

I sat straight up in bed. "Dad. Let's not talk about this."

"If I didn't know it probably wouldn't matter," he said, "but since I saw, I feel the need to ask whether he's treating you in a way you deserve to be treated." He wasn't, but that had nothing to do with the marks. "Are you all right? I just want to know if—"

"*Dad.* Who was the one running so much equipment with his girlfriend up there that my lights flickered?"

He jerked his head back in surprise. "They *flickered?* Really? You should put in a call to your landlord. There could be something wrong with the circuit."

"I don't think you of all people are in any position to pass judgment on what I do. You have forfeited the right to play the dad card with me."

"I'm not saying I haven't made mistakes," he said. "But as your parent I have a right to ask. Does he force you to do things against your will?"

"No!"

"It's just—as much as Elizabeth educated me as to the ways of—desire—when I saw those marks, it made me feel like—like a failure as a father."

"Let me get this straight," I said. "That made you feel like a failure as a father but sleeping with your daughter's best friend and then being found out didn't?"

He paused with his mouth hanging open and then he patted the blanket, stood up, and said, "Maybe you're right. Maybe it's best we not explore this area of conversation."

He ducked under the shade. I heard the sofa bed creak as he lumbered in. We lay there in the darkness. I could hear him breathing through the wall since there wasn't a door. Every time he turned over it made a noise and I lay awake another hour before I finally drifted off.

TSHUVAH

M Y dad decided the way back into my mom's heart was gradual. He spent the next week on the phone to her all the time, having long, drawn-out conversations on his cell, down on the stoop so I wouldn't hear. I only got snippets—things like "give it another shot" and "not a good-bye affair" and "happy to come in and talk to your therapist"—but it was obvious from the way most of them ended that she wasn't budging.

One night, though, he informed me she had agreed to let him come over, because she wanted to talk face-to-face. He took this as a sign that there was a tiny crack of hope so he got really dressed up in a collared shirt and Dockers with a belt, and slicked his hair back with gel. I told him he looked great and said to call me if he needed me. An hour went by, then three, and he finally came back around eleven looking twenty years older. He hung his head and sat on the couch.

"It's over," he said dully, like he didn't believe it himself.

"She won't even agree to couples therapy?"

He shook his head no. "She's reading some book, on infidelity, and she's decided that this was the kind of affair she couldn't forgive. She says she's realized how small I made her feel for so long, and how enriched she's been with all her groups, and she said the best thing she can do now is be on her own. She said she doesn't need me anymore." He wasn't even crying, which for my dad was a really dangerous sign. He seemed numb, shell-shocked, like someone had grabbed him by the throat.

I knew that if she really felt this way then it didn't have to do with

Liz but I couldn't help blaming her anyway. I could tell myself this was best, that my parents had problems anyway, but I didn't really believe it.

"I hate her so much," I growled.

"Mom?"

"Liz! It's all her fault. She drove you apart."

"You can't think of it that way. I had a choice to make and I made the wrong one. I knew I was playing with fire when I started. Mom was always a one-strike kind of person. But when it ended I held out hope that Mom would love me too much to reject me. Shows how much I know." He ran his fingers through his hair and said, "What's left for me, Rach?"

"What do you mean what's left for you?"

"I mean who am I kidding? I'm a loser."

"You're not a loser."

"Yes I am! I'm beginning to feel like I destroy everything I touch." He put his head in his hands and then lifted it, his eyes wild and desperate. "I've made such a mess of my life!"

"No you haven't."

"I have! I've been unemployed for almost four months, I'm fifty-five years old, and I'm living with my twenty-six-year-old daughter."

"Wait a minute," I said. "Who said you're living with me?"

"Where else did you think I was going to go?"

"To your own apartment!"

"One-bedrooms start at fourteen hundred," he said, "and I'm living off my unemployment. I had the checks forwarded to Elizabeth's but Mom froze me out of our joint account."

"Isn't that illegal?"

"How should I know? I guess eventually we'll have to start"—he choked a little—"proceedings, but until then I'm living on $405 a week."

"I can't have you here! It's barely big enough for me!"

"You won't even notice I'm here," he said. "I promise I'll be neat. I'll make the sofabed every day and close it up. Whaddaya say, Rach? Please?"

Though his face was poised in questioning mode, eyebrows knit,

there was a hint of a glint in his eye. I knew why. My father had gotten exactly what he had wanted from me since the moment I left for
college: proximity. He could never get enough of me. When I saw
them once a week he'd ask me to come twice, when I saw them
twice a week he'd call every other day. On one level he was falling
apart but on another he'd gotten his heart's desire.

This was every parent's fantasy: to live four feet away from their
kid, close enough to be able to watch her every move. Now everything I did would be on display for him to evaluate and judge. Every
night I'd have to fall asleep to the sound of him peeing and shaking.
He'd feel he had full license to nag me about my bartending job and
try to convince me to get back into Jewish education. He'd harass
me about Powell no matter how little I told him. It was his greatest
fantasy and my greatest nightmare. He'd flown out of his empty nest
right into mine.

I T took a week for him to get all his stuff moved in. Once I prom-
ised my mom he wasn't going to try to contact her again she scheduled time for him to come and collect his belongings. I cleared a few
shelves for him in the armoire and pushed all my winter clothes to
the side of the closet.

He got to shower first in the morning but he had to make coffee
for both of us, and he started buying cereal, which was better for my
diet than bagels and cream cheese anyway. He helped me wire my
stereo system so that the sound from the TV came out of the speak-
ers, and I taught him to hang his towels on the hook on the back of
the bathroom door instead of over it, and to light a match after he'd
taken a shit. He bought some T/Gel dandruff shampoo, which I reluctantly began to use once I got over the tar smell, and I even bor-
rowed some of his hydrocortisone when the eczema on my elbows
flared up.

I changed the message on the machine to the automated one so
headhunters could call him about jobs, and he set up a table for his
iBook where he could use my Internet access to e-mail résumés. I
bought him the Sandy Koufax biography, which he devoured in just

two days, and at night we would rent DVDs. One night I made the mistake of selecting *Blame It on Rio,* thinking it would cheer him up, and halfway through he got so upset I had to eject it.

Powell and I still had breakfast together but when I asked to see him at night he always begged off, saying he was busy with Nora and *The Brother-in-Law.* I wound up spending all my free time with my father instead, listening to him recount his sob story, helping him shop for interview clothes, and trying to insure he didn't do something really stupid like kill himself.

My mom started taking my calls again and a few times we went to dinner to talk about things. She was still folk dancing and leading Koffee Klatsch, and when I suggested that maybe it was a good time to lighten her extracurricular load, she said the groups helped her because they gave her distraction from her problems. Although she never said she forgave me, she stopped implying like the affair was my fault and once in a while she even asked about him, and his job hunt, which I thought was a decent sign even if it was rapidly becoming clear there was no way they were getting back together.

For a while Liz seemed to have disappeared. I didn't know whether she was trying celibacy or living at her parents', but I stopped hearing her footsteps in the morning and she never seemed to be around the building.

One night at dinner, my dad and I were sitting at the kitchen table eating takeout from the Fountain Café. He was flipping through a *New Yorker* chuckling at a Roz Chast cartoon when there was some spirited moaning from up above. He jerked his head up to the ceiling like he'd gotten a shock to the chest, and a male voice cried, "How'd you like me to come all over your tits?"

"Why don't you do that?" came the response. "Why don't you do that and then I'll rub it in with my hands!"

"You could use a little moisturizer!" the man said, and by the way he pronounced the word "moisturizer" I realized it was Gordon, the cowboy.

"Oh brother," my dad groaned, his face frozen in anguish.

"Keep jerking it!" Liz said. "Jerk that *shvantz!*"

"I am. I'm jerking it for you. You see me jerking it?"

"This is torture," my dad said.

"It sounds like it'll be over soon," I said.

"That's supposed to make me feel *better?*" he howled, angling his head up like he was afraid the ceiling was going to drop in.

"Mmmmmmmmm," Gordon said.

"I can't believe this!" my dad cried. "I was trying to console my-self with the thought that she might have some regrets, but the girl's like Edith Piaf!"

"Maybe she's just trying to forget you by throwing herself into something else before she's really ready."

"This one's gonna be a good load!" Gordon said. My dad's brow knotted and he looked like he might have a seizure himself.

"Why don't we go get a beer?" I said, and before he could argue I ushered him quickly out the door.

T H A T whole night I kept tossing and turning. I always kept my window open a little bit because otherwise I couldn't sleep and around one in the morning I heard someone tapping at the door. I pulled the window shade open and saw Liz crouched on my fire es-cape, beckoning me out. She was smoking a cigarette and the smoke was coming in through the window.

I heard my dad murmuring faintly in his sleep, something like twenty-eight K, and I worried he might wake up if I talked too loud so I climbed out. Her hair was messier than usual and she was wear-ing a tight blue T-shirt that said PORNSTAR with a rainbow decal un-derneath it, and a hooded Juicy zip-up she was holding around her body. It seemed strange that someone so skinny could be capable of ruining three people's lives.

"Hey," she said, lighting a cigarette and taking a long, deep drag. She waved the smoke away from my window like it would make a difference.

"What do you want?" I said, crossing my arms over my chest.

"I wanted to talk. What happened with your parents? Are they back together?"

I shook my head no. "He's been living with me."

"What?" she said.

"You should keep your voice down. He's in the next room."

"I don't understand," she said. "I told him he should try to reconcile with your mom."

"He did. But unfortunately it's not a one-person decision."

"She wouldn't have him?"

"Would *you?*"

"I figured after this many years they'd find a way to stay together." I shook my head no. I hated her figure, her gaunt evil cheeks. "This—this makes no sense," she said. "I thought she was still into him. I knew she'd be mad for a while but I thought she'd find a way to forgive. This really sucks."

"Yeah, well, it's a lot worse for me than it is for you."

She looked at me with a kind of strange compassion and her face contorted into something foreign and anguished. "I'm sorry," she said.

Her eyes were lonely and sad and she didn't look like a raging bitch so much as a really fucked-up person. "Why did you do it?" I said.

"I'm not totally sure. I'm trying really hard to process it right now with Dr. Fromberg. She says I violate boundaries because I'm afraid no one will like me if I don't relate to them sexually."

"It's just the opposite," I said.

"I know, but it still takes a while to figure that out."

She was acting like *I* was supposed to feel sorry for her. It was completely unfair. "I just don't understand why you did it," I said. "I mean you can't pretend he was just some random guy. So what did I do to make you hate me so much?"

"I dunno," she said, curling out her lower lip and taking a deep drag. "Dr. Fromberg thinks I felt some weird jealousy of you because you didn't seem to have any of the problems with men that I did."

I snickered. "Yeah, right."

"I know that's not true *now,* but I didn't then. And that night on Smith Street when your dad asked me out for a nightcap I thought, *Well, let's just see where this goes,* and then we started talking and there was this chemistry, and it all . . ." She shrugged. "I don't know. I wasn't like consciously trying to hurt you. I guess I just—I felt like you were so superior all the time—"

"What did I ever say that gave you that impression?"

"When I'd talk about guys you'd look at me with pity. Like I was completely psycho for being attracted to blue-collar men. Or for fucking on the first date. You never said anything but I could feel you judging me."

"But I didn't!" I said. "It was the opposite. I always thought you were so cool for being able to fuck like a guy. *I* wanted to learn how."

"Well, I don't think it was all in my head. Sometimes I'd tell you a story and you'd just look at me like I was trash. So I guess—I decided to prove you right."

"I don't think you're trash," I said, "but I wish you'd said something to me so we could have talked about it or something. That might have been a slightly simpler solution."

"Look. I'm not saying what I did was justified. For goodness sake, Rachel, I'm the one who's going to have to live with it for the rest of my life, cringe every time I pass your mom in the neighborhood. It's not like I was thinking this whole thing through. I just—fell for him."

I still couldn't see it, couldn't make sense of what they had. How could anyone use the term "fell for him" when referring to my dad? "I know it's hard to believe but he treated me like he cared. And he made it sound like there were problems at home anyway. For all I knew, you knew they were struggling. And then I ran into him that night, and it—started, and then your mom found out, and before I could decide if I wanted my unborn child's father to be eighty when she graduated college, he had already moved in."

"So if you cared about him so much then why'd you break it off?"

"Because as soon as he moved in I realized we were just too different. I mean, did you ever think the two of us were actually compatible?"

"No! I just wished you'd cut it off before you two got spotted!"

She looked out at the sky and flicked some ash down onto the pathetic garden behind the building, which consisted of some sad-looking grass, a slab of concrete, and a couple picnic tables. The wrinkles between her eyes seemed prominent in the moonlight and her skin was pale and blue.

"I did a shitty thing," she said, "and I had suspicions of its shittiness early on but sometimes even though you know you're making a big mistake it's hard to turn back." She sighed and licked her lips. "I know you can probably never speak to me again. And if I were in your position I probably wouldn't either. I'm really sorry, Rachel. I know it sounds trite and probably doesn't count for anything but I didn't know it would end like this." It had gotten chilly and she pulled her sweatshirt tightly around her. "Do you think I'm a total cunt? Do you think I'm a home wrecker?"

"Definitely at least one of the two," I said.

"Yeah," she said sullenly. "You know what the worst part of this is?"

"What?"

"I was really thinking of getting out of analysis and now I'll never be able to."

There was a groan and then a yawn from upstairs and a voice said, "Liz? Where'd you go?"

"I'm down here!" she called up to her window. "Talking to Rachel! Be up in a second!"

"I hope you and the cowboy can be a little more quiet," I said. "We heard him coming all over your tits."

She clapped her hand over her mouth. "Rachel," she said. "I swear to God I didn't know your dad was living here."

"Please get some eggshell. His heart just isn't that strong."

"I will. I promise. I'll go to Canal Street tomorrow." I knew she wouldn't but it counted for something that she probably thought she would.

"So are you two, like, a couple now?" I said, pointing up to the ceiling.

"Not officially," she said offhandedly, "but judging by the stinging sensation in my ass, I'd definitely say we're seeing each other." She gave me a wink and climbed back up the stairs to her apartment.

A   C O U P L E   days later when my dad was out at a job interview, Powell called and said he wanted to come over. His tone was urgent. "Are you OK?" I said.

"Yeah," he said. "I just wanna see you."

I ran to the bathroom and checked to see if there was any spinach in my teeth but all was clean for my dirty old man. At the door he seemed sweaty even though it was a chilly day. "The subway ride did me in," he said, leaning against the jamb. "It always takes a lot outta me."

"Then why do you ride it?" I said.

"Because one year when I was doing my taxes I saw that I'd spent five thousand dollars on taxicabs and I realized I had to rein it in."

"You rearranged," he said when he came inside. My dad and I had moved the couch to the opposite wall, at the end of the entrance hallway, so there was room for it to open up at night. His pillows and blankets were stacked on top of it and I delicately carried them into my bedroom.

We sat on the couch and Powell said, "So how've you been getting along with your pop?"

"And I was just getting in the mood to see you."

"I'm sorry," he said, and put his thumb in my mouth. I sucked that thumb and turned my head so I could suck it deeper. I liked him looking up at me with those watery blue eyes. I slithered my way down and unbuckled his buckle. It only took me a few seconds to get the pup out of the kennel. "Maybe we can pick up where we left off that time," he said.

"Sounds like a good idea."

I felt so happy to see him, so happy he'd come over voluntarily. It made me feel like maybe things between us would be romantic again and that sometimes when men said they were busy they really meant it. I rubbed his cock, which was already hard.

"Did you take a Viagra?" I said.

"Don't ruin this," he said.

"Is that a yes?"

"*I'm a natural man!*" he said. "*My cock does not require the assistance of synthetics!*"

I bent down to suck it and he said, "Oh that's good," and rubbed the back of my neck. I moved my head up and down like a seasoned whore, working the spot on the bottom of the shaft just below the head, and then he put his hands under my armpits and pulled me up on top of him. "You wanna be a guy again?" he said.

"Way to put pressure on me," I said.

I got a condom from the bathroom and rolled it on him quickly before he could complain, and then straddled him and ground around. He sunk his hands into my ass and buried his face between my breasts. I could see the jail out the window and imagined I was imprisoned in an all-women's facility and Powell was a warden I was fucking in exchange for a good-behavior write-up.

He got harder inside me and kept moving his face from breast to breast, making a muffled growling noise, and then he said, "I'm right on the edge." I knew this meant it was my turn to come, so I pressed my pelvis hard against his. I sniffed the sweat in his neck and clawed at his hair and ten minutes later I came. It wasn't as good as the first time but still I saw it as a hurdle.

I made a noise so he'd know and he grabbed my tits really hard, threw his head back and said, "Oh, I'm right there, I'm almost there."

"That's good," I said, my hand on his back.

"It's coming up inside me," he said, and as his mouth fell open and his eyes rolled to the back of his head, I heard a key in the door. I jerked my head over my shoulder to spot my father standing in the doorway, his mouth forming the O Powell would never have.

"Whoops a-daisy," he said, and shut the door as abruptly as he'd opened it. I leapt off of Powell and threw on my shirt, while he jumped to his feet and yanked on his pants. "I can't believe this," he said. "It's impossible for a guy to get his rocks off in this apartment!"

"But I wasn't expecting him!"

"You shoulda had a system," he said, straightening his hair. "Something on the door. I'm gonna have blue balls."

"There's no such thing," I said.

"Tell that to my prostate!"

"Can I come in now?" my dad called.

"Just a second!" we both shouted at the same time.

"I can't take this," Powell said. "I'm too old." He threw his coat on and stormed to the door, where my dad was still standing with the same rattled expression he'd had before. "How you doing, Hank?" my father said, but he brushed past him down the stairs.

I chased after him but he yelled, "Just leave me alone!" I stormed back into the apartment past my father into my bedroom and threw myself down on the bed.

"I know 'I'm sorry' won't cut it," my dad said, coming in and sitting on the edge. "But—"

"I thought you'd be home at four!"

"My interview was canceled. I would have called to tell you if I thought I might be interrupting something."

"You're ruining my life!" I sat up in bed. "I can't live like this!"

"I'm prepared to let go of what I saw today," he said. "Just block it out."

"I don't know if I can."

"I—I don't understand," he said. "Haven't these last few weeks been fun? I mean, playing Scrabble at night, and going to the Fountain Café and listening to Garrison?" I loathed Garrison Keillor and his arch-narcissism and nose breathing but saying that would be like saying something anti-Semitic or anti-Brooklyn; I just couldn't do it.

"It's not that they haven't been fun," I said. "It's that I can't have a life. You gotta leave."

"Can't you just wait till I get a job?"

"No." As I spoke it I felt stronger and more revved up. "I think you gotta get out or I'm going to kill you."

He looked at me like he was hearing me for the first time, his eyes wide and wounded. "You're—evicting me?"

"Yes. I'll help you find a new place but you gotta get out. As soon as possible."

He didn't say anything and then he looked at me and said, "Rachel, you know that if there were any way I could press rewind, go backward, and undo the whole thing I would. You know that, right?"

"Yeah."

"Do you hate me? For everything that's happened?"

I wanted to hate him but I couldn't. He was intrusive, clueless and stagnated, self-hating, parasitic, and unemployed, and still I loved him. Maybe this was what family meant, that in the precise moments you felt most misunderstood and violated, you were angry not because of what your parents did but because you loved them in spite of it.

"I don't hate you."

"So does that mean I can stay?"

I shook my head no. He nodded slowly like he didn't like it but was prepared to accept it. "I understand," he said, rising to his feet, his chin up in an imitation of dignity. "I'll pick up a *Voice* tomorrow," he said, and ducked out under the shade.

I N the morning I walked down to D'Amico. The two old Italian guys were sitting at a table in the back, reminiscing about how cheap haircuts used to be. "Now they don't even give you a shave," said one of them. "You gotta pay extra. It used to be a service culture."

"It's a different world we live in," said the other.

A few tables away a nerdy Jewish guy was reading *The New Yorker* and he eyed me as I came in. Powell was at the table next to his, his head slightly obscured by the paper. I walked right up to him and leaned over the top. His eyes moved up to mine and he gave me the kind of slick smile he gave all the ass kissers at the cast party. It was like he didn't know me.

"Good morning," he said formally. There was a cold blackness behind his eyes.

I went up to the counter, ordered a bagel, fixed myself a cup of coffee, and sat down opposite him. "I'm sorry we got interrupted," I said. "But believe me, it was worse for me."

"I don't want to talk about it," he said.

"Are you all right?" I said. "What's with you?"

"What did I just say?"

He lifted his newspaper and read silently, like I wasn't there. I nibbled my bagel and watched him and after a few minutes the silence got so deafening I opened my trap. "Are you still working on *Who Killed My Wife?*"

He threw the paper down and glared. "Why?"

"You haven't mentioned it in a while, so I was wondering if, you know, you were only working on *The Brother-in-Law*, or—"

"I'm working on the new one."

"Because you have a deadline or because you're blocked on the other one?"

"Jesus H. Christ."

"I guess you are."

"I didn't say I was blocked!"

I felt totally panicked, like he was going to throw something at me, or punch me in the mouth. So I did the thing I always do when I get scared: kept talking. "Well, look on the bright side," I said. "The less money you make the less you'll have to give to your ex."

"Why are you bringing up money?" he roared.

"I don't know," I said.

"You act like you're so sensitive all a the time, like I should tread lightly with you, but you're the insensitive one. Your behavior is boorish."

His eyes were angry and insane. I had seen this side of him before and I always felt like I just had to switch him around, calm him down enough so that he'd act normal. But Powell wasn't normal. It was the best part of him and the worst. He was who he was and more than fifty percent of the time he was a jerk.

"You know what?" I said. "You can be a real asshole sometimes."

"What did you say?" he hissed, leaning in, as though daring me to dig myself in deeper.

"You pass yourself off as so enlightened but you're just a grump. You're obnoxious and moody and you expect everyone around you to just suck it up and be grateful to be around such a genius. You're totally full of yourself. And mean. And old."

"You don't know a goddamn thing about me!"

"Sure I do! I just never said any of this before because I knew you'd act like even more of an asshole."

"I act this way because you have no grace! I always have to put you back in line because you're always doing the *wrong thing*."

"If you hate me so much then how come you keep asking to see me?"

"That's a *very good question*." He stared sullenly at the wall as the Italian guys behind us got quiet. They probably lived for drama like this.

"I don't understand how you have any friends when you're this obnoxious," I said.

"You have no right trying to make *me* feel guilty when *you're* the one violating my boundaries."

"I'm not violating your boundaries," I said. "I'm telling you what I think. And even if I don't say the exact right thing all the time I'm a human being. You make me feel like I have to follow some script with you, some perfect script. It's like I can't ever be honest or myself. You just want an audience telling you how great you are every second of the day. And you *are* great. You're funny and smart and endlessly entertaining. But I don't want to be a clapping seal all the time. It's not that it's hard to appreciate you. It just gets . . . *really boring.*"

"You're vile!" he said. "You know what the problem with your family is? Nobody taught you any manners!"

With this foul scowl on his face, his eyebrows twisted around, the saliva glistening at the sides of his mouth, his hair matted and unkempt, he didn't look so dashing or brilliant anymore. He just looked ugly and angry.

Powell was the wrong kind of sadist. It wasn't the tying-me-up part I hated. It was this, the snarls and the temper. It wasn't fun. I wanted the good stuff without any of the bad but he had told me who he was all along and it was my fault for never listening. The whole point of having someone was to feel better around him than you did with everyone else but when I was with Powell I always felt worse.

I stood up and stared down at his thinning hair. I didn't want to say good-bye. I wanted him to love me, to be sweet. I wanted him to apologize for being mean and irritable, for blaming me when my dad had walked in, for being sporadic with his affection and cruel when I didn't kiss his ass. But Powell was like Popeye and if nobody else had been able to change him I wouldn't be able to. This knowledge hit me in the stomach like failure and instead of hating him I felt the tragedy of it not having worked.

"I don't think I can see you anymore," I said.

"That's fine by me." He turned his body away toward the wall and flipped a page of the paper with a loud rustling noise. I walked out past the coffee barrels. Through the window I could still see him, frowning, bent down intently. From far away he looked like a crazy man.

A c o u p l e days later I got a call from my mom asking me to come over. She wouldn't say why and when I got there she and my dad were sitting at the kitchen table laughing. "Hel-lo," she said as I came through the door.

"Hi," I said. "Is everything OK?"

"We're doing just fine," she said, tossing her head back to him. "Right, Richard?"

"I'd say more than fine." They were acting like it was Rosh Hashanah dinner all over again.

"What's going on?" I said. "This is really weird."

"Mom and I had a talk and figured out a lot of things." He patted one of the kitchen chairs and I sat down reluctantly. I didn't know if they were going to say they'd gotten back together and I didn't know if I wanted them to. "For starters," my dad said, setting his plate down on the table, "I'm going to be living here again."

"You guys made up?"

"Are you crazy?" my mom said. "I found a rental on the Upper West Side and Dad's going to stay here. I want to be closer to Symphony Space and this place is too big and empty for me anyway. I was willing to give it up but Dad said he could handle it."

"The rent's less than yours, Rachel, and I've got the whole place."

"But what about Koffee Klatsch?" I asked my mom.

"What do you care?"

"It's important to the neighborhood!"

She shook her head like I wasn't making any sense and said, "Nina's going to take over. She has a bigger living room anyway."

My mom seemed far away then, like a stranger, like someone I didn't know. Her face was pink and she looked so optimistic, like she'd just graduated high school and was moving into her very own apartment.

"So what do you think?" my dad said.

"I don't know," I said.

"It was strange for me too at first," he said, "but then I accepted the fact that Mom doesn't want me back and there's nothing I can do about it."

"You're making it sound like this is my fault," she said, "when you're the one who brought it on. I didn't cheat. Who's the one who displayed such a total lack of self-control he felt the need to take off with the Jewish Happy Hooker?"

"I'm not saying I didn't make a mistake, I just—"

"You can't even be accountable now, even after all this, even after I agreed to give up the place for you? That is so like you."

"Maybe if you'd showed a little more awareness during the past year of what I was going through—"

"Oh, so it's back to the cause-and-effect," she said. "I am trying really hard to move through my acute stage into the integration but you—"

"What?" he snarled.

"I can't believe you blame me. Even now you can't even look at the mirror and see what you did. You're just going to keep denying, denying, denying, because even to this day you cannot be accountable for your own actions!"

As they kept going back and forth I stood up quietly, went into the living room, and lay on my stomach on the couch. A little while later they must have realized I was gone because they shut up and came over. And then my mom was lifting my head up and sliding under me so my head was resting on her lap, and my dad was sitting on the other end of the couch and squeezing the arch of my foot.

I remembered when I was little and I used to crawl into their bed on weekend mornings and wake them up and tell them I wanted to make a peanut butter sandwich. They were the bread and I was the peanut butter and I would squeeze in between them and tell them to crush me, and it was that feeling of being suffocated in the best way, smothered by love.

I knew then what scared me so much. I hadn't wanted to admit it because it was too unsettling and weird, but for the past few years I had been dating my parents. I chose to move back into the neighborhood not because of the hipsters but because of them. They were my steadies, the ones I could count on, and as much as I griped about the dinners and obligations, I craved their company like it was a drug. Now that their marriage was over I was afraid that as they disintegrated I would too. I'd just wander around like a soldier whose arm's been shot off but doesn't know it.

My mom brushed her hand across my forehead. "Aren't you glad to have him get out of your apartment? Now you can have some privacy with Hank." I started bawling. "What is it?"

"It's over," I said. I had told my dad I ended it but when he pressed for details I hadn't given any.

"That's terrible," she said. "I thought the two of you had something really special. What were the issues? When did this happen?"

"Maybe she doesn't want to go into it, Sue," my dad said. The only time my dad was willing to give me an ounce of space was to get one over on my mom.

She leaned forward and said, "You can tell me all about it when you come to visit in a few weeks."

"Why's she going to talk about it with you when she won't talk about it with me?"

"Stop playing the victim," she said.

I looked from one to the other, the steeliness in their gazes, and I could see that they were no longer a couple. There was a formality in the way that they looked at each other, even under the fighting, that reminded me of a customer and a bank teller. The glaze of love was gone.

I couldn't fix them, I'd never be Hayley Mills in *The Parent Trap*. The most boring, static, dorky, public radio–ified boomer couple in the hood was no longer a couple. And whether it had happened because of his affair, or just because, I probably wouldn't know in my lifetime.

They were two entities now and I would have to come at them in a new way. I felt the terror of this and at the same time the possibility. I'd spent years feeling frustrated that I couldn't tell one of them anything without having them pass it on to the other and now it seemed maybe I could. Maybe they had to separate in order for me to separate.

M Y mom had me over for dinner at her new place soon after she moved in. She cooked salmon and pilaf and I brought over a bottle of white wine. It was small but charming, in a prewar building with a rickety elevator and that uniquely New York blend of dust and noodles that so many Upper West Side buildings have. She seemed mellow in a way she hadn't in all the time I had known her, like a woman who'd been single for twenty-five years instead of just two months.

Over dinner I told her a little about what had happened with Powell and when I finished I said, "I know it sounds stupid, but I still miss him. Even though I know he was crazy and wrong for me."

"Why would you want to be with someone who didn't want you?" she said.

"A million reasons," I said.

"But that should be prerequisite." She frowned tightly. "It makes me worried when I hear you say you could love someone who didn't love you back."

"Hello?" I said. "It's called being in your twenties?"

"I know," she said. "It just makes me feel like I should have been clearer with you when you were younger, told you not to go for a guy who wouldn't give you the time of day, not to go for jerks."

"He was a jerk in some ways but not in others."

"That's the very worst kind."

We ate in silence for a little and it had that same awkward feeling it often did, where we had to struggle to find things to talk about. "So do you have a boyfriend?" I asked. She blushed. "Oh my God. You act fast."

"I wouldn't call him a boyfriend," she said, "but yes, I am seeing someone."

"How old is he?"

"Fifty-two."

"Yeah? And what's his name?"

"Stan." This could not be good. Stan was not a name pulsing with sexuality and promise. Stan was the name of Dorothy's ex on *The Golden Girls*.

"Where'd you meet?"

"At a Wednesday-night dancing group I go to at Metropolitan Duane. He came up to me and said, 'Is your name Sue?' Turned out we were in the same folk dancing group at NYU when I was a student. He remembered me. He said I hadn't changed a bit." I swallowed. The guy sounded way too oily. "He's divorced with two sons.

We've gone out twice and so far we seem to be enjoying each other. We're taking it very slowly."

I couldn't say I was overjoyed that she'd gotten back in the saddle almost as quickly as Liz had, but I wasn't as angry as I expected to be either. It just seemed like yet another aspect of her life that I didn't completely understand, but wasn't prepared to give her a hard time about. "I'm—really happy for you, Mom."

"You know," she said, setting her napkin down next to her plate, "one of his sons is your age. He went to Oberlin and works at a dot-com. Stan and I were thinking maybe the four of us could get together some night next—"

"Mom. That is sick."

"It's not a setup! I just thought the two of you might—" I shot her a look. "All right," she said. "Why don't you think about it?"

I poured myself some more wine and as I did she said, "I want you to know that I don't blame you."

"You don't?" I said.

"It took me a lot of processing with Dr. Fern, that's the woman I've been seeing, Nina recommended her, she's feminist and wears the most beautiful caftans, but I don't think it's your fault. I wanted to believe it was your fault, for introducing the girl to Dad, because I wasn't ready to look at what Dad—did, but I have a more evolved understanding of events. And then when Dad moved in with you I felt like I was going to lose not only him but you. But now I see that . . ." Her voice trailed off.

"You what?"

"That hasn't happened." She made a noise, and covered her face, and I could tell she was crying a little. It was such a strange, cocka-mamie world. My mother was crying and my dad was living on his own. But I knew better than to humiliate her about it. I started clearing the plates and asked what she had for dessert.

T H E day my dad moved out was bright and sunny. He insisted on renting a U-Haul van since he had passed his driving test, and we loaded his boxes into the back. I asked him four times if he was cer-

tain he was comfortable driving a van and he said he'd called Mr.
Goddard and gotten a few pointers so I shouldn't worry.

There were only two near accidents along the way—a bicyclist
zoomed around us as we were about to turn onto Warren, and a kid
ran in halfway down the street to get a ball—but no one was killed.
By the time we had pulled up at the house it felt like we'd gone
three hundred miles instead of six blocks.

We found a parking spot around the corner and unloaded the
stuff together. The house was stark and empty; she'd left a lot of the
furniture like the etageres, the TV, and TV stand but removed personal stuff like her photos.

When we were finished hauling the boxes in we sat on the stoop
and watched the people bustling by, women shopping and kids on
little scooters and wheelbarrows and tricycles. I could smell a fire
burning in somebody's house and I found myself comforted by the
smell instead of disgusted. Cobble Hill makes the most sense in the
fall; the houses look more right and the air feels crisp but not too
cold.

"There's been something I've been meaning to tell you," he said,
"and I haven't known how."

"You're dating T. Russell in Apartment Fifteen?"

"These past few months I've been thinking about how much
trouble I have in conventional job situations and how I've always
wanted to work in a Jewish environment. So . . ." He winced and
wrung his hands. "I want to run it by you but I'm afraid you might
discourage me and I just don't know if—"

"Just tell me!"

"I was thinking of everything I've been through, and how I'd do
things differently the next time, and how much more I understand
about choices, and consequences, and what it means to live a meaningful life, and I thought, *What kind of person gets to help people
figure out all that stuff?* Because I think it's something I could be
good at. Or at least better at than I was before. And it hit me. Maybe
I could be a rabbi."

It was weird what happened next—I let out this hollow sob, a
noise I hadn't made before then and haven't made since. There was

a rush of love in my chest that made me dizzy and I felt the kind of pride that a parent feels for their kid, except it was my dad so it was mixed with awestruck admiration. He was hunched over, his shoulders low and his beard speckled, a new patch of dermatitis forming on his forehead, but in that moment he seemed large to me, like a giant.

I leaned over and hugged him hard, gripping my two hands together, my chin jutting into the bone of his shoulder. "You're not upset?" he said, muffled, into my neck.

I pulled away. "Why would I be upset?"

"I thought you'd feel like I was stealing your thunder."

"You're such an idiot," I said. "It doesn't work like that."

As I looked over at him and saw how happy he was I understood for a second that love was like blood. It coursed through you no matter how many layers of anger and pain it was buried under. It might run thin sometimes or get blocked but it was in you and it kept you going even when there were times you wanted to purge yourself completely.

My father had pushed me too hard all of my life and maybe this was the reason, because he'd never had any faith in himself. But now he was going to do something he wanted to do and even if it meant he had to apply five times before he got in it was a start. The fact that he had figured this out made me less angry at him for all that pressure because it explained it a little, and the truth was, he hadn't nagged me about my job situation in a pretty long time. I knew he wasn't happy with me bartending but I wasn't going to do it forever anyway. I doubted I'd be a Hebrew school teacher, or do anything involving organized religion, but maybe someday I'd do something partially rabbinic, like write a guide to dating crazy men.

"I was thinking about writing my essay on *tshuvah,* on repentance," my father said.

"What do you know about *tshuvah?*" I said, impressed.

"I've been reading up. The Grand Army branch has an excellent Judaic Studies section. So you'll help me with my application?"

"Of course I will."

"You think I stand a chance of getting in?"

"Sure. Half my classmates were middle-aged. With the job market the way it is more and more people are going into the rabbinate as a second career. I think this could be a really good move for you."

"You think so?" he said, his voice cracking.

"Yeah. I like the ring of it."

"What?"

"Reb Dad," I said, and held my hand up like I was seeing it on a marquis.

He choked up and cleared his throat. "I'm sorry," he coughed. "It's just—uh—a chest cold."

"Before you can be a rabbi you're going to have to learn not to cry so easily," I said, but as usual it was too late.

A COUPLE weeks later around four in the morning when I was coming home from my shift, I saw something very strange in front of the building. A black SUV with shaded windows, the kind that belong only to rock stars, pulled up in front and Liz stepped out. She turned around and leaned her head into the window.

"When I fall asleep tonight," a melodic and oddly familiar southern-accented voice said, "I'll be thinkin' 'bout my fingers in your sweet beav."

"I love the way you say that," she said.

"Be good, you hear?" he said, and something about the sexy paternalism of the tone made me realize in a click of an instant who it was.

The car sped off into the night and as she waved goodbye she saw me standing in the shadows. "Hello, Rachel," she said nervously.

"Who was that?"

"What are you talking about?"

"Was that who I think it was?"

"That depends," she said, biting her lip. "Who do you think it was?"

"The forty-second president of the United States?"

She turned a deep pink and said, "You caught me."

"Jesus! Doesn't he care about being spotted?"

"Not too many people are around at four AM in Cobble Hill. Brooklyn's very protected that way."

"What happened to Gordon?"

"It was good while it lasted but then we started fighting again. He never introduced me to any of his friends, and he started getting really protective about his ass. It was just too much of a downer."

"So how did you meet him?" I said, my curiosity taking precedence over my shock.

"You knew he liked Jewish girls."

"I mean, what happened?"

"I was at this Israel benefit in Chappaqua a couple weeks ago with my parents and he was one of the guests. Everyone was talking the whole time about how he was going to show up but I didn't believe it. My parents left around ten but I figured I'd stay because there was this semihot investment banker named Jon Metzger there I'd been flirting with. Just as I was debating whether or not to leave with him, the door opened and you-know-who came in with two Secret Service guys. Immediately everyone started crowding him but I hung back, not wanting to be too obvious. There was a little space between the heads and like the Red Sea had parted, I saw him eyeing me.

"Eventually the guests started to leave. I told the investment banker I was going to stay a little longer so he jetted, and as I was standing by the buffet table eating a cheese stick Mr. C. came up to me. The first words he spoke were, 'You've got the prettiest blue eyes.' So I said the only thing I could think of: 'Back atcha.'"

"I bet he's never heard that before."

"What can I say?" She shrugged as we went into the building. "I was lust-drunk. I mean what you've heard about his presence does not do justice." She sighed blissfully. "He looked so amazing I barely recognized him. He's dropped like forty pounds. I said, 'I gotta tell you, you've lost a lot of weight,' and he beckoned me close and said, 'South Beach.' We kept talking—about Israeli politics, eating disorders, and what he thinks of Chappaqua. He asked if I had a boyfriend and I told him I was just getting out of something. He said he knew what it was like, that it could be hard to bounce back right away. I said I had a habit of dating persecuted minorities like blacks, Jews, and dirty old men, and he said, 'I definitely fit the last category.' Then he asked if I wanted to come over to his place for a drink. He said his wife was in Washington so there wasn't a problem."

We were standing in front of my apartment door and my mouth was hanging open, a bit of spittle forming at the corner. "He had this Mies daybed in the living room," she said, "and we got down on that because he didn't feel comfortable in the conjugal bed. I know this sounds crazy but I think he could really be the one. I don't mind that he travels, that he's married. I feel like this could really give me the space I need to finish my dissertation."

I was aghast, agape. I needed details. "When you say you *got down,* you mean you went all the way?"

"Of course not," she said. "You know he has intercourse issues. He still has that twisted southern morality even though they've been in couples counseling long enough for him to know better."

"So what *did* you do?"

"Everything else," she said wickedly. "And yes, I swallowed. I'm not an idiot. He had one of his guys drive me back and before I left he said he wanted to see me again but I should know that dating a married guy could be complicated. I said, 'That's all right, I've been through it before.' Aren't you happy for me?"

I wasn't sure. On the one hand I felt guaranteed she'd never have second thoughts about my dad, on the other I was concerned for her welfare. "This could be bad," I said. "If he thinks you'll leak he could have you murdered. That's what they did to Marilyn. With HRC contemplating a presidential bid and—"

"I don't care!" she cried. "It would be a fitting way to go out! Death by beege."

"So does he have Peyronie's? The distinguishing characteristics?"

"I'll never tell," she said smugly.

"You gotta give me something. Would you say it's wider than it is round, or—"

"I am so not sharing."

"Is he going to come over?"

"Number Forty-two is not going to be having dirty stay-outs in Cobble Hill!" She hesitated, like she wanted to ask me something.

"What is it?" I finally said.

"Do you want to come upstairs for a second? I'll make you a drink."

I was curious but I hadn't forgotten what she had done. I was afraid to let her back in even a little but at this point there was nobody left in my life for her to steal.

"I—I'm not sure," I said.

She paused for a second, then said, "I'll show you some pictures I took of him naked."

"You've got a deal," I said, and we ran upstairs.

T H E next afternoon before work I went to the deli by the park for a cappuccino. It was a chilly December day, too cold to sit in the park, but something made me want to stop by. I brought my cup and as I headed past the park I saw Powell sitting on a bench next to a young woman with short hair.

The woman was in her early thirties, and she wore a long flowing skirt with laced-up boots, the kind of outfit that screamed actress. His body was turned intently toward hers and I waited for him to notice me but he was totally engaged in what she was saying. She was speaking very animatedly with her hands, and then he said something back and she laughed, and put her hand on his knee. He didn't touch it but he didn't move it away and after a few seconds she took it back. It wasn't clear how intimate they were—he seemed formal enough that I could wager they hadn't slept together—but I could see him enjoying the captive audience, getting off on her enjoyment of him, her appreciative smile.

I felt jealous of their intimacy, of how easy and low-maintenance she seemed. I wondered whether maybe he'd be able to open up to her in ways he never would to me, whether someday I'd have to read their announcement in the single woman's porn: the weddings pages.

But as she flashed her teeth at him I realized that the only part I envied was this part, when Powell's company felt like a shiny blue ribbon. I would have given anything to be her in this moment, when he was outrageous and surprising and when being around him made you feel like the luckiest girl in the world. It was the other part I wouldn't miss, the later part, the fighting and vindictiveness. I missed the beginning of Powell, not the end. I watched them a little longer and then I went to work.

T H A T   night I had my best night in tips since I'd started at Roxy. I wasn't sure why it was so crowded since it was bitingly cold and that usually made people stay inside—but by eleven I'd already cleared three hundred dollars. Blimp and a few other guys from the PJs were holding court by the front, laughing loudly. A few gay boys sat on the pews by the window feeding ice cubes to a Brooklyn mutt, and about twenty white hipsters were spread all over, playing Patsy Cline and Wilco on the juke, drinking beers, and complaining about their jobs.

Jasper and Delia were in his usual place and he had his arm slung around her protectively. He'd told me they were starting to get serious—they'd gone on three more dates but she still hadn't slept with him, and he decided this was a sign that she really cared.

A Betty Page wannabe had just come in alone, looking glum, and ordered a Stoli and cranberry. She'd actually ordered a "vodka cran" but lately I had started asking people what kind of vodka they wanted and half the time they picked something top-shelf, which meant better tips. As I put down her drink she passed me the money with a glum frown. You have to worry when you see a cute girl alone in a bar on a Saturday night; usually they come in with girlfriends.

"You OK?" I said.

"Not really," she said, lowering her chin.

"What is it?"

"It's about my ex-boyfriend."

Normally I wouldn't have pried but she seemed lost and I decided there was a chance she actually needed help. "Hit me." She eyed me anxiously like she wasn't sure she'd be able to talk about it without crying and then she heaved in and said, "You see—"

A Goth-looking chick was beckoning me from the other end of the bar. "Hold on just a second," I told Stoli Cran.

"Can I order some food?" the Goth girl asked. "Am I allowed to eat here?"

"Absolutely," I said, grabbing the menu book. She opened up and began flipping through the pages. I figured I'd help her a little. "Baluchi, the Indian, is good but they charge for the rice, Zaytoon's is the cheapest but don't order lamb, and if you need comfort food you could try 247 Smith. I recommend the crab cakes."

I was on my way back to Stoli Cran when a hostile fat guy in a Chinese rice-picker hat waved his arm. He'd had four Brooklyn Lagers and so far he'd tipped me a buck. "Can I get another?" he said.

I poured it, brought it over. He laid down a five. I brought the single and he left it there like it was some sort of generous gift. I picked up the bill and held it in front of him. "You've ordered four drinks and tipped me a dollar," I said. "I'm a little confused. Have I been surly?"

"No," he said like a reprimanded schoolboy.

"Late with drinks?"

"No."

"So the service was all right, then."

"I guess so."

"Well the standard tip on a sixteen-dollar tab is four to five dollars."

His face got red as the gay boys leaned over and laughed. "You tell him, Rachel!" a black guy named Barry said, doing the snaps.

The rice-picker guy reached into his pocket and laid down another four dollars. People were easy. You just had to know how to work them.

I went back to Stoli Cran. "I'm sorry," I said. "You were saying?"

She looked needy and more urgent than before. "My ex-boyfriend left all this stuff in my apartment five months ago when we broke up. I've called him like ten times to get it but he keeps making excuses."

"The answer's very simple," I said.

"It is?"

"Sure. If you want to sever ties with your ex you need to call UPS and have them come pick up your boyfriend's shit because you're only holding on to it as a way of holding on to him."

"Really?" she said. "You think so?"

"Absolutely," I said. "Even though you're saying it's his fault for not picking it up you're clinging to those remnants of him because it insures a future dialogue. You have to let go. You think it's romantic to flounder but a girl that flops like a fish is unappealing."

"I'm over him," she said.

"Not if you still have his stuff in your place after five months."

"I never saw it that way before."

I nodded and leaned back, surveying the room. I had a pulpit now but a more honest one. I would never be a messenger of God but I was doing an all right job of ministering to the masses. I was a rabbi at Congregation Inebriation. Everyone there needed help in some way and though I still had a hard time not screaming *You're such an idiot!* when someone told me their sob story, it had been weeks since I'd driven a customer to Boat and I no longer dreaded coming to work. I had learned how to listen a little and I even liked them.

"I know it sounds extreme," I told Stoli Cran, running the cloth over the bar top. "But you gotta clean house. His boxes are the baggage weighing you down and preventing you from meeting somebody else. Until ya move them out every guy you meet's gonna see for himself that you're clinging to some otha guy's cock."

"Do you have an accent?" she said.

"It comes out sometimes," I said. "Think a yourself as a monkey in a forest. You gotta let go of the first vine before you can swing to the next. I know it's tempting to think you could bring him back but when it comes to love the best thing you can do is admit failure. Nobody can turn anybody else around."

"That's pretty good," she said. "Did you make that up?"

"Yes I did," I said, feeling a sudden rush of energy. "That's Aphorism Number One of Rachel's Aphorisms."

"How many are there?"

"I don't know yet."

Someone had put that Replacements song "Kiss Me On The Bus" on the jukebox and everyone was shouting and laughing. I leaned back and scanned the room. The hungry Goth girl was talking on her cell phone, reading off an order from one of the menus. The guy with the mutt was coming up to the bar for more ice, and Jasper and Delia were getting up out of their seats. I could tell they were going to do it by the way he winked at me as he helped her with her coat.

There was a shout from the back as someone won a pool game. I heard the coin tray sliding in and out, and the balls clackety-clacking down the ramps. The room seemed to be humming and when I closed my eyes it sounded like a chant.

The author wishes to thank the following individuals:
Daniel Greenberg, Marysue Rucci, David Rosenthal,
Tara Eggert, Charles Miller, Rabbi Hara Person,
Rabbi Niles Goldstein, Rabbi Jon Malamy,
Rabbi Mark Kaiserman, Rabbi Steve Shulman,
Rabbi Shira Stern, Amy McFarland, Rebecca Hargreaves,
Polly Yerkes, John Currin, and Kimball Higgs.
This book would not have been possible
without the encouragement, wisdom, and friendship
of Will Blythe.

AMY SOHN is the author of the novel *Run Catch Kiss* and the *New York* magazine column "Naked City." She has also written for *Playboy, Premiere, Harper's Bazaar,* and many other magazines. She wrote the film *Spin the Bottle* and co-created the Oxygen television series "Avenue Amy." She lives in Brooklyn and at www.amysohn.com.